LADY ALEXANDRA'S
EXCELLENT ADVENTURE

LADY ALEXANDRA'S EXCELLENT ADVENTURE

A Summersby Tale

SOPHIE BARNES

AVONIMPULSE
An Imprint of HarperCollinsPublishers

Excerpt from the next Summersby Tale copyright © 2012 by Sophie Barnes.

Excerpt from *How Miss Rutherford Got Her Groove Back* copyright © 2012 by Sophie Barnes.

EPub Edition JUNE 2012 ISBN: 9780062190314

Print Edition ISBN: 9780062190345

10 9 8 7 6 5 4 3 2 1

To my parents, for always believing in me and encouraging me to follow my dreams. I love you.

CHAPTER ONE

London
May 15, 1815

Sir Percy Foxstone took a slow sip of his single malt whiskey, savoring the rich flavor as it warmed his chest before he sank down into one of the deep leather armchairs in his office at Whitehall.

Lazily swirling the caramel-colored liquid, allowing it to lap against the edges of his glass, he regarded his friend with caution. "I'm deeply sorry it had to come to this, old chap," he told him quietly.

Bryce Summersby, Earl of Moorland, nodded, his forehead furrowed in a thoughtful frown. "Do you see now why I never wanted Alex to get involved?" He shook his head in disbelief.

Bryce's son William had joined The Foreign Office four years earlier when he was twenty-three years old. He'd had a number of successful missions during that time and had been personally thanked by The Prince Regent for uncovering a French spy who'd managed to infiltrate parliament.

Which is why it was so difficult to now believe that William was handing over valuable information to the French.

He'd gone to Paris in March, as soon as news of Napoleon's escape from Elba had reached the British shores. Accompanying him on his mission was his longtime friend, Andrew Finch, who'd joined The Foreign Office a couple of years earlier, on William's recommendation.

Percy picked up the most recent letter that Andrew had managed to send out of the country. "Judging from the tone of this, it seems Mr. Finch was completely caught off guard by William's behavior."

Bryce grunted before taking a swig of his whiskey. "I'm just not buying it," he muttered, piercing his friend with a hard stare, his mouth set in a grim line.

"Is that an objective opinion or one based on the fact that William's your son?"

"Bloody hell, Percy!" Bryce shouted, glaring at his friend. "Do you seriously believe William has betrayed us—that he's a traitor?"

Percy let out a deep sigh as he leaned forward, his elbows resting in his lap as he studied the glass between his hands. "I have to accept all possibilities." His eyes settled on Bryce's in a hard stare. "My position demands it."

"Who are you sending, Percy?"

Percy paused for a moment. The only reason he'd sent for Bryce in the first place was because he considered him a close friend. He'd already shared the details regarding William's mission with him and was beginning to wonder how much more he ought to divulge. "I've settled on Michael Ashford, Earl of Trenton."

"Thomas's boy?"

Percy nodded, knowing Bryce was familiar with the Duke of Willowbrook.

"Thomas is a man of great integrity," Bryce said rather stiffly. "I hope the apple didn't fall too far from the tree."

"Would you like to meet him?"

"What's your *plan*, Percy?" Bryce asked, ignoring his question. "Are you sending this Ashford fellow to kill my son?"

Percy sighed. "I'm not sending Ashford to assassinate your son, Bryce. I'm sending him to bring William back home so that he may face the charges against him. My hands are tied, old chap. You know treason's an unpardonable offense."

"And if he resists?"

"Let's hope he's wise enough not to." Percy said softly, giving Bryce a meaningful look.

"Michael will assume he's guilty of all charges and will do what must be done by all means necessary. Is that it?"

Percy nodded reluctantly. "Something like that," he said, in little more than a whisper.

"Then by all means, show Lord Trenton in so I may meet the man."

It was a delicate situation—one that Percy wished to have no part in. But now since he'd started down this road, what could he do other than hope it would soon be over?

He was inclined to agree with Bryce when it came to William's character. William had always been an honorable man. It seemed unthinkable that he might have turned traitor. Then again, Percy had seen it happen before. As he went to the door and called for Michael to enter, he sent up a silent prayer that he would somehow manage to bring William home in one piece.

A moment later, Michael strode into the room with a confidence that made it clear this was no fledgling.

Before them stood a tall figure of a man, well over six feet, with broad shoulders, a powerful chest, and strong arms. In short, he looked like he could slay a dragon with one hand while protecting a damsel in distress with the other. His hair was dark and ruffled, his eyes sparkling with boyish anticipation.

"Gentlemen . . ." Michael followed his greeting with a slight nod.

"Lord Moorland," Percy said, "May I present Michael Ashford, Earl of Trenton."

Bryce rose to his feet, all the while assessing the man who'd soon be determining the fate of his son. After a moment's pause, he grasped Michael's outstretched hand in a firm shake.

"I've heard a great deal about you, Lord Moorland, from my father in particular," Michael said. "He's a great admirer of your military endeavors—says you're quite the strategist." He released Bryce's hand with a wry twist of his lips. "He also says he's never managed to beat you at chess."

Bryce feigned a polite smile. It had been a while since he'd last seen Thomas, but he had fond memories of the poor man's numerous attempts at beating him at his favorite game. "How is your father?"

Michael shrugged as he reached for one of the decanters on the side table. "Do you mind?" he asked Percy.

"Not at all. Help yourself."

Pouring a glass of port, Michael glanced over at Bryce. "Still going strong," he told him. "He will be sixty-two in a couple of months, but he's still running around like a young lad. Trouble is, his limbs are stiffer than they used to be. I can't help but worry he might hurt himself. In his mind, he's no more than twenty years of age."

"Just wait until you are as old as we are," Bryce told him. "You won't believe your eyes when you happen to catch yourself in a mirror. Indeed, you will most likely draw your sword wondering who the devil that stranger is staring back at you." He raised his glass to Michael. "Enjoy your youth while you have it, Trenton. Lord knows it will be gone before you know it."

"I briefed Trenton on his mission this morning," Percy said, apparently deciding that it was time to get on with the business at hand. Bryce could only hazard a guess at how uncomfortable this whole dratted business must be for him. Nothing could be nastier than having to decide the fate of somebody's child—especially not when that child was like family. But he also understood that responsibility weighed heavily on his friend's shoulders. Percy would not be able to leave the matter alone—he *had* to investigate. As Bryce watched him sit back down in his dark brown leather chair, he desperately hoped that he truly did know his son well enough, and that Andrew was somehow mistaken about William's actions. "He'll be ready to leave in the morning."

Bryce moved to the side table to refill his glass. "How long have you and my son known each other?" he asked Michael.

"Well, er . . . actually, I . . ."

"Trenton has never actually met your son, Bryce. You know we don't allow our agents to meet unless they are working on the same assignment. It helps protect their identities when they are in the field."

"Well, I certainly don't mean to point out the obvious," Bryce remarked, his voice laced with annoyance. "But how the devil is he supposed to find him when he doesn't even know what he looks like?"

"There are ways."

Bryce scoffed. "We both know that William is quite skilled at deception. He works well undercover—hence the reason you gave him such an important assignment in the first place." Bryce took a large gulp of his whiskey to calm his nerves. "I want Ryan and Alex to accompany him."

Percy's mouth dropped open. "But you always said—"

"That was then and this is now. They will be able to identify their brother."

"And you are certain that you want Alex to go as well?"

Bryce had no desire to let his daughter get muddled up in this mess, but she was a better horseman, a better swordsman, and a better shot than Ryan had ever been. In fact, the only reason he was sending Ryan at all was to act as her chaperone. "Quite certain."

Both men turned to Michael. His expression was impossible to read as he absorbed the news that Bryce's children would be tagging along. "It will be a perilous journey," he stated. "They will have to hold their own. I have no desire to babysit anyone."

"You won't have to," Bryce grumbled. "Alexa—"

"Is the best swordsman you're ever likely to come across," Percy said as he cut off his friend.

Bryce followed his lead and held silent, realizing that it would probably be a cold day in hell before Michael would ever agree to bring a woman along, no matter how much he and Percy might vouch for her. In truth, he'd likely quit first, and if Bryce knew Percy as well as he thought, then that was not a risk that he was willing to take.

"Henry Angelo is a good friend of mine," Bryce added. "He's spent a number of years at Moorland Manor polishing Alex's skills."

Mentioning the famous dueling master had its desired effect. Michael nodded his approval. "But what if Summersby *is* guilty of treason? . . . What if he fights back? I can't afford to have his siblings standing in my way if I'm forced to take action." He paused. "Do you think they'll be willing to stand idly by while I kill their brother, or will they turn on me in a foolhardy attempt to save him?"

Bryce's blood ran cold at Michael's detached tone. He didn't doubt for a second that the man before him was prepared to carry out his orders. Would Alex and Ryan let him kill their brother, even if he were a traitor? Absolutely not, but they gave him hope that he might see William again, and for that reason alone, he was prepared to say anything to ensure that they would be in a position to help their brother. "If they were to discover that he has been consorting with the French, then I cannot imagine that they would try to stop you."

"Very well then," Michael acquiesced. "We leave at dawn. Will they be ready by then?"

Bryce nodded. "I have already told them to prepare themselves in the event that they would be joining you."

"There's a tavern on the outskirts of town—The Royal Oak. Are you familiar with the place?"

"I am."

"Good. Tell your sons to meet me there at five. I have no intention of waiting for them, so if they're late—"

"They will be there," Bryce told him sharply. "You have my word," he added, reaching out to shake Michael's hand.

"And you have my word as a gentleman that I shall act fairly," Michael responded. "Sir Percy tells me that both of you find it unlikely that William's a turncoat. I will discover the truth of the matter, and I hope you will trust me when I say that I would never dream of harming an innocent man. Furthermore, my prerogative is to bring him back alive, so if all goes well, you will see your son soon enough, Lord Moorland."

"Thank you," Bryce told him sincerely. "I shall await your return." He raised his glass in a final salute before gathering up his coat and heading for the door. "You will keep me informed?" he asked as he looked back over his shoulder at Percy, his hand already on the door handle.

"You will hear from me as soon as I have any news. I promise."

With a heavy sigh and a thoughtful nod, Bryce left Percy's office with growing trepidation. He wasn't a gambling man, yet here he was, willing to risk everything dear to him in order to save his firstborn child.

Though he had faith in both Alexandra and Ryan, he hated having to sit idly by in anticipation. If only he could go in their stead but that was impossible. He'd grown too old to be of use on rescue missions, particularly with his left leg paining him as much as it did these days.

No . . . he had no choice but to send his children, and in spite of himself, he suddenly smiled. This was exactly the sort of thing that Alexandra had been dreaming about for years, and now he was finally ready to indulge her. If only the stakes weren't so high.

CHAPTER TWO

The air was wet with rain as Alexandra and Ryan waited below an outcrop in front of The Royal Oak. A gaslight on the side of the building brightened the darkness with a shimmering orange glow as the tavern's sign squeaked from side to side on its hinges.

Alexandra's cloak was drawn tight across her shoulders, the edge of her hood lowered to just below her eyebrows. About her nose and mouth, she wore a scarf, the damp chill serving as a perfect excuse for her to conceal her face.

She and Ryan had purposefully arrived early, but they were now both shivering with cold and eager to be on their way. Alexandra watched the water drip from her hood—large, heavy drops that landed against her horse's mane. "Have you met him before?" she asked Ryan, hoping to learn whatever she could about Michael Ashford, a man she was determined to hate.

"Trenton? No . . ." Ryan admitted, "I haven't had the pleasure."

"But surely you must have heard *something* about him," she prodded.

Ryan nodded. "He is—from what I understand—the sort of man who makes an excellent acquaintance. In fact, I've never heard a single word said against him from any gentleman."

Not exactly the negative description of his character that Alexandra had been hoping for.

"However, he's not the sort of man that any reasonable parent would trust to as much as dance with their daughter."

Alexandra's interest peaked.

"I daresay he's quite possibly the biggest rakehell in all of England." Ryan told her.

"Oh?" she asked, hoping that he might elaborate on that.

"It has been said that he has no fewer than nine mistresses at any given moment—one for each day of the week, with a couple to spare for variety's sake."

Oh my.

Ryan glanced over at his sister, a look of surprise crossing his face as he realized what he'd said. "Forgive me. I know this is not at all the sort of thing I ought to discuss with you. It's quite inappropriate really."

Alexandra stopped herself from rolling her eyes. What a silly thing to say when she was sitting there dressed like a man, about to tear off to France in the company of spies. This entire situation was inappropriate. "Not to worry," she quipped. "I am confident my constitution can handle it."

"Yes, well . . ." Ryan said somewhat skeptically. "If I may give you a word of advice—stay away from Lord Trenton as much as possible. He will only give you trouble."

"Are you suggesting he will try to take advantage of me?"

Ryan darted a nervous look in her direction. "It is a fair assumption to make when one considers the man's reputation," he told her. "And once he discovers you are not a man, but an attractive, young woman instead . . . well, I think you get the idea."

Cold anger flickered behind Alexandra's eyes. "He will never succeed."

Not in this lifetime.

Ryan muttered something beneath his breath that Alexandra could only assume must have been a curse.

Silence followed, dragging on for what seemed like an eternity, until Alexandra finally noticed her horse's ears perk up. He began shifting restlessly from side to side beneath her, his front hooves clawing at the muddied ground in agitation. Looking up, she spotted a lone figure emerging from beyond the darkness. He sat astride the most magnificent horse she'd ever seen—a velvety black stallion with powerful ropes of muscle that flexed with every move it made.

"The Summersby brothers, I presume?" The figure moved toward them until his head was under the shelter of the outcrop. He then threw back his hood and wiped the water from his face with the palm of his hand.

Alexandra tightened her grip on the reins, her whole body tensing as she stared at the man before her. His eyes were dark beneath dense black hair that hung in messy tresses to his broad shoulders. His nose was straight, his mouth set against a perfectly sculpted jaw line. Not a flicker of humor graced his features. Indeed, he was as grave as he was handsome—not at all the sort of man Alexandra had expected, for her vivid imagination had conjured a far more toady fellow instead. He was unnerving to say the least, especially since her experience with men was basically limited to her brothers.

Her eyes narrowed ever so slightly as she studied Michael's features in much the same manner that a botanist might study a shrub. Well, if she had to be tortured by his company for an indefinite amount of time, it was just as well that he wasn't too sore on the eyes. Still, when he turned his deep brown eyes on her, she felt a sudden flutter in the pit of her belly that she wasn't at all comfortable with. She disliked surprises, and discovering that her treacherous body responded to a mere glance from this cad was not only unpleasant but also completely unfamiliar territory for her. She had no idea how to handle the situation short of nodding and allowing Ryan to answer for her.

"Indeed we are," Ryan told him. "And you must be Lord Trenton."

Michael nodded, his eyes moving over both of them in an assessing manner. Alexandra's heart hammered against her chest as she cast her eyes down, fixing them upon her horse's mane. She knew that he wouldn't be able to make out much of anything about her, thanks to the scarf and hood, but her nerves were still on edge as she waited for his approval.

"Are you ready?" he finally asked.

Again Alexandra only nodded, though the sudden surge of relief she felt was quite overwhelming. She darted a quick look in Lord Trenton's direction, just in time to notice a look of disappointment crossing his face. Too bad. For now the most important thing was to make it to Brighton. With just a little bit of luck, they would be in France by tomorrow.

Setting off, the group left London far behind, mud flying about the thundering hooves of their horses as they galloped through puddles and along muddied roads, the dirt caking their horses' flanks. Michael led the team onward, while Alexandra had taken up the rear, content to keep as much distance between her and Lord Trenton as possible. Consequently, she didn't mind at all that the only thing she could see from her present position was Ryan's billowing cloak.

By midmorning the rain had stilled, yet they kept up their pace until they reached Crawley, where they finally allowed themselves a well-deserved break. The horses were tended to in the stables of a roadside inn, while the three companions each paid a penny for a pint of beer and a chunk of bread to ease their aching bellies.

Allowing her brother to make the necessary excuses, Alexandra walked away from him and Michael, her hood drawn down and her scarf still in place to conceal her face. She had no intention of letting Michael know that she was a woman until they were safely in Paris where it would be nearly impossible for him to send her back home. It wouldn't be easy to keep him in the dark for that long, but she'd have to manage.

She'd also decided that the less time she spent in his presence the better, regardless. Her father had put a lot of faith in her ability to bring William home safely. It was an important mission—one that would mean life or death for her brother. She couldn't afford any distractions, least of all something as superficial as a handsome man's face. The mere thought of him was enough to make her scold herself.

Kicking a couple of pebbles carelessly about with the tip of her boot, she glanced back at Ryan. He and Michael seemed to be getting along well enough, though she couldn't begin to imagine what the two of them might possibly be talking about. Lowering her gaze to the ground, she quickly reminded herself that she didn't care. Michael was her nemesis, no matter what. But just as that thought had taken shape inside her head, she looked up to find him staring right back at her with piercing dark eyes—that same assessing look upon his face.

On a sharp intake of breath, she spun around and looked away, her stomach flip-flopping so violently that she thought she might be sick. Things were clearly not going as smoothly as she would have hoped. She'd learned to master her emotions years ago. Granted, these were new, unexpected emotions— the sort she'd always dreaded—but they were emotions all the same. One way or the other, she would have to find a way to overcome them.

"He's a bit of an odd fellow, your brother," Michael said as he took a bite of his bread and followed it with a large gulp of beer.

Ryan eyed his sister for a moment, still wondering if it wasn't a huge mistake, bringing her along to France. He knew that she was better skilled than he, but she was a woman, and as such, one simply couldn't ignore the fact that she would always be at greater risk. Here she was now, preparing to travel into male dominated territory. And not just any men, but soldiers who might not have seen a woman in months.

It was complete lunacy to put her in that situation. God only knew what might happen if she found herself outnumbered and he couldn't be there to protect her. He shuddered at the thought of it. "Alex is a bit of a loner," he said in response to Michael's question.

"Not much of a conversationalist I take it?"

"There's a time and a place for everything. Alex has never liked distraction. Indulging in idle conversation while on the move would be, according to Alex, a distraction."

"But not according to you?"

Ryan shrugged his shoulders. "I never had the same discipline my siblings have. Hence why I'm not as quick with my sword or as fast on the trigger, but I can still manage to win a good fight," he grinned. "You need not worry about protecting me. I can hold my own."

"I must say I'm glad to hear it, because where we are going, I doubt I'll have much time to waste on novices."

Ryan's eyes gleamed with mischief. Clearly, Michael had underestimated both of them. He suddenly looked forward to showing him what they were both made of, but more than that, he couldn't wait to see the befuddled look on his face when he discovered that one of the best swordsmen in all of England was in fact a woman.

He watched now, with some degree of apprehension, as Michael cast a careless glance in Alexandra's direction. Following his gaze, he noted that his sister was standing as if rooted to the ground, her bright blue eyes staring right back at them. *Turn away, damn it*, he wanted to yell. If she kept on standing there like that the earl would certainly grow suspicious and . . . she finally turned her back on them. *Thank God.* But when Ryan glanced back at Michael, he couldn't help but notice that his expression had grown rather unsettled, almost as if he'd noticed something his conscious mind had yet to come to terms with.

"Call your brother," Michael said, his thoughts once more concealed beneath a stern facade as he patted Ryan roughly on the shoulder. "We have a boat to catch." He then emptied the remainder of his beer and strode away in search of his horse.

Ryan watched him go, unable to shake the unnerving sensation that Michael might pose a much greater threat to his sister than the French soldiers ever would.

They reached Brighton by lunchtime—the salty scent of the sea greeting them before the town itself came into view.

Slowing their horses to an easy gait, they made their way through the cobbled streets toward the docks. The sea looked calm as it lapped against the pier, sending a soft spray of seawater onto the wharf. Alexandra breathed in the pungent smell of discarded fish, increasingly thankful for the scarf that she wore about her face. A pair of seagulls squawked as they bobbed up and down overhead like a couple of marionettes, their beady eyes searching for an easy meal. Teams of men busied themselves with hauling crates back and forth, yelling instructions while a handful of street urchins ran to and fro between them.

"We'll be sailing with Captain Grover," Michael said. "Would you two see if you can get us a table at that pub over there while I make some inquiries about his whereabouts?"

After tethering their horses to a couple of iron rings that were set in the outside wall of the tavern, Alexandra followed

Ryan inside, her eyes squinting against an onslaught of smoke as they adjusted to the dim lighting. The place was teaming with noisy and hungry men, all pushing each other about to attract the attention of one of the waiters.

Ryan elbowed his way past a couple of brawny chaps and made his way toward the back corner of the room to an empty table with a couple of benches alongside it.

Striding after him and stepping over a grizzly canine in the process, Alexandra was just about to sit down when she felt a heavy hand settle upon her shoulder. "I believe that table is ours," a mocking voice grumbled behind her.

Instinct roared to life inside her like a furnace. She spun smoothly away, ducking low to avoid the blow that she sensed would be coming. No man would ever lay a hand on her without facing the consequences. Metal flashed as she unsheathed her sword in so swift a movement that the man was caught completely off guard. He'd had no time to gather his wits about him and now stood staring down at the tip of Alexandra's blade where it pushed against his chest, pressing into his coat. Her scarf had loosened, exposing most of her face as she stood there now, staring up at her adversary with eyes of steel, her mouth drawn tight in a menacing smirk.

"You . . . but you're a . . . a . . ."

Alexandra cocked her head to one side, only slightly amused by the man's apparent awkwardness. "And you're a bully." Her voice was as cool as an autumn breeze. "I suggest you find yourself another table before I decide whether or not you're worth troubling myself over."

The man shot a hasty look in Ryan's direction, but Ryan

merely threw up his hands and took a step backward. "I would do as she says if I were you," he said with a lopsided grin.

To underline her brother's statement, Alexandra added a hint of pressure to the man's chest and raised a challenging eyebrow. It took no more than a second for her assailant to quietly back away to the safety of his comrades. They'd undoubtedly ridicule him later, but for now, none of them were eager to draw attention to themselves. Five minutes later, they gave up on their food and left, passing Michael in the doorway.

The moment she spotted him, Alexandra immediately lowered her eyes to the table, her face once again concealed by her hood.

"Our ship's not far from here," Michael told them as he seated himself next to Ryan. He cast a quick glance at Alexandra, once again wondering at how withdrawn Ryan's brother seemed. He wasn't anything like what he might have imagined based on Sir Percy's description. In fact, he'd been sure that Alex would have been arrogant—too big for his own boots so to speak. But the man who sat across from him appeared to be anything but. And then there was his peculiar habit of constantly wearing his hood.

Michael shrugged. Who was he to question the man's reasoning? Perhaps he had an ugly scar that he was somehow embarrassed about, or pockmarked cheeks. He remembered the glimpse he'd caught of his eyes. Surely his face must be handsome with eyes such as those.

His thoughts were interrupted by Ryan, who'd finally managed to draw one of the waiters' attentions. A potbellied man swaggered toward them and lazily asked them what they'd like.

"We'll have three stouts—Barclay's if you have them," Ryan told him. "And then something to eat. What do you have to offer?"

The waiter scratched the back of his head while his belly bounced up and down. "I have some pan-fried fish and vegetables if that'll do. If not, I can offer you some cheese and cured meats."

"The fish will be fine," Michael told him, not sure of when they'd be having their next hot meal. Whatever the case, they would need something to keep them going until they were well out to sea later on in the evening.

As it turned out, the food wasn't even warm—in fact, it had most likely been sitting around for the last couple of hours, but the flavor wasn't too bad, so they did their best to finish what was there, following each bit with a sip of Barclay's.

"You're not much of a conversationalist, are you?" Michael asked, his eyes pinned on Alex. His head was bent over his plate with his hood pulled so low that not even his nose could be seen.

Michael was surprised to see him freeze—his fork hovering between his plate and his mouth. What was wrong with him? The question hadn't been meant as an insult. Michael turned to see Ryan's fork move with a lazy slowness as he pushed his food about his plate, just as uncomfortable as Alex clearly was.

And then, before Michael could manage to say anything else that might alter the mood, Alex simply pushed the chair back from the table, got up, and left without uttering a word.

"I apologize," Michael muttered after a few moments. "It wasn't my intention to offend him."

"You ought not worry about it," Ryan replied. "Alex can be a bit . . . difficult at times. I'm quite sure you two will get along soon enough. You'll see." But even Michael could hear the trepidation underlying Ryan's hopeful tone.

CHAPTER THREE

Alexandra leaned against the railing of James Grover's ship while she looked out over the oily waters. She listened to the sound of the crew hoisting the sails as they slid out toward the open sea, their feet a soft pitter-patter upon the wooden surface of the deck. A couple of lights from other vessels were visible in the distance. But what fascinated her most was the night sky upon which were scattered a million stars—like specks of silver on an artist's canvas.

So lost in thought was she, when Michael's sudden voice coming from no more than a yard behind her, it startled her. "Summersby?" His voice was soft and cautious, as if he half expected her to turn around and lash out at him.

Alexandra caught her breath, her heart thumping so wildly she thought it might burst from her chest.

"I'm sorry about earlier," he said with an element of sincerity to his voice that surprised her. "It's just . . . well . . . we'll be spending quite a bit of time together you and I, so I was rather hoping we might be able to get along."

She remained perfectly still, as if she feared that the

slightest movement would give her away. She heard him shift—could almost see the frown that surely graced his face at her lack of response.

"Listen," he insisted. "I can understand your apprehension, but you must believe me when I tell you that your brother's case will be treated with the utmost fairness. I'm not the sort of man to act rashly. I'll look at all the evidence first before deciding how to proceed. If you help me, it would make my job a lot easier."

Alexandra turned to face him with a glower.

Michael stepped backward as if she'd physically shoved him, seemingly stunned by the blatant anger that shone in her eyes.

"Help you?" she muttered, keeping her voice low and muffled beneath her scarf. "You must think that I am a complete blockhead."

"No, of course not. After all, I barely know you," Michael said in a voice of clear exasperation. "But if we work together, we might be able to return to England sooner rather than later."

Less time spent in each other's company—it is tempting.

"Lord Trenton, I—"

Michael winced. "Ashford," he said.

"What?" Alexandra asked, momentarily thrown by his comment.

"I'd prefer it if you'd call me Ashford," he told her. "Lord Trenton's too formal . . . too . . ."

"Old?" Alexandra offered, unable to resist the chance to provoke him. She regarded him with some degree of curiosity—it was impossible to discern what he might be thinking.

Unfortunately, he didn't seem to take the bait. On the contrary, he merely stood there, watching her in an annoyingly condescending fashion, until she felt herself quite silly. "Very well then . . . *Ashford*. Let me ask you this—Do you think my brother is guilty or innocent?"

"If Finch's letter holds water . . ." His words trailed off when she narrowed her eyes.

If the man was hoping to forge a lifelong friendship, then this was certainly not the conversation that would facilitate it.

He sighed. "I have to be honest with you. The evidence thus far doesn't look good."

"Then we have nothing further to discuss," she told him haughtily.

A couple of crewmen ran past them, conveying orders for the ship's sails to be hoisted. Michael waited until they were well out of earshot before lowering his voice and saying, "Be reasonable, Summersby. Suppose your brother has indeed been supplying the French with information they can use against your own countrymen. Do you honestly believe he should go unpunished?"

"He's innocent," Alexandra ground out. "That is the whole point."

"And you know this beyond any shadow of a doubt?" His voice was barely a whisper on the breeze.

Alexandra tensed her shoulders. She would *not* be distracted by his nearness. Even now, in the middle of their argument she could feel her heart rate begin to rise.

Ridiculous.

She gave a curt nod and did her best to ignore the effect he was having on her.

"I must say your loyalty's quite remarkable. There isn't a trace of doubt in your words." He paused for a moment. "Do you think Finch is lying?"

"Unlike you," she said quietly. "I won't speculate or make assumptions before all the facts are known. I will find William, and once I do, I'll know the truth."

"A bold statement, Summersby."

Michael served her a patronizing smile that rankled her to no end. He clearly thought her naive. Whatever his opinion of her, however, he had no cause to doubt where her allegiance lay. After all, she'd made herself quite clear—she would protect her family with her life, no question about it. "And you," Alexandra muttered. "From what I understand, you've never met him. You know nothing of his character. Hell, you don't even know the color of his hair. And yet you're so eager to accuse him—to find him guilty of a crime I can promise you he did not commit."

"Shall I simply take your word for it?" His lips curled upward to form the beginnings of a smile.

"That would indeed save us all a great deal of trouble."

"Hm . . . I suppose it might," he conceded. "Tell me though, for I am curious now—Why do you presume that I have already found your brother guilty?"

She balked at that. "You just said—"

"Actually, I didn't. You drew that conclusion entirely on your own."

"But—" She stopped to think. Had he not told her that William surely must be guilty? He'd implied that he probably was, but he hadn't actually said it. "I don't trust you," she finally said.

Michael stared back at her with a steady gaze. "Why?"

"Because of the sort of man you are," she snapped. She was beginning to lose her patience.

Michael's eyes narrowed into two angry slits. "Would you care to elaborate on that?" he asked, crossing his arms as if in preparation for the verbal attack that was sure to come.

"You're a whoremonger, Lord Trenton," she told him plainly, using the name that she knew he disliked, with slow deliberation. "The worst sort of man there is—the kind who has no respect for women whatsoever and who—"

"Stop right there," he gruffed, effectively cutting her off. "I will not allow you to speak of my mistresses in such a degrading fashion." Michael scowled.

"Why?" Alexandra pressed. Her tone was out right mocking. "Because of how much you *care* about them?"

"Precisely," he told her in a clipped tone.

Few things had ever been able to shut her up, but this certainly did the trick. Alexandra's blue eyes stared blankly back at him. She felt as if someone had just shoved a stocking in her mouth. Having two brothers, the idea that a gentleman might have a mistress was unlikely to surprise her. The fact that he might actually concern himself with their welfare did. She tried to compose herself but found it damned difficult.

Michael apparently couldn't help but smirk. "It's not all about sex, you know," he finally said as if he were discussing the weather.

What could she possibly say to that?

"I . . . er . . . I see," she murmured. Thank God she was wearing both a hooded cloak and a scarf about her face. Surely her whole body must be blushing by now. Though she'd momentarily forgotten herself in her anger, it wouldn't do to have him discover her now. How the devil had they arrived at this subject anyway?

"I'm not entirely sure you do, Summersby." There was a twinkle in his eyes that made her catch her breath. "For as much as I love an ample bosom and a pair of soft thighs, my mistresses also offer me a great deal in terms of companionship."

"Really?" she asked incredulously.

He stared back at her, his dark eyes locking onto hers. "You don't have much experience with the fairer sex, do you?"

Was she really required to answer such a question?

"Not to worry," Michael grinned. "We'll rectify that soon enough. No need to be embarrassed about it. You are after all only what . . . twenty years of age?"

"Twenty-two," she told him hesitantly.

"Much too old to be a virgin," he muttered. He seemed to study her for a moment—his eyes narrowed. "Do you by any chance prefer men?"

Yes!

She caught herself just in time.

"Of course not," she lied.

Could the conversation possibly get more bizarre?

A look of relief came over Michael's face. "Good. Then we'll find a pretty little strumpet for you the minute we reach Paris."

Alexandra groaned inwardly. Apparently, it *could* get more bizarre. If only there were a way to change the subject.

Again Michael stared at her.

What is it? Why do you keep looking at me like that?

"Is there a particular reason why you choose to hide your face?" he asked quite suddenly.

"My nose and jaw are disfigured," she told him without thinking. And then, to add to the lie, "I was born this way."

As if it weren't enough that Ashford thought her a man . . . well, how else was she supposed to explain her odd scarf-wearing habit?

"I'm sorry to hear it," he told her.

The look of sympathy in his eyes went straight to her heart.

Oh hell!

If there were one thing she didn't care for, aside from the way he could turn her legs to jelly with no more than a glance, it was feeling guilty toward the very man that she was so determined to hate.

"You needn't be," she said in a tight voice. Her conscience was beginning to nag at her. This was the only way though. If Ashford discovered who she was before they reached Paris, she could bet a fair sum that he'd send her back to England one way or the other.

The silence seemed to stretch between them until Alexandra decided that it was time to put an end to their strenuous rendezvous. She was just about to bid Michael a good evening when his face suddenly brightened. "Your father and Sir Percy are quite proud of you, you know."

Alexandra shifted against the railing of the ship. She'd come up on deck to be alone, not to engage in an endless amount of meaningless conversation with a man whom she wished might vanish to the opposite side of the planet. Perhaps then she'd be able to focus her full attention on William, rather than the way in which Ashford's cheeks dimpled when he smiled.

Before she could predict his next move, he stepped closer, put his arm about her shoulder in a companionable fashion, and began steering her toward the stern. It was the same sort of gesture she'd seen her brothers use with their friends countless times over the years. From Michael's perspective there should be nothing wrong with behaving in such a way. After all, as far as he knew, Alexandra was a young gentleman.

But Alexandra had no time whatsoever to prepare herself for his touch. Her knees practically buckled beneath her. But that wasn't the worst of it. In an attempt to steady herself, she reached out and grabbed onto the nearest thing she could find, which of course happened to be Michael's chest. She clawed at it, trying to latch on, but her hand kept slipping until he finally caught her by the elbow.

"Are you all right?" he asked. His breath was warm against her face.

"A touch of seasickness I suppose," she murmured—yet another lie.

He chuckled. "I gather you haven't been aboard a ship before."

She shook her head, her hand still resting upon his chest. All she could think about at that moment was how firm his muscles seemed beneath his shirt and how fast her heart was suddenly beating. She feared it was so loud, he might actually hear it.

For heaven's sake, pull yourself together.

She wondered if she were the only one affected by their

brief entanglement and quickly snuck a look at Michael. He was standing with his legs planted firmly upon the deck, his hand still bracing her arm, and the look in his eyes was . . . disconcerting to say the least. Never in her life had anyone looked at her quite like that. She'd no idea what it meant, but she knew that she didn't like it. It made her feel highly uneasy.

This is madness.

A thought struck her—*he knows.* Surely that had to be it, if his perplexed expression was anything to go by. She'd thought he'd be angrier when he realized the truth, but instead he simply looked confused and perhaps even a little sad. Odd at that.

She briefly wondered what might have given her away, until, quite suddenly, things took a turn for the more bizarre.

"I love women," Michael blurted out, his eyes still firmly locked on hers.

"I never said that you didn't," Alexandra replied, not certain of how else to respond to such a statement.

"I've always loved women and always will. This . . . this . . ." He shook his head as if to rid it of something unpleasant.

"Er . . . Lord Trenton? Sorry, I mean Ashford." His eyes seemed to clear at the sound of his name. "Are you all right?"

With a soft nudge, he distanced himself from Alexandra. "Yes, quite." he said. "Do you think you can manage?"

"I believe so," she told him, relieved that the awkward moment had finally passed.

"Good, because I was hoping we might have a small contest." A glimmer of mischief flickered in his eyes.

"What sort of contest?" she asked, her curiosity peaked.

An impish smile spread its way across his face. "The sort wherein we throw knives," he told her.

It was impossible for her not to laugh. This was precisely the sort of thing that she enjoyed most. "You're a brave man," she jibed. "You know I dislike you intensely—after all, I've made no secret of it. And yet you trust me to throw a knife and not hit you with it."

"Should I be afraid?"

"Very," she said in the gravest voice she could manage.

But inside, she laughed with glee. She turned to Ashford who was clearly doing his best to feign a frown. He failed miserably though and eventually laughed instead. For just about the hundredth time since setting out that morning, Alexandra felt a disturbing attraction toward him. She would have to be careful, she reminded herself, or she might very well find herself falling for him, and that would be a most unfavorable outcome indeed, under the circumstances.

She watched now as Michael pulled a deck of cards from his coat pocket and selected the ace of spades. He pushed the top of it onto a nail protruding from one of the masts and stepped back to admire his work. "This will do," he said, casting a sidelong glance in Alexandra's direction before shouting a warning to the sailors on deck to stay out of the way. "The object of the game will be to hit the center of the spade with the tip of your blade, so it sticks. If your knife falls to the ground, you lose.

"We'll start here." He indicated the designated spot with the tip of his boot. "And move backward in one-yard increments."

"Two-yard increments" she told him, her competitive spirit taking over.

"Are you quite certain?" Michael asked. "Two yards will make a huge difference in terms of—"

"Are you getting cold feet?" she asked.

"Certainly not. Two-yard increments it is then."

Alexandra was the first to throw her blade. It hit its mark just as she'd known it would. So did Michael's. Within twenty minutes they'd reached a distance of twenty-seven feet—about as far as they could go without falling over the railing. The sailors had long since paused in their duties and were either standing to one side or hanging from the roping in eager attempts to get a clear view of the ensuing competition. Alexandra lifted her blade, took aim and . . . the knife began to take flight just as Ryan called out her name, distracting her enough to make her hand flinch. All she could do was look helplessly on as her knife continued past its mark before landing on the deck with a loud thud.

A roar of cheers filled the air from those who'd been supporting Michael. "Too bad," he told Alexandra with feigned remorse as he gave her a sympathetic pat on the shoulder.

She wanted to scream.

"What the hell did you have to do that for?" she yelled, her fury directed at none other than her brother. "I could have won!"

"Hm . . . I'm not so sure you would have," Michael remarked. He tossed his knife with practiced ease before she could voice a response. It hit the spade, dead center. "There . . . see? It would have been a draw."

Alexandra clenched her fists. She could practically feel

the steam coming out of her ears. Not only did she have to suffer her brother's stupidity but now she had to contend with Ashford's arrogance as well.

"Except it wasn't a draw of course," Michael continued. "You obviously lost, and I won."

Angry sparks ignited behind her eyes. "This is far from over," she muttered in a low tone.

"Come on, Alex," Ryan said as he sauntered toward her. "Try not to be such an addle plot. There's no harm in losing every once in a while. As long as you do it with dignity."

She glared at him. "I take it you speak from experience," she snapped, before she could stop herself.

A fleeting look of pain swept over Ryan's face, and she instantly regretted her words. How could she be so cold and unfeeling? She knew it couldn't be easy for Ryan to acknowledge that even his sister always bested him whenever weapons and horses were involved, yet he never took it to heart and always voiced his pride in her. She wanted to pummel herself for being so insensitive. "Sorry," she murmured, unable to meet her brother's gaze.

An uncomfortable silence followed.

None of them knew what to say.

Eventually, Alexandra shrugged her shoulders and strode off. She paused before reaching the staircase, picked up her knife and then headed below deck in search of her cabin.

Michael and Ryan stared after her. "A bit of a sore loser, your brother," Michael remarked.

"I do believe this is the first time he's lost at anything in the past five years," Ryan told him thoughtfully.

"You must be joking."

Ryan shook his head. "No, he's the best I've ever seen when it comes to such things—better than William even. Just wait until you see him brandishing a sword. You'll never forget it, for it is truly a remarkable thing to watch. It's the reason why my father insisted he join us." He turned to look at Michael. "But he's young, with a tendency to act rashly. That is why I've come—to keep him out of trouble."

Michael grinned. "Well, I think he's quite fortunate to have you around." Then, in a more serious tone, "I have the feeling, though, he and I are unlikely to get along. A pity since I happen to quite like him."

"Can you blame him? After all, you do pose a very real threat to our brother—you, the man who'll bring him home to face charges . . . unless of course you find an excuse to kill him first."

Michael narrowed his eyes. "It seems even you are against me. And here I thought we were becoming friends."

"I respect you, Ashford, and I understand you're merely doing your job, but you and I are *not* friends. Whether we will be or not, will very likely be determined on how this whole affair plays out. William is family. How would you feel if you were in our position?"

Michael was quiet for a moment, as if he were giving Ryan's question some serious thought. He eventually nodded, conceding the point. "Will you try to stop me from completing my assignment?"

"No," Ryan said, with a shake of his head. "I won't. But keep an eye on Alex. I can't vouch for him."

Michael nodded. "A game of whist before bed?" he asked hopefully.

Ryan chuckled. "Why not?" he said, then paused. "The stakes?"

"The same as what they were with your brother. If you win, I'll promise not to harm as much as a hair on William's head. He'll be returned to England, unscathed."

Ryan stopped, dead in his tracks. "No wonder she was so peeved," he murmured.

"What was that?"

"Er . . . nothing . . . just that I now understand why Alex was so upset about losing."

Perhaps he could right this wrong though. After all, whist was one of his favorite games and one of the few things he'd always been better at than his siblings. With a sudden smile on his face, he picked up his pace. It seemed as though there might still be hope.

A couple of hours later, Alexandra awoke to the mad hammering of someone pounding furiously against her door. She leapt from her cot, threw her cloak around her shoulders and pulled the hood down low to cover her eyes.

"Alex!" It was Ryan's voice, hollering away at the top of his lungs. "Are you in there?"

"Maybe he jumped ship," another voice said. It was Michael's. "After such a heavy loss, I probably would have."

"Do you sup . . . suppose he might be bobbing about The Chanel then?"

Some bawdy laughter followed. There were some scuffling sounds and then a loud thud against the wall, which told Alexandra that one of them had probably lost his footing.

They're in their cups. Both of them.

Pulling her hood close against her face to mask as much of it as possible, she eased her door open.

"Ah, there he is," Michael muttered as he swayed slightly from side to side. "You missed quite the game of whist, you know."

Leaning forward, Alexandra glanced about in search of Ryan. She found him sitting on the floor, looking up at her with a loopy grin. "What the devil have you been up to?" she asked. "You're both completely foxed. How will you manage tomorrow?"

"Do you know . . ." Michael responded. He closed his eyes as if to overcome the need to vomit. "Do you know . . . you . . . you often sound rather like a woman?"

Alexandra stared back at him in horror. How could she have been so clumsy to forget her female voice? "What do you mean?" she asked, lowering her voice another octave for good measure.

"Well," he drawled. "You're just as touchy and scarcely any fun at all, unless you get to have your way. All the men of my acquaintance are far more laid back. And they would *never* disapprove of all my conquests."

Oh dear.

She hadn't considered that her personality might interfere with her plan of deception. There was really nothing for it but to add another lie to the ever-increasing pile.

"What I disapprove of is the idea of having several mistresses all at once. I find it dishonorable. A gentleman ought to have either one mistress alone, or, a string of women left behind him in the wake. Women with whom one *never* forms an attachment. I for one prefer the latter."

She could see Ryan's eyes bulging out of his head as soon as she'd said her piece, but it had to be done. If Michael were really going to think her a man, she'd at least have to tell him she'd bedded a few ladies over the years, no matter how disgusting she found it. Was this really what men discussed with one another? How utterly base and vile.

Michael grinned. "Now that's more like it, Summersby. For a second there, I thought you might be a backgammon player . . ."

Alexandra gave him a blank stare.

"I thought you might prefer men."

This again.

"I already told you that I don't," she snapped. "I love a woman's company just as much as you and my brothers."

"That is . . ." Michael seemed to fumble about his brain for the correct word. "Quite reassuring."

There was a moment's pause, which was soon smothered by another bout of laughter from both men. Alexandra rolled her eyes. "If that's all," she said. "I should like to return to my bed."

"Is that all?" Michael asked Ryan. "I could have sworn we had something more to say. My brain is so damn fogged I cannot seem to think straight."

"I think it had something to do with a game of cards," Ryan remarked.

Alexandra was even more confused now. "Cards?"

"Ah yes, so it did. Whist, to be precise." Michael looked

quite smug all of a sudden—as if he were the keeper of a great secret. "Your brother's a remarkably good player. I dare say he won. Beat me fair and square."

Alexandra's gaze shifted to Ryan, who'd finally managed to gather himself up off the floor and was now giving her a toothy grin. "William shan't be harmed. Ashford has given me his word on it."

"Is that true?" Alexandra asked warily, returning her attention to Michael. She wasn't quite ready to trust anything he said just yet.

"It is indeed," he slurred, nodding his head in a less than elegant fashion.

"Thank you," she said, after a moment's hesitation. "I'm much obliged. Now, if you don't mind, I'd like to get some rest before we set out tomorrow. And judging from the state you two are in, I'd certainly advise you to do the same."

"Duly noted," Michael said, with an overstated salute. He then turned about somewhat awkwardly until he found Ryan. "Come along, Summersby. We have our orders."

Alexandra stared after them as they wobbled away down the corridor. Remaining indifferent toward Michael was quite possibly the most difficult thing she'd ever had to do. As much as she was loathe to admit it, he occupied far too many of her thoughts. Her attraction to the man was starting to get annoying. It's not as if they'd ever form an attachment.

Get a hold of yourself.

She was Alexandra Summersby after all—not some simple country girl about to be sucked in by a handsome face. Besides, he wasn't even charming, but rather . . . ugh, she didn't know what he was exactly, but he certainly wasn't worth wasting precious hours of sleep over.

She and Ashford? Ha! It was impossible, hopeless, mad . . . indeed, the most awful notion that had ever entered into her head. Still, she couldn't quite stop her wretched mind from wondering what it might be like to be held by those strong arms of his. She let out a sigh of undeniable frustration before closing her cabin door and slipping back into bed.

"I abhor him, I despise him, I . . ." she whispered to herself before drifting off to sleep, yet the very last image to drift through her treacherous mind before sleep claimed her, was that of a dark-haired rogue with a cheeky smile.

CHAPTER FOUR

The following morning, Alexandra was surprised to find both Ryan and Michael waiting for her on the quay. They did not look well though. "I thought you two would still be asleep," she said with a smirk.

"And we probably would be if it hadn't been for those god-awful seagulls squawking so loudly—I almost felt compelled to shoot one of them," Ryan grumbled.

"I couldn't agree more," Michael moaned, pressing his hand against his forehead in an attempt to ward off an apparent headache. "The world would be well served indeed if those evil birds would become extinct. I should be more than happy to assist."

Alexandra hid a grin. Although they only had themselves to blame, she couldn't help but feel sorry for them. It was going to be a very long day indeed for Ryan and Michael. "We need horses. You can wait here while I make some inquiries at the tavern over there." She nodded toward a rundown building on the other side of the road. A crooked sign above the door claimed it to be LE VIEUX DOUELLE.

It was late morning, so the place was mostly empty, except for a handful of customers still lingering over a late breakfast. Alexandra paused in the doorway and pushed back her hood. She then pulled down her scarf. She'd decided that her feminine wiles might serve her better in this instance than the disguise she wore for Michael's benefit alone.

Looking around the murky place, she quickly spotted a man who fit the bill of innkeeper—an older, portly fellow with a grizzly beard and rolled-up shirt sleeves who was drying off some freshly washed glasses with a dish towel.

Alexandra straightened her back and strode toward him. "*Excusez moi, monsieur,*" she said in flawless French—the result of a very determined tutor.

The man glanced up at her, one eyebrow slightly rising as he took in her overall appearance. He paused at his task, and then set the glass he'd been holding down on the bar counter. He said nothing, though the corners of his mouth began to twist themselves into a mocking smile.

Alexandra chose to ignore it. "I was hoping you might be able to help me."

"*Oui?*"

"My companions and I are in need of transportation. Do you have three horses available for purchase?"

"As it happens, I do have a few horses in my stables. But they are champions and will not come cheap." The man leaned toward her until she could smell the wine on his breath. "How well are you prepared to pay for them?" His eyes wandered over her, then came to rest upon her chest. There was no misinterpreting his meaning.

Alexandra flinched in spite of herself, a faint taste of bile rising in her throat. "I'm terribly sorry," she told him between gritted teeth. "I believe I may have come to the wrong place." She wasn't looking for trouble, and the mere act of allowing this awful man to look at her was making her feel sullied enough to want to poke his eyes out. She turned to leave, only to find herself face to face with a skinnier man who, if his eyes were to be believed, was having the exact same notion as the innkeeper. Alexandra pasted a haughty expression onto her face. "May I help you with something?" she asked as she placed both hands on her hips and gave him a look of disgust.

Perhaps not the correct thing to say, she realized a moment too late when the skinny man's face broke into a rather disturbing smile. Given the chance, she would have taken a step backward, but in this case, that would have landed her straight in the arms of the innkeeper. She threw up her hands instead. "I have no desire to cause any trouble," she said in a voice far calmer than she felt.

She'd always considered herself to be on equal footing with her brothers and had never considered that other men might treat her differently. It was true that she was skilled at handling weaponry, but this situation turned her stomach. Somehow, it had never occurred to her that she might have to fight to protect her innocence. It was not at all what she had expected and the possibility of losing was most assuredly a fate far worse than that of dying in battle.

"Oh, it won't be any trouble at all," she heard the innkeeper say.

A moment later, she felt his grubby hand upon her backside. Instinct overruled any lack of confidence that the situation might have stirred in her. Without so much as turning her head, Alexandra jabbed her elbow backward and up into the innkeeper's neck. She then ducked to avoid the blow she knew would follow from his friend. The skinny man's punch flew over her head and made contact with the innkeeper's nose.

"*Putain!*" the innkeeper wheezed.

Taking quick advantage of the situation, Alexandra sprang to her full height, drew her sword and rammed the hilt of it down until it made contact with the back of the skinny man's head. He uttered a loud groan before sagging to the floor in a sorry heap of unconsciousness.

Swirling around in one fluid motion, she pinned the angry innkeeper with her sword, her glare speaking volumes about her feelings toward him.

He looked like a rabid dog, eager to attack. Alexandra paid him no heed. She was now in full control of the situation—her momentary lapse in confidence completely evaporated without a trace. "One should never underestimate an opponent . . . or a potential victim, as I believe you intended me to be." She was conscious of being watched by the few guests present as they'd abandoned their food in order to take in the whole scene. Nobody moved a muscle. The room was shrouded in silence.

"Only a woman with no morals would dress like that." The innkeeper almost spat the words at her. "Indeed, you are no lady, and you should be treated accordingly."

Alexandra merely cocked an eyebrow. She would not allow this sorry apology of a man to see just how offended she was. Instead, she pressed the tip of her sword against his chest, drawing what little gratification she could out of watching him flinch. "I was willing to pay handsomely for those horses of yours—though I now believe you ought to give them to me as some form of . . . shall we say compensation?"

The innkeeper's eyes darkened with rage. Alexandra merely smiled at him as she needled the tip of her sword a little closer. A single drop of scarlet blood beaded around the tip before trickling down the frightened man's chest. He winced before nodding vigorously, his eyes quickly flooding with fear.

"Excellent," she said, easing back a little. "Now then, would you be kind enough to show me the stables?"

Ten minutes later, Ryan and Michael spotted Alexandra racing toward them, leading two large stallions and one smaller mare along by their bridles. "Hurry up," she yelled, her voice conveying the urgency of the situation at hand. "We've no time to lose. Hell will be on our heels before you know it."

"What the blazes?" Michael muttered. He still looked pretty groggy.

"I suggest you do as she says," Ryan said, jumping to his feet with enormous effort as he grabbed his bag. He took Alexandra's too and tossed it to her. "I see an innkeeper who looks quite displeased. He has a pistol, Ashford."

That got Michael's legs working. Picking his own bag up off the ground, he hurried after Ryan, taking the reins of one of the stallions from Alexandra. "What the devil have you been playing at, Summersby?" he asked as he swung himself into the saddle.

"I don't like to be insulted," Alex called out over her shoulder, her mare already carrying her off down the road. "I suggest you keep that in mind."

For a split second, Michael couldn't help but stare at the disappearing back of the reckless youth.

Bloody hell!

With a quick kick to his horse's flanks, he raced after the two siblings, just as gunfire rang out behind him.

The lad is going to get us all killed before we even reach Paris.

CHAPTER FIVE

It was six thirty in the evening by the time they reached Rouen. They'd ridden hard, pushing their horses to the limit and were all extremely exhausted. To top it off, it had begun to rain—a steady downpour that had them soaked to the skin within minutes.

Forced to slow to a more measured pace as they entered the city, they clopped along the streets, heading toward the cathedral that rose like a beacon from the town center.

Rounding the corner, Alexandra drew a sharp breath as she took in the magnificence of it—the spires, beautifully adorned in lacy stonework and the flying buttresses a testament to the skill of the craftsmen who had once made them. "Isn't it incredible?" Michael asked as he drew up beside her.

"It is indeed," Ryan remarked.

"Remarkable," Alexandra muttered.

Michael grinned. "Just wait until you see the one in Paris. It's far grander." He looked about and then nodded toward a hotel on the opposite side of the square. "Come along . . . let's get out of this miserable weather."

Water trickled down Alexandra's forehead as she dismounted—her boots splashing a puddle as she hit the ground, wetting her breeches even further. She wiped her eyes with the back of her hand and glanced around the darkened town. A couple of lone figures roamed between the gaslights, lighting them as they went—the yellow glow of each lantern casting a shimmering glare upon the wet cobbles.

Leaving their horses with one of the grooms, they went inside, their clothes dripping and their boots squelching as they walked across to the front desk.

"Shall we meet downstairs for dinner in say . . . half an hour?" Michael asked a short while later while they headed upstairs in search of their rooms.

"Certainly," Ryan said. "Though I do believe I'd like to make an early night of it. In truth, I don't believe I've ever felt this rotten in my life."

"More so than when you and William emptied Papa's case of champagne last Christmas?" Alexandra asked.

"I suppose not. There's still much that I don't recall about that incident, except that I was practically bed-ridden for a full week after."

"Hm . . . I must admit my heart went out to the poor maids who had to clean up after you two," she said. "*That* cannot have been a pleasant job."

They reached the landing and as they waited for the porter to show them to their rooms, Alexandra turned to Michael. "I will take my dinner elsewhere."

A puzzled expression came over his face as if he were putting a great deal of effort into figuring out *why* she would choose to eat alone. "I will have to remove my scarf," she continued, in answer to his unspoken question. "I doubt that the lighting will be dim enough to conceal my features, and I would hate to be the cause of someone losing their appetite."

Michael visibly balked at that. "Surely it's not that bad," he said. "And your brother and I won't mind—that goes without saying. If some of the other guests have an issue however, then to hell with them."

Alexandra wanted to creep away under the carpet and die. Why the devil did he have to be so damned pleasant about it? It just compounded how awful she felt for all the lies she kept dishing out at him. She felt rotten to the core—especially because she'd begun to acknowledge that he wasn't quite as bad as she'd hoped he'd be. How easy it would have been if he'd truly been the monster she'd conjured in her head. Instead, he was kind toward those who were less fortunate. He probably took in stray puppies and donated money to the homeless. She groaned inwardly, because once he discovered that she'd tricked him and lied to him over and over and over again . . . he'd probably despise her for the remainder of her days.

"I insist," she told him as she stepped inside her room. "I shall see you both in the morning. Bright and early." The door closed.

Too bad.

Michael sighed in frustration. He'd taken a liking to Alex, and it bothered him that the lad still feared showing his face in front of him.

"My brother's a bit self-conscious about his appearance," Ryan said, offering Michael an apologetic smile.

"He need not be," Michael muttered. "I wouldn't think any less of him for the way he looks."

After a quick dinner, Michael headed out. He needed some fresh air, if for no other reason than to ease the headache that still bothered him. Besides, he was too agitated to be able to sleep. Something about Alex Summersby troubled him. He couldn't put his finger on what it was, but instinct told him to stay on alert. It seemed as if Alex was keeping something from him. He shook his head to rid it of the uneasiness that plagued it. Perhaps it was nothing. And with Alex's condition, having a face he dared not show in public, it was probably natural for him to be unsure, awkward, and skittish. Still, Michael decided that it would be wise to keep an eye on him—just in case.

Alexandra marched along the rain drenched street, water splashing about her booted feet as she went. She was in a furious temper. When she'd gotten out of bed yesterday morning, she'd *known* that she would dislike Michael Ashford. She hadn't doubted it for a second.

But then he'd come riding along, knocking the stable little planet she'd been living on right off its axis—with nothing more than the features that a very generous mother nature had bestowed upon him. It was enough to make her sick to her stomach. And the lies! God help her, but she'd never told such outrageous tales in all her life. She'd only planned to pass herself off as a young man, yet somewhere along the line, that had been greatly elaborated upon. Now it seemed that she, who was an innocent virgin, born without a single blemish upon her flesh, was pretending to be not only horribly malformed but also to have a voracious appetite for sex.

Good grief!

However, he would soon discover the truth, and once he did, their relationship would very likely take a drastic turn. In truth, she'd be lucky if he didn't tear her limb from limb.

She picked up her pace to clear her head.

Before all else comes duty—her father had always said— *toward one's family and toward one's country.* Hers lay toward her family, while Ashford's lay toward their country. She could not allow something as trivial as her growing attraction for him to come in the way of either of their responsibilities.

Alexandra was just passing by the Veuve Lorraine when the front doors to the place sprang open, and two men tumbled out, knocking her sideways. Before she had a chance to get her bearings, more men joined in the fight, while somebody else pushed her forcefully into the midst of the ensuing melee. Unsure of how it had all come about, she suddenly found herself dodging punches and doing the best she could to stand her ground. This was, she conceded, one of those rare occasions when men held the clear advantage. Her punches just didn't carry enough weight behind them to make a difference.

Spotting an opening in the scuffle, she edged toward it. She was just about ready to make a run for it, when a large hand gripped hold of her ankle and pulled.

Alexandra's heart leapt with the knowledge that she was about to fall.

Her cheek hit the pavement with a loud crack that sent shockwaves through her jaw. A sharp pain followed as she fumbled about, doing her best to gather her wits about her. This was not the time to be lying sprawled out on the ground while a hoard of buffoons were getting ready to trample all over her.

There was only one way for her to protect herself in this case.

Deciding that she wasn't going to be stampeded for one more second, she sprang to her feet, coolheaded, and seemingly annoyed. She then drew a dagger from her left boot in one swift motion while unsheathing her sword at the same time.

Enough is enough.

"Sword!" someone bellowed.

As if by magic, all action came to an abrupt halt as darting eyes hurried to locate the piece of weaponry. A moment later, Alexandra found herself the center of attention.

"*Quest ce que tu fait?*" a loud voice yelled.

"I have no desire to hurt anyone," Alexandra began. "Just let me go. This is not my fight, so I'd rather not suffer any further injury because of it."

"Would you look at that?" a burly fellow snorted with much disdain in his voice. "A little chit in men's clothing." They all caught a good look at her face before she could manage to rearrange the scarf that had come loose during the scuffle.

"Aye, I wouldn't mind givin' her a tumble," another said.

Grins broke out as the men, suddenly united in a different cause—their previous skirmish completely forgotten—turned on Alexandra. She rolled her eyes. This really wasn't going the way she'd planned it at all.

Holding her sword at arm's length to keep the men at bay, she tried to back away from them, but with little success. All were now grinning from ear to ear, likening the spectacle no doubt, to that of seeing a bear dance about the town square.

"Come now, *mademoiselle* . . . What exactly do you hope to accomplish with *that?*" one man asked, pointing to her sword.

"Stole it from her brother most like," another commented. "Or a poor sod who was fool enough to fall asleep after a healthy bout of lovemaking!" a toothless fellow chimed in.

Roars of laughter filled the air.

"You a virgin then?" the first man asked as he ogled Alexandra from head to toe with eyes that seemed ready to leap from their sockets.

Alexandra swallowed hard, a soft prickle scurrying over her entire body. She suddenly felt more filthy being victim to these men's rude remarks than if she'd been mucking out a pigsty. Well, she wouldn't have it, not by any stretch of their pathetic imaginations. Squaring her shoulders, a sudden urge for recklessness washing over her, she stared straight back at them and held her ground. "Are any of you dimwits fortunate enough to own a weapon equal to mine?"

The challenge was unmistakable. There was a murmur among the crowd before a tall rather thinly shaped man with angular features and a sharp pointy nose stepped forward, brandishing his own sword. *"Oui!"* he exclaimed.

His companions immediately raised a cheer of encouragement for him.

"Very well then," Alexandra remarked, the feeling of control back in her hands. A familiar need for danger filled her as she looked back at the expectant crowd. She was holding them captive in the palm of her hand, and she loved it. "I shall allow any one of you fools to have your way with me without offering a single complaint in return—if your friend here can beat me in a fair fight."

After a moment's silence, the exact amount of time that it took for everyone present to digest such a shocking proposition, the small group burst into cheers and began wishing their friend the best of luck, patting him enthusiastically on the back and shaking his hand.

"If, however, I win," Alexandra continued. "You will give me free passage. You will not stand in my way, and you will not follow me."

A roar of laughter filled the air and the terms were agreed upon with a quick handshake.

Looking about, Alexandra knew that none of them doubted the outcome of the upcoming fight—except, perhaps, the fellow holding the sword. If Alexandra weren't entirely mistaken, he was beginning to look far less confident than he had done a moment earlier. His friend's on the other hand seemed quite convinced that their victory was already in hand.

Returning her knife to her boot, Alexandra took an en garde stance, her saber held firmly in her right hand. "Let us begin," she suggested. She then cocked an expectant eyebrow and beckoned for her opponent to engage her.

Rounding a corner, Michael stopped short as he took in the scene before him.

What the devil?

It seemed as if a duel was taking place right there in the middle of the street, though in the dim lighting it was impossible for him to make out the participants.

Highly unusual, especially since dueling was just as illegal in France as it was in England. His curiosity piqued, yet with no desire to get himself embroiled in the battle, he stayed within the shadows of the buildings and moved hesitantly forward in order to get a closer look. Two men were having a go at each other, though one appeared to be handling his weapon far more proficiently than the other.

What on earth could have brought this on?

Whatever their differences, a duel still seemed a bit . . . *theatrical*, for lack of a better word.

It took a while for him to get a clear look at what was happening. The large crowd of onlookers concealed most of the action from Michael, until one of the duelers was suddenly forced backward by the other and out into the street. Michael took in the sight with growing interest. One of the men was well over a head taller than the other, which ought to have given him a clear advantage, yet the smaller of the two held his ground with expert footing, giving as good, if not better than he got.

Moving closer still to the ensuing spectacle, Michael's eyes moved over the figure that seemed to be effortlessly parrying every blow that came from his opponent. He was skilled. Very skilled. In fact, it was virtually impossible for his opponent to keep up. Each time he struck out his sword, the smaller man escaped him.

A small suspicion crept over Michael.

Can it be?

The body type was certainly similar . . . the arms, just as slim. . . .

The pair of duelers turned, the glow from a lantern bathing their faces in a soft glow, and then there was no longer any disputing it. Michael was watching Alex Summersby in full action as he danced about with an expertise and agility that he couldn't recall ever having witnessed before.

Remarkable!

Ryan had certainly been right when he'd praised his brother's swordsmanship. There wasn't a single man that Michael could think of who might be able to compete with that level of proficiency.

He wondered how Alex might react if he saw him watching him and considered turning and walking away. But he could scarcely tear his eyes away—watching Alex was simply extraordinary. His body seemed to move with more ease than most people could manage when they were taking a mere stroll down the street.

Stepping onto the edge of the pavement, he watched, enthralled as Alex swept gracefully aside, sending his attacker stumbling with nowhere to go. The minute his adversary fell upon his knees, Alex ran up behind him, quick as a fox and delivered a good and solid kick to his backside, putting him flat on his face and bringing up a roar of cheers from the crowd.

Support has clearly shifted to Alex.

A helpless grin was spreading to Michael's cheeks.

"Do you surrender?" Alex asked in perfect French while he poked his opponent in the back with the tip of his saber.

He sounds like a bloody native, Michael thought with a growing sense of awe.

And he seemed so comfortable too, so relaxed and carefree—not at all guarded like he tended to be toward Michael. This was clearly his element.

Michael started to turn away, but a pair of sharp blue eyes caught hold of his. They seemed to sparkle with glee—so much so, that Michael had no trouble imagining the triumphant smile on Alex's lips. Well, now that he'd been spotted, he might as well wait. Indeed, it would probably be rude not to.

"*Oui*," came the faint sound, carried on the breeze.

Alexandra eased away from her target and reached out her hand to help the poor man to his feet. His friends quickly surrounded them both, teasing him and congratulating her.

"An impressive display of swordsmanship," Michael remarked when Alexandra came toward him a few moments later.

"Thank you," she said. She regarded him for a moment. "Does it surprise you?"

"I have to admit," Michael told her. "When your father and Sir Percy recommended you, I thought they might be exaggerating when they said you were the finest swordsman in England. But I do believe they may be quite right. I've never seen anyone else perform as well as you just did."

Alexandra could feel her ears grow hot from blushing. It was the grandest compliment he could have paid to her. She'd struggled so hard over the years to be the best that she could be. Now, hearing Michael's praise was a true reward.

"Shall we walk back together?" he then asked.

She tilted her head as if considering the pros and cons, then nodded—after all, what would he think of her if she said she didn't want his company on a mere walk? "Yes, I'm quite ready to get myself to bed." She gave him a sidelong glance. "And with last night's activities in mind, I trust you must be feeling much the same way."

He grinned at that. "I *am* exhausted."

CHAPTER SIX

Alexandra stood next to her brother and Michael, regarding the building in front of them. It was so much better than what she'd expected. Then again, they were employed by The Foreign Office, and they were all members of the *ton*, so they couldn't very well be told to live under a bridge, could they? At any rate, the handsome apartment building with matching towers at either end looked quite welcoming. "Shall we?" she asked, as she glanced toward the massive iron gates.

Stepping forward, Michael rang the bell and waited for the caretaker (a skinny man with very little to say) to let them into an open courtyard where a groom was ready to take their horses.

"I must say, I've yet to see an apartment building in London to rival this," Ryan said as they wound their way up a large, spiraling staircase.

"I was just thinking that very same thing," Alexandra told him. "This has enough lavishness to compete with the vestibule at Chesterfield House."

"It's one of the reasons Paris is as famous as it is. The architecture is simply dazzling," Michael remarked as they reached the fifth floor landing. He gave a hard knock on the door.

A moment later, it opened, and they were greeted by a middle-aged woman who immediately introduced herself as Mrs. Bell. She was a short, round thing with a seemingly cheerful disposition, twinkling eyes, and dark grey hair. "I shall be your housekeeper, maid, and cook," she announced in a fine Yorkshire accent. "No need for a large staff in a place this size."

"An Englishwoman," Ryan exclaimed in obvious relief before lowering his voice to a whisper. "Do you speak French?"

Mrs. Bell looked a bit put out by his question but quickly recovered. "Yes, Mr. Summersby, I don't see how we'd manage if I didn't. After all, we don't want to attract attention to ourselves, do we now?"

"We certainly do not," Michael agreed while he frowned at Ryan. "Is there a man about who might serve as a valet by any chance?" he then asked, his eyes searching the front entrance for any sign of a butler. "The Summersbys and I can easily share, but we will need for our clothes and boots to be tended to, and perhaps a little help in dressing on occasion."

Mrs. Bell nodded. "Mr. Bell will be joining us shortly. He just stepped out to run a quick errand." Her voice was more than a little apologetic.

"No need to trouble yourself over it," Alexandra told her. "We will manage well enough until he returns. In the meantime, however, would you perhaps be kind enough to show us to our rooms?"

"Certainly, sir," Mrs. Bell replied. "There are only three, so it's just a matter of individual preference."

Mrs. Bell turned toward a long corridor. "Here's the first room," she said as she opened a door on the right. "Mr. Bell and I are staying in the servant's quarters just behind the kitchen, so you'll have plenty of privacy at this end."

Ryan popped his head inside the room for a quick look. "I will take this one," he announced without bothering to look in Michael's or Alexandra's direction. "See you in a few minutes." The door closed smoothly behind him.

Mrs. Bell then opened a door opposite Ryan's. Michael and Alexandra stepped forward at the same time to take a look at it, his arm inadvertently brushing against her side.

An unfamiliar warmth floated through her, calming her senses and easing her mind—she felt momentarily light-headed. Praying that he hadn't noticed, she quickly stepped back and broke contact. This was ridiculous. She barely knew the man, yet he suddenly had the power to make her heart flutter and her brain lag desperately far behind.

"You can have this one," Michael told her, then added, "If you would like it."

Alexandra stepped inside. It was a very spacious room with a wide canopy bed dressed in light blue and silver tones. A chest of drawers stood next to it. There was a tall closet next to where they were standing by the door. A comfortable sitting area comprised of a sofa, a table, and two chairs had been set in one corner of the room, and at the wall opposite them, were a pair of French doors leading out onto a balcony.

"The balcony runs along the length of the building connecting all the rooms on this side," Mrs. Bell said as if reading her thoughts.

"It will do nicely," Alexandra muttered, not knowing what else to say to that. She knew that there was only one room left. It was next to hers and it would belong to Michael. The thought shook her more than she dared to admit.

Damn it all.

She would very likely drive herself mad because of this man. It was absolutely infuriating.

"Needless to say, the next room will be yours, Lord Trenton," Mrs. Bell chirped. "Now if you don't mind, I'll leave you both to get settled. Supper will be ready in about one hour." With that, she sauntered off in the direction of the kitchen, her whole body swaying from side to side as she went.

Michael hid a smile. "I will see you later, Summersby. Perhaps then we can begin discussing how best to go about finding your brother."

I dare say, it won't be the only thing we shall be discussing, she thought, but she merely nodded in approval as she closed the door behind her. Poor Michael—he was going to be in for one hell of a surprise when she showed up for dinner without her cloak and scarf.

She dropped her bag on the floor with a heavy thud, and then let out a slow sigh.

Never in her life had she felt so self-conscious and so uncertain of herself. In no more than two days, Michael Ashford had managed to unnerve her more than she was willing to acknowledge. This wasn't like her at all. No man had ever held such power over her, and it vexed her beyond compare.

With a groan, she opened her bag and rummaged through it. Pulling out the only two dresses she owned, she carefully laid them out on the bed and stood back to take a good look at them. She'd packed them as an afterthought, hastily throwing them into her bag on her way out the door. Looking at them now, she couldn't help but wince. Not only were they more wrinkled than an old, withered apple but they were also completely drab. In truth, they were more likely to attract a swarm of horseflies than a man as refined as Ashford.

She blinked.

Had she just been worrying about whether his lordship might find her attractive? Was she seriously concerned about what he might think of her if she showed up in one of these dresses?

Not that it was likely to matter. Once he found out that she'd hoodwinked him, the fact that she stood before him dressed like a potato would probably go completely unnoticed. All the same, she decided to stuff the dresses back in her bag and put on a clean shirt and a pair of brown breeches instead.

If Ashford was ever going to see her in a gown, better to wait until she had one that would be sure to astound him.

Michael and Ryan were sitting in the parlor enjoying a bottle of claret, when Alexandra walked in, as nonchalant as ever. Ryan was the first to glance in her direction, a look of panic creeping into his eyes. Noticing the change in his expression, Michael turned in his seat until his gaze landed on Alex.

It was a moment Alexandra would not soon forget.

At first, he looked confused, as if uncertain as to whom this woman might be, suddenly standing there in the middle of the room. It looked as if he might ask, but then his eyes narrowed, they locked onto hers, and then his whole demeanor changed. "What the hell is going on?" he asked as his eyes darted between the two siblings.

"I . . . well, you see . . ." Ryan seemed to grope about for the right words, if his perplexed expression was anything to go by. Eventually he just said, "This is my sister, Alexandra Summersby."

Michael didn't move a muscle. He did not look shocked or even the slightest bit surprised. It was the oddest thing, his face was like a mask, completely concealing whatever it was he might be thinking. "Please tell me that this is a nightmare from which I will soon awaken," he finally managed to say.

"Unfortunately, it is not," Alexandra told him quietly.

Michael's eyes found hers again. "I should have known," he said. "I have yet to meet a man with eyes like yours. Those are a woman's eyes."

And then he said nothing. He merely stared at her until she felt herself grow hot and uncomfortable. There was something in his eyes . . . a look that made her heart beat just a little bit faster. She wasn't sure of what it was exactly, but it was similar to the way in which he'd looked at her the other night on the ship—that same disconcerting stare.

"I cannot believe that we've brought you along to France." He seemed quite angry. "You had best give me a bloody good explanation for this," he told them in a tight voice.

Alexandra shrugged her shoulders as she plopped down onto a chair and crossed her legs. "You would never have agreed to let me come if you had known."

Michael's eyes narrowed as he glared back at her. "So you decided to trick me instead—how very noble of you."

"Don't forget that this whole thing is Sir Percy's doing," Ryan reminded him. "If anyone is to blame, it is he and our father."

"And I shall have a very pointed discussion with both of them upon my return," Michael stated. He shook his head while he looked at Ryan. "I was a fool to trust you."

Ryan looked momentarily pained by Michael's harsh words, but he said nothing, no doubt deciding that he couldn't deny them without making matters worse. Michael did have a point after all. They had both betrayed him.

Seeing the hurt expression upon her brother's face, Alexandra decided to make an attempt at smoothing things over. "Look, I realize that what we did was underhanded, but it was really the only way for us to go about it. I am sorry, Ashford. We both are."

He stared back at her. "You will get us all killed," he muttered, rising to his feet and stalking angrily across to the side table to pour himself a drink.

She scoffed at that. "And why is that? Because I happen to be a woman?"

"Well, at least you are smart enough to realize *that* much," he told her sarcastically.

Alexandra held his gaze, furious. Ryan looked as if he was trying to think of an excuse, any excuse, to leave. "You saw me fight in Rouen," she said. "You thought me quite proficient then. 'An impressive display of swordsmanship,' you said—if I am not mistaken."

"I thought you were a man," he shot back.

"So now that you know I am not, but that I am a woman instead, my swordsmanship is suddenly *less* impressive? Is that it?"

"You are missing the point entirely, *Lady Alexandra*."

"And you, *Lord* Trenton, are suddenly willing to dismiss me on account of my gender. Well, suffice it to say that you are the most arrogant and despicable man that I have ever encountered." She held her ground; she was so angry her blood practically boiling in her veins.

"Alex," Ryan cautioned her in a low voice. "Ashford has every reason to be vexed by all of this."

"By the fact that we deceived him, yes. But he has no right to insist that I will get us all killed, just because he has suddenly discovered that I am a woman. I dare say he's a bigot."

Ryan groaned, apparently acknowledging that it would be hopeless to try and reason with his sister and that there was nothing left to do but ride out the storm.

Michael frowned, but he didn't take her bait. Instead, he must have decided to make an attempt to explain himself, for when he next spoke, his voice seemed overly calm. "All I know is that we're likely to face battle. In that event, you will be nothing but a liability to us," he said as if he were explaining a potential danger to a child. "You are a woman, Lady Alexandra—a stunningly beautiful woman, as it happens. Ryan and I simply cannot afford having to stick our necks out on account of you. We shall have enough trouble keeping ourselves safe." He settled back against his chair with a rather pleased look upon his face, as if she'd certainly be able to see the logic behind his reasoning now.

But Alexandra just gaped at him. Ryan looked as if he might throttle him.

Michael's gaze shifted from one to the other, then frowned, his lips parting in dismay. "Please excuse my candor," he told him smoothly. One had to give him credit for maintaining his composure. "But I would rather if we didn't beat about the bush in this instance."

"Point taken," Ryan muttered with an edge of annoyance.

Alexandra paid them no mind. All she could think about were Michael's words. Nobody had ever remarked on her looks before, and she couldn't help but be pleased by it. And that such a compliment should come from a man as dashing as him, was . . . well . . . she dared not even think of what it made her feel.

She shook her head and made a desperate attempt to focus on the matter at hand. There just wasn't room for this kind of distraction. Besides, she now definitely disliked the man. Intensely.

Or so she kept telling herself.

"I do not need for you *or* Ryan to protect me," she protested.

Michael groaned. "I realize that, but what *you* don't seem to understand is that you shall be faced with far more danger than either one of us."

Alexandra paused. "What do you mean?" she asked cautiously. "If I can fight as well as either of you, perhaps even better, then why should I be in more danger than you or Ryan on this assignment?"

Michael threw up his hands in exasperation. "Because you're a woman, Lady Alexandra. A rather lovely English-woman who's about to walk right into the midst of Napoleon's army—an army full of men who would gladly give their right arm to bed you."

Ryan drew a sharp breath while Alex's jaw dropped open once again. She *had* to stop doing that. The implication of what Michael was saying began to dawn on her as she thought back on the encounters she'd had over the past two days with men who'd discovered she was female. Alexandra felt a rush of heat coloring her cheeks. She cast a quick glance in Ryan's direction. He was white as a sheet.

Oh dear.

"Forgive me. I did not mean to embarrass you," Michael apologized.

Alexandra drew a deep breath. "We have indeed shocked one another, have we not, Lord Trenton?" The edge of her mouth drew upward to form a partial smile.

"We have indeed, Lady Alexandra, though I am merely being honest." His eyes did not budge from hers. She knew he intended to intimidate her, but she would have none of it. How dare he? What right did he have?

"My lord, do I perhaps owe you something?" she asked, her voice now laced with ice. "Anything at all, in fact? No, I don't believe that I do," she said, answering her own question. "I do however owe my brother everything, and I *will* do whatever I must in order to help him." She crossed her arms and gave him a venomous glare. "You have no authority over me. Please don't make the error of presuming that you do."

To her brother she said, "I will be in my room if you need me."

She got up to leave.

"Shall I ask Mrs. Bell to send in a tray for you?" Ryan asked.

Alexandra paused in the doorway. She glanced back at the two men. "No need to bother," she remarked. "As it happens, I have completely lost my appetite."

What the devil is wrong with this woman? Michael wondered as he watched Alexandra saunter off, her blonde curls spilling down her back. *Has she no common sense whatsoever? Is she completely devoid of all reason?*

She clearly had no idea of the perils that awaited her . . . a lady of breeding heading into enemy territory . . . it was preposterous. Then again, the fact that she was dressed in men's breeches was enough to send any respectable person's head spinning. There was a carelessness about her, coupled with an attitude that spoke volumes about her character. It seemed to Michael that Alexandra Summersby was a very unique young lady indeed.

He couldn't help but wonder how the stringent rules of society could possibly have allowed for such a creature to flourish.

Well, it's unlikely that society has any clue of her existence.

She would have long since become the talk of the town

if it did, since this was precisely the sort of thing that all the gossip mongers would positively drool over—a lord's daughter dressing as a boy and prancing about with loaded pistols and swords. Surely nothing could be more absurd.

"I dare say I need a bit of fresh air on top of this," Michael told Ryan. "I believe I shall take a walk." Michael strode from the room, still unable to comprehend what he'd just learned—or to quite get Alexandra's beautiful face out of his mind.

CHAPTER SEVEN

Alexandra was so furious she was practically shaking, balling her hands into tight fists and pacing about her room. Michael had done nothing but patronize her. He didn't care how adept she might be—that she might even be as capable if not more so than any man when wielding a sword and pistols. But no . . . Michael Ashford had simply decided, based on her gender alone, that she would become a liability, and she absolutely hated him for it. She hated him for making her realize she'd been hoping for his approval . . . his admiration.

Perhaps a tiny part of her did, but it was such a tiny part that she chose to ignore it. In fact, Michael Ashford ought to be completely ignored for the foreseeable future. He had proven himself to be just as she'd feared and had swiftly become a thorn in her side. And when she factored in her unexpected reactions to him, well . . . it would simply be best to try and avoid Ashford altogether.

She set her mind to the task at hand instead. William was in trouble and needed her help. Was it possible that he might have turned? That he might be assisting Bonaparte?

Surely not.

She would bet her life on William's loyalty. But given what she now knew of Michael's opinion of her gender, she would need concrete proof. Alexandra groaned as she flopped down onto her bed. There was no doubt in her mind that this was going to be a very unpleasant assignment indeed.

Michael returned to the apartment two hours later still angry, but most of all at himself. Being made a fool did not sit well with him at all.

Though there had been plenty of signs. They were so easy to recognize now—in hindsight. But he'd ignored every single one of them—the eyes, the voice, the constant need to wear that damnable scarf. He muttered a series of oaths as he yanked the front door open and slammed it shut behind him.

The most vexing thing of all of course, was that feigning indifference toward Alexandra Summersby would, in all likelihood, prove to be a task of monumental proportions. It was true that she was without a doubt the most annoying female he'd ever met. She cursed like a sailor, dressed like a man, ran about like an unruly child. She was opinionated—insufferably so, in fact. But in spite of all her flaws, he was drawn to her. She didn't seem to care about what people thought of her and to top it off, she didn't seem to be at all intimidated by *him*, as women—indeed, most everyone—oftentimes were. She was refreshing. There it was. He'd never met anyone like her, and it intrigued him. He simply couldn't help it.

Returning to the parlor, Michael spotted Ryan reclining in one of the armchairs with a book in his hands. He looked up the minute Michael walked in. "Look . . ." he began. "I owe you an apology, Ashford. Indeed, we both do. It was wrong to deceive you, but we had our orders, just as you have yours."

Michael nodded thoughtfully. "I know," he said with some reluctance. "Perhaps, it might be wise for us to start over."

A smile began to tug at Ryan's lips. "That is awfully big of you," he said. "And greatly appreciated."

Again Michael nodded, then gestured toward the book that Ryan still held. "Anything interesting?" he asked.

"Just a bit of Shakespeare," he said, and then gave a wide grin. "*The Taming of the Shrew* as it happens. You ought to try it."

Michael rolled his eyes. "Is she always like that?" he asked.

"Pretty much," Ryan told him.

"I know that Sir Percy must have had a damn good reason for allowing her to come along, but really . . . I do believe that something must have clouded his better judgment."

"He has known us our whole lives, you know. He's watched Alexandra grow up. In fact, he's approached Papa before about recruiting her for The Foreign Office. He would not have done so unless he thought she was the very best."

"Then why didn't she join? Something must have stopped her, and I can't imagine that it was her lack of interest."

Ryan grinned. "No, it was not her lack of interest—far from it. It was Papa. He simply wouldn't allow it."

"And she listened to him?" Michael asked with much surprise.

"She has a great deal of respect for him. In fact, *he's* just about the only person that she *does* listen to."

"Well, he was right to forbid her from joining," Michael said. "I wonder why he changed his mind."

"I suppose he must be worried that you might act rashly. He decided to send Alex along as counter balance."

"Why not simply send you?"

Ryan looked momentarily embarrassed. "She's a better swordsman, shot, equestrian . . . indeed a better soldier than I could ever hope to be"—he paused for a moment—"I don't begrudge her for it. In fact, I'm very proud of her."

She really must be something, Michael thought, *if her brother is willing to admit that to someone he has only just met.*

"I admire your honesty," Michael told him. "Most men would deny that any woman might be better than them at such things. Tell me though. Has she always been so difficult to handle?"

"I suppose she can be quite a handful, but I wouldn't say that she is difficult to handle . . . it makes her sound like a spoiled child."

"And you don't think she's spoiled? It sounds to me as if she's been allowed to run wild for far too long. Indeed, she's not a child. She's a young lady who ought to be dressed in fine muslin gowns and—"

"Go for strolls in the park or sit about painting water color pictures and such?" Ryan interrupted. "Good luck convincing her of that."

"You don't agree?" Michael asked with much surprise.

"I think I might have a different perspective because of my closeness to her." Ryan told him. "You see, I admire Alexandra tremendously. She's not only thwarted the stringent rules of society but she's done it so remarkably well. In truth, I don't understand how you can fail to respect her for that."

"It's not that I am not impressed by her. Indeed, it's rather difficult not to be, but surely you must admit that sending a woman into harm's way like this is irresponsible."

"I am certain that you must have attended your fair share of balls where you were introduced to hordes of young ladies—very eligible ones with a proper upbringing. Ladies who could sing for your amusement while playing the pianoforte, as if they'd never done anything else but that their entire lives. Ladies in exquisitely cut gowns, bonnets tied with bright ribbons, and hands that have never done anything more strenuous than write a letter in perfectly lined calligraphy. Ladies who will never argue your point, but always nod their heads in agreement because their sole purpose in life is to please *you*."

Michael frowned. Yes, he knew precisely the sort of women Ryan referred to, for he had met them all. It was one of the reasons why he kept his mistresses and refused to marry.

"To put it plainly," Ryan continued. "They are all exceedingly dull. Not a single one has an adventurous spirit like Alex, not one dares to speak her mind; and whenever one of them laughs, her heart is not in it—it's rather a trained sort of sound that they must have practiced at for hours in order to perfect.

"I for one have scoured the ballrooms of Mayfair in search of a lady who does *not* fit the description I have just given you. After all, where is the fun in having the same wife as everyone else? Is it not better to find a woman who is unique? Who stands out?" Ryan asked. "I do believe that I would find myself lucky to meet a woman with as much spirit as my sister. After all, life might become a touch unbearable with a dull wife to see to every day for the remainder of my days."

Michael couldn't help but see the truth in what Ryan was telling him. "And how does William feel about this?" he asked. "Being the eldest, he has a duty to fulfill. Or does he plan to shirk it as I do?"

"Not at all, but he does share my opinion of the ladies we have met thus far. He too hopes to marry someone with a bit more character than those women whose only ambition in life is to marry well. Growing up with Alex has made us realize women have much more to offer than society trains them to express."

"I must admit you have a point," Michael muttered, though it did very little in strengthening his resolve to stay away from Alexandra. "Although I would never have thought to consider it, I must agree that your sister would certainly make for a more interesting companion than most. However, it does seem to be beside the point."

"Perhaps," Ryan mused.

"Besides, she's by far the most unruly woman I have ever met," Michael said.

Ryan chuckled. "I am sure she is. However, given the circumstances, I would still like to know what your intentions are."

Michael stiffened. "My intentions? What the devil are you talking about, Summersby?"

"Well," Ryan began, "judging by the way the two of you went at each other's throats, I suspect you'll either wind up killing each other or getting married. I would like to know which it is going to be in case I need to make arrangements," he added casually.

"I'm afraid to disappoint you, but with even the littlest bit of luck, it won't be either," Michael told him rather adamantly.

"Oh?"

"I have no intention of marrying anybody and most certainly not a woman I've only just met. Hell, you know my reputation, Summersby. I am quite content with my life as it is. I have no desire to find myself leg shackled—least of all to a boisterous hoyden like your sister. No offense."

"None taken, though I must admit that I rather thought a man such as yourself might find her . . . refreshing."

Michael scowled at Ryan. The man apparently knew his mind better than he would have thought. Still, he loved his freedom. He enjoyed having whichever one of his mistresses struck his fancy, visiting his club, and whiling away the hours of the night with gambling and drink whenever he felt like it. The last thing he needed was to tie himself down to an opinionated woman. He shuddered as he thought of all the men he'd known . . . how they'd been reformed the minute they'd said "yes" at the altar. It would be a cold day in hell before he wandered down that path.

"And if my presumption is correct"—Ryan continued in an even tone, bringing Michael out of his reverie—"then I merely wish to inform you that whatever it was you were thinking when you looked at her—yes, Ashford, I do have eyes in my head—you'd best stop it right away unless the word *matrimony* is on your mind as well."

Well, I'll be damned. The pup has teeth.

"I won't see Alexandra ruined," Ryan told him brusquely.

"I hope you understand that. I know she's not the conventional sort of woman, but she's my sister all the same, and I love her. I have her best interests at heart, so if your intentions toward her are noble, then I shall be happy to discuss them with you."

Michael drew a deep breath as he handed Ryan a new glass of claret. Taking a large gulp of his own, he considered Ryan's words.

Marriage.

Not in this lifetime.

Yet he'd also come to realize that Alexandra Summersby was beyond anything he'd ever encountered before. "She's getting to me," he said suddenly, surprising even himself.

Ryan nodded. "That is understandable. She does leave a lasting impression." He got to his feet and walked over to the large windows. "I think you ought to give her a chance, Ashford. I think you would be well suited for each other, though if you tell her I said that, I will most assuredly deny it," he said, giving Michael a sidelong glance.

Michael grinned before taking another sip of his whiskey. "What you are implying is complete lunacy. She and I barely know each other. Hell, we've only just met, and you are suggesting that—"

"That you get to know her," Ryan said, cutting him off. "That is all I am saying for now. But my promise still holds. If you as much as lay a finger on her without the right intentions in mind, I will personally string you up by your ballocks. Do I make myself perfectly clear?"

"Perfectly," Michael conceded as his eyes met Ryan's. The pup wasn't kidding he realized. Not by a long shot.

CHAPTER EIGHT

Three days went by without the slightest hint of where they might find William. They'd each scouted the parts of the city that were frequented the most by Napoleon's men, but there was simply no sign of him anywhere. On top of that, the tension between Alexandra and Michael had stretched the air thin. She refused to so much as be in the same room as him, and whenever Ryan confronted her about it, she'd cross her arms and proceed to recite a long list of all the things that were wrong with him. It was steadily growing and currently affirmed that Michael was the most arrogant of all men, the most despicable, the vilest, a scourge on the aristocracy, a scraggy nick-ninny. He was also bracket-faced, a jackanapes, a numskull, and, most recent, too much of a Friday-faced twiddle-poop.

It was exasperating.

Michael, however, seemed to take it in stride. "The best I can do is to let her get it out of her system. She obviously resents me, so chasing after her is hardly likely to help."

"She's being unusually stubborn about this, even for her," Ryan stated.

"I've wounded her pride. And in all fairness, I would be greatly annoyed too, if I were in her place. But she really *is* more vulnerable than you and I. I wish she would only realize that."

"What do you plan to do?" Ryan asked.

"Wait. For now, that is all I *can* do."

"Well, don't wait too long before you make your peace with her—this place has practically become uninhabitable thanks to you two."

It was true, Michael knew. Besides, he missed the way he'd bantered with Alexandra when he'd thought her to be Alex. Indeed, he'd liked the lad a great deal. Why shouldn't he like the woman as well? If only she'd give him the chance to make it up to her. They could be friends, though anything more was out of the question, clearly. He valued his freedom, and to have a woman as boisterous as Alexandra as his wife . . . but heaven help him—he'd never find a moment of peace again. Still, she *was* unique, and that in itself was enough to make him want to fix this.

On the fourth day, Ryan was feeling a bit under the weather, or so he claimed. In truth, he'd simply had enough of Alexandra's constant bickering and decided to stay in bed.

Michael on the other hand, had no intention of remaining indoors. It was a beautiful spring day, the sun was shining—no sense in remaining cooped up.

Grabbing his jacket, he headed out into the hallway, only

to spot Alexandra, who was just now opening the front door. "Heading out?" Michael asked in an authoritative voice as if he expected her to tell him exactly where she was going.

"As a matter of fact, I am," she replied as she turned toward him. She appeared to be doing her best to hide not only her annoyance but also the blush that was quickly creeping into her cheeks, turning her a delightful shade of pink. "Mind if I join you?"

Oh yes, this is precisely what I need, he imagined her thinking as he studied the frown that presently creased her forehead. *Why won't he leave me alone?*

A valid question, he supposed, his eyes still fixed on Alexandra who seemed to be growing more and more distressed by the second. She was probably trying to decide how rude she could allow herself to be without feeling too guilty. Was the prospect of an afternoon spent in his company really so terrible then? He clenched his teeth in an attempt not to laugh, realizing that he really did find a rather unusual pleasure in tormenting her.

"If you must," she finally replied in a resigned tone as she walked out of the door without waiting to see if he might follow.

He grinned and shook his head in open amusement. "Are you always this charming?"

"Oh no, not always," she said while she hurried down the stairs, not bothering to hold the door open for him. He barely managed to dodge out of the way before it slammed back into place. "You get special treatment, my lord."

"I see," he muttered. "Then I cannot help but pity the man who might have angered you."

"I'm sure that no such man exists for I am not at all prone to anger," she quipped.

"I think you're in denial," he said as he ran after her. "Either that or you actually find pleasure in being contrary all the time."

Good God the woman was walking fast. This was more like a sprint than a stroll.

"And you are free to think whatever you wish, my lord."

"Might we not be friends then?" he asked, rushing to keep up with her while dodging a man who was coming toward them.

"*Friends?* Ha! Friends do not make it their sole priority to belittle one another at every given opportunity. They do not consider themselves superior. So no, my lord, I am *not* your friend, and you are most assuredly *not* mine."

"For someone who insists she's not prone to anger, you certainly do sound rather agitated. Would it by any chance help if I apologized?"

Alexandra stopped walking so abruptly that Michael nearly crashed right into her. She turned to him with open astonishment, clearly not believing what she'd heard. Michael noticed that she was doing her best to hide a smile, but her efforts fell short just a fraction, in spite of the scowl she attempted to send him. "It might," she told him haughtily, though her tone was clearly now one of amusement.

"Very well then," he told her cautiously. "I'm sorry for the way I insulted you the other day—for suggesting that you are incapable of taking care of yourself, and that you'd pose a liability toward this mission. I spoke without thinking. After all, your display of swordsmanship in Rouen truly was quite impressive, more so now *because* you are a woman. And as loathe as I am to admit it, your skills at deception are quite remarkable as well. You had me completely fooled. So, it seems I have been too critical in my way of thinking. Please accept my humblest apologies for my gross miscalculation."

Her crisp demeanor finally crumbled, and Alexandra served him a dazzling smile that almost made his heart stop, right then and there. "Nicely done, my lord," she said, no doubt happy to have seen him grovel. What was it with women? "Now that is settled, you may accompany me."

"I thought I was already accompanying you?" he remarked a little uncertainly.

"You most certainly were not, my lord," she exclaimed with a mounting sense of humor. "You were imposing yourself on me, and in case you are not aware, there *is* a difference, you know."

She really was a handful. A charming one in some ways, perhaps less so in others. Her attitude toward him certainly left a lot to be desired, but he was working on that. At least it seemed his words of regret had managed to placate her a little, even if he felt that he was equally deserving of an apology. He was willing to bet his entire fortune however, that the sun would rise in the West before that was likely to happen.

"Might I at least ask you where it is that you are going?"

She stopped then, turned to face him and offered him a stern look. "To find my brother," she told him plainly. "If you will recall, that is our primary objective in coming here." She turned away and recommenced walking.

After a moment's shocked pause, Michael hurried after her. "It's a large city, Lady Alexandra. Your brother could be anywhere." When she failed to respond, he decided to try a different approach. "Have you ever been to Paris before?"

"No, never," she admitted.

"Well, in that case there's something that I really ought to show you," he told her as he hailed a carriage.

"Whatever it is, it will have to wait," she insisted. "William is my first priority, and I won't—"

She wasn't given the chance to complete her sentence before Michael had her by the arm and was practically shoving her inside the awaiting carriage.

She glared at him with unabashed contempt. "Are you always this gallant?" she asked, half-mockingly.

"Not at all, Lady Alexandra," he told her with a wide smile. "You get special treatment."

Without another word, she turned her face away from him and stared out of the window, and that was when Michael noticed . . . if he wasn't mistaken, she was trying desperately not to laugh. Well, this was certainly unexpected. He leaned back against the opposite bench, a crooked smile playing upon his lips as he regarded her profile. In spite of everything, he'd somehow managed to break through her tough exterior and make her laugh. Loathe though he was to admit it, it filled his heart with warmth.

"Oh!" Alexandra exclaimed half an hour later as she looked out over the rooftops of the city below. "It's so incredibly beautiful, Ashford."

"I thought you might like it up here," he murmured as he walked up beside her to share the view. "I came across this place on my last visit here, purely by chance. It's a bit outside the city, so few people even come here, though I don't see why that is. The view is really quite remarkable and the wine is excellent too. I've been told it's made by a group of local nuns."

Alexandra gave him a sidelong glance before brushing a few wisps of hair from her face with her fingers. "Hm . . . I wouldn't mind a taste, if you're up to it," she said.

"Certainly, my lady, your wish is my command."

"And what do you call this area, if I may ask? Surely a place this wonderful must have a name." She shot him a smile that left him momentarily speechless. She truly was unbelievably stunning.

"Montmartre," he replied, feeling quite flustered by his body's helpless response to her. If only he could manage to slow his heartbeat to a more acceptable pace.

"Well, my lord, thank you for sharing it with me," she said, looking back at the view one last time before turning to follow him. "I think I'd be very content if I had the freedom to sit and just look out over all those rooftops all day."

Her response surprised him. He would have thought her the sort who might appreciate it for a while, but who would then surely tire of it for lack of excitement. It seemed as if there might be more to this woman than met the eye—a sentimental streak that she kept well hidden. It pleased him immensely to have discovered it.

Chapter Nine

They had lunch at a small restaurant where the wine was just as good as Michael had promised it would be. By the time they decided to make their way back to the apartment, it felt as if they'd known each other for years, thanks to all the stories they'd shared with each other. Michael could tell that Alexandra still held a grudge against him, but he was confident that with a little effort, it might soon be behind them.

Still, he didn't want her to lose her edge. As exasperating as he'd found it in the beginning, he'd really taken a liking to their friendly banter and to his amazement, Alexandra had begun to show a side of herself that he never would have dreamed existed.

As he already knew, she was smart, witty, and extremely interesting to talk to. But she was also a very good listener, and this was something that Michael *truly* valued. Most women he'd known were so busy chatting about nonsensical issues of little importance, like who might be marrying who, which dress a certain lady might have worn to a particular ball, which children of their acquaintance were the best behaved, which were the worst behaved, and so forth. They had no interest in politics or in what might be happening outside of their own little confined universes.

Alexandra, on the other hand, was the complete opposite. She had no interest in any of the ridiculous topics that most ladies liked to talk about, but rather every interest in whatever they were discussing. Indeed, she was always completely focused on what he had to say.

As they walked along the River Seine later that afternoon, on their way back to the apartment, they talked about warfare and Alexandra told him about some of the military campaigns that her father had helped lead. She had a lot of in depth knowledge about the early years of the Peninsular War—the last war of her father's career, the one that had injured his leg, and forced him into an early retirement.

From the tone of her voice, Michael sensed that she loved and respected her father greatly. She never mentioned her mother, however, and Michael didn't feel comfortable enough to ask, though he was growing increasingly curious.

He knew that he was seeing Alexandra in an entirely different light than when they'd left the apartment in the morning. In fact, he suddenly realized with much surprise that he actually liked her. Not only that, but he couldn't quite remember a more enjoyable time spent in anyone else's company.

Perhaps, he ought to reevaluate his feelings and intentions toward her. Whatever the case, he certainly needed to think a few things over, because it was becoming increasingly clear that the woman who was presently smiling up at him had somehow, against all odds and to his complete consternation, managed to wheedle her way past his defenses.

After dinner that evening, Alexandra, Ryan, and Michael sat together in the parlor, contemplating their lack of progress in finding William. "I had a thought," Alexandra finally said, looking from one man to the other. "William has always said that he prefers to keep close company with his targets. Perhaps, he's actually staying at the Tuileries Palace as Bonaparte's personal guest." It was a long shot of course, but one that seemed as good as any other at that point.

"You know, you're probably right," Ryan told her. "It wouldn't surprise me in the least if he and Bonaparte are sharing childhood memories over a bottle of cognac as we speak."

"Especially if they've come to some form of agreement," Michael added.

Alexandra glared at him. The man didn't seem to waste an opportunity to remind them that William might be a traitor. "Even if that is the case, I can assure you that William would only strike a deal with the French in order to help his country."

"You seem very sure of yourself."

"I've no reason to be anything else. Unlike you, I have known William my whole life. I know the sort of man he is." She fixed her eyes on Michael's. "I would trust him with my life, my lord."

Michael strode across to the sideboard and refilled his glass. "And unlike you, Lady Alexandra, I am of an objective opinion."

"No, you're not," Alexandra told him angrily. "You are determined to find William guilty, and I simply will not stand for it."

"Alex," Ryan cautioned her. "Ashford takes his job quite seriously, I assure you. He will not condemn William without proof. You have to admit that he has a valid point. We must not assume anything, Alex—doing so would not only be dangerous but indeed quite stupid."

"Well, I see you two have come to quite an agreement," Alexandra snapped. "How reassuring."

Michael grinned.

"What the devil are you laughing at?" she fumed.

"Alex!" Ryan exclaimed, clearly aghast at his sister's language and her lack of respect.

Alexandra ignored him while her eyes trailed after Michael.

"My dear woman," Michael replied. "I was merely wondering what it might take to earn such loyalty from you. The way in which you defend your brother is indeed quite admirable."

Alexandra could do nothing but gape at the man. Had he just paid her a compliment? This was not the retort she had expected. It almost seemed as if he understood her point of view. But that was of course impossible. Or was it?

As she sat there now, watching Michael, she felt something . . . quite unfamiliar—a slow warmth seeping through her. The feeling was so unsettling that she involuntarily shrugged her shoulders to rid herself of it, only to find that it persisted. Alarm bells began going off in her head. Was she actually beginning to *like* Lord Trenton? It was true that they'd shared an enjoyable day together, but she hadn't had the time to put much thought into it before now. What if she was slowly beginning to grow fond of him? Where did that leave her? He was impossibly good looking as it was, even when she despised him. If she were to start *liking* him . . .

Fear stopped her from dwelling on that thought any longer.

"So?"

Startled, Alexandra saw that both Ryan and Michael were watching her, the latter with a rather amused expression upon his face as if he knew precisely what was troubling her. Heat flooded her from head to toe and her heart quickened as it always did when she noticed Michael studying her. "Forgive me, my mind was elsewhere," she said.

"Well," Michael told her. "While you were so preoccupied with your woolgathering, I was saying that I intend to make a social call at the Tuileries Palace tomorrow afternoon in the hopes that William will be there."

"Are you completely mad?" Alexandra gasped, stunned that she'd been so lost in thought to have missed this piece of information. "What if he's not there? Or, what if Ryan and I are entirely mistaken and William is indeed collaborating with the French? Though I hate to do so, I must consider that possibility in this instance. What if the true purpose of your visit is discovered? What will you do then? You'll get yourself killed!"

Michael stared at her intensely. "I would think that might please you," he said.

Unable to meet his gaze for once, Alexandra turned toward Ryan. "I merely think it unnecessary to take such a risk," she said. "Do you not agree?"

Through the corner of her eye she could see that Michael was watching her quite closely. *What on earth must he be thinking?* she wondered. She silently cursed herself before directing another curse at him for good measure.

"I think it may be worth the risk," Ryan remarked. "We haven't come up with anything else so far and we must determine what is going on before Bonaparte decides to ride into battle, as he undoubtedly intends to do sooner or later."

"Well, then I suppose the matter is settled," Alexandra stated, crossing her arms in front of her. "If you don't mind, I shall leave you two to work out the details of this harebrained scheme of yours, since I'm clearly not needed. I am off to bed."

Without another glance in either man's direction, she got up from her chair, hoping Michael wouldn't notice the hint of concern in her voice. "Men!" she huffed as she strode out of the parlor and headed toward her bedroom.

Alexandra paced about her room. What could she do? How could she stop the stubborn fool from endangering himself? There was nothing for it—she had to speak to him. She had to try to make him see reason. It was a mad scheme. Absolutely mad. Decision made, she went to the French doors . . . and paused. Maybe she was being too hasty. Maybe he'd come to his senses on his own. She went back to her pacing and pondering—her eyes constantly seeking out the doors. He'd think her insane if she sought him out now . . . on the balcony no less. It was a silly idea. She ought to forget all about it, she ought to . . . oh, dash it all!

Ten seconds later, she found herself knocking on his door, and then immediately wondered if it were too late to run back inside her own room and hide. Apparently, it was, for no sooner had she thought of doing so, than the door was yanked open, revealing a rather annoyed looking Michael. "What is it?" he asked her in a gruff tone that clearly marked his irritation.

"Not so happy to see me I take it?" she offered what she hoped to be her most dazzling smile, and for a moment he froze—or seemed to at least—and just stood there, staring at her in that same unsettling fashion she'd seen before.

And then the moment passed, and he said, "I'm tired, so please make it quick—whatever it is."

And she would have, except that she was suddenly at a remarkable loss for words. So instead she just stood there, staring at Michael, searching for something, but with no idea of what. He seemed more tense than usual, and she couldn't help but wonder why.

Something deep inside her sprang to life in that moment, with such force that it nearly knocked her off her feet. It struck her with sudden clarity, that she wanted his approval—not just professionally but as a woman. She wanted for him to find her just as enticing as any other young lady he might fancy, and it shook her to her core.

Heaven help her—she must be vainer than she'd ever imagined. It had never mattered to her what anyone thought of her, least of all any men. The interest in seeking approval from the opposite sex had simply not been there, particularly since she'd long since vowed that she would never marry. She didn't fear becoming a spinster like all the other young ladies her age apparently did. She felt confident that retaining her independence would suit her rather nicely. And she had no interest in subjecting herself to the emotional turmoil her father had suffered upon her mother's death. The whole tragedy had virtually torn their family apart. Their father had grown distant and introverted—not even protesting when Alexandra refused a season three years earlier. Her aunt had been outraged when she'd last visited and discovered how little care was being directed at the children, but she'd voiced a particular concern for Alexandra.

"A young lady should not be running rampant the way she does," she'd told Bryce. Her father had merely shrugged his shoulders in response and asked, "What would you have me do, Virginia? I can barely take care of myself right now."

Alexandra cringed just remembering his depressed tone, so clear that he'd lost all will to do anything. Penelope had died and so had Bryce's strength to go on.

"Let me take her for a while," Virginia had said as she'd cast a firm glance in Alexandra's direction. Her aunt had clearly planned to turn her into her own pet project, and to Alexandra's horror, her father had agreed. Not a week had passed however, before Alexandra was back home again, having stolen a horse and ridden haphazardly through the night, returning to Moorland at dawn.

Alex realized that something had changed inside her that very evening—Michael had told her that he admired her, and just like that, her eyes had been opened. In fact, just standing there in front of him now was turning her stomach inside out.

She'd been trying for five days to ignore how attractive she found him, but she no longer had the willpower. It was time to face reality. Michael Ashford was having a serious effect on her, and she still didn't know what to make of it or what to do about it, though she was very eager to find out. "I want to discuss your plan for tomorrow, because I still think that walking into the lion's den is complete lunacy."

"Oh?" He studied her for a moment. "Do you have a better idea?"

"Let me go instead."

Michael would have laughed had she not looked so serious. Deadly serious. What the devil was the matter with her? He thought he'd begun to understand who she was, only to discover that he wasn't at all sure he was even *beginning* to figure her out. "I can't let you do that," he said simply.

"Why on earth not? I'll be far more discreet and far more capable of wiggling my way out of danger. You on the other hand will be in constant peril the minute you step through the front door."

"And this concerns you why exactly?" he couldn't help but ask. He had a growing suspicion, but he needed to push her just a bit harder to see if he was right or not.

She rolled her eyes at him. "Because, if you're found out, William will be in immediate danger. Think of all the information he might have gathered. They'll skewer him for certain. On the other hand, if you are correct in your assumption that William is guilty, he will no doubt have you served up for Bonaparte on a silver platter. Who knows what the French might discover if they put you under torture. Don't you see? You'll be compromising everything if you fail."

"First of all, failure is not an option and second of all I must tell you quite adamantly that I would never divulge any secrets under torture. That you would even make such an assumption—"

"Are you really such a fool, my lord, as to think for one

minute that you would not talk if your nails were being pulled out and your limbs cut off," Alexandra cried in exasperation as she interrupted him. "Why do men always presume themselves to be so invincible all the time?"

Michael stared at her in disbelief. He could not ignore what she was saying, regardless of how much he wished to deny her accusation. It was true that he had never fallen prey to an enemy, but he'd always believed that if he ever did, he would withstand anything for the sake of his country. Alexandra had just cast serious doubts on that and it shook him rather violently to acknowledge her point of view.

She sighed. "I'm sorry, my lord. I find that I am being quite rude of late. It's not my place to question your sense of duty or your honor. Please understand that it's this whole dratted business that has me so out of sorts. I'm quite worried about our potential for success, and I happen to care about . . ." She stopped herself instantly and there was suddenly a very perplexed look upon her face, as if she'd been about to say something that she knew she'd come to regret.

"What?" he asked.

"Hm?" Her eyes took on a look of complete incomprehension as if she was doing her very best to feign ignorance.

"What is it that you care about?" he asked in a low murmur.

"Oh . . . er . . . nothing really . . ." She made a sound much like a nervous chuckle before sticking her hands in her pockets and shrugging her shoulders dismissively.

Nothing indeed?

"It wouldn't happen to be my welfare would it?" He moved

a little closer and couldn't help but smile when he spotted the telltale blush upon her cheeks.

She snorted. "Of course not . . . that would be preposterous, Michael." Again she chuckled with apparent uneasiness. "I mean really . . ." She turned her head away as if something of far more interest had suddenly caught her attention.

Michael, however, stood as if nailed to the ground. That one simple sentence had given him a world of insight. Alexandra had not only used his Christian name but she had also made that small uneasy sound that women tended to make when they were shy or embarrassed about something. However, the Alex *he* knew was *not* the sort of woman to be shy or embarrassed about anything, which led him to deduce that she must have finally taken a liking to him. The thought pleased him to no end. In truth, it surprised him just how much it pleased him, but there it was. It simply did.

Now, to test the theory.

Pushing the thought of Ryan hunting him down and beating him to a bloody pulp from his mind, he took a step forward, toward Alexandra. She didn't move.

So far so good.

Feeling a bit more confident, he took another step until they were standing no more than half an arm's length apart. She remained where she was, gazing up at him, expectantly. It was almost as if she *wanted* him to kiss her. The realization stunned him. Alexandra Summersby, the most unruly, feisty hoyden he'd ever encountered in his life, was presently gazing up at him with that same doe-eyed expression that he'd seen a hundred times before. He felt the corners of his mouth start to twitch with the beginnings of a chuckle. It really wouldn't do to laugh now, he warned himself. It would be most unfair, ungentlemanly and unkind to say the least. Yet for some annoying reason he couldn't seem to stop himself. The expression on her face was so completely out of character. Never in a million years would he have imagined her to look at him like that—eyelids batting of their own volition and her lips puckering in expectation as she leaned slightly forward. Yet here she was doing precisely that—it was much too comical to stop the smile crossing face.

And that was when she hit him.

It wasn't a faint slap on the cheek. No, Alexandra put all her weight behind the right hook that landed squarely across his jaw, throwing him completely off balance.

Damnation!

"What the devil are you—"

"Who the hell do you think you are?" she hissed, cutting him off.

"You hit me," was all he could think to say as he raised his hand to his rapidly bruising cheek.

"And you bloody well deserved it," she said, seething with rage.

He supposed he did. Still, he never would have expected her to hit him . . . or to do it so painfully well. Besides, he hadn't actually laughed, he'd just smiled . . . a bit more than usual perhaps. And he'd felt like laughing, but she couldn't possibly know that, could she? Judging from her expression, perhaps she could read his mind. He met her eyes, and looked a bit deeper—beyond the anger—and what he saw filled him with guilt. She was hurt. *He'd* hurt her, and he'd never regretted anything more in his life.

Blast!

Rubbing her sore knuckles with her hand, she turned to go. He didn't want her to—not with this bad air between them—he had to explain. She cursed under her breath and was just getting ready to step back into her room when he broke from his trance and reached for her wrist, wrapping his fingers around it. "Let go of me," she cried in clear frustration as she tried to yank herself free.

"Alex," he said, pulling her toward him. "I'm sorry I laughed, truly I am . . . it was badly done of me and not at all meant as an insult. Please stay." She eyed him skeptically, not at all ready to fall into his arms. Well, it seemed as if an explanation was in order. "The look on your face was so . . . well, you looked as if you were hoping I might kiss you, and it just seemed funny because . . . well, to be perfectly honest, you're just about the last person I ever expected to find looking at me like that."

There, that should do it.

The look on her face however, told him that he might be dangling over the railing in another second unless he did something drastic to alter her state of mind. With a quick tug, he drew her into his arms. Then, before she had the chance to launch into another verbal attack or give him yet another beating, he closed his mouth over hers.

Heavenly.

She struggled like a caged animal at first, but a heartbeat later, he felt the tension flow from her body and she sagged against him. He tightened his hold and pulled her closer, his right hand resting on the small of her back while the left remained upon her shoulder. She smelled of lavender.

Testing the waters, he ran the tip of his tongue along her lips and felt her quiver—a delightful response that made his own pulse quicken. When she put her arms about his neck, he knew she wasn't about to run away from him. He pulled back a little to take a look at her. Her eyes were still closed, her perfect lips slightly pursed from kissing. He ran the pad of his thumb along her cheekbone and watched her sigh in response. What a charming creature she was.

Without another moment's pause, he crushed his lips against hers.

During the course of his life, Michael must have kissed at least a hundred women. But this was different. This was new and refreshing and it was . . . he wasn't sure exactly what it was, but it felt *better* somehow. Strange choice of word perhaps, but there it was.

Pressing her closer, he deepened the kiss with his tongue. He felt her stiffen for a moment, but then she sighed, allowing him to coax her tongue to follow.

He'd know for a while now that he wanted to kiss Alexandra, but he never would have guessed just how captivating he would find it. In fact, he'd thought himself capable of keeping it brief, his only intention being to sample what she had to offer, but this was proving far more difficult than he'd anticipated. She was so soft and pliable beneath his touch—all traces of her prickly, tomboyish character completely evaporated, save for her choice of clothes. And he'd been overly surprised to discover that there was something quite erotic about the fact that she was wearing breeches. Her legs were clearly defined beneath them, but more importantly, so was her firm and perfectly rounded backside.

His right hand drifted down to grasp onto one of her buttocks. She groaned faintly in response, arousing him even further.

Good God.

He had to stop this now before he took her right there on the balcony for all of Paris to see.

And that was when the stabbing sense of guilt that he'd thus far managed to contain, suddenly surfaced in full force. He'd given Ryan his word of honor that he would steer clear of his sister unless he intended to court her. Well, he had no intention of doing any such thing. Indeed, now that she'd shown her interest, he was very likely to tire of her rather rapidly he knew.

He was just about to pull away, when she beat him to it.

"Well," she said as she looked him dead in the eye. "That was far better than I would have expected."

Michael blinked.

"However, it's growing exceedingly late, and I must be off to bed. Alone—before you get any ideas in that presumptuous head of yours."

She sent him a coy smile as she slipped from his arms and walked away. "Good night, Ashford," she called over her shoulder as she sashayed back inside her bedroom and pulled the door closed behind her. He heard the lock click.

Well, that was a first, Michael thought to himself. He had always been the one to walk away, leaving the girl staring after *him*. With a sigh of exasperation he leaned against the railing to look down upon the street bellow. The nights were growing warmer though the slow breeze was leaving him quite chilly now that he was standing there alone.

Damn.

Alexandra was unlike any other woman he'd ever met and she was beginning to get under his skin. It was a rather disconcerting admission for him to make, but there it was.

Still, he was only just getting to know her, he reminded himself. Perhaps, he would still discover that she wasn't nearly as appealing as he presently found her to be. Besides, the whole attraction was very likely based on the fact that there were no other women around to draw his attention.

Feeling as if he'd finally solved a great mystery, he headed back inside. There was nothing for it. He would simply have to control his urges and keep his distance from her or he'd find himself heading for the altar before they even managed to complete their assignment.

Chapter Ten

Michael stepped down from the carriage that he'd hired to take him to rue de Rivoli. He paused for a moment as he regarded the large palace that lay before him—a vast and magnificent edifice that seemed to dwarf Carlton House in both size and opulence. Straightening his back and taking on an air of arrogance that only those of extreme wealth and importance were capable of managing, Michael strode toward the sentry that guarded the imposing entrance of the French Emperor's residence.

He handed his calling card to one of the guards and stated his purpose. It identified him as Monsieur Michel Laurant, having purposefully avoided taking a title that might be known among Bonaparte and his cronies. The man, who appeared only marginally less arrogant than Michael (due in no doubt to the fact that he was not only French but Parisian to boot) stepped inside to convey the message to a higher authority who remained invisible to the public.

After ten minutes, the guard returned and gave Michael a haughty glance before opening the door just wide enough for Michael to step inside. "Monsieur le Docteur will receive you now."

Michael squeezed past the insufferable man, trying terribly hard to hide the beginnings of a wide smile. He had asked to see a Monsieur Philippe Allaire, who Sir Percy had assured him would be William's cover name. Well, it appeared as if the would-be double agent had turned himself into a doctor—perhaps Bonaparte's very own private physician.

Michael stifled a grin as he followed a footman up a long flight of stairs. He must remember not to underestimate his opponent, for it did appear as if Lord Summersby was a very determined man. Then again, should he really have expected anything less of Alexandra's eldest brother? He wondered what she would think of William's ingenuity. In any event, he had newfound respect for the man, traitor though he may be.

Michael's shoes clicked sharply against the polished marble floor as he followed the footman down a corridor flanked by partially nude sculptures of what he presumed were renditions of various Greek or Roman gods. The images immediately drew his thoughts to Alexandra and the captivating question of how her breasts might compare with the perfectly rounded ones of the statue. He cursed beneath his breath when he felt himself begin to strain against his breeches. This really wasn't the sort of thing he ought to be thinking of as he readied himself to meet with her elder brother. There was a code of behavior among gentlemen, and besides, he'd promised Ryan that he would keep away from her.

Bloody hell!

It wasn't as if Ryan was a close friend, but still, he liked the young lad and as he reminded himself, he'd given him his word—the word of a supposed gentleman. Not to mention that, despite appearance, Alex *was* a lady.

He wasn't even supposed to have kissed her!

Michael's mental haranguing came to an abrupt halt when the footman suddenly stopped before a heavy wooden door and gave it a loud knock. A muffled murmur that Michael couldn't quite distinguish sounded from within. An instant later, the door was opened and Michael was ushered into a splendidly lavish drawing room with plush rugs full of elaborate floral patterns in varying shades of blue. Silk upholstered furniture in gold tones and beautifully carved tables inlaid with mother of pearl occupied the space. The walls were filled with gilt-framed paintings of biblical scenes resplendent with images of angels, beams of light emerging between puffy white clouds, and gowned figures gazing heavenward in a mixture of fear and reverence. It was all a bit too gaudy for Michael's tastes, though he didn't give this much thought. After all, he wasn't the one who had to live there.

There were two people present in the room, a sturdy man whom he took to be none other than the infamous Lord Summersby himself, and a lady with whom he appeared to be in the middle of a rather animated conversation. Michael quickly noted the resemblance between William and Ryan, though William's hair appeared to be a shade darker. The lady sat with her back toward the door, dressed in a lilac walking gown and a matching Spencer jacket.

Michael hid a smug smile. What a pleasure it would be to finally encounter a true lady of breeding, just the thing to prove to himself that the only reason he found Lady Alexandra in the least bit enticing was because she had, until now, lacked any competition.

He stepped forward just as William looked up. "Monsieur Laurant. Please join us," he said as he got to his feet and gestured toward a comfortable looking divan.

Michael inclined his head in acceptance while he watched William's gaze shift toward the footman who was still holding the door ajar. "That will be all," he said stiffly.

The footman paused momentarily until William's look hardened, and he waved his hand in an effort to shoo the impertinent man away. "*Allez . . . vite!*" he hissed at him.

Muttering an almost imperceptible "*Oui monsieur, Le Docteur,*" the disgruntled footman quickly exited the room.

"Tea?" William asked as Michael sauntered toward his designated seat. He flashed him a lopsided smile. Funny how ridiculous such a question sounded under the circumstances.

"May I present my sister, Lady Alexandra Summersby," William said. "I believe the two of you have already met."

Michael's mind screeched to an abrupt halt that seemed to stretch for all eternity before slowly whirring back to life again. His head came around at a snail's pace until his eyes settled upon the woman who was seated in one of the two armchairs. She was gazing up at him with a . . . he couldn't tell if her smile was one of triumph or mischief. Her eyes sparkled as she raised one eyebrow. "Lord Trenton. How good of you to join us."

How good of you to join us?

The little hoyden.

He had a good mind to wring her neck just then, though

he wasn't quite certain that William would look too kindly on such a maneuver.

Instead, he gritted his teeth and bent over her outstretched hand, brushing his lips against her knuckles. This was not the Alexandra he'd grown accustomed to. No, indeed he was used to seeing her garbed in breaches and a loose fitting shirt, her hair carelessly tied back with a ribbon.

The transformation was nothing short of astounding. She appeared to be the very paragon of what a true lady ought to look like. Hell, even her hair had been perfectly arranged in a tight chignon—not a loose strand in sight. How she'd managed that feat without a lady's maid confounded him. He supposed that Mrs. Bell must have stepped in and been of some assistance.

"Well, my lord?" Her eyes bore into his while her smile edged slightly more upward. "What do you think? I picked it up in a small boutique. The modiste assured me it was quite à la mode."

"It suits you remarkably well, my lady. In fact, I dare say it's quite an improvement."

Why he'd added that last bit was beyond him. Well, perhaps not entirely.

Though he'd grown rather fond of seeing her in the snug breeches that shamelessly put her hips, thighs, and backside on constant display, he wasn't about to let her know it. Besides, he enjoyed jibing her. Particularly when his efforts were so easily rewarded with that scornful glare she seemed to reserve entirely for him.

"I couldn't agree more," William stated. "Really Alex, you

can be quite the lady when you put your mind to it. Brandishing swords and pistols, as fun as that may have been when we were children, is not entirely befitting for a lady your age. Frankly, I don't understand why father still allows it."

"Well, he did try his best by sending me off to Aunt V," she reflected. Her tone was light, yet Michael still managed to catch the hint of bitterness that laced her words. "Perhaps, it was simply because I made it plainly known that I was happy as I was. Boys always have all the fun you know, and when given the choice between studying fashion plates and climbing trees . . . well, the fashion plates always came up rather short I'm afraid."

William chuckled. "Then it's a miracle indeed that you have any sense whatsoever in regards to what a lady ought to wear."

"I am not a complete idiot," Alexandra shot back. "I *can* tell the difference between a chemise and a petticoat, though I was not at all comfortable with being strapped into my corset—unnaturally confining thing that it is." Michael's and William's mouths fell open, and she rolled her eyes. "Oh for heaven's sake! It's not as if I'm not wearing one. After all, they did manage to squeeze me into the dastardly contraption in the end. However, I—"

"Alexandra . . ." William cautioned her in a tight voice as he cast a glance in Michael's direction.

"Well, you know, I've never paid much heed to dressing appropriately," she continued. "So naturally I managed to get the darn hooks caught on my chemise and . . ."

"That is *enough*, Alexandra!" William said, his voice so tight it might just snap.

Alexandra stared at her brother's outraged face, but he wasn't looking at her. Following his line of vision, her eyes settled upon Michael's smoldering expression. The man looked as if his cravat might suddenly strangle him.

Heat washed over her, prickling her skin from her hairline down to the tips of her toes as understanding dawned on her. She'd seen that look the night before—as if she was a delectable desert that he was getting ready to sink his teeth into. Heavens! This must be the wicked face of desire, Alexandra realized with a shudder, and it was so plain in Michael's eyes that the words *I want you* might as well have been written in bold letters upon his forehead.

In spite of how wonderful their kiss had been the night before (and it had been earth shatteringly wonderful to say the least), Michael's expression still surprised her. Not that it didn't please her—after all this was what she wanted: for him to like her—but she'd somehow imagined having to work a little harder at it, given that she had all his previous experiences to compete with.

A churning warmth settled in the pit of her stomach as she recalled the way he'd held her on the balcony. What had her plan been? To throw it all back in his face once she'd proven to him that she was just as agreeable as any other warm-blooded female? Yes, that was exactly what her plan had been. *But is that still what I want?* she wondered.

She had no desire to marry or bear children and since it would be William's duty to produce an heir at some point in time, she'd always imagined having a brood of nieces and nephews to dote upon—all the joys without the hassle, so to speak. And then of course there was that constant nagging fear of getting too close to another person—to allow herself to care . . . to *love*.

She watched Michael carefully for a moment as he sat down, realizing with a sudden urgency how desperately she longed for him to hold her again. His reputation was that of a notorious rake—the sort that every Mama would warn her chaste daughter to stay away from.

However, since marriage was not on Alexandra's list of priorities and, more to the point, never would be, she considered Michael Ashford in a very different light. Indeed, he could be the very man who might enlighten her in an area where she was suddenly very keen on being enlightened. And though a man like Michael *must* marry, being the rake that he was, it shouldn't be too difficult to get him to ignore the proprieties.

Would it be possible, she wondered slyly, to convince him to take their kiss one step further? It would certainly be scandalous. She would face the very real threat of ruination, not to mention that her brothers would undoubtedly kill both of them if they realized what was going on. But it was precisely the sort of danger and impropriety that spoke to her adventurous spirit. And, if she were to experience the true goings on between man and woman at least once in her life, who better to show her than a handsome man with plenty of experience?

Recalling where she was, she pushed the thought from her mind and favored the two gentlemen with her most winning smile. "Suppose we continue where we left off?" She turned toward Michael. "My lord, we were just admiring this wonderful piece of weaponry when you arrived. Tell me, what is your opinion of it?" She lifted a harquebus that she'd been cradling in her lap and then looked across at Michael, hoping for an answer. Instead, it seemed as if he were finding it difficult not to laugh. Irritating man. Donning a disapproving frown, she merely said, "my lord?"

"Forgive me," Michael chuckled. "But to see you sitting like this, dressed in all you finery while holding a rifle in the same manner that any other young lady might be holding her embroidery . . . it really is rather amusing."

Deciding to ignore him, she turned to her brother instead, only to find that he was having much the same problem as Michael. For lack of anything better to do, she rolled her eyes in response. "Sixteenth century I presume?"

"I do believe it is," William said with a cough that immediately ironed out his expression.

"One of Bonaparte's?"

"Mine actually. I acquired it the other day with the intention of adding it to my collection back home."

Reaching forward, Michael took the musket from Alexandra's hands. It had clearly been well looked after if the sheen of the wood was any indication. "I agree. It's quite something to admire." He handed the weapon back to its rightful owner.

"Now then, Ashford, what is it that you would like to discuss?" William inquired, returning the harquebus to its velvet-lined case.

Michael spared a quick glance in Alexandra's direction. She could feel herself growing tense and nervous. "Surely you must be able to imagine why I've come," he said.

"Indeed, I believe I know precisely why you have come, though I really wish you would have stayed away. Your interference is likely to ruin everything."

"Are you telling me that you are *not* in league with the French?"

William leaned back against his chair, pressing two arched fingers against his lips and regarded Michael from behind hooded eyes. "I have no intention of telling you anything—at least not yet," he replied.

Alexandra took a sharp breath, but if Michael registered it, he didn't react. Instead, he kept his eyes pinned on William. "There are many who would consider such a statement a confession of your guilt."

"And what, pray tell, are you suggesting that I am guilty of?" William asked with genuine curiosity, so genuine in fact that Alexandra could see that Michael was momentarily thrown.

"Treason."

Alexandra gasped, horrified by Michael's casual bluntness. She didn't miss the tightening of William's jaw, however, and knew in that instant, without any shadow of a doubt, that her brother was innocent. He had just taken great offence to Michael's accusation, though she knew he was trying his best not to show it.

"And I suppose Sir Percy sent you to verify this?" he asked, then continued without waiting for an answer. "By the by, would you care telling me *why* you would suspect such a thing?"

"Mr. Finch was kind enough to inform us that you might be tempted to indiscretion and that an investigation might be necessary. In fact, I should like to have a word with the man myself if I may. Do you know where I might find him?"

William stared at Michael for a moment as if wondering how much to tell him. "I do not know," he finally muttered. "In fact, I have not seen him in over a month."

"Listen, William"—Alexandra cut in—"why not simply explain the whole situation to Lord Trenton. I am sure you can easily convince him of your innocence. And once you do, we will be more than willing to help you in your cause."

"And just what exactly *is* my cause, Alex?"

"Why, to stop whatever attack Bonaparte is planning from ever happening."

"A tall order, wouldn't you agree?" William's eyes flashed with something that Alexandra didn't recognize, or like for that matter. "You should not have come. Quite frankly, I do not know what you were thinking. It's much too dangerous."

"But—" Alexandra began.

"Please excuse me. I have other matters to attend to today." William's cool gaze held hers before turning to Michael. "I trust you will see yourselves out?"

Unable to hide the shock or disappointment that she felt at her brother's words, Alexandra rose to her feet and turned numbly toward the door.

CHAPTER ELEVEN

"Are you all right?" Michael asked.

It seemed like a silly question, considering all that had happened in the course of the past hour, yet it was better than the relentless silence that filled the carriage.

"I know he's innocent," Alexandra persisted. "I just don't understand why he chose not to convince you of it when he had the opportunity."

Her faith in her brother really was quite remarkable under the circumstances. Then again, it was only natural that she wouldn't want to believe him capable of any crime. He was her brother. Alexandra had probably admired him her whole life. "Are you quite certain that you have not misjudged him?" he asked.

Her eyes immediately skewered him. "I realize how skeptical you must be after what just happened, but I assure you, William is *not* collaborating with Bonaparte."

"Then how do you explain his reluctance to include us in his plans? He had the chance but chose instead to send us on our merry way. I'm sorry, my lady, but what reason do I have to trust him when he did not make the slightest attempt at defending himself?"

"I don't know," she whispered, turning her head to look out of the window at the glistening water of the River Seine. "I just know what my heart tells me."

Biting back a remark that would do nothing but widen the rift he felt forming between them, Michael chose instead to lean forward and place his hand on hers in comfort. "I hope you're right, I truly do. I just hope that you will not bear any ill will toward me, should it turn out that you are not."

"Well." She managed to smile at him, her eyes twinkling with sudden mischief. "We shall just have to find out the truth about the matter, shan't we?"

Michael was instantly on edge. He should have known this woman might have something up her sleeve. "I suppose you have a plan?" he asked.

"A very simple one, now that you mention it."

"Really?" He wondered if his voice sounded as dubious as he felt. "What is it?"

"We will simply have to ask Mr. Finch and see what *he* has to say about the matter. If he's disappeared, then perhaps there's more to this than meets the eye."

Michael would have laughed had she not been so thoroughly serious. Instead, he groaned, for he knew Alexandra well enough by now to understand that if he didn't help her, she'd attempt something stupid on her own. "Simple indeed," he muttered.

"Well, yes. Of course there is the minor detail of finding out where he is."

"And just how exactly do you propose that we go about discovering Mr. Finch's whereabouts?"

"Not sure, but perhaps it's time for me to use my feminine wiles," she said with a wry smile.

With a deep sigh, Michael leaned back in his seat and pretended to look out of the window. What the devil was he going to do about this woman? One thing was for sure, he thoroughly disliked the idea of Alexandra using her *feminine wiles* on anyone other than him. God help him if somebody else put their filthy hands on her . . .

Casting a sideways glance in her direction, he couldn't help but take in the lovely curve of her breasts as they pressed against her Spencer. Once again, he wondered how they might compare to those of Aphrodite's . . . how soft they'd feel beneath his touch . . . the taste of them as he . . .

With an inward groan, he thought of Ryan, and then of his own sisters and how protective he'd always been of them. If he succumbed to temptation, then Ryan would naturally force him to marry Alexandra. After all, that was what *he* would do in his place.

It was true that he'd had more mistresses than anyone might consider reasonable, but that didn't alter the fact that he was a gentleman to the bone. None of those women had been ladies of breeding, and those who had been were widows. None of them had been extraordinary and none of them had offered him their innocence.

He cast another glance at her, this time focusing on her profile, her long eyelashes, her delicate nose, and her luscious, oh-so kissable lips.

Would it be such a hardship to marry the woman?

He was genuinely stunned to discover that he wasn't actually trembling with fear at the sudden thought of marriage. What a peculiar thing. He loved his life; the freedom he had to be gone from home all night, no questions asked as he roamed the city—visiting his club, his favorite gambling hell, or one of his mistresses. It was true that he was his father's heir and that the old man had more than once broached the topic of Michael seeking a wife, but settling down just sounded like such a bore. The way he saw it, he'd be more than happy to name his nephew Gareth his heir once the time came for him to draw up a will. As it was, the eight-year-old already seemed more responsible than Michael imagined he would ever be. All he really wanted was to enjoy life. Marriage . . . well, it just seemed so confining.

Yet, his run in with Alexandra, the kiss they'd shared, not to mention his rather serious conversation with Ryan, had forced him to reevaluate his priorities. It was very odd indeed, but as far as Alexandra Summersby was concerned, the notion of marriage seemed to thrill him more than the prospect of a possible seduction did. Life with Alexandra would never be dull or boring. She was simply too boisterous and adventurous, too unruly and vivacious. She was a force to be reckoned with, and Michael knew to the very depth of his soul that she was the only woman he'd met he would ever consider making his wife.

And since Alexandra would be required to find a husband sooner or later anyway, why shouldn't that man be him? Which made his desperate attraction to her far less of a hardship. Judging by her reaction to his kiss last night, she had to feel the same way about him. But was he willing to get himself leg shackled for the sake of satisfying his own carnal needs? It was preposterous. And yet, Michael found his heart suddenly racing with keen excitement, so rapidly in fact that he was forced to wonder if it might be damaging to his health.

Marriage. It was the only honorable way to go about tackling the problem that had been forever plaguing his mind this past week. And considering that she was a lady—albeit an unusual one who was bound to give him trouble—the *only* way to go about it without ruining her.

"**D**o you know where your brother might be?" Michael asked Alexandra upon returning to the apartment and removing his gloves. Now that he'd decided what to do, he had every intention of approaching the task in the correct manner. He would ask for Ryan's permission to court her.

Immediately, and with great haste.

Indeed, he wasn't sure how much longer he might be capable of restraining himself, knowing full well that she slept with nothing more than a thin wall between them.

He watched her now as she unbuttoned her Spencer with a slow laziness that made him want to tear the jacket from her shoulders himself. As it fell away, however, he saw that his patience had been greatly rewarded. Letting out a steady breath, he clenched his fists in an effort to gain control of his disobedient body. Already he could feel blood rushing toward his groin while his eyes settled helplessly upon the rise and fall of her bosom.

Lord, give me strength!

Her waistline was high, as fashion decreed, her neckline

scooped low . . . too low—if such a thing was possible. But who was he to complain? His mouth had grown dry several seconds ago and his . . . Michael quickly removed his hat from his head and held it in front of himself, hoping the gesture wouldn't seem too obvious.

"I believe he mentioned he had an appointment of some sort," Alexandra said.

"Hm?"

She laid her Spencer on the nearest chair. "Ryan . . . you asked me where he might be?"

Michael watched as she turned her gaze on him for the first time since entering the apartment, her eyes widening as though she was suddenly startled by something. Unable to help himself, he served her a crooked smile in response. He knew he was staring, and judging from the sudden blush upon her skin, he also knew that the hunger he felt for her must be quite visible in his dark brown eyes.

She sucked in a sharp breath, but in doing so, she naturally forced her breasts even higher—increasing the swell they made as they lurched against her restraining bodice. It was all Michael could do not to start drooling.

"Would you like me to take that for you?" she asked, gesturing to his hat.

"I'm not entirely certain that would be a good idea," he managed as he felt himself tighten even more.

Her eyes stared at his hat, narrowing slightly as if she found the positioning of it rather peculiar, then widening as she quickly looked away.

"I er . . . I . . ." she faltered and seemed to drag her gaze back to his face, presumably determined not to appear too flustered, yet she couldn't possibly have appeared more so. It was all too much—he didn't want to smile or laugh even, but he simply couldn't help but grin at her *very* apparent discomfiture.

Was that a gulp? Good Lord, she really was having a difficult time of it. Funny thing that. He was the one standing at attention, yet for some absurd reason, he felt completely calm and collected at present—presumably because she was being so wonderfully distracting right now.

She took a deep breath, and then exhaled it very, very slowly. Michael remained silent, allowing her a moment to calm her nerves. She still looked flustered, though, and more than just a little uncomfortable. What would she do next? Presumably make an excuse of some sort before running off to hide in her room. He realized that he was still smiling, which really wasn't fair at all. He made another attempt at a serious expression, and failed, yet again.

And then the most remarkable thing happened. Squaring her shoulders, Alexandra met his gaze dead on. Whatever discomfort she'd just been feeling had completely vanished—swept away beneath a sultry veneer that made his heart leap. Why wasn't she busy making her escape? She gave him a little smile and a scorching heat flooded him from his head to his toes. Did she realize that she was playing with fire? He ought to warn her, but the words wouldn't come. All he could do was watch her face, her lips, which seemed to dimple ever so slightly in one corner, her eyes, which seemed to draw him in. And then she blinked, as she drew a tight breath, and he realized with great fascination that she wasn't nearly as confident as she was trying to let on. Whatever her agenda might be, she was clearly trying to appear more sophisticated and knowledgeable than she was, and there was something very charming about that somehow. He couldn't help but admire her efforts.

"My lord," she whispered in a rather seductive voice as she took a step toward him. His skin began to tingle. She looked determined, and he knew then, beyond any shadow of a doubt, that she was trying to seduce him. *Good God!* He held his breath. He didn't want her coming any closer, but he didn't want to move either—indeed, he didn't think himself capable. Yet he was the more experienced of the two. He had to stop her; he simply had to.

Her gaze was unwavering, the edge of her lips curled upward in an almost predatory smile. His stomach tightened as she paused before him—so close, he could almost see the sparks of energy flowing between them.

"May I take your hat, my lord?"

A whoosh of air escaped Michael's lungs at that one simple question. It wasn't so much the question itself, but the way in which she'd asked it, her voice low and inviting. He'd be lucky if he survived to see another day. *Lord, help me.*

She tilted her head a little, as if she was pondering something, then licked her lips before biting down ever so gently on her bottom lip—a mesmerizing motion, that Michael could not tear his eyes away from. More blood raced toward his groin, hardening him even further. He held onto his hat with all his might, trying desperately to gain some semblance of control before it abandoned him completely.

Alexandra reached down and tugged at the brim, her hands brushing softly against the smooth fabric of his trousers.

"Lady Alexandra, I—" he said, his voice sounded distant in his own ears. He had to pull himself together—for both of their sakes.

"Please, call me, Alex," she murmured.

He cleared his throat and took a step backward, determined to put an end to this while he was still able. He watched as she straightened, her eyes narrowing as if with confusion.

"Very well then . . ." he said, deciding that it might be time to start explaining things to her. Surely she would understand. "Alex . . . you are a lady, and I . . . well, this is highly irregular, don't you agree? Besides, your brother will most likely kill me, or worse, if he discovers us together . . . like this. After all, I promised him that I wouldn't . . . I was hoping that . . ." he said as he raked his hand through his hair in agitation. "Dash it all, there are consequences, you know!" His voice wavered on the last part—not very convincing at all, he realized.

He watched her, hoping that she'd find his words a bit more believable than he did, but apparently she didn't, because instead of turning away, she raised a challenging eyebrow and edged toward him once more, her eyes watching him closely as he felt his resolve begin to falter. When she leaned into him, every last honorable contemplation of stopping the inevitable fled. He dropped his hat, his hands reached for her and his head dipped toward the pure delight she so willingly offered. All rational thought abandoned him, and he knew that he was lost—completely and utterly beyond saving.

Finally.

His lips brushed against her skin, searing her with kisses, his pulse quickening with every touch he made as he breathed her in. He heard her sigh in response—such a lovely sound.

Abandoning her cleavage, he tightened his grip on her waist and buried his head against the curve of her neck. Once again, the scent of lavender enfolded him in its sweetness. He reached for her face, allowing his fingers to run along the delicate edge of her cheekbone. She leaned into his caress, letting out a slight murmur of pleasure that aroused him more than a kiss or touch ever should.

Enough.

Easing back, he watched her closely, examining each and every one of her features. Her face was flushed, her lips slightly parted, and when her eyes fluttered open, there was a look of want within them that almost had him embarrassing himself like a boy in short pants.

Without a word, he took her hand and dragged her along with him, almost tripping on a rug in his haste to get out of the hallway. He found the door to his room and pushed it open with such force that he nearly unhinged it.

Yanking her inside, he kicked the door shut with the heel of his shoe before thrusting her up against the wall. She looked mildly dazed, though by no means perturbed by his rough handling, although a few strands of her hair had come loose to trail down her neck.

"What do you want?" he asked her, his voice low and gravelly as he braced his arms on either side of her.

Alarm bells were ringing a deafening symphony in his head and as much as he wished it, he could no longer ignore them.

Alexandra peered up at him, her brilliant blue eyes swimming with desire. "You," she whispered. "I want you, Michael."

Had his name ever sounded sweeter? By God she was even more brazen than he'd come to expect.

Bloody hell!

If only he had the strength to walk away. Instead, he leaned forward, resting his forehead against hers. "Such things have consequences," he told her. "Are you prepared to face them?"

She shifted slightly as if unsure of how to answer. He'd given her a good reason to pause. "I've no desire to trap you," she murmured as her warm breath flowed toward him, penetrating the thin linen of his shirt before diving beneath his skin—a soft heat that grew, spread, and filled him to the brim. "I merely wish to enjoy whatever it is you have to offer."

Michael squeezed his eyes shut and counted to three, forcing his heart rate back to a more disciplined pace than it had been at for the past five minutes. He let out a slow, lengthy sigh. She was an innocent after all, regardless of how she wished for him to perceive her, and even though he may have just decided to ask for her brother's permission to court her, he sure as hell wasn't about to deny her a wedding night. Some things were sacred, even to him.

Still, he had to make her understand where this path she was so determined to take was bound to lead them. By God he was more than happy to oblige her, but it was still imperative to him that she made her choice, fully aware of what the repercussions would be. "You're a virgin," he told her. "I won't change that."

"Why?" she asked, her voice held a note of despair that shot straight through him. He squeezed his eyes even tighter and groaned in physical anguish. Did she have any idea of the effect she was having on him, he wondered.

"You're a lady, Alex, and regardless of what I may have done in the past, I have never taken an innocent to my bed. Doing so would ruin you in every way imaginable. Even if nobody finds out, your eventual husband will discover the truth quickly enough, and he will despise you forever." The look of disappointment on her face was undeniable, but he rushed on. He had to tell her of his own intentions before he lost his nerve. "I cannot deny that there is something between us—an attraction more powerful than any I have ever known. It's for this reason that I have decided to ask for Ryan's permission to court you."

Alexandra froze, pondering his words briefly before saying, "Yes, I believe a courtship will serve us nicely."

Michael frowned at her odd choice of words and considered a more direct approach. He needed to make sure that he'd made himself understood—that by agreeing to an intimate attachment with him, she was agreeing to so much more—a courtship and eventually marriage. On the other hand, the woman wasn't an imbecile, and he loathed treating her as such.

Looking into her eyes, her need so naked in that gaze of hers, he leaned back on his heels and took her hand in his.

Enough talk.

She wanted him, and he wanted her. Let the cards fall where they may.

Alexandra's pulse quickened as Michael led her brusquely toward a burgundy velvet sofa and with a gentle tug on her arm, encouraged her to sit, her mind still trying to digest his proposition.

A courtship?

She didn't want marriage, but did a courtship necessarily have to lead to that? Clearly, Michael was an honorable man—more honorable than she'd imagined, given his reputation. She was confident that marriage would be the last thing he desired for himself, though she had to respect him for trying to do the right thing for *her*.

However, even if he wouldn't take her to his bed, perhaps the pretext of a courtship would put his mind at ease enough to allow him to . . . her stomach fluttered at the thought of what he might do to her. When they returned to England they could always call the whole thing off.

She watched him now with growing interest as he pushed the table before the sofa a little bit closer. When that was done, he walked across to a standing mirror and pulled it away from the corner in which it stood, moving the heavy thing across the floor until it faced Alexandra. Stepping back, he admired his work, giving it a faint nod of approval. He then reached up to loosen his cravat, his eyes seeking hers. God he was handsome—dangerously so as he stood there now, his hair more ruffled than usual, his eyes burning with something that turned her legs to mush and his jaw tightening as if he was trying desperately to rein himself in. His gaze drifted down until she realized with a start that they had settled on the gentle rise and fall of her bosom.

Was that a soft groan she heard?

She glanced up and gasped at the blazing heat that shone in his eyes, her hand absently reaching for something with which to support her weight before her legs gave out completely. There was something raw and primitive in it that sent an instant rush of shivers coursing through her body.

Regarding the odd arrangement of furniture, she wondered once again what he might have in mind. Clearly, he must be quite experienced, for she could not imagine requiring anything other than the sofa itself.

She didn't have a chance to consider it for long, before he was beside her, his arm circling about her waist and drawing her toward him. There was no more room for thought, no chance to back away or to flee. With the confidence of a man who knew what he wanted and intended to have it, Michael lifted her chin with his fingertips, tilting her head backward until the soft promise of his lips was but a hair breadth away from her own. She quivered ever so gently beneath his hand and inadvertently caught her breath as she waited expectantly for him to make his move.

A moment later his tongue swept slowly over her lower lip—his hand falling to rest alongside her breast. Cupping her gently, he pressed his hand against her before crushing her mouth in a fierce, heart-stopping kiss that shattered the stillness. She was alive—more tantalizingly so than she'd ever thought possible. Without thought for anything other than that very moment, she allowed him to deepen the kiss, his tongue twisting its way around hers, stroking the inner depths of her mouth with seductive pleasure.

Alexandra groaned beneath his touch, reveling in the musky sandalwood scent that encompassed him while his fingers danced gently across her breasts. Feeling the friction of her gown's fabric against her increasingly tender nipples as they strained against her bodice, she arched her back in a silent plea.

Michael responded immediately, lifting her onto his lap and bracing her back firmly against his chest as he began pressing tender kisses against the nape of her neck. "You have no idea how often I've thought of this moment," he whispered against her ear. Caressing her head with one hand, he ran the other over each of her curves, all the while searing her skin with heated kisses. She gasped when he adjusted her position against him, and then again when he gently lifted her legs and placed her feet on the edge of the table in front of them.

An unfamiliar sensation swam through her. It was a hot and molten burst of desire that crept swiftly between her thighs, where it grew to a highly sensitized awareness—a wantonness and wickedness that surely would have shamed even a demimondaine.

With tender slowness, Michael's nimble fingers unfastened the buttons of her bodice, until the back of it gaped open. Lowering his mouth against the curve of her spine he planted a row of kisses. All that remained to be done now, was for him to pull away the fabric that held her body captive— and he did so slowly, but without hesitation, exposing two perfectly rounded breasts in all their glory. "Mm . . . so beautiful," he murmured as his hands slid over them, stroking and teasing while she pressed herself against his hands.

He kissed her neck once more. "Open your eyes, Alex," he said, his voice was thick with desire. "Look at yourself—at how beautiful you are."

She barely dared to do as he suggested, fearful that once she did, she'd be forced to acknowledge her shameful behavior. Yet she couldn't disobey his needy whispers, and so she complied, her eyes locking onto his in the mirror, surprised to discover that her own state of dishabille, added to the thrill of it all, exciting her even further. Her hair was partially undone, a few loose strands draped carelessly over her brow, her bodice slightly askew. Fascination lit her eyes, and she relaxed completely, content with the knowledge that at that precise moment, this was what she wanted more than anything else in the world.

Abandoning her breasts, Michael reached down and took hold of the hemline of her gown, gathering the fabric as he pulled it upward until it settled about Alexandra's waist, exposing the very core of her desire. "Ah, yes," he breathed, his eyes wandering over her reflection while an impish grin played upon his lips. With gentle care, he placed his hands between her thighs, nudging her legs apart until she opened up completely.

Alexandra could barely breathe. Tingling warmth sifted through her most intimate part, giving way to a need she'd never before known and had never thought she possessed. She could scarcely believe that she'd allowed herself to fall into such a compromising position, but was perhaps even more shocked that it didn't seem to bother her in the least. A deep yearning had taken root within her, and as a consequence, all her inhibitions had apparently vanished without a trace. "Please," she now murmured, digging her fingers into Michael's legs, her hips rising ever so slightly in search of something she couldn't at all comprehend. "I don't . . . I cannot . . . I . . ."

Running his fingers playfully along her inner thighs in

a constant upward swirling motion, Michael pressed a kiss against her ear. "Shh," he whispered. "Soon, my sweet. Very soon. Be patient and let me show you."

Alexandra watched with growing fascination as Michael's fingers slid over her.

Just when she thought she would surely die, he finally allowed one lone finger to trail its way along her sex. A tremor gripped her as he stroked her again, parting the soft flesh. A finger went in, and she sagged against him, her breath so ragged while an unearthly delight moved through her—wave upon wave in ever increasing intensity.

"Please," she breathed, without knowing what she demanded. All she knew was that she needed something that felt so close she could almost touch it, yet somehow, it still remained out of reach.

"Soon, Alex. Just relax and let yourself go. Embrace your need."

Raising her hips against the thrust of his finger, Alexandra felt the tension expand to a tautness that suddenly burst. Shivers of ecstasy rippled through her, sending her soaring on a wave of pleasure so intense and so dazzling that she knew she must have caught a glimpse of heaven.

The only thing that Michael could do was hold her. Alexandra had shuddered against him, voicing her passion with moans that had brought him close to the edge himself. No other woman could ever claim to have had such an effect on him. His blood had been on fire. Hell, it still was; his need so intense he could barely imagine not burying himself inside her. Yet he must, for her sake. This moment was about her—a lesson in sexual pleasure.

It had taken every cell in his body to rein himself in so as not to topple over. One thought reigned supreme in his mind however. He *would* marry this woman, if for no other reason than to experience this very thing every day for the rest of his life.

Unfortunately, his line of thought came to a rather abrupt halt when a most unwelcome and extremely unpleasant sound echoed through the air—a knock at the door.

CHAPTER TWELVE

"Ashford, are you . . ."

The door swung open just as Alexandra managed to pull her skirts down and her bodice up in an effort to make herself just a tad bit more presentable. A second later, Ryan stepped into the room, the smile on his face falling away the moment he laid eyes on his sister. His whole countenance changed in that instance—his jaw clenched, his eyes darkened, and his lips were suddenly drawn tight in a grimace of complete and utter fury.

"What the hell is going on here?" he asked.

He did not shout or yell. Indeed, his voice was low and even more frightening than if he'd bellowed the question like a madman.

Alexandra shuddered, taking a small step backward while she clasped the bodice of her gown against her chest. She sensed Michael getting to his feet beside her, but she couldn't look at him.

This was that most horrifying moment of her life. Her face was flushed; she could feel it. Her hair was in disarray, and her dress . . . well, to be frank it didn't much resemble a dress at all anymore but rather a length of crumpled fabric that she'd hastily draped about herself. In short, her humiliation was complete.

Or so she thought.

"What does it look like?" Michael asked.

Alexandra could *not* believe her ears. Was he seriously about to embark on a verbal battle with Ryan? They'd been caught. The least he could do was apologize like any other reasonable gentleman.

Then again, no gentleman would have allowed for such a situation to arise in the first place, she reflected.

No, Michael Ashford was a rake—a notorious one at that. He'd just made that shamelessly apparent. Then again, *she'd* been the one encouraging *him*. To be fair, she'd acted no better than a harlot.

"Do you want him to hit you?" she ground out between clenched teeth.

"He will do so anyway," Michael replied, resigned. "And, having a hoard of sisters myself, I cannot think of a single reason why he shouldn't. I only hoped to help him quicken his resolve."

Alexandra gaped at him. "You *want* him to hit you?" She frowned, realizing she'd just asked that very question a mere second ago.

Michael grinned at her, just as Ryan closed the distance between them and buried his fist in his left cheek. He went down without pause, his grin twisting into something quite painful to look at.

Alexandra gasped. "Good God, Ryan," she yelled as her

eyes shifted between the heap of limbs sprawled out on the floor and her brother. He seemed to be more interested in attending to the reddening knuckles on his right hand, than he was in regarding his handiwork.

"Watch your tongue, Alex," Ryan told her morosely. "I have had just about enough of you acting any which way you please. We've all done what we could to humor your antics, but we're out in public now, not hidden away behind the walls of Moorland Manor. I won't have you bringing our name to shame, no matter your excuses." He let out a heavy sigh as he slumped down on the very sofa where Alexandra and Michael had just had their little tryst. He didn't seem to notice and Alexandra was definitely not about to point it out to him.

"Should we perhaps help him up?" she asked as she looked down at Michael who was presently trying to pull himself together enough to stand.

"I believe he can manage," Ryan muttered. "Do you know, I'm really quite angry with you, Alex, for putting me in a position where my only option was to bloody the Earl of Trenton's nose."

"Really, Ryan, it's not as bad as all that. He will have a nasty bruise to be sure, but you didn't bloody his nose."

"Ah, then at least I have *that* to be thankful for," he snapped sarcastically.

"Summersby." Michael had finally managed to drag himself off the floor and haul himself into an empty chair. "I must apologize to you, though you ought to know her innocence remains intact."

"I am so relieved," Ryan growled. "You say it as if that makes it all right."

"Well, I merely wished for you to know that as compromising as this situation might appear, there are certain things that even a man like me considers holy."

Alexandra gaped at him. Was he really sitting there discussing her innocence with her brother? *Inconceivable!*

Michael cleared his throat. "I like you, Summersby, and I am sorry, truly I am. I didn't mean for it to happen like this."

"Like *this?*" Ryan arched a brow as he pushed himself out of his chair, his hands clenching into tight fists while he regarded his adversary with silent disdain. "That, Lord Trenton, would imply that you meant for it to happen sooner or later. It *implies*, that you had no intention of heeding my warning and staying away from my sister at all. Do I take your meaning to be correct, sir?"

"You *warned* him?" Alexandra cut in, drawing the attention of both men. They turned their heads toward her, and she shot them both a tight, somewhat awkward smile. "As you can see, I am still here."

Michael smirked at her disheveled figure, his cheek already showing signs of puffiness.

Goodness gracious it looked painful.

Without comment, he turned back to Ryan, ignoring Alexandra and her loud sigh of annoyance. "As I was saying, I did not mean for it to happen like this. In truth, I meant to begin a courtship with her first. Unfortunately, it would seem we got a little . . . carried away. However, I would like you to know that, given the circumstances, I have every intention of standing by her and doing the right thing. I shall marry her as soon as we are safely back in England."

"You'll *what?*" Alexandra squeaked, staring at Michael in shocked disbelief.

Ryan looked suddenly transformed—a brilliant smile of relief lifting his features. "I'm so relieved to hear it," he exclaimed, giving his soon to be brother-in-law a sound nod of approval. "So, very, very relieved indeed."

"I'm happy to hear that, Summersby."

Ryan gave a nonchalant wave of his hand. "Ryan, please."

"Well, then you must call me Michael. Agreed?"

"With pleasure. However, I must apologize for hitting you. I lost it for a moment there. I'm afraid it's beginning to look rather horrid, if I may say so myself."

"No matter. It hardly came as a surprise, you know. But, I dare say a glass of whiskey might do the trick."

"To numb the pain you mean?"

"What else?" Michael laughed as he patted Ryan on the back. The two men had begun heading for the door. "After a few glasses, I'm sure I won't feel a thing."

"I must admit I can't abide the stuff myself," Ryan said—his hand already on the door handle.

"How about a glass of claret then?" Michael asked, ready to follow Ryan out of the room.

Alexandra blinked. This could not be happening. She didn't want to marry. Not now, not ever. It didn't matter if the man proposing to save her from spinsterhood was the most handsome man she'd ever laid eyes upon. Indeed, it didn't even matter that she had begun liking him, even if it was only just a little bit. She quickly reminded herself how much he annoyed her and that he happened to do so the majority of the time. Like right now for instance. Without as much as a glance in her direction, he'd planned her direct route to the altar for her.

Never mind her opinion on the matter. Clearly that was of no importance to Michael *or* her brother. And now look at them. They were best friends all of a sudden.

Really?

Did they have any idea of how ridiculous they appeared to an observer? After all, that was what she'd become. She'd practically been forgotten and it simply couldn't go on. She *would* have her say whether they liked it or not, and she rather suspected that it was going to be the latter of the two. Straightening her spine, she uttered one word just as Ryan's hand pushed down upon the door handle.

"No!" she said.

Both men turned their heads and looked at her in puzzlement. They'd either forgotten she was there, or they couldn't quite comprehend what she was talking about. Both possibilities seemed equally likely in that instance—so much so in fact that Alexandra decided to quickly elaborate.

"I won't marry you," she explained.

"Won't marry him?" Ryan asked in a partially choked voice. "Alex, you cannot be serious."

"Oh, but I am, Ryan. Indeed I am quite serious. I won't marry his lordship or any other gentleman who offers me a life consisting of little else than making babies and putting on a farce of the perfectly bred wife. It's not for me."

Ryan simply stared at her. Michael, on the other hand, looked angry. Surprisingly so in fact. "Have you lost all sense of reason," he ground out. "You *must* marry me, for the sake of your reputation if nothing else."

"My reputation?" Alexandra offered him a coy smile. "Really, how is my reputation to suffer? Nobody has seen us, save for Ryan, and he's highly unlikely to mention it to anyone. He wouldn't risk tarnishing our good family name for anything in the world. That leaves you, my lord, and you hardly seem the sort to spread gossip. Least of all gossip in which you figure quite prominently yourself. Am I correct?"

Michael stared at her, his eyes darkening into black thunderclouds. *Is it possible for a man's head to explode?* she wondered with a small amount of curiosity while she faced him without pause. Michael's head certainly looked as if it were about to do just that.

"We spoke of the consequences beforehand." His tone held an iciness to it that seemed to have a more immediate effect on Alexandra than his expression did. A slow sense of anxiety began to form in the pit of her belly—an odd sensation that she hadn't felt in years—not since she was a child. "I told you I would court you, and you agreed. Don't pretend you did not know where such a courtship would eventually lead."

Alexandra shrugged her shoulders, hoping that the gesture would distract him from noticing the panic that was creeping through her. "And I told *you* that a courtship would serve us nicely. It would allow us to engage in certain activities that might otherwise be considered improper. The whole affair would naturally have been called off the minute we returned to England. That goes without saying."

Michael and Ryan seemed equally appalled by Alexandra's outrageous confession. Neither man said a word for a number of seconds. They simply didn't appear to be quite capable of processing the magnitude of what her words implied. Alexandra on the other hand, felt oddly pleased with herself.

She was certain that she'd just achieved two very important things. Number one, she'd made it very clear that she had no intention of ever marrying anyone, and number two, she'd painted such a despicable picture of herself that she was quite confident Michael would run screaming in the other direction.

Her mind was quickly returned to the present however, at the sound of her brother's words.

"Have you no shame?" he asked, pinning her with an accusatory stare that was clearly meant to make her squirm. "You're . . . you're no better than a . . . a . . . !" His voice was shaky, his hands clenched tightly at his sides. "I cannot bring myself to say the word that comes to mind, for I will surely regret it." He shook his head in disbelief, staring at her as if he was seeing her for the very first time.

It stung more than any blow ever would. Perhaps he was right in his assessment of her, as hard as that was to accept. She'd lusted after Michael for days. She'd set out to purposefully lure the man into bed without any intent of ever marrying him. Now, because she was a woman, she'd backed herself into a corner by doing so. Panic gripped at her insides. She needed a means of escape.

"I wish to challenge you." Michael's words were spoken with composed calm in spite of the rage that still flickered in his eyes. They hung in the air, hovering between them so clearly that Alexandra was certain she just might catch a glimpse of them at any moment.

"I beg your pardon?" Ryan asked before Alexandra could manage it.

"Your sister has offended my sense of honor by prohibiting

me from doing the only respectable thing I might have done in this instance. She has deliberately trapped me in a way that is bound to cause a great deal of disgrace to my family. Who in their right mind will think that *she's* the culprit? No," he said, shaking his head as if to clear his mind of the whole entanglement. "Everyone will point an accusing finger at me, especially given my reputation. So yes, as unusual as it is, I demand satisfaction."

"You cannot mean that," Alexandra whispered, her whole body going numb.

This was the man who'd kissed and touched her so intimately a mere moment ago, now challenging her to a duel. It was absurd.

She stared back at him and suddenly realized with abrupt clarity how much she'd truly wounded him. He did his best not to show it. For that she commended him, but his eyes betrayed him. Was it possible that he'd really *wanted* to marry her? It couldn't be. She was sure he'd have grown tired of her by the time they returned to London. He didn't even like her, and he couldn't possibly think that she liked him—even if she did . . . just a little. Still, there was something undeniable between them and as she'd pointed out to herself earlier, perhaps she did like him just a bit more than she was allowing herself to admit.

But marriage?

Why on earth would he want to marry her when he could surely marry any lady of his choosing? After all, his wealth and title went a long way.

Even if for some unfathomable reason he'd decided that she was the one, she had made her choice a long time ago. She'd witnessed the pain that her father had suffered when her mother had died. She and her brothers had suffered his emotional withdrawal for years—a depression from which he'd only recently begun to emerge. Indeed, it was as if she'd lost both parents at once, and it had been devastating.

Now that she finally felt as if she had her father back, she was faced with the fear of reliving it all over again. The pain of losing a parent was inevitable. It was bound to happen sooner or later if nature followed its natural course, but that hardly made it any more bearable. Already, she dreaded the day when it would happen once more. Her father was hardly getting any younger and watching him recently with the trouble his legs were giving him . . . it made her want to weep. He'd always been the strongest of men, capable of anything—her hero. Yet every day she saw him, she could almost hear the sands of time rushing through a giant hourglass, bringing her closer to yet another impossibly painful loss.

Why anybody might choose to put oneself in such a precarious situation—to open their heart and allow love in, only to face the inevitable dread of having it all snatched away in an instant, she couldn't imagine. One would almost certainly outlive the other, to be left behind in constant heartache, and Alexandra couldn't possibly imagine anything more awful.

As sorry as she now was for having wounded his pride and as shocked as she was at the turn of events, Alexandra knew that Michael had just given her a means of escape. Funny how such things worked out. If Ryan had applied just a little more force by threatening to tell her father what she'd been up to, she probably would have agreed to marry Michael without a second thought. Yet here they were. Michael had challenged her, and as unconventional as that might be, she had no intention of turning him down. She would have the choice of weapons, and she knew without any shadow of a doubt that she could beat him.

"Oh, but I do," Michael smirked. He looked as though he was truly enjoying himself now.

Out of nowhere, Ryan suddenly laughed. In fact, it was closer to a howl. Alexandra blinked, her lips parting in startled bewilderment.

What the devil is so amusing?

"Oh, this is perfect!" Ryan chortled as he wiped tears of mirth from his eyes. "Absolutely perfect. Really, Michael, you must allow me to be your second. I wouldn't want to miss this for the world!"

"You wish to be *his* second?" Alexandra asked with a note of disappointment clinging to her words. "I rather thought you might be mine."

"So sorry, Alex, but I'm afraid Michael needs me," he said, his apology didn't sound at all convincing and Alexandra was getting more than a little annoyed about how much Ryan seemed to be enjoying the whole scenario. His anger at this unlikely turn of events had clearly evaporated. "Besides, you did bring this on yourself, dear sister. Now, it's time for you to pay the price."

A sparkle of mischief brightened his eyes. It was almost as if he was taking some sort of twisted pleasure in this calamitous outcome. This was one moment that he would very likely savor for the remainder of his days, she reckoned—the one instance when his sister who excelled at practically everything had finally been bested. It was infuriating enough to make her want to stomp her feet in protest.

Her mind snapped to attention at the mention of her name.

"Are you even listening to me?" Ryan was asking with a somewhat exasperated look upon his face.

"Yes, of course," she lied, noting that Michael's jaw seemed to clench with marked annoyance.

"You wish to act like a man, dress like a man, and fight like a man." Ryan said, forcing her attention back to him. "Indeed, you desire all the privileges that men enjoy and yet, you do not wish to face the consequences. From what I've been able to piece together, you were even the instigator in what transpired this evening.

"So you see, Alex, you are the one who has compromised *his* reputation and on top of that, in spite of the fact that he is willing to do the right thing, you've gone and tossed his honor right back in his face! And that, in spite of the fact that you've always seemed so honorable yourself . . . I just don't understand it."

Ryan's voice trailed off, the amusement gone, which made Alexandra feel even more chastised than before. The fact that he put her sense of honor into question, the shake of his head when he'd said he didn't understand it . . . it all made her feel so undeniably small.

"If you had any sense of honor, you would be racing to the altar right this minute with his lordship in tow," he went on. "However, since it appears that you have no intention of doing so, you will face him at dawn tomorrow instead and, God willing, come to your senses." And with that, Ryan strode from the room, no doubt in search of the claret Michael had mentioned earlier.

Alexandra stood as if glued to the floor.

How has everything managed to go so horribly wrong?

In a matter of mere seconds it seemed she'd managed to lose all the respect that Ryan had ever had for her. He'd called her a . . . well, he hadn't said the word, but she'd known what he'd meant, and that was enough. A tight lump filled her throat at the thought. She felt as if her heart had just been torn from her chest and smashed to pieces. The most disturbing thing was that she had been the one doing the smashing.

How could she possibly be so stupid? She was refusing the one person who might just make the perfect husband for her if she'd only give him half a chance. She shook her head. It was out of the question and now she was faced with having to hurt him as well. Ryan had given her that little speech about honor. Really! What on earth was so honorable about getting up at the crack of dawn to spar with somebody in a deserted field? It hardly seemed like the most intelligent way in which to settle a dispute. Then again, it might be quicker than a well thought out debate. For the first time since Ryan had walked in on her and Michael, Alexandra grinned.

Would it not be fun to do both?

"There's still the matter of choosing your weapon," a dry voice told her.

Looking up, she spotted Michael. He was watching her with a steady gaze as if trying to discern what she was thinking. There was no warmth in his eyes however. Not anymore. A heavy silence hung between them while he waited for her reply. "Swords," she finally told him. "I shall have to ask William to be my second."

Michael nodded. "We will head to the Bois du Bologne together. I trust William can meet us there?"

"I'd better send him a note." He turned toward the door, but Alexandra stopped him with a question. "Will it be to the death?"

"What?" he asked as he turned back to look at her.

"The duel. Will it be to the death?"

Michael stared at her in complete and utter disbelief. Not only was she perfectly stunning as she stood there now, her dress still dangling awkwardly on her slim figure, but heaven help him if she hadn't just said the stupidest of all things. "I have no desire to kill you, my lady." He paused as he waited for her to comment, but when she merely stared back at him saying nothing he added, "Whoever draws first blood wins."

He wasn't quite sure, but it did seem as if she breathed a huge sigh of what could only be relief. Was she possibly worried about the outcome? And if so, why? He knew her well enough by now to know that she would be confident about winning, which meant that if she was alarmed, it was only because she knew she'd cause him bodily harm. Michael allowed himself to wonder what that might mean and arrived at only one conclusion—Alexandra Summersby actually liked him—quite possibly more than she was ready to admit, even to herself. A velvety warm feeling settled in his belly at the thought of it. There was still hope for everything to turn out the way he wanted them to after all.

"Chin up," he told her as he turned back toward the door. "Your freedom is within your grasp. All you have to do is win." Hiding a lopsided grin, he then quickly exited his bedroom and went in search of Ryan before he managed to say or do something else that he might come to regret.

CHAPTER THIRTEEN

A misty drizzle filled the air in the early hours of the morning as the three riders set out toward the park. Alexandra kept a fair distance behind her brother and Michael, her mount hanging its head as if aware of what was about to take place. Alexandra had no desire for conversation at present, nor did she wish to share an uncomfortable silence. Instead, she looked straight ahead, watching Michael's and Ryan's backs while wondering what they might possibly be talking about at a time like this.

She was furious with both of them of course, though she wasn't quite sure which of them had made her angrier—Michael for challenging her or Ryan for practically placing a sword in her hand and pushing her into combat.

When Michael had shared his intention to court her with Ryan, he'd caught her completely off guard. But as flattering as such a notion might be, it was equally horrifying when the thought of marriage or God forbid love, happened to go hand in hand with it. And if there was one thing that Alexandra absolutely did not want, it was to fall in love—she especially did not want to face each day with the same worry: *How much longer do we have together?*

Will it be decades? Years? Months, or mere days?

She simply would not be able to live with such a concern, particularly in light of the fact that he clearly enjoyed going on dangerous missions that would forever put him in peril. As it was she could barely stand it whenever William went away, not knowing if it would be the last time she saw him. Her brother always rolled his eyes each time she insisted that he write her daily letters to ensure her of his welfare, telling her he'd be fine and that she was overreacting. Well, it wasn't *his* heart that had practically stopped when those letters had ceased two months earlier. And when she'd found him grinning at her upon her arrival at the Tuileries Palace, as if he hadn't a care in the world, she'd very nearly throttled him. Living on constant edge like this, forever filled with panic that tragedy might strike at any moment, was no life at all.

She didn't intend to live out the rest of her days as a virgin, however. Perhaps she *was* being wicked and immoral, but she really didn't care. She'd always believed in getting what she wanted out of life, even if it did send gasps of horror through the higher ranks of society.

She wasn't acquainted with very many men though, since she'd never had a London season, her father being too preoccupied with his sorrow to notice that she was turning into a woman. So instead of learning how to embroider, she'd climbed trees and balanced along the rooftop of Moorland Manor. Instead of continuing with the piano lessons her mother had been so adamant about, she'd spent hours with the horses, galloping across the fields. And instead of visiting the dressmakers and learning to carry herself with the grace of a lady, she'd practiced at firing pistols until she could kill a bird in flight without pause. The only reason she'd learned to dance was because her brothers needed someone to practice with. It had been fun in a way, and she'd certainly honed her skills, but it had also been incredibly lonely. She'd missed her mother desperately and had rarely seen her father. Even Ryan and William had been away much of the time, both attending Eton. So all things told, remaining chaste hadn't seemed like much of a problem. She certainly wasn't one to go for the stable boy.

But then she'd crossed paths with Michael. It would be the biggest lie of the century to deny that sparks went flying whenever he as much as glanced in her direction. He annoyed her to no end and was by far the most arrogant man she'd ever come across . . . but, somehow he'd managed to wiggle his way under her skin, to do the unthinkable. He'd actually made her fall for him in a ridiculously short amount of time and without any apparent effort on his part. "Damn!"

"Are you all right?" Ryan had turned in his saddle to look back at her.

"Fine," she muttered. "I just remembered something." She felt like hitting her head against a brick wall at that statement. Why would she say such a thing?

"What?" Michael asked, pulling his horse to a halt so he could wait for her.

"I said I just remembered something." She tossed him a scowl.

"I know." Michael smirked, clearly struggling to keep a

straight face. She knew that he was still angry with her of course, though the intensity of it had apparently faded. "I was inquiring as to *what* it was you just remembered."

"Oh." She glared at him with what could only be unmistakable annoyance. "It's not important."

Thank heavens I shall not marry, she thought. The man was likely to drive her insane! All she'd wanted was to know what went on between a man and a woman, and he, England's most talked about womanizer, rake, rogue . . . call him what you will, had gone and grown a conscience. She wanted to scream!

As if that wasn't enough, he'd decided that she'd wounded his pride or his honor or whatever it was that had them leaving the comfort of their beds at this ungodly hour. And now, it had even begun to rain. Somebody must be looking down on them and having a merry time at their expense. And for nothing less than a duel.

A duel!

A duel between an English lord and an English lady on French soil! Surely she wasn't the only one who thought the whole thing bordered on insanity.

"Oh, but it must be," Michael told her seriously as her horse came up between his and Ryan's. "Judging from your scowl, I dare say it must be very important indeed."

"Perhaps you're right," she conceded. "Though I doubt you will ever know."

Ryan let out a muffled laugh beside her while Michael merely muttered an oath that was more offensive in nature than most. Alexandra on the other hand remained quiet, satisfied in knowing that she'd managed to vex him yet again. Somehow, that little bit of knowledge made her feel a whole lot better.

Alexandra was the first to see William when they entered the park. He was wearing a heavy cloak with the hood drawn low over his head to protect him from the rain. The minute Alexandra spotted him, he nudged his mount toward them. The animal protested with a rough shake of its head, stepping in place with great agitation before bowing to William's command. "What's all this nonsense about?" he asked in a stiff voice while he drew up alongside Alexandra.

"It appears as though I have offended his lordship's honor." She paused for a moment as a smile crept over her lips. "He's challenged me to a duel in the hope of defending it."

William cast a glance over her shoulder at Michael. "It must have been quite an offense indeed if you felt compelled to challenge her."

"I didn't make the decision lightly," Michael ground out. His eyes were unflinching as he stared back at William.

"You made it quickly enough," Alexandra remarked.

"That is beside the point," he shot back.

"I hardly . . ." she stopped herself with a sigh. An argument wasn't going to solve anything right now. She looked at William. "Thank you for coming. I was not sure if you would be able to manage it."

"I must admit I was quite taken aback by your hasty letter, but it goes without saying that I would do whatever it took to be here right now. After all, it's not every day that my little sister asks for my assistance." He smiled affectionately at her, but when his eyes shifted to Ryan, it dropped from his face. "What I would like to know is why the devil *you* are not her second."

"Michael asked me first," Ryan said simply and much too nonchalantly for Alexandra's liking.

"He did not!" she exclaimed as she spun around, her eyes pinning him with an accusing stare.

He shrugged. "Well, then I suppose it's because I thought it the right thing to do after you had just insulted him so distastefully."

"Did you?" William asked her in a low tone that demanded an honest answer.

Alexandra's eyes met Michael's. They glistened with a mixture of anger, regret, and desire that tore at her heart with a vengeance. She nodded solemnly. "I'm afraid I did."

"Well, then I suppose there's nothing for it, although, as your second I must inform you that this entire business may be settled with an apology." William frowned as he looked at his sister. "Do you wish to apologize to Lord Trenton so we might put this whole—"

She shook her head. "No," she whispered.

Her eyes were cast down. She couldn't look at any of them anymore. There was no one to blame for it but herself. She shook her head in an attempt to clear it.

"Very well then," William sighed. "There's no point in wasting time. Let us begin."

Turning his horse around, he trotted along a footpath to a large lawn that was both flat and devoid of trees and bushes. It would serve nicely as a sparring ground.

Alexandra followed close behind him, dismounting and tying the reins of her horse to a nearby bench. She felt a heavy hand settle upon her shoulder and looked up to see William looking down at her, concern marking his eyes. "Will it be to the death?" he asked her.

She shook her head. "No, only until first blood."

He let out a sigh. "I imagine that must come as quite a relief to you. As far as I know, you've never killed a man before. I should hate for your first time to be somebody you actually care about."

"I don't . . ." she gasped defensively.

William raised an eyebrow. "Do not lie to yourself, Alex. I do not know all the details about your relationship with Trenton, but I have seen enough to know that what *is* between you two, is very far from hate. If I were bold, I might venture to suggest that you have fallen in love with the man." Alexandra's jaw dropped at her brother's forthright observation. How could he possibly think that when she hadn't even allowed herself to consider such a prospect?

"Don't say anything," he continued in a low whisper. "I'm sure you have your reasons for doing what you're about to do, yet I thought it necessary to tell you that I do believe you're making a terrible mistake."

Alexandra's lips drew together in a tight line. This really wasn't helping her at all. "You're right, William. I *do* have my reasons, and I *do* have to do this."

William handed her a saber. "Keep telling yourself that, and you just might believe it." He paused before adding, "Go easy on him, Alex. First blood doesn't necessarily mean a wide gash."

Alexandra stared back at him for a moment, then gave a quick nod before turning about and heading out onto the grass. "Ready?" she called to Michael.

"I believe so," he called back, picking up his own saber and heading toward her. He was a mere foot away from her before he stopped, his eyes latching onto hers as if pleading for something impossible. "Be reasonable, Alex," he murmured. "I . . . you . . ." He paused as he ran a hand through his hair. Alexandra felt her stomach tighten before it suddenly flipped in a most uncomfortable fashion. Her skin prickled and the urge to rush into his arms, to feel the warmth of his body wrap itself around her, overwhelmed her with such a force that she could scarcely breathe.

"Why are you torturing me like this?" he finally managed. "Do you have any idea how I—"

"En garde!" Alexandra yelled, cutting him off. The last thing she wanted right now was for him to declare his feelings for her. She knew her resolve would waiver if he did so. In fact, if she waited a moment longer she'd find herself melting into a hopeless pool of lament before his very eyes. She couldn't allow for that to happen. Her fear was too strong, too powerful, too relentless, and although she'd always feared the idea of love in general, she especially feared it now that she'd met Michael. He was not the sort of man who would say no to danger. On the contrary, he'd eagerly face it head on, pistols blazing while she would have to live in constant dread.

The clash of metal sharpened her senses in an instant. It felt good to wield a sword again, the weight of it in her hand an unexpected comfort. Her lungs filled with a rush of cool dawn air while she sidestepped Michael's attack. She twisted smoothly out of the way, only just managing to turn about before he was upon her again, already pushing her to the limit.

Reality began to seep in. This was no ordinary adversary. Compared with Ryan and William . . . Well, they were good, very good in fact, but Michael, he was simply excellent. Concern poured through her. He had stamina and a marvelous technique that was proving more and more difficult to outmaneuver. She'd never seen him fight, and she'd assumed that she would easily best him. There was no doubt that she'd made a serious error in judgment.

She performed a quick inquartata in response to Michael's lunge. Inertia kept him moving, allowing her a brief yet necessary moment's reprieve. "You're better than I'd expected," she told him honestly. Her breath was already coming quickly.

"One should never underestimate one's opponent, my lady," he replied with a note of confidence that brought her immediately on edge. "I recently learned that lesson myself."

She knew he was referring to her interpretation of what might constitute a courtship. "I'm sorry, Michael," she muttered.

"What was that?" he asked, his eyes shone with amusement. "I couldn't quite hear you."

"You must have selective hearing then," she quipped as flippantly as she could muster while he advanced on her again.

"Do you know, it almost sounded as if you just apologized. But knowing you, that cannot possibly be right. Can it?"

She favored him with her best scowl, pushing a sudden advantage she'd found in an opening. "Clearly you cannot fight and talk at the same time, my lord. You've just given me the advantage."

"Hm . . . I see your point."

"You do?"

"Certainly, though I thought that *you* might be smart enough to consider *why* I would choose to do such a thing."

Blocking Alexandra's sudden attack and forcing her blade sideways, he didn't miss a beat. With a quick application of pressure, he pushed her off balance until she toppled backward. She landed with a loud thump on her bottom, her hands sliding out behind her in the wet grass.

Alexandra was not an idiot. She knew when she'd been beaten fair and square, but that didn't make it any less infuriating, or humiliating for that matter. She muttered an oath just as she felt the prick of Michael's saber against her shoulder, forcing her back upon her elbows. Tilting her head backward, she reluctantly looked up only to find him gazing down at her with a rather annoying look of satisfaction.

"You let your confidence get the better of you, my lady," he said.

She moved to sit up, but he only applied more pressure to the sword point.

"Not so fast." He smirked. "First blood, remember?"

Before Alexandra had a chance to consider the significance of what he'd just said, he pressed forward just enough to puncture her skin. A drop of scarlet blood sprang forth to redden the white linen of her shirt. "Ow!"

Tilting his head sideways, Michael stared down at her for a moment. "Just wanted to be clear about who won," he told her.

"You had an advantage, you know," she muttered as she glared up at him. "You saw me fight in Rouen. You knew what you were getting into, yet I had no idea about your level of skill."

"I hope you're not implying that it wasn't a fair fight."

"No, not at all, but I do feel as though I've just been had."

"Not so pleasant, is it?" Extending his free hand, Michael reached down to help her up. She looked at it as if it might as well have been diseased. "Come on. The least I can do is offer my assistance."

Looking none too pleased, Alexandra reluctantly took his hand, allowing him to haul her to her feet. She was in the middle of brushing dirt off herself when both William and Ryan strode up to where she and Michael were standing. "That was brilliantly done, Michael," Ryan grinned. "You know, I was hoping you might win."

Alexandra just glared at her brother. She wondered if having him drawn and quartered would satisfy her sudden need to hurt him. As if reading her mind, Ryan took a small step in William's direction. "No offense, Alex, but it's just so damn satisfying to watch somebody best you."

"He's right you know," William chuckled. "I wouldn't have thought it, but by all that's holy, this really has been very rewarding." Turning to Michael, William made an elaborate show of bowing before him. "It's an honor to know you, Ashford."

Michael suddenly laughed. He couldn't help himself. By God they were an odd bunch, the Summersbys. He knew he ought to act with more reserve, especially since he was meant to be investigating the loyalty of the eldest sibling, but this was just too much of a farce to be taken seriously. He'd practically been caught molesting the men's sister, but apparently all had been forgiven just because he happened to have beaten her in a duel.

A smug look crept over his face as he now recalled the reason behind the duel. *He* was the victor, which meant that . . . he turned to Alexandra. "I hope you realize this means marriage," he told her.

There was no denying the panic that swamped Alex at those words. If she could only run away from it all. She glanced toward him and as she did, his pleased expression faded. He must have seen the pain upon her face, for he suddenly seemed to take on a look of apology and regret. "Look at me," he said. His words were soft and gentle.

Raising her gaze toward him, her eyes met his, and as they did he seemed to shiver. The wind perhaps? She couldn't tell, but for some reason she liked to think that he'd somehow responded to the anguish she felt at that very moment.

"I will do whatever I can to make you happy," he said, reaching for her hand. "You'll never want for anything, and . . . you shall never have to endure the embarrassment of a mistress."

She started a little at his promise. It was unexpected, to be sure, yet somehow, in spite of everything, it filled her with an immense amount of relief. She knew she could never share him, but she also knew that it was not a promise he'd made lightly, as was evidenced by the stunned expression upon his face. He clearly was surprised by what he'd just said, and she appreciated the value of it so much more because of that. She didn't fear that he might go back on his word either, he was too honorable for that, and besides, he'd spoken the promise in front of her brothers. There were witnesses now.

"Will you ride with us for a bit?" Alexandra asked as she turned to William. She felt emotionally drained. Freedom had been within her grasp. She could almost feel her fingers closing around it, only to have it ripped away so unexpectedly.

William shook his head. "I ought to get back before my absence becomes too noticeable. Nobody's shown any sign of suspicion yet, and I certainly have no desire to draw attention to myself. I'm an Englishman after all, and I will hang as one if they discover the truth."

"And what *is* the truth?" Michael asked him, his brow knit in a studious frown.

William grinned. "I won't make it that easy on you, Ashford. However, I will give you these invitations." Reaching inside his jacket pocket, he pulled out three sealed envelopes. "They're for the ball next Friday."

"Bonaparte is having a ball?" Ryan asked with no small degree of surprise.

William nodded. "It's the first since his return from Elba, perhaps his last before his next campaign. Who knows?" He flashed Michael a meaningful look that immediately pushed the cogs in his brain into action. "In any case, it promises to be a big bash indeed. Bonaparte doesn't do anything in half measure. All the gentry in Paris will be invited, including foreign ministers and ambassadors. Not ours of course, for obvious reasons."

"Do we even have one here at the moment?" Alexandra asked.

"No. Lord Whitworth was the last, but that was ten years ago." A moment's silence hovered over them until William finally tightened his hold on the reins and pulled his horse about. "Enjoy your victory, Ashford. I hope for your sake that it will be the first of many." He grinned as he looked across at his sister. "She can be a handful you know."

"I know," Michael agreed with a heavy sigh. "But if all our disputes can be settled with a duel, then perhaps I stand a fighting chance."

Alexandra caught herself rolling her eyes. "I am not *that* difficult to deal with," she muttered.

"My dear sister," William announced with great fervor, "you tire even the most energetic of men. Indeed you are the most wearing female of my acquaintance. However, I for one would not have it any other way, for you are truly unique, and I do love you beyond all rhyme or reason. That said, I am thrilled to finally deposit you in another man's care— absolutely thrilled!"

Ryan grinned while Michael took on an unexpected look of uneasiness. "She'll give you a run for your money," William continued. "But I hazard a guess that it will be well worth it. I will see you all at the ball."

Alexandra watched him ride off in the opposite direction to where she would be going. She gave Michael a sidelong glance. He'd managed to snare her so easily. She hated him for it, but most of all she hated herself and her stupid arrogance for landing her in this mess. The life she'd always imagined for herself, free of society's strictures, was now out of reach.

Worst of all was the rigid knot of fear that was presently tightening in the pit of her stomach. She took a deep breath to steady herself.

"Are you all right?" It was Michael's velvety voice that asked the question.

"I'll be fine," she managed as a vision of standing at the altar and promising to love this man until death did them part sneaked up on her, filling her with dread. She felt suddenly overcome with dizziness. Bringing her hand to her forehead in response to the pain that now sliced its way through her skull, she couldn't help but wince. Her heart was pounding so furiously she could almost hear it.

Michael watched Alexandra with a growing degree of concern. She looked panic-stricken and quite ill. Casting a quick glance in Ryan's direction, he saw that he had noticed the same thing, but before either of them could reach out to help her, her body sagged sideways, and she toppled from her saddle.

"Alex!" they both called out in unison, as if their words would slow her descent to the ground.

"Good God, Ryan," Michael exclaimed, dismounting as fast as he could manage. "Her foot is caught in the stirrup."

They were beside her dangling body in an instant.

Scooping her up, Michael cradled her against his chest while Ryan untangled her foot.

"She's out cold," Ryan murmured. "I wonder what happened. She's never fainted before in her life."

"Hold her for a minute will you," Michael said as he settled her into her brother's arms. He got back on his horse, moving as far back in his saddle as he could manage so that Alexandra would have enough room. "You can hand her up to me now," he told him.

CHAPTER FOURTEEN

It was noon by the time Alexandra's eyes fluttered open. The early morning rain must have cleared, for the brightness that was blinding her could only be the sun's sharp rays protruding through the window. She squinted slightly as her hand moved up to clasp her head.

The pain was still there.

"Welcome back." She recognized Michael's voice in an instant and immediately groaned her displeasure. Rolling over onto her side, she pulled the pillow over her head.

"Not so pleased to see me I take it."

There was a question in his statement that she refused to answer.

"What happened?" she asked instead.

"We had a duel. I won, and then you fainted. That sums it up fairly accurately."

"Just fairly?"

"Well, I *could* give you a more detailed account of how I beat you, but I've decided to take pity on you—because you fainted of course."

"Of course," came her sarcastic reply.

She knew he was grinning from ear to ear. She could feel it.

A short silence followed. She could hear him shifting restlessly in his chair before finally getting up and walking across the room. "This did not turn out at all the way I'd hoped it would," he muttered.

"Oh?" She snatched the pillow from her face and tossed it aside so that she might be able to see him. He was leaning with his shoulder against the wall by the window as he looked down toward the street.

"You annoy me more than any woman I have ever met. You're as troublesome as an unruly child who refuses do as she's told—a hoyden in the extreme. You have the breeding of a lady, but choose instead to thwart all rules of polite society. Hell, you curse worse than me for heaven's sake!"

"I hope that's not a compliment, for if it is, you're not only terrible at it but I would also hate to know what it's like to be insulted by you."

He threw her a chastising glance, but there was humor in his eyes. "Do you know what the most annoying thing about you is? The thing that has me truly vexed?"

"I shudder to think of it."

He ignored her jibe. "The thing that irks me more than anything else, is that in spite of all this, for some bizarre reason that I cannot possibly hope to ever comprehend, I actually happen to like you."

Alexandra knew her heart must have stopped. Her mouth was certainly gaping wide open in dismay. Had Michael Ashford just confessed to liking her?

Impossible.

She knew he desired her. She knew he was honorable enough to marry her to save her reputation, but that he actually might like her . . . with a slow thump, thump, her heart slowly began a steady beat once more. He was right. It was absolutely beyond comprehension—but then, so had been the realization that *she* liked *him*.

The worst part was that she liked him more and more the more time they spent in each other's company. Blast it all. Things weren't at all moving in the direction that they were supposed to. She watched him turn toward her, his head tilting in a thoughtful pose. "Aren't you going to say anything?"

Never.

Not in a million years.

"I really ought to get changed. My clothes are terribly dirty not to mention bloodied thanks to you." She shot him a look of irritation. "Would you please excuse me so I might see to it?"

He watched her for a moment without moving, as if considering whether or not to grant her such a wish. There was a quick flicker of something in those dark eyes of his. Pain? Regret? "Yes, of course," he said suddenly as he straightened himself and strode toward the door. "I shall trouble you no further."

With that he was gone.

Alexandra sank back down onto the bed, knowing full well that she'd somehow managed to wound his pride again. Could the day possibly get any worse?

Following his disastrous attempt at a conversation with Alexandra, Michael headed for the parlor to seek comfort in a very full glass of brandy. He found Ryan there, his legs thrown casually up on the table while he leaned back in his chair, book in hand.

"What are you reading this time?" Michael asked, though not particularly interested.

"Some nonsense by Molière," Ryan muttered, snapping the book shut and placing it in his lap. "Funny nonsense, I have to admit, but nonsense all the same."

"I take it you do not like him much?"

"He's French," Ryan mused. "I'm not supposed to like him."

Michael hid a tentative smile with subtle ease while he took a sip from his glass.

"Any luck taming the shrew?" Ryan suddenly asked with a clear nod in the direction of Alexandra's closed door.

Michael sputtered a bit at that. Clearing his throat, he brushed the drops of spilt brandy from his breeches. "Not really, no," he admitted.

Ryan nodded sympathetically. "May I offer a bit of advice?"

"By all means," Michael told him as he straightened himself in his chair and set his glass on the table.

"Make an effort to show a genuine interest in her. Court her."

"I beg your pardon."

"May I speak plainly?"

"I thought you were speaking *quite* plainly," Michael muttered.

Ryan gave him an assessing glance. "Let me put it like this then shall I? So far, you've argued with her at every available opportunity. And when you weren't doing so, you were lusting after her like a dog in heat."

Michael merely arched an eyebrow in response. He could not deny the claim without an obvious lie.

"Clearly, you like her, for if you didn't, you wouldn't have been so determined to make her your bride. But, rather than court her with flowers and bouts of conversation like any other decent gentleman might have done, you rushed in and trapped her.

"It was neatly done, I have to give you that, but you certainly haven't dealt yourself an easy hand. You'll have to work at winning her forgiveness now, and I daresay the way to do it is by courting her."

"But she's a hoyden!" Michael exclaimed before he could help himself. "A desirable one, but one nonetheless. You really think she'd be swayed by flowers and poetry?"

"Look past it, Michael," Ryan urged him. "She's a woman, a unique woman, whom, I don't believe, has ever received much flattering attention from any young gentleman before."

"She's never received a gentleman caller?" Realization struck Michael. He could scarcely believe that a woman of her beauty and with her figure would not have caught the eye of somebody by now.

"She's never had a season in London." There was something distressing about the way he said it that instantly sparked Michael's curiosity. "We haven't had any social gatherings at Moorland in the last few years, not since . . ." Was that pain in his eyes? Michael wasn't sure, but whatever it was, he quickly recovered. "Papa has been very . . . withdrawn for a number of years and . . . well, the last thing on his mind, I suspect, was to turn a boisterous chit of a daughter into a lady refined enough for the London ballrooms."

Michael couldn't help but frown. How could Lord Moorland have allowed his responsibilities toward his daughter to slip in such a way? It seemed unforgivable.

"I know it sounds harsh," Ryan continued. "But it is what it is. Sometimes circumstance steps in the way and trips one up, causing one to fall so hard it's almost impossible to get back up again."

What the devil is he going on about, Michael wondered. He didn't say anything though, sensing that Ryan might have more to say.

Ryan paused for a moment to take a sip of claret. He looked at Michael and there was something very emotional behind those bright blue eyes of his—something protective, if Michael wasn't entirely mistaken. He knew that Ryan loved his sister tremendously—he'd told him so in fact—so it was only natural that he should concern himself with her welfare. "The point is that if you care for Alexandra," Ryan was now saying. "And if you want her to be happy, then you ought to make the effort to sweep her off her feet. She deserves at least that much, don't you agree?"

"Do you know, Ryan—I never would have taken you for a romantic, though I haven't the faintest idea why. But you *are* a romantic, and I do believe you've just given me the soundest advice I have ever received. Shall we drink to my success?"

Ryan grinned and held his glass forward to clink against Michael's. "We shall indeed."

It was well past midnight when Alexandra finally decided to get out of bed. She couldn't sleep and had finally had enough of the endless tossing and turning. Taking her wrapper from the hook behind the door, she tied it firmly about herself before stepping quietly out into the hallway.

She found the kitchen easily enough and, pushing the door open with a soft squeak, she advanced, her eyes seeking out any furniture that might pose as an obstacle. The bare floor was cold and smooth against her naked feet, forcing her to inadvertently curl her toes. Perhaps she should have worn slippers? Well, she wasn't going back for them now.

Lifting the lid of a large chest that stood against the wall, she opened what she presumed to be the icebox. It was. The light was too dim for her to make out the contents, so she reached inside, fumbling around between stored meats, butter, and cheeses, until she found the bottle of milk she'd been seeking.

Now, if she could only find a mug.

She opened one cupboard containing dishes—all neatly stacked, side by side. In the next there were pots and pans and what appeared to be a kettle. Closing the door, Alexandra glanced about, drumming her fingers thoughtfully upon the countertop. There! Against the opposite wall she spotted the vitrine—the glass doors casting off a warped reflection in the darkness. *I should have brought a candle*, she thought as she opened its doors and reached inside for the desired mug.

Her wrist brushed against something that quietly shifted before giving way. A soft clang of glass hitting glass followed, just as a cold sweat swept through her. She pulled her hand back to catch the tumbling glass, but it was too late—her hand clutched at empty air instead. And then the silence splintered as the glass shattered upon the floor.

Damn!

Alexandra took a deep breath and carefully pushed the vitrine doors shut. She knew the worst of the shards would be scattered at her feet, so if she could just take a big step over them.

The kitchen door swung open, light flooded the room and Alexandra jumped.

"Ow!" A sharp pain tore through the sole of her right foot. She lifted it reflexively and in so doing put all her weight on her left. "Ow!" she cried again as a piece of glass sliced through that one as well.

Before she could stop herself, she was jumping from foot to foot in an impossible attempt to escape the fragments embedded in her feet.

"For the love of God, stop moving!" Michael implored. "You're making it worse."

She sent him a scowl that would have sent the hounds of hell scurrying. "Easy for you to say," she hissed. "You're not the one with bloodied feet. Besides, I wouldn't have jumped if it hadn't been for you startling me."

Setting his lantern on the table, Michael moved to Alexandra, picked her up and carried her across to one of two chairs. He pulled it out from under the table and dropped her into it. Without a word, he fetched the remaining chair, brought it round to her side of the table and placed it before her. She watched, stupefied as he eyed the bowl of fruit on the table, then picked the thing up, emptied out the fruit and marched across to the sink where he filled it with water instead. He then grabbed the two white linen towels that hung next to the sink and returned to take his place in the empty chair.

"Put your feet up," he said, clapping his hand against his thigh.

Alexandra stared at him. "Surely you must be joking."

"I hardly think so. Come now, Alex, put your feet up so I can have a look at the damage."

"I couldn't possibly," she cried. "Look at them, they're bleeding all over the place. I shall damage your clothes."

He gave her a stern look of authority similar to that of a father dealing with an unwilling child. "You are being more than just a little bit silly about this, do you know that? Now stop arguing and put your damn feet up."

With a heavy sigh of resignation Alexandra lifted her legs and placed her feet in Michael's lap.

"Good God," he exclaimed. "There *is* blood everywhere!"

Alexandra rolled her eyes and moved to remove her feet, but he held on to her ankles. "Don't move," he told her. "For the love of Christ just sit still will you?"

Soaking one of the towels, Michael wrung it and began dabbing gently at the bloodied mess. Alexandra winced as he inadvertently pushed against a piece of glass. He looked up at her, concern visible upon his face. "Sorry. I just need to clean it a bit so I can get a better look."

She gave a quick nod of consent, gritting her teeth against the pain.

"It looks as though you've got a couple of pieces lodged in

your right foot, but there's only one in your left. With a bit of care, I ought to be able to pull them out without causing you too much pain."

"Well, there's little sense in wasting time," she breathed, pasting a brave smile on her face. "Let's get on with it."

"Very well," he muttered.

With the nimblest of touches, Michael set about his work while Alexandra squeezed her eyes shut and concentrated on taking deep, regular breaths. She cursed her own stupidity for not bringing a light with her on her midnight errand. How dimwitted he must think her. She was hardly the vision of grace and sophistication that she'd been hoping to portray two days ago in her smart day dress and Spencer. He'd kissed her with greed in his eyes then, but had made no attempt to do so since. Not once.

Who can blame him?

It was true that she'd been unconscious for half the day yesterday, but still. She flinched as a sharp pain cut through her foot. They were betrothed now, which very likely meant that he'd lost all interest. Well, he'd said he liked her, but hell, people liked their friends and their pets . . . not in the least bit reassuring. Then again, what should she expect? She'd practically thrown herself at him like a harridan of the worst order. How many times had she heard her brothers talk about the "chase" being the most enticing aspect of a relationship—the challenge, so to speak. Well, she certainly hadn't posed much of a challenge for Michael, had she?

Damnation.

"That should do it," Michael told her while he gently wiped her feet. "I'll have to clean the cuts, which will most likely hurt like blazes, but it must be done I'm afraid. I'll be back in just a moment. Stay right where you are."

She grimaced as she watched him go. Somehow she'd find a way to escape marrying him. Already, her brain had become a muddled mess because of him, her heart more so. She'd already accepted liking him. What if she fell in love with him? An unthinkable outcome that she must avoid at all cost. Even now, the very thought of it sent her pulse racing as familiar fear clutched at her insides, lacing through her ribs to constrict her lungs. She gripped the seat of her chair in a desperate attempt to gain control.

"Alex?" It was Michael's voice.

Just focus on his voice, Alex. Easy does it.

Her breathing slowed.

"Are you all right?" he asked.

"I'm fine," she gasped. "It's just my feet."

He sat back down and opened the bottle of whiskey that he'd brought with him. "They're about to hurt even more I fear. Time to disinfect the wounds, Alex."

She looked across at him with wary apprehension. "Tell me about your family," she told him suddenly. "I understand that you have what, four sisters?"

"Five, actually," he replied, pouring some of the alcohol over a white towel.

"And you are number?"

"Two," he told her. "Claire's the oldest. She's married to the Duke of Heinsworth. After her there's me, naturally, followed by Chloe who's married to Viscount Harrington, Charlotte who's married to Lord Devon, and finally Caroline and Cassandra who are both yet unmarried."

Alexandra stared at him for a moment. "Your parents certainly had a liking for names beginning with the letter C. I cannot help but ask, why is your name Michael?"

Michael's eyes held hers for a moment, the alcohol doused towel suspended in his hand. "I have no idea," he told her plainly. "Though I must admit I'm quite relieved they didn't brand me with either of the names they initially had in mind, or I would have ended up a Charles or a Cyril. They named me after my paternal grandfather instead, thank God."

Alexandra snorted. Her hand flew to her mouth to cover the sound, but her eyes danced with merriment. "Cyril?" she half choked. Michael frowned at her, which only made her laughter bubble up even higher in her throat. She thought for a moment she might choke on it. "Charles isn't all that bad—but Cyril?"

She snorted with laughter again.

"I'm sorry, Michael," she grinned. "But such a name brings to mind a dandy with his nose up in the air."

"I'll get you for that." And before Alexandra could utter another word of insult, Michael pressed the towel against both feet at the same time.

"Yeaow!" she screeched, tears springing to her eyes. "I hate you, Lord Trenton," she muttered as he set about binding her feet in another linen towel that he'd torn into two equally wide strips.

"I know, my lady, but you will thank me for it tomorrow when there's no sign of infection."

Alexandra merely groaned as she pulled her feet out of his lap and placed them carefully on the floor.

"Now, if you do not mind my asking—what were you doing rummaging about in here in the dark anyway?"

"I was unable to sleep," she muttered miserably. "So I thought I'd have some milk." She glanced at the bottle that stood on the table. She couldn't remember putting it there and wasn't sure if she had, or if Michael had taken it from her and put it there himself.

"I see." He regarded her for a moment before continuing. "And were you planning to heat it?"

"What? Oh yes, of course, I was."

"Aha. And you were planning to do so in the dark?"

"I suppose so," she said cautiously.

"So let me get this straight. You were planning on operating the stove, in the dark—an appliance filled with red-hot coals and putting out an average temperature of four hundred degrees. Is that right?" Alexandra responded with a faint nod. "Are you absolutely mad? You couldn't even retrieve a mug from the vitrine without injuring yourself. Lord only knows what might have happened if you'd set about such a thing!"

"You really needn't remind me," she groaned. "I am clumsy enough as it is. I'm sure you must think me a complete imbecile."

Michael's gaze softened marginally, for which she was truly grateful, considering how embarrassed she felt, but he apparently couldn't stop himself from adding one last thing. "You truly are the most stubborn woman I have ever known, Alex, but I would never think you an imbecile. I wouldn't have the courage," he grinned. She sent him a doubtful frown. "I think instead your passionate nature has a tendency to war against your logical reasoning. It forces you to forge ahead despite your better judgment, though your intentions are always noble. On top of that, you won't allow the dictates of society to control your life. You want something more, though you don't always consider the consequences that such wants might have."

Alexandra stared at him in amazement. She felt what he described to the very depth of her soul, but this was the first time that somebody had captured the essence of her being with mere words. Somehow Michael Ashford understood her better than anyone else ever had. It was shocking yet comforting all at once.

"Now then," he added with a chuckle that instantly lightened the mood. "How about that warm milk?"

"I've no idea how to work a stove," she admitted, not daring to meet his eyes.

"Then it is fortunate that I do," he said.

Somehow, she wasn't surprised. She was grateful that he didn't reprimand her further, and so sat quietly on her chair instead, watching him open up the vents and stoke the coals. There was something very domestic about it that warmed her heart.

He found a pot for the milk, and a few minutes later, he placed her cup before her with a smile. He moved the chair he'd been using around to the other side of the table so he could sit across from her instead. "Try it," he suggested, nodding toward her cup.

She took a small sip, savoring the warmth of the liquid as it flowed down her throat, heating her insides. "Perfect," she murmured.

"So tell me about *your* family," Michael prodded, wiping his mouth with the back of his hand.

"Well, there's not that much to tell really. I don't have a very large family, and when Mama passed away nine years ago, it seemed to shrink significantly." Alexandra stared at the table for a moment, caught up in her own thoughts. "She was awfully good at keeping in touch with everyone, but then she got so terribly sick, and when she finally died . . . well, Papa just didn't have the energy to host the kind of soirees and house parties she'd been so renowned for."

"How did she die?" he asked in a quiet voice.

Alexandra grimaced. "From the usual ailment that targets even the healthiest of us."

"Consumption?"

She nodded and lifted her gaze to meet his.

"I'm so sorry, Alex," he told her in an earnest voice.

She shrugged, suddenly overcome by emotion but trying desperately not to show it. "It was a long time ago," she whispered.

"It must have been very difficult for you. You can't have been more than what . . . twelve?"

"Thirteen, actually." She rapped her fingers nervously on the tabletop. This was ridiculous. It had been so long and yet she felt those awful tears pricking at her eyes again.

"A difficult age for a girl to lose her mother," he told her sympathetically.

She nodded slowly before taking another sip of her milk. As she put the mug down, she brushed the back of her hand against the corner of her eye, wiping away the wet spot that had been forming there. "However difficult it was for my brothers and me, I believe it was so much worse for Papa." Her voice quivered, and she tried to smile, fighting for control. "Children eventually leave the nest in search of their own destinies, but Papa had already found his. He lost it the day she died.

"She was the love of his life, his best friend, his future. She was his shoulder to lean on, the mother of his children, the very epicenter of what he considered to be his family. It broke his heart. The whole ordeal tore us apart . . . he locked himself away in his study, avoiding the world and drowning himself in lament. It took time for him to heal—such a terribly long time."

"At least you had your brothers."

Alexandra forced a smile. "Ryan was fifteen and William was seventeen—they both attended Eton and weren't home much during that time." She looked across at Michael whose vision seemed to have clouded as if he were trying to picture what it must have been like. She appreciated his efforts, even though he couldn't possibly understand.

"He eventually recovered though—Papa that is. One day he simply emerged from hiding. He took one look at me and then pulled me into his arms. He kept berating himself for letting me down, for deserting me when I needed him most.

"We spoke for hours that day, but not about my mother. To this day he refuses to talk about her. I think he's afraid he might cry. He doesn't want anybody to see that."

Michael watched as Alexandra stared off into a distant past he couldn't see. The sense of loss was etched upon her face. There was pain there, but there was something else as well—something much more powerful.

Fear.

"What are you so afraid of, Alex?" he asked her in a soft whisper.

"What?" she darted a panic stricken look in his direction.

"Perhaps I can help. If there's something you'd like to talk about—"

"No! It's nothing." The force of her tone startled him. He suspected he must have touched a raw nerve. Whatever the case, it clearly wasn't something that she wished to discuss, at least not with him, at this moment. Not over a warm cup of milk anyway.

"I'm going to bed," she told him as she staggered to her feet in a most inelegant fashion, wincing as she did so.

"My apologies. I . . . Alex, let me help you." Getting up, he was beside her in a second. He lifted her into his arms, took the lantern and carried her back to her room. "I'm surprised we didn't wake Mr. and Mrs. Bell with our ruckus. You especially—you're not very dainty you know."

She grinned at that, much to his relief. He'd enjoyed their conversation and was sorry to have ruined it for her, though he still wasn't quite sure how he'd managed it. "They must be sound sleepers I suppose."

"A valuable piece of information, should we ever decide to raid the larder." Again she smiled, though she didn't respond. "Here we are then, my lady, right to your doorstep."

"Thank you," she said softly, biting ever so gently down on her bottom lip. "I'm sorry I got upset before, it's just . . . I can't talk about it . . . sorry."

"No worries," he told her. "I won't press you. Sleep well, Alex. I'll see you in the morning."

Kissing her gently on the forehead, he moved away in the direction of his own room. He cast a quick backward glance just in time to see her door close. With a heavy sigh and a great deal to think about, he then made his way to bed.

CHAPTER FIFTEEN

The next week flew by in a haze with each day swallowing up the next. Michael had insisted that Alexandra stay in bed and allow her feet to heal, promising to visit her daily to help her pass the time. Alexandra naturally found it ridiculous to remain abed for an entire week. Her injuries really didn't warrant such fussiness, but she was pleased to find that Michael kept his promise, so she decided to humor him.

Each morning, Michael would arrive at her bedroom door with a fresh bouquet of flowers for her. These varied, though they generally consisted of yellow tulips—which, Alexandra soon discovered, happened to be Michael's favorite.

Shortly after Michael's arrival, Mrs. Bell would bring in a tray with tea and biscuits for them to share and would then depart, leaving the door slightly ajar for propriety's sake. Ryan had been very firm about following this convention.

They talked of everything between heaven and earth during those days, discovering which artists and musicians they each preferred, which books were their favorites, and which places they each dreamed of one day traveling to. Alexandra had made a few sketches on a couple of occasions and when Michael had hesitantly asked if he might have one of the drawings, she'd happily obliged him after scribbling her name in the bottom right hand corner.

Six days after cutting her feet, Alexandra sat propped up against a couple of pillows, leafing through a book of poems by Robert Burns. She couldn't concentrate on any of the poems however—she was simply too anxious about seeing Michael to be able to focus her mind on anything else. It was already well past ten, she noted as she looked over at the clock for the hundredth time. What on earth was taking him so long? He was never this late in coming to check on her.

She was just about to call for Ryan to come and sit with her for a while when a gentle knock at the door made her stomach flutter.

Each day, her feelings toward Michael increased tenfold. Her heart pounded in her chest whenever he touched her in the slightest way. It terrified her, but it was becoming increasingly difficult for her to ignore her growing feelings toward him. The worst of it was that he clearly didn't seem to feel the same way. He never gave her more than a peck on the cheek—no doubt he probably regretted the code of honor that presented him with little choice but to marry her. But she had to give him credit for making the most of a situation that he obviously found to be quite undesirable. Not once had he complained about his predicament. Instead, he treated her like a true lady. He brought her flowers, listened to her with interest and treated her with respect. It was clear that he wanted to make her happy.

And she was happy—terrified but happy.

"Come in!" she called out. The door eased open, giving way to Michael's sturdy frame. Alexandra's eyes widened. She couldn't help it. He was just so drop-dead gorgeous that it almost sent her head spinning like a fair ground carrousel.

"Good morning," he said as he came toward her and dropped into the chair beside her bed. "Sorry I'm a bit late."

"Oh? I hadn't noticed," she told him, feigning indifference. She hoped her voice hadn't betrayed her. "In fact, I was quite busy with Burns."

"I see . . . well . . . er . . . Where is the tea?" he suddenly asked, looking about for the tray.

"I'm sure Mrs. Bell will bring it in shortly. Are you hungry?"

"Ravenous," he admitted. "I missed breakfast this morning in order to run an errand of some importance."

"Really?" her eyes narrowed as she looked at him. "Something to do with William? Did he send word by any chance?"

"No, no, it's nothing regarding him. We'll see him soon enough." Alexandra stared at him in bewilderment. "Bonaparte's ball . . . remember?"

"Good grief!" Alexandra exclaimed, slamming her book shut and throwing back her covers. "I'd completely forgotten. I have to decide what to wear, how to do my hair, I—"

"Easy does it," Michael cautioned her as he put a restraining hand on her arm and eased her back down onto the bed. "There'll be plenty of time for that later."

The door opened again and Mrs. Bell trundled in with a tray piled high with a teapot, cups, sandwiches, and freshly baked cookies. "How are you doing, Dearie?" she asked, setting the tray on the nightstand. "Ready to dance the night away this evening?"

"Apparently, everyone seems to have remembered the ball except for me," Alexandra moaned.

"Just goes to show what a hoyden you really are," Michael grinned, dodging the punch that Alexandra aimed at his shoulder.

"Now, now," Mrs. Bell scolded in a lighthearted voice. "There'll be none of that. His lordship has been very kind to you of late, so you'd best be on your best behavior if you don't want a scolding, my lady."

Alexandra rolled her eyes while Michael chuckled. She was well aware that he'd been giving Mrs. Bell flowers too in the course of the past week and could see that he was clearly more than just a little delighted to see his efforts pay off.

"And don't you worry about what to wear either. I'll be here to assist you this evening." A dreamy look filled the older woman's eyes. "You'll be the belle of the ball, I assure you." With a lazy sigh followed by a girlish giggle, she then hurried from the room.

"Well, she certainly likes you," Alexandra remarked as she leaned over to pour the tea.

"And what reason would she have *not* to? I can be quite charming when I put my mind to it, you know." He waggled his eyebrows mischievously.

Alexandra ignored this last comment and offered him a sandwich that he greedily accepted. He took a bite and a combination of relief and immense satisfaction flooded his face.

What is it about men and food?

"So, tell me about your sisters," she said. "How old are they?"

"Well, Claire's two years older than me, so that would make her thirty-two. Chloe's twenty-seven, Charlotte's twenty-three, and the twins—Caroline and Cass—are eighteen." He picked up another sandwich and wasted no time in sinking his teeth into it.

"So then they must be just about ready to enjoy a busy season—the twins I mean."

"They were certainly looking forward to it when I left London. In fact, I must admit I was quite relieved to be given this assignment." He sent her a wayward smile. "It gave me the excuse I needed to escape."

"Escape?" She looked confused. "Surely it can't be that bad."

"You've no idea," he shuddered. "I remember Charlotte's coming-out ball as if it were only yesterday. Before the season had even begun, the house was overrun by dressmakers, cobblers, and milliners. The parlor was transformed into a fitting room. It was impossible to find the furniture for all the fabric that was forever lying about. And then, once the season *did* begin, the house was suddenly infested by hoards of eager young men vying for Charlotte's hand in marriage. Not a surface remained without a bouquet of flowers upon it—a myriad of scents all clamoring for attention."

"It doesn't sound like much fun at all," Alexandra said. "Thankfully, it's not something I had to endure. Besides, it never really caught my interest—all the fuss and being put on constant display. My aunt was very pushy about the whole idea for a while, but that was years ago. Still, I suppose if you truly are in the market for a wife or a husband, then there's not much choice but to endure the whole menagerie."

"Most young ladies enjoy it tremendously, Alex. You're quite the exception, trust me. The trouble is when it comes to Cass and Caroline . . . well, they're very different from each other, even though they're twins. They're not identical, even their personalities are at opposite poles." It looked to Alexandra as if Michael was mulling something over in his head. He suddenly looked at her with great intensity. "I know Caroline will have no trouble—she's so refined and delicate. I worry about Cass though."

"Why? Is there something wrong with her?" Alexandra blurted out before she could stop herself. Her hand came up to cover her mouth just as her eyes grew big with shock at her own words. "I beg your pardon, I didn't mean to be so rude."

Michael grinned and shook his head. "There's nothing wrong with her as such, Alex, but the girl can't even go for a walk in the park without getting grass stains on her dress or mud on her slippers. Her hairpins are forever falling out. She's a terrible mess and no matter how hard we all try, we just don't seem to be able to do anything about it."

Alexandra bit back a smile. "And you're worried she'll not attract as many gentlemen as Caroline, and that she'll be crushed. Is that it?"

"In a nutshell." He nodded with obvious relief. He'd known she'd understand. After all, she and Cassandra were quite similar in some ways.

"I don't think you ought to overly concern yourself. I have a feeling your sister Cass has spirit, and if I'm not terribly wrong, then any man worth having is more interested in a spirited wife than a demure one." She lifted her big blue eyes to stare directly at him from behind her thick, dark lashes. "Isn't that correct, Michael?"

There was so much meaning in that one question that Michael felt sure he could write a whole book on it. Was she really asking him point blank if, given the choice, he would pick her over a more dispassionate woman? Well of course he would. In fact, he already *had*, but she didn't know that yet. She thought he was marrying her for the sake of honor. "Yes," he heard himself say. "Yes, you are absolutely right."

She sank back against her pillows with a small sigh of what he assumed to be relief. "I'm glad to hear it," she muttered. "In fact, I'm quite certain Cass will find a husband who will make her very happy."

"You're probably right," Michael agreed as he cleared his throat. The tension eased a bit and he suddenly remembered why he'd been later today than all the other days. Reaching inside his jacket pocket, he pulled out a small velvet box.

"I almost forgot. This is for you." He placed the box in Alexandra's hand. She stared down at it for a long moment as if unsure of what to do with it.

"Go ahead," Michael urged her. "Open it."

"Oh, Michael," she whispered after flipping back the lid. "They're beautiful. Oh, it's too much. You really didn't have to."

"No? Very well then." He shrugged as he reached for the box. "I'll just have to return it then."

"Absolutely not, you fiend!" She grinned, snatching the box away from him and keeping it out of his reach. Once again she looked inside at the filigree pendant and matching earrings, each with a bold sapphire in its center.

"I thought you might like to wear them this evening," he told her. "They'll bring out the color of your eyes." Michael barely refrained from rolling his eyes—at himself. When had he ever churned out such romantic drivel before? She'd turned him from a carefree womanizer into a lovesick puppy in no time at all.

"Thank you," she said on a whisper of breath. "I'll cherish them forever."

And then she reached for him, her hand curling about his neck and pulling him ever so gently toward her.

Michael felt his heart stop. Or was it beating so fast that he could no longer feel it? He wasn't sure. Either way, he was quite certain that he was about to expire from anticipation. She was about to kiss him and as far as he could tell, she wasn't aiming for his cheek. No, this would be a proper kiss—the first of its kind since they'd been caught by Ryan. He sucked in a breath at the very moment that her lips touched his.

It was as if an explosion of energy burst through him at that very point of contact.

Alexandra began to pull away, but Michael wasn't about to end their intimate encounter, this gift that she'd bestowed upon him, so swiftly. With lightening speed his arms were about her, pressing her against him as he crushed her lips with his own.

She stiffened, no doubt uncertain, but desire must have finally won her over. At any rate, she clung to him with an almost desperate hunger, as if she planned to gobble him up alive. It thrilled him to no end, filling him with a feverish need of his own. He brushed her lips with the tip of his tongue, begging for entry, and was quickly rewarded with her surrender.

"God, Alex," he murmured against her mouth.

He knew he was hard for her. Hell, he could feel himself straining against the seam of his breeches. If only they could . . . no, he mustn't think of it. But it was of the utmost importance that they return to England as soon as possible so that they could get married and end this madness once and for all. How he hoped to survive that long, God only knew, but she was a lady after all—not some hussy he could simply take for a tumble. *Christ!* He had to stop himself from thinking along those lines.

Releasing her swollen lips, he set his mouth against her neck, licking ever so gently while she shuddered and moaned in response. He pulled back to look at her. Oh, there was no doubt about what she wanted. Her eyes were glazed over, her skin pink from blushing and her nipples were impossible to ignore as they puckered beneath her nightgown.

He pulled her against him in a tight embrace, his hands steadying her as he leaned into her. "I want you, Alex. Oh God, if you only knew how much I want you." She whimpered slightly at the sound of his words. "My blood's on fire . . . I can't . . . I can't think of anything else. Please tell me you feel the same way."

Her breath came raggedly as if it was almost too difficult for her to speak. "What you did before . . . the way you touched me . . . I can't get it out of my mind. I find myself wanting more. But not with just anyone, Michael. With *you* . . . only with you."

Her honesty almost undid him. He took a deep breath, inhaling her sweetness before drawing away from her. "We have to wait," he told her in an even tone that spoke of monumental restraint on his part. "This is not the proper time or place for this, and I've already insulted your brother once. I can't do it again. But once we're back in England and married, you have my word that I'll indulge you as often as you please."

She nodded, her disappointment evident upon her face, and he'd never felt more frustrated in his life. There was some measure of consolation to be had however. She still wanted him. That much had just been made abundantly clear. She might not care about him the way he cared about her, but she wanted him. At least that was something.

CHAPTER SIXTEEN

That evening, Michael and Ryan waited in the parlor for Alexandra to appear. "I don't understand why it's taking so long," Michael muttered. "You and I have to share Mr. Bell between us, yet we managed to be ready half an hour ago."

Ryan grinned. "You of all people ought to know how long it takes a woman to ready herself for a ball with as many sisters as you have."

"Of course, I do. But that doesn't mean I understand it." He threw back his glass of brandy, savoring the bite of it as it swirled around his mouth.

The sound of a door opening and closing brought both men to attention. They stared at the parlor door, holding their breaths while it slowly opened. Mrs. Bell appeared. "Gentlemen," she announced with a gleaming smile on her face and a twinkle in her eyes. "May I present, Lady Alexandra Summersby."

Stepping aside, Mrs. Bell made way for Alexandra.

Michael gasped. She was dressed in the most splendid ball gown that he had ever seen. It was a frost blue creation made of the finest mull. Silver tinsel embroidery dotted the fine fabric—a wide border of the glittering needlework adorning the hem in depiction of wispy, springtime bouquets above a wavy border of flowers.

The sleeves were short puffs set just below the shoulders, the high waist emphasized by a long twisted chord, tied in a knot at the front. But what had Michael struggling for air, was the shocking, plunging neckline that set Alexandra's cleavage on very prominent display.

"You're not married yet, Ashford." Ryan snapped. "I hope you'll try to remember that."

"You drive a hard bargain, Summersby," he drawled, taking a step in Alexandra's direction. "My dear, you look lovely. Absolutely lovely."

"Does she have a cloak?" Ryan almost yelled, his voice rising to an alarmingly high pitch. "A cloak if you will, Mrs. Bell."

"Ryan . . . honestly, you're too fussy." Alexandra rolled her eyes at her brother's efforts to protect her modesty.

"Not fussy enough or you wouldn't have dared to don such a gown in the first place."

"It's French, you know," she teased.

"Even more reason not to like it," Ryan muttered. "Mrs. Bell?"

Alexandra giggled with amusement as Mrs. Bell stormed in with a black velvet cloak hanging over her arm. "You can't keep me covered up all night, you know," Alexandra said as she pulled the cloak across her shoulders. Ryan groaned. Apparently he knew all too well that he might as well concede her point.

"Not to worry, old boy," Michael told him with a slap on the back. "I'll keep a watchful eye on her, as will you. Together I am sure we'll manage to chase away the hounds."

"It won't stop them from looking," Ryan grumbled.

"That's enough, you two," Alexandra exclaimed, slapping her fan furiously against her cloak as she all but stomped her feet in protest. "Yes, my gown is more risqué than any I have ever seen in England. However, I do believe that I am brave enough to wear it." She said, taking a deep breath to calm herself.

"Now then, as I've never been to a ball before, I'm fully set on enjoying this one. *You* won't ruin it for me by acting like a couple of stuffy old matrons." She pointed a gloved finger at both men. "Do I make myself perfectly clear?"

"Absolutely," Michael muttered.

It was overlapped by Ryan's, "Of course."

"Good." She sent them a dazzling smile that instantly brought out the gentleman in each of them. "Then you may escort me to the carriage."

The throng of carriages lined up along rue de Rivoli and spilling into the palace courtyard kept the three companions waiting for close to an hour before they finally managed to alight and make their way inside. A footman took Alexandra's cloak just as Michael and Ryan both offered her their arms. With a girlish giggle she accepted, stepping between them and allowing each of them to guide her up the stairs.

Soft notes of music already filled the salon de la Paix—the long gallery that stretched toward the hall des Maréchaux where the ball was being held. Already the hum of voices warned them of the crush that awaited them inside. A few couples stood by the tall open windows that flanked the hall, enjoying a short reprieve from the heat in the ballroom or simply eager for a little privacy.

As they stepped beyond the gilded doors, Alexandra found herself swept inside a dreamlike fantasy of sparkling opulence and riches beyond her wildest imagination. This was a far cry from any of the English estates she'd visited over the years—they seemed so utterly dull and dismal by comparison.

Five crystal chandeliers of extraordinary size weighed heavily on chains that looked too thin to bear them. The vaulted ceiling, painted with blue skies and drifting clouds stretched to infinity between four ornately sculpted ribs. The room paid homage to the heroes of war, its walls filled with paintings of Bonaparte's marshals and a parade of busts depicting his generals. At the far end, looming above the crowd, stood four imposing figures—replicas of Goujon's *Caryatides*.

Jewel bedecked women shimmered in the lamplight, their gowns overflowing with silk, lace and enough beads and ribbons to open a whole chain of haberdasheries. Alexandra squinted, allowing for her eyesight to adjust. "I've never seen anything more spectacular or more"—she paused while she searched her mind for the right word—"opulent."

"Few people have," Michael remarked. "I fear no other ball will ever live up to this."

"Let's move away from the door," Ryan suggested. "We're very rudely obstructing the entrance."

They strolled toward the refreshment table, all the while

scanning the room for any sign of William and not at all oblivious to the eyes of uniformed men that followed in their wake. "You're causing quite a stir, my dear," Michael whispered in Alexandra's ear. Heat scorched her face at his words. She could not think when he was so close to her.

"*Madame. Messieurs.*" A tall gentleman with dark, sprouting hair and a pleasant smile stepped in front of them. He was resplendent in his navy blue coat tails, embroidered in gold thread and sequins and decorated with proof of his valor. His breeches were a dazzling white, and his boots of polished black leather that shone. About his waist he wore a wide sash of gold, while a crimson one slashed its way across his frame, tying at his side.

"Allow me to introduce myself," he said. "I am Comte Bertrand, His Imperial Majesty's Grand Marshal."

Alexandra's fingers clenched around Michael's arm as her eyes held the count's.

Stay calm, just stay calm, she intoned to herself, ignoring the dread that swamped her.

This man was among three of Bonaparte's most entrusted soldiers. He was not only in charge of the entire imperial household but he was also the very one entrusted with procuring any woman that happened to strike the emperor's fancy.

"It's a pleasure to make your acquaintance, *Monsieur*," Ryan told the man with a hearty smile. "My name is Renard Gravois. This is my sister Sandrine and her husband, Michel Laurant."

"*Enchanté,*" The count reached for Alexandra's hand and pulled it toward him, placing a soft kiss upon her gloved knuckles. "Might I have the pleasure of this dance?" he asked.

There was nothing that Alexandra wanted more at that very moment than to decline, but how could she without offending the man? Besides, perhaps the answers to all their questions had happily materialized in the form of a smartly dressed dance partner. Surely, he would know what had become of Mr. Finch—if Bonaparte had indeed had a hand in his disappearance. She might also be able to gather further information regarding her brother, but she would have to tread lightly as far as he was concerned. She wanted to help him, not push him in front of Napoleon's firing squad.

"Indeed, nothing would delight me more."

With a stiff smile, Michael reluctantly handed her over to her fate. "Can she even dance?" he asked Ryan when they were well out of earshot.

"I damn well hope so," he muttered, craning his neck as if trying to pick his sister out from among all the dancers. "Oh bloody hell. I should have known."

"Known what?" Michael asked, looking to see what had put Ryan in a sudden sweat.

"I dare say it's the bloody waltz!"

Michael groaned. Of course it was. Well, he wasn't about to stand around watching Alexandra in a much too close embrace with a Frenchman while she swirled about the dance floor. Muttering an oath, he continued on toward his initial destination—the refreshment table. A drink was clearly in order.

"So tell me, *Madame*, what brings a woman of such extraordinary beauty to Paris? You cannot live here, or I would have noticed you already and, I must declare, I have never set eyes on you before this very evening." His words were soft against her forehead, yet Alexandra couldn't help but feel like he was prodding her.

Oftentimes the best lies were the ones resembling the truth as closely as possible. They were the ones that she could make herself believe enough for her to act her part convincingly. She saw no other choice but to dive in. "I see I have presented you with quite a mystery, my lord."

"And, will you willingly enlighten me, or shall I have to squeeze it out of you?" He pressed her closer until she felt his jaw graze against her cheek. She stifled a shudder.

"*Monsieur*, may I remind you that I'm a married woman. I do not dally." Thank God for Ryan's sense in telling this man that she belonged to Michael.

The count laughed. "*Madame*, you are as prudish as the English. We Frenchmen never allow a husband or a wife to deter us from the greater pleasures in life. Indeed, *Madame*, husbands exist in order to provide for their wives, while wives exist in order to dote upon their husbands. It's a symbiotic relationship. But, when it comes to passion, decadence, and unadulterated sex—the kind that makes you writhe between the sheets . . . then, *Madame*, it's not a husband you need, but a lover."

Alexandra could feel her stomach roil. Never before had she thought herself more close to being violently ill. Had it been Michael who had spoken such filth, it might have stirred her, but to find herself so shamelessly affronted. Few things agitated her, but this . . . this was beyond all sense of decorum.

"Might I offer my services?" the count whispered as his wet tongue swiped against her earlobe.

Yuk!

This was by far, more than she was willing to endure. And yet, she had to remember her primary goal in attending this evening.

Pulling back slightly, she gazed up at the man who'd just declared her to be nothing but a slab of meat. She batted her eyelids to the best of her ability and prayed to God that she would not vomit. "To answer your first question, I am here this evening as a guest of *Monsieur le Docteur*. He's my brother, *Monsieur*."

The count raised an eyebrow, surprise clearly evident upon his face, but then he narrowed his eyes and looked at her more closely as if he hoped to read her like an open book. "I've enjoyed several interesting conversations with him, I must admit." He swept her in a wide circle and tightened his hold on her hand. "His Imperial Majesty is quite taken with him, you know, but then, he admires all men who've studied at the Sorbonne. He's a great advocate of higher learning, you see."

Alexandra spotted the trap immediately. She didn't know why this man was deliberately trying to set her up—the only thing that mattered was that he was and that could only mean one thing. He suspected her of something or he suspected William. Fortunately, her brother had been farsighted enough to mention this detail when they'd last spoken. "I fear you must be mistaken, my lord," Alexandra smiled as they glided to a halt. She placed her hand on Bertrand's arm and allowed him to lead her off the dance floor. "I'm quite certain that he studied at Leiden."

"Ah, yes, I do believe you are correct. One must admire him for managing such a feat. After all, it can't have been easy for him to study in a foreign language." Bertrand's eyes glittered like those of a wolf preparing to spring a trap. "I don't believe *Monsieur le Docteur* speaks Dutch."

Alexandra's smile tightened. There was no longer any doubt. This man was clearly trying to prove that William wasn't who he claimed to be. It worried her to no end. Her brother's situation was clearly more precarious than she'd imagined. "My lord, the last I heard, medicine is taught in Latin—a language which my brother happens to be quite proficient in."

"Well done, *Madame*," the count exclaimed. "You do appear to have passed the test. Come, walk with me."

Alexandra let out a small sigh of relief. Her head was feeling rather dizzy from the strain of it all. She'd been ready to make a dash for it the minute the count had caught her out. Thank heavens she'd managed to remain calm.

"I do apologize for questioning you like that, but you must understand that His Imperial Majesty's safety is of the utmost importance. Having never seen you before, I was naturally concerned."

"I completely understand," she muttered as she glanced about, hoping to spot Michael, William, or Ryan . . . anyone who might save her from her current companion.

Bertrand led her out onto a small deserted balcony. The cool breeze that wafted against her was a refreshing change from the oppressive heat in the ballroom. "Might I ask *you* a question now, *Monsieur?*" She stared out over the Place de la Concorde, her back ramrod straight and her chin held high. She was about to risk everything with one simple question.

"I believe you've earned the right," Bertrand chuckled at her side as he placed his hand over the one she'd placed upon the railing in front of her.

"My brother Renard and I were recently admiring all the Emperor's achievements," she said, angling her face in his direction. "You were with him at Elba, were you not?"

Bertrand nodded, his eyes darkening with the memory of it.

"Then I admire you as well, my lord." The corner of her mouth curved upward into the most alluring smile that she could muster. "You've been so very brave."

Turning fully toward him, her hip resting against the balcony railing, Alexandra pushed her chest as far out as possible without risking permanent damage to her gown. Bertrand's gaze fell instantly to her prominent cleavage. "You must forgive me for my curiosity tends to get the better of me." She gazed up at him before running her index finger lazily down the front of his jacket.

"I was wondering if you've captured any of those horrid Englishmen who seem to have become such a menace to our beloved country, indeed to our very Emperor," she drawled. Her finger, having arrived at his waist, fell away. Bertrand stiffened, mesmerized by her forwardness. She turned back toward the view of Paris.

Bertrand cleared his throat and edged close enough to her for their shoulders to touch while they both stood looking out over the city. "May I ask why such a thing might interest you,

Madame? To be frank, you're the first woman to have asked me such a question."

"Well then," she murmured. "Suffice it to say that my reasons are of a rather personal nature."

Let him make what he will out of that.

He paused for a moment before leaning toward her. "Does the thought of holding an Englishman captive against his will . . . of torturing him . . . does it arouse you, *Madame?*"

Alexandra stood stock still. She simply didn't dare move, because if she did, she was either going to laugh hysterically or punch the man. Well, she had laid it on a bit thick, so really, who could blame him from drawing such a conclusion?

I can do this, I can do this, she told herself.

There was nothing for it. She had come this far, and she wasn't about to turn her back on that vital piece of information now. Would she risk her innocence to gain it?

Hell no.

But, she wasn't opposed to misleading this man even further if that was what was required of her.

"I cannot deny it," she told him bravely, her voice hushed as if the confession shamed her—which of course it did.

Eugh.

She felt as if she was being slobbered by a wet poodle.

"Then perhaps . . ." he lifted his finger to trace a steady line between her breasts.

The nerve!

" . . . I ought to tell you that we do happen to have an Englishman imprisoned—within these very walls in fact."

Alexandra gasped ever so slightly, but loud enough for

him to hear her, and interpret it as a sign of her growing excitement. Before she had a chance to gather her wits about her, he'd placed his hand against her bottom.

This had better be worth it!

She gritted her teeth, ready to do battle. "Tell me more," she whispered in a saucy voice that would have horrified anyone with a single ounce of respectability.

"He's a spy. A vicious, vicious little man, whose very life has proved to be a threat to ours."

He ran his tongue against her neck.

She almost jumped out of her skin at the sliminess of it . . . rather like being assaulted by a snake, though that might be considered an insult to the poor snake. "Will you torture him, my lord?" she murmured, hoping that he didn't hear the sting in her voice.

"Yes, but not here. The Emperor's a reputable man, *Madame*. He'll want him moved to La Conciergerie first." He reached his arm around her waist and finally settled his hand upon her breast.

Oh no. No no no . . . I cannot . . . please do not.

He squeezed and before Alexandra could help herself, she leaned over the railing to cast up her accounts upon the ground below.

"*Madame Laurant! Qu'est-ce qui se passe?* Are you all right?"

"*Oui, oui . . . ce n'est rien.* I must have eaten something that didn't quite agree with me. Forgive me, my lord." She intentionally turned her head toward him as she spoke that last sentence, hoping that the pungent smell of her breath might be enough of a deterrent.

"*Madame*, there's absolutely nothing to forgive," he said, stepping away from her. "May I escort you back to your husband? He must be terribly worried about you."

Alexandra hid her grin well as Bertrand hauled her back inside the ballroom and dragged her along behind him, pushing his way through the crowd with a hint of desperation in his stride. She knew she'd just been dropped like a hot potato and she didn't mind it one little bit.

"*Monsieur Laurant! Monsieur Gravois!*" Bertrand called out as soon as he spotted the two men about to save him. "*Madame* has taken ill. Terribly sorry, *Messieurs*, she claims it's something she ate."

Michael and Ryan were at her side in an instant, both questioning her to no end about her health, or sudden lack of it as they politely relieved the count of his duties and sent him on his merry way.

"Would you like some lemonade to ease your stomach?" Michael asked her, his face filled with concern. "Or perhaps some tea?"

"What happened?" Ryan asked.

Alexandra waved her hands impatiently at both of them. "Where's William? Have you seen him?"

"He's standing right over there." Ryan pointed toward a group of men who seemed to be deep in conversation with one another. "We were on our way over there to greet him when you arrived."

Alexandra pierced Ryan with a meaningful look. "Come with me," she whispered, latching onto Ryan's arm and pulling him along with her. She never once looked at Michael, confident that he would follow.

When they reached the salon de Paix, Alexandra glanced warily about. The gallery was still sparsely filled with people. Slowing her pace, she lowered her voice to a barely audible whisper. She felt Michael step up beside her, no doubt in order to hear what she was saying.

"William's in danger," she told them, her face betraying nothing of what she felt. "Bertrand was trying every which way to make me trip up once he discovered that we were acquainted with each other. He's suspicious. He has no idea that William's English." She paused for a moment as she considered this piece of vital information. "This can only mean one thing—he's *not* collaborating with them."

She darted a look in Michael's direction to gauge his reaction, but his expression was inscrutable. "If he were," she continued, "it would be impossible for him to conceal his identity while providing them with information only the British would be able to know about."

Passing a group of people who were on their way toward the ballroom, they nodded politely and exchanged a few pleasantries before moving on. "There's something else afoot here, but it makes little sense to me," she murmured. "I believe William is working on discovering something terribly important." She lowered her voice even further. "Mr. Finch is being held prisoner somewhere in this building, so clearly his position has been compromised. What I cannot explain, is the letter he sent to Percy."

They fell silent again as they passed yet another group of people.

"It's possible that even Mr. Finch was not privy to your brother's ideas," Michael muttered. "Perhaps your brother thought it best not to allow anyone into his confidence. Such actions would very likely have made Mr. Finch suspicious—especially if they're as good friends as I've been led to believe that they are."

"You may have a point," Alexandra acknowledged with a great deal of thoughtfulness. "But whatever the case, he can't remain here. They intend to remove him to La Conciergerie. Once that is done, it will be much more difficult for us to gain access."

Michael and Ryan both groaned in trepidation of what she was about to suggest.

"We'll have to rescue him," she said. "Tonight."

The two men froze in their tracks, their sudden stop jolting Alexandra to a halt. "I knew you were mad," Michael hissed between clenched teeth. "But I had no idea that you were suicidal."

"Come now, lads." She sent them both a bright smile. "Don't tell me that the thrill of adventure doesn't excite you. Yes, there will be some risk involved, but it would be terribly boring and hardly adventurous at all if there were not. Now, are you with me or not?"

Michael and Ryan sent each other a hesitant look. "I believe I'll have to give you a paddle for your wedding," Ryan told Michael. "This girl is in dire need of a good spanking if you ask me."

"I'll take that as a yes," Alexandra grinned, her eyes already brimming with excitement. "So, how do you suggest that we proceed?"

Both men stared at her as if she belonged in an asylum. "Er . . . Alex," Michael drawled. "This was your idea . . ."

"Yes, I know." She looked at them both expectedly, her gaze shifting from one to the other while they in turn continued to regard her in stupefied disbelief. "Oh . . . you expect *me* to have a plan?" They both nodded dumbfoundedly. "All right, I suppose I can improvise if you're not up to it."

Before either man had a chance to defend himself in the face of such an insult, Alexandra ploughed ahead, relentlessly. "Ryan, you must return to the ballroom to warn William—make it clear to him that Bertrand is sniffing about, and that he needs to watch his back. Also tell him that if he has discovered something vital, he should consider informing Sir Percy of it as soon as possible.

"Michael and I will see to Mr. Finch. We'll meet you outside and head on back to the apartment together."

Ryan grabbed his sister's arm and leaned toward her, his face so close to hers that she could smell a hint of champagne upon his breath. "I'll go with Michael while you speak to William," he said. "This is far too dangerous for you, Alex. I cannot allow it."

"Out of the question," she told him, staring firmly back at him. "Bertrand believes I'm unwell. He'll expect me to leave. If I return now and he sees me speaking with William after all the questions he's just asked me about him— No, it's too obvious."

"And what of me? I am not obvious?"

"No, Ryan. You are merely his brother, informing him that we were forced to depart earlier than we intended. You will let him know that my husband is tending to me after I fell ill and that we're awaiting you downstairs. You simply wished to make your farewells. Now, somewhere along the line, you'll have to pass on the message about Bertrand. Do you think you can manage it?"

Ryan looked about ready to salute. Alex realized she was like a general giving orders. "Yes, Alex, I believe I can." Squaring his shoulders, he turned and walked away.

"There's not a moment to lose," Alexandra said as she caught hold of Michael's arm and steered him toward the stairs.

"Do you mind telling me how you discovered all of this information," he asked, striving to keep up with her quick steps.

Alexandra shuddered as she thought of how she'd come by it all. "I told you my feminine wiles would work."

"Good God woman! I hope you didn't have to bare yourself."

"It came awfully close as a matter of fact, but it seems I simply couldn't stomach the man." She threw Michael a grim smile. "Fortunately, I'd already learned everything I needed to know by the time I vomited for all of Paris to see. Except of course for the prisoner's name."

"*What?*" Michael skidded to a halt behind Alexandra just before they reached the stairs.

"We can't go that way," she muttered, ignoring his question and now peevish attitude. "There must be a minor staircase we can use without being seen. Come along. This way."

They turned left and headed down another corridor until they reached a rather plain looking door at the end. "What do you mean you don't know the prisoner's name, Alex? How do you even know it's Mr. Finch? For that matter, how will we even *find* him in this place? He could be anywhere."

"Oh for heaven's sake, Michael, stop being so difficult.

How many English spies do you suppose Bonaparte is housing? Even if it's not Mr. Finch, should we just leave him here in the hands of the French, to torture while we live happily ever after? Hm?" She challenged him with her eyes, her hand on the doorknob while she waited for his response.

"I see your point," he admitted.

"Good. Now let me see . . ." she opened the door onto a narrow stairwell. "My lord, it seems we are in luck."

Alexandra beamed a smile in his direction that made him clutch at the wall for dear life. His legs were ready to give out beneath him. She was completely disarming as she stood there now with her big round eyes, imploring him to follow. Heaven help him—he would have followed her to hell and beyond in that instance.

"In answer to your other question, the dungeons tend to be below ground," she said. "Shall we have a look?"

Muttering an oath, Michael couldn't help but ask himself how this mad woman had managed to drag him along on this haphazard, wild goose chase, at the very core of the enemy's lair in the first place. If this was what love did to a man, one had to wonder how the human race had ever survived, because this was plain and simple lunacy.

CHAPTER SEVENTEEN

Pierre Dupont was seated on the painfully uncomfortable chair his superior had issued him. Why somebody needed to remain outside the Englishman's cell was beyond him—he was hardly about to make a run for it, and nobody would be mad enough to try and rescue him. Besides, the door was firmly locked with the key that dangled from his belt.

His duties pertaining to the prisoner were few. Occasionally, he would have to refill the man's water jug, serve him his meal, or empty his chamber pot—the latter being the least appetizing of the three by far.

Well, at least the *sous sol* of the Tuileries Palace was comfortable compared to most. The floors were marble, the ceilings high and vaulted. Grand pillars surrounded by cherubs flanked the main stairway leading down to it and the cells were not only clean but also contained proper beds with sheets upon them.

Hell. The prisoners are better off here than most of the Frenchmen I know are in their own homes.

The sound of clicking footsteps approaching at a run

caught his attention. He straightened his back and rose to his feet, his hand falling automatically to the hilt of his sword.

What the—?

Coming toward him, her hair in disarray, her eyes wide open in fear, and her bloodied hands pressing against her midsection, was a woman—the loveliest he'd ever seen.

"*Aidez moi!*" she cried, rushing toward him. He felt momentarily stunned. "You must help me, I beg you."

Pierre couldn't help but be shocked. He wasn't expecting a damsel in distress with a stab wound, no less, to be roaming about in that part of the palace. "*Madame*, what happened? Who did this to you?" he asked as he hurried to her aid.

"It was a lover's quarrel." Her voice was breathless as she clutched at his outstretched arm for support. "His wife . . . oh God . . . she saw us!"

The woman's legs buckled beneath her, but Pierre managed to catch her in an awkward hold. The poor thing needed help, but how was he to . . .

Before he managed to complete that thought, something hard came crashing down over his head, his eyes rolled backward, and everything went dark.

Alexandra landed in a heap on the floor when the guard released her. "Well done," she said, looking up at Michael. He was rubbing the fist he'd used to render the man unconscious. "I told you a bit of drama would serve to distract him."

"So you did," Michael conceded. "Do you have the key?"

With a big sigh and a shake of her head, she began fumbling about for the key, all the while muttering a string of oaths that were only occasionally interrupted by words to the effect of useless git and ungrateful oaf. Michael merely watched her in silent amusement, his arms crossed in front of him. If she would have looked up at him at that very moment, she would have seen his lips twitch.

"Here!" she finally snapped, thrusting a large iron key toward him. "See if it fits."

Michael stooped to snatch up the key and then placed it in the lock. He turned it, the lock clicked, and the door swung easily open to reveal a large spacious room beyond it. "Mr. Finch?"

A man of medium height with straw colored hair and a full beard rose from a chair. A single candle flickered on top of a worm eaten table, sending puffs of smoke toward the ceiling. The man stepped toward Michael. "Yes, I'm Andrew Finch," he said. "And who, may I ask, are you?"

"I'm Michael Ashford, Earl of Trenton, come to rescue you. "And this . . ." he gestured toward the doorway expecting to find Alexandra standing there, but there was nothing but empty space. "Alex?"

"Do you mind giving me a hand, or do you plan to stand about chatting while I do all the work?" an annoyed voice called from the hallway.

"Excuse me a moment," Michael told Andrew as he popped his head back out the door. Alexandra was bent over, pulling frantically on one of the guard's arms in an attempt to haul him along with her, but every time she stepped forward, her slippers slipped backward on the slippery marble floor. Michael tried desperately not to laugh at the sight of her walking in place, her face scrunched up in determination while the lax guard shifted only from side to side. It was like watching Sisyphus and his infamous rock played out in a cloud of lace and ribbons.

"Well, don't just stand there grinning like a bloody idiot!" she fumed. "Help me move him into the cell."

"Right," Michael complied as he donned a serious frown. He gently pushed Alexandra aside and picked up the floppy guard, carrying him into the cell and laying him carefully on the floor. He righted himself before turning once again toward Andrew. "As I was saying, this is Lady Alexandra. You really owe her a great deal of gratitude, Mr. Finch. This whole rescue mission was her idea."

"It appears I am in your debt, my lady."

"Think nothing of it," Alexandra said as she brushed his words aside with self-conscious embarrassment. "Now, put these clothes on so we can all walk out of here without raising too many alarms." She began tugging at the guard's jacket as both men bent to help her.

"Er . . . Lady Alexandra . . . are you all right? That's an awful lot of blood you have there." Andrew commented as he looked across at Alexandra with marked concern. He was in the middle of pulling off a shiny black hessian. The boot suddenly gave way, projecting Andrew backward onto his bottom.

Alexandra grinned. "Not to worry, Mr. Finch. It's only tomato soup. We found a big bowl of it near the kitchen—on its way upstairs to fill the stomachs of the French, no doubt. Have you ever seen a treacherous bowl of soup before? It warms my heart to know that those French toads will be slurping away at the very thing that helped you escape. Unfortunately, my gown had no choice but to sacrifice itself and shall have to be deemed a casualty. It's positively ruined!"

Andrew nodded as if in a daze, then turned to Michael. "Is she always like this?" he asked him curiously.

"No, not always," he chuckled while he glanced in her direction. "Sometimes she can be quite pleasant."

Alexandra apparently chose to ignore that last comment so Michael turned his attention back to the task at hand. They weren't there to banter with one another. In fact, the faster they moved, the quicker they could get the hell out of there before someone happened to notice a missing guard and he dared not even consider what might happen to them then.

"Here," Alexandra said, tossing the guard's navy blue jacket to Andrew. "I'm not sure it will be a perfect fit, but it will have to do. I'll step outside while you change."

"We're ready," Michael told her when he and Andrew emerged from the cell a moment later, locking the door behind them.

"Very well." She paused for a moment while she gave Andrew a quick once over, followed by a nod of approval. She then turned an assessing gaze on Michael. "May I have your jacket please?" she asked.

He must have followed her line of thought, for he didn't question her. Instead, he merely shrugged out of his jacket and draped it over her shoulders. She was practically drowning in the heavy garment, but they simply had to cover up the suspicious stain on her dress. Without another word, they moved silently toward the same back staircase they'd used before and climbed all the way back up again.

Reaching the floor from which they had come, Alexandra eased the door open until she had a clear view of the hall-way beyond. She could just make out the corner of the grand staircase leading from the salon de Paix to the foyer and the freedom that lay beyond it.

A couple of voices caught her attention and she stiffened. Coming toward them was none other than Bonaparte himself and his Grand Marshal, the distasteful Comte Bertrand.

She quietly held her breath and pulled the door shut. What if they decided to use this very staircase? How the hell was she going to explain their presence in it? That she was having a threesome with her husband and a soldier? Or that she'd enlisted them both to rid her dress of tomato soup? Both explanations were outrageous.

She could feel Michael breathing heavily behind her, his breath gently tickling her skin in a most annoying fashion— under the circumstances. She knew he had enough sense not to question her reasoning behind closing the door again, and silently prayed that Mr. Finch did too. Pressing her ear against the door, she strained to hear what was happening behind it. There was nothing that stood out—just muffled conversation as if Bonaparte and Bertrand had stopped right in front of their hiding place for a nice little chat.

Damn!

There was nothing to do but wait.

It was the longest five minutes of Alexandra's life. In fact, she was positively sure that her hair must have turned gray by the time she heard Bonaparte's and Bertrand's voices receding.

She eased the door open again and looked about. There was nobody around. With a sigh of relief, she quickly stepped out from behind the door and held it open for Michael and Andrew to follow. Together, they hurried along the corridor toward the top of the grandiose staircase. Taking Michael's arm and clutching his jacket against her as if she'd caught a chill, she started down the stairs. "*Chérie*," she said to Michael. "Was it not the best Champagne you ever tasted?"

"Indeed, I believe it was, my dear," Michael responded with a tilt of his head.

"And thank you, *Monsieur*, for retrieving my earring for me," she continued, briefly touching Andrew's arm in a sign of gratitude. "Heaven knows how I managed to drop the thing, but I do know that I would have been quite lost without your assistance."

"It was a pleasure, *Madame*," Andrew said as they swept past the guards and out into the cool night air.

"Oh, and the music," Alexandra exclaimed as they waited for their carriage to pull up. "It was a wonderful selection, was it not? Really, we must remember to send our thanks. Don't you agree?"

"Indeed, I do," Michael said. "It would be very rude of us not to."

Oh, he was so proud of her. She was born for this, he realized. She'd single-handedly pulled together a rescue mission at a moment's notice and without hesitation. They weren't out of the woods yet, that was true, but he had no doubt that they would be very soon. His heart tightened with pleasure at watching her carry on as if standing there in front of the Tuileries Palace with two agents from the British Foreign Office was the most natural thing in the world.

He knew she did not feel for him what he felt for her. Indeed, he very much sensed that she never would. Something about their conversation in the kitchen when she'd cut her feet had told him so—the way she'd described her mother's passing and her father's heartache. He sensed that she was terrified of feeling such grief—that she would push love away with all her might, rather than open herself up to inevitable pain.

It was heartbreaking, knowing that they would enter into marriage this way—he, hopelessly in love with her and she quite indifferent. Well, not indifferent perhaps. There was passion in her eyes when she looked at him, but she would never let her guard down and allow herself to love him, of that he was quite sure.

A carriage pulled up in front of them, just as a loud shout rang through the air, followed by another. Michael turned his head to see what all the commotion was about. He spotted Ryan and then he spotted William, both men hurrying toward them at an alarming pace. *What the devil?* A split second later, Bertrand emerged in the doorway, his arms frantically waving about. He seemed to be issuing orders of some sort, and then he heard the man holler at the top of his lungs *"Arrêtez-les!* Don't let them get away!"

Bloody hell!

He sensed Alexandra move at his side and quickly turned to warn her, only to discover that she was three steps ahead of him. How she'd managed to clamber onto the coachman's seat of the awaiting carriage and push the driver aside he couldn't imagine, but what he did notice was that her skirt was hiked up over her knees. He watched in astonishment as she elbowed the helpless coachman in the face, upon which, he quickly fled.

"Don't just stand there," she said, looking very serious and determined. "Get everyone on board!"

Michael blinked as he fell back to reality, the rattling sound of swords being unsheathed coming closer. Without another moment's hesitation he called for William and Ryan to hurry. They'd just reached the bottom of the steps when another shot rang out, shaking the air. It was Bertrand, his pistol still trained on them from no more than twenty paces away. Another shot rang out and Michael's ears were filled with an agonized yell. He turned, searching for the source and found Andrew, his mouth gaping open and his eyes widening in terror. He wobbled a little before tilting sideways and Michael realized that he must have been shot.

They'd just managed to save the man, and now this? He mustn't let him die. In one fluid motion, Michael had his arms around him, holding him upright as Ryan and William came up beside him. Behind them, his face bright red with anger, came Bertrand followed by a dozen soldiers.

"Hurry up!" Alexandra called down to them from her perch on the coachman's seat. "Stop twiddling you thumbs and get in. We haven't much time."

"Let me help you," Ryan offered, taking hold of Andrew's other arm and easing the load for Michael.

"Leave him," William snapped. "He'll only slow us down."

"What?" Michael and Ryan exclaimed at once.

"You can't be serious," Michael added, not moving as much as an inch in spite of the fact that Bertrand would be upon them shortly. "We can't just—"

He didn't have a chance to finish before William's large hands grabbed hold of Andrew's jacket and snatched him out of Michael's grasp, discarding him with a careless shove.

"Are you coming or what?" Alexandra yelled, her impatience quite audible in her voice.

"I'll explain later," William muttered as he caught Ryan by the arm and steered him closer to the carriage before shoving him inside. He then snapped his eyes back to Michael and nodded in Alexandra's general direction. "Up you go."

Michael wasn't one to miss a cue, not when his life and those of others depended on it, yet he still couldn't help but pause at the sight of Andrew who was writhing and groaning upon the ground. It was a damnable mess to be sure, but if William insisted on leaving his friend behind, he must have a good reason. With one final glance over his shoulder he leapt up onto the coachman's step just as Alexandra whipped the horses into motion, barely escaping the tip of Bertrand's sword. A loud curse filled the air behind them, forcing him to look back. Bertrand was already clambering aboard another carriage and shouting instructions. Would it really have been too much to hope for that the blasted man would just let them slip away?

"Is everyone accounted for?" Alexandra asked as he scrambled up beside her. She didn't look at him, her eyes completely trained on the two horses as she steered them along at an increasingly haphazard pace. A shot sounded from behind

them—too far away to make much difference, yet a solid reminder that they were being pursued.

"Everyone except Mr. Finch," Michael told her. He
watched as her jaw clenched and her hands tightened against
the reins, whipping them a bit more roughly to mark her irritation.

"What happened?" she asked, her voice carried a detached
coolness that Michael couldn't help but note as the mark of a
true soldier. Fact and logical reasoning. Once again, he was
more than a little impressed.

"I'm not sure." He stared forward, bracing himself as she
jerked the reins to the right at a hard angle that almost sent
the carriage careening sideways as the horses did their best
to follow, turning down a narrower street. "He got shot and
William insisted we leave him behind."

She looked at him then, her eyes narrowing as if she
thought to learn more by simply regarding his face. Her
cheeks were flushed and her hair had half come undone—
strands flying backward in the wind. And all Michael could
do was stare—she looked magnificent.

"Here," she said, thrusting a pistol into his lap. "It was
under the seat. I suggest you take a look back there and let me
know how we're doing. We can't keep riding about until the
horses give out. Somehow we have to lose them."

Nodding his understanding, Michael turned half about
and braced his hand against the hood of the cabin. It was a
precarious position to say the least—especially with the way
Alexandra was driving, but it afforded him the necessary
backward glance.

"Well?" she asked just as the carriage lurched left and turned down another street.

Michael couldn't help but wonder if he ought to start praying as he held on for dear life, fearful of toppling overboard. Straightening, he soon managed to regain his position just as the other carriage rounded the corner. "They're still after us . . . and gaining, it would seem." In fact, he was rather sure of that detail since he was now able to make out the murderous twinkle in Bertrand's eyes as he raised his pistol and . . . "Get down!"

The shot rang out with a deafening force. "Are you all right?" Michael asked.

Alexandra nodded. "I think it's about time you did something."

Under normal circumstances, he would have shot a remark right back at her, but he knew she was right. Besides, this was no time for lightheartedness and if they didn't get rid of their pursuers they'd very likely find themselves killed. Resuming his position, he noted that Bertrand was busy reloading. It wouldn't take him long, but it might just give Michael the reprieve he required. Stilling himself as much as possible against the bumpy ride, he took aim and fired. A loud yell sounded, and he watched as the other carriage lurched, the coachman gripping his arm while Bertrand shouted a string of oaths in utter rage. Michael took advantage, aimed again, and fired. "*Merde!*" Bertrand roared as something clattered away in the distance.

"What happened?" Alexandra asked, whipping the reins to increase the horses' pace.

"I believe our count has dropped his pistol. His coachman's wounded and his carriage seems to have slowed marginally."

"Just marginally?"

They rounded yet another corner to the sound of splintering glass as one of the side lanterns struck a wall and shattered. "Good God, woman! We'll be lucky if we don't lose the wheels the way you're handling this thing."

She shot him a glance that was clearly meant to admonish. "If you think you can do better, then by all means, be my guest."

"Gladly!" he replied, trying not so smile in response to the look of annoyance that wrinkled her features. Grabbing the reins, he kept up the pace while smoothing the horses' gait and, he hoped, allowing for a less bumpy ride.

"Is that you, Michael?" he heard Ryan call from somewhere inside the cabin. Or perhaps the younger Summersby was hanging out the window, he really couldn't tell.

"Yes," he shouted back.

"I knew it!" And Michael couldn't help but hear the note of appreciation in Ryan's voice—apparently, he hadn't been the only one who'd thought Alexandra was a far worse coachwoman than most. She said nothing in response, though Michael sensed that she probably rolled her eyes.

"Turn here," she suddenly said, and he did.

"Where are we going?"

"I've no idea, but we've a better chance of losing them if we don't keep to the same road indefinitely."

It made sense.

A few turns later, at Alexandra's direction, they barreled out onto rue du Louvre, barely managing to dodge another carriage which, luckily enough, managed to block Bertrand, increasing the distance between them by another five seconds. Michael maneuvered the horses to the left until they were running parallel with the River Seine.

"We'll have to jump!"

Michael recognized William's voice coming from behind him. "What did he say?" he asked Alexandra as he whipped the reins to encourage the horses. He wasn't at all sure he'd heard him correctly.

"We have to jump," she repeated. "Bertrand won't stop, and as long as we're sitting in this carriage we're nothing but a big target. He'll catch up with us eventually, of that you may be certain."

Michael gave her a sidelong glance. Her face was serious—deadly so. "Very well," he said. "We'll jump in the water, but we'll need cover. If we jump now, he'll see us."

"What do you propose?"

Something stirred inside him as she asked the question. For a moment he couldn't tell what it was, but then it dawned on him. She trusted him implicitly, and it warmed his heart and soul in a way few things ever had. "I'll make a sharp turn at the next bridge. We'll have to be quick, no doubt about it, but if we can manage, the carriage ought to shield us when we jump." He began securing the reins so the horses would keep on running once he let them slip. "Do you think you might be able to climb down to your brothers? I know it won't be—"

She was already on her way, no doubt balancing in a

highly dangerous fashion as the carriage bounced along the street. All Michael could do was hope that she didn't fall off when he made the turn.

Approaching the bridge, Michael glanced back one last time, his eyes squinting against the darkness. Bertrand's carriage was still visible, though not as clear as it would have been in the light of day, and that gave Michael hope. Now, if only he could find some means by which to distract him as well. Turning the horses onto the bridge, he angled himself, aimed his pistol at the carriage lantern that hung just left of Bertrand's shoulder, and fired—a loud crack sounded, followed by a splintering burst. And then, without a moment's hesitation or further thoughts for his own safety, Michael turned around and jumped.

CHAPTER EIGHTEEN

The water was freezing—much colder than Alexandra would have expected as she splashed about, gasping for air. She'd have to make a mental note that swimming in an evening gown was not the easiest thing in the world.

"This way," William said in an urgent whisper, pointing toward a spot where the embankment appeared to be completely shrouded in darkness.

Alexandra watched as Ryan followed. "Where's Michael?" she hissed, looking about as she began making slow, even strokes through the water. If anything had happened to him . . .

"Right here." Her heart skipped a beat at the sound of his voice coming up behind her, and she suddenly realized with shocking alarm, just how frightened she'd been for his safety. "Miss me?"

"Just making sure we all made it," she muttered, reaching the shore in another two strokes and grabbing hold of Ryan's outstretched hand. Michael was beside her in a second, his dripping wet hair falling into his eyes.

"And here I was, thinking that you might be just a little concerned for my safety," he said and sighed in a highly disappointed fashion as he placed his hand against his chest in mock pain. "I'm crushed."

"Michael, I do believe you missed your calling—the theatre," Ryan said, grinning.

"Really? I always did wonder how I might fare in the role of Romeo," Michael said, as if he was seriously contemplating such a drastic career change.

"Now *that* I'd like to see," William said, his eyes darting toward the bridge. "Do you think he fell for it?"

"Bertrand?" Michael asked, his voice returning to the severity of their present situation.

Alexandra was stunned as she tried to follow their odd conversation, unable to wonder if Michael had even as much as glanced at the pages of *Romeo and Juliet* before.

"I believe he did," Michael was saying. "Though it might be wise for us to get moving—he won't be fooled forever."

"Well, we can't go back to the apartment," Ryan said. "It's too risky."

Michael's face seemed to harden. It looked to Alexandra as though he was going over all their options in his head. "Agreed." His voice was low but assertive, and then his eyes shot toward William. "Any ideas?"

"What about the house?" William suggested.

Alexandra stared at him. *What house?* What was he talking about now?

Michael nodded, apparently quite aware of what William was referring to. "I did consider it myself. I just wasn't sure if—"

"Come along," William said, already striding away. "We'd best hurry."

Alexandra blinked. She hated to just tag along without knowing every little detail of where they were going or what to expect. She looked at Ryan, but found no dumbfounded ally there. Instead, he merely shrugged his shoulders and headed after William.

"Do you plan to stand there for the rest of the night, or will you join us?" Michael asked.

She felt her feet begin to move. "Will you please tell me where we're going?"

He grinned ever so slightly, and it was enough to force her head around to look at him. But his expression wasn't one of amusement as she'd expected. Instead, his eyes were sweeping over her in a most approving fashion. "I do believe we ought to get you wet more often," he murmured, so seductively that she couldn't fight the flash of heat that assaulted her body.

"Please answer the question," she said, trying for an unaffected voice and failing miserably. He chuckled, quite openly enjoying her sudden discomfort. *Annoying man.* If only she had a club so she could hit him over the head with it.

"Very well," Michael said, his voice returning to a more serious tone. "There's a small house on the outskirts of the city—a place the foreign office keeps in the event that an agent's cover becomes compromised. There won't be a staff, so we'll have to take care of ourselves for however long we remain there." He paused. "I hope you can handle food better than you handled heating milk."

Alexandra halted in her tracks. "What—" she barely managed.

"You know—the process of making food."

She searched for the humor in his eyes, convinced that he must be mocking her somehow, but there was none. Apparently he really expected her to start keeping house. "Urgh!" Would anyone really blame her if she strangled him now? Clenching her hands at her sides, she raised her chin and turned away to march off after her brothers, muttering a string of unveiled oaths that were very clearly directed at the man she'd just walked away from. Her gown clung to her body while her hair flopped in a most ungraceful manner, the water from it dripping down her back. And if she would have turned, if she would only have looked back at Michael, she would have seen that he was smiling with unabashed pleasure.

Two hours later, they were all settled in the small house that Michael had mentioned. As it turned out, *small* might have been an exaggeration. The truth of the matter was that it was tiny, though it did have three rooms and a kitchen. William and Ryan had immediately suggested that they share the larger of the three rooms, in spite of the fact that it had no beds since it had clearly been intended to serve as a drawing room of sorts. They'd merely shrugged however, claiming that the sofas present would do well enough, at which Alexandra had looked rather dubious. For a good minute she'd tried to determine how her brothers' large figures could possibly manage to fit into the confining spaces that the sofas offered. However, she could hardly complain, given the fact that this afforded her with a comfortable room of her own while Michael had taken the other.

"I think it's time you told us what happened," she found herself saying as they all convened in William's and Ryan's makeshift bedroom. Of all the things the house had to offer, Alexandra had been most relieved to discover that there were dry men's clothing of varying sizes in the closets, along with some money, hidden away in a box beneath a floorboard. Percy really did think of everything, she mused, even if the clothes had probably been there for a good number of years without being used. "Why did you insist on leaving Andrew behind, William? He doesn't stand a chance on his own, especially not as wounded as he was."

Silence filled the room as they all turned to William for an explanation. His eyes darkened. "Finch wasn't who we thought him to be," he muttered after what seemed to be an unbearable amount of time. "He let me down in the worst possible way. Indeed, he let us all down. You came here, intent on accusing me of treachery." His eyes turned to Michael who seemed to want to deny the claim, but William stopped him, saying forcefully, "I would never dream of betraying my country or my people . . . my family for God's sake. Though I must admit that in your situation, Ashford, I probably would have had my doubts as well—especially given the fact that you didn't know me. However, the true culprit as it turns out, was Andrew. *He* is the double agent, not I."

"*What?*" Alexandra gasped, her hand flying to her mouth. It couldn't be—surely not. "You two were such close friends—you've known each other for years. You went to Oxford together for heaven's sake. Why on earth would he do such a thing?"

"Because, as it turns out, Finch was too greedy for his own good." William's mouth was set in a grim line. "He requested an exorbitant amount of money in exchange for the information he was selling, and was very swiftly locked away as a result. Apparently, Bonaparte was not to be fooled. He knew Andrew would run straight back to England, only to sell whatever secrets he'd learned about the French."

Alexandra stared at her brother for a long moment. "So what you're telling me," she finally managed to get out. "Is that I risked all of our lives to save a man who should have been left exactly where he was."

"Yes," William said simply. "That pretty much sums it up."

Alexandra buried her face in her hands. "I am by far the biggest idiot there is," she mumbled.

"Well, perhaps not the biggest idiot," Ryan put in. "There was that Hatchfield fellow who married the Italian woman— the one who took off with all his family heirlooms. I never did understand why he failed to see that one coming when everybody else did. But to put it bluntly, you're not far behind."

"Urgh," Alexandra groaned. She was disgusted with herself. She'd been so wrong, so foolishly stubborn and headstrong. She'd blown William's cover and . . . dear Lord, had he even managed to complete his mission before she'd done so? If not, then she'd single-handedly ruined everything. She dared not even look at Michael.

"I'm terribly sorry about this mess," she muttered, wishing that there was a carpet for her to crawl away under.

Alex, you mustn't put all the blame on yourself," Michael

said, grabbing her attention. "Truth is we're all to blame for this mess."

"But it was my idea."

"And Ryan and I went along with it quite willingly, did we not?"

"I feel like I coerced you," she moaned, looking away.

"Alex?" he asked her seriously. "Did you know that Finch was attempting to sell information to both the English and the French before we helped him escape?"

"No," she groaned. "But if I'd only spoken to William, then—"

"Stop blaming yourself," Michael exclaimed with a small degree of frustration. "It wasn't your fault any more than it was mine or Ryan's."

"He's right, you know," Ryan told her gently. "None of us knew."

"I need a drink," William suddenly stated.

"I could make some tea," Alexandra offered. At least she knew how to do that much, as long as Michael would see to lighting the stove.

William snorted. "Seriously?" He turned to Ryan. "Have a look in that cabinet next to your chair, will you? Surely, Percy will have supplied us with some stronger stuff."

"It seems we are in luck," Ryan announced with the delight of discovery. "It's only half full, but it is indeed a bottle of whiskey."

William strode over to him, taking the bottle from his brother's outstretched hand with a smile of glee. "Fetch some glasses will you?"

His request wasn't directed at anyone in particular, but

since neither Ryan nor Michael seemed to stir, Alexandra eventually got up and went to the kitchen. Returning with glasses in hand, she placed them on a table and watched as William began to pour himself a large glass. "How about the rest of you?"

"I'll have a glass too," Michael said.

"Just half a glass for me," Ryan added.

"To victory," William then said, raising his own glass as soon as he'd supplied both Ryan and Michael with theirs.

"What about me?" Alexandra asked, feeling quite left out. How typical of them to think she wouldn't care to join in. The three men turned to her, their glasses paused mere inches from their lips, their look of surprise unmistakable. She tried not to smile too much at their befuddlement and shrugged instead. "Why not?"

"Why indeed?" Michael muttered, his eyes brightening with amusement as he offered her his glass. "Pour me another, Summersby."

William did and then repeated his toast. "To victory!"

Alexandra watched as they each tossed back their glasses, before following suit.

A split second later, she thought she might die. Heaven help her. This was not at all like the wine or champagne she was used to. This . . . Lord have mercy . . . but it burned. She opened her eyes, realizing that she must have closed them in anguish, only to find the men trying terribly hard not to burst into fits of laughter.

"You truly are too stubborn for your own good," Ryan choked out.

Inwardly, Alexandra couldn't help but agree. But her pride forced a different reaction. "Laugh all you want," she said carelessly, holding out her empty glass toward William. "In the meantime, I'll have another."

William complied without question, knowing full well that arguing the point would come to no avail. Instead he re-filled his own, took a large gulp, then set his glass down and began to pace. There was still an awful lot of information that he had to get out, and he couldn't do it sitting down or standing still. He needed to move.

"Bonaparte will begin his campaign tomorrow," he finally said as he glanced about, taking in all of their expressions. He was glad to find that they didn't look worried or startled by his statement. Instead, they waited for him to continue. This was, after all, the reason they were there.

"When Bonaparte returned from Elba," he continued. "He had about fifty-six thousand troops, of which only forty-six thousand were ready to do battle. As of last week, that number has risen to a staggering one hundred and ninety-eight thousand with another sixty-six thousand in various training camps around the city. How many men does Wellington have? Do any of you know?"

"I believe it must be roughly ninety thousand," Michael replied.

William nodded. "And Blücher?"

"The Prussian?" Alexandra asked, with a frown. "I've no idea."

"I would give an estimate of one hundred thousand if I were to place a bet on it," Ryan said.

"That's fairly accurate," William agreed. He retrieved his glass and took another swig. "It's important you see, because *that* is who Bonaparte will be attacking."

Alexandra sank back against the sofa with a deflated sigh. She bit her lip as if she was trying quite hard to make sense of it all. "Tell us the rest," she finally said as she looked to her brother for answers.

Stopping for a moment to gather his thoughts, William's eyes went to each of them in turn as he continued with slow deliberation. "Bonaparte is hoping to bring the Seventh Coalition—Great Britain, Austria, Prussia, and Russia to the peace table."

"By attacking them?" Alexandra asked. William turned to her with a frown. Was it too much to hope for that she might just sit there quietly and listen? "Sorry," she muttered. "Please go ahead."

"He believes," William continued. "That he can cause enough damage to their armies, so they'll be willing to listen to whatever it is he has to say. It goes without saying that what he's interested in obtaining is peace for France with himself as its Emperor. If the Coalition rejects his proposal, he'll merely continue the war until the Coalition armies are defeated."

"And he's marching on Belgium because of the odds?" Michael asked with a great deal of curiosity.

"Precisely," William agreed. "He's learned that the British and Prussian troops are not only widely dispersed, but that the British armed forces consist primarily of second—line troops since all the soldiers who fought in the Peninsular War were sent to America three years ago and have yet to return."

He ran his fingers through his hair in frustration. "Then of course, he's also counting on French-speaking Brussels sympathizing with his cause. He thinks a French victory might instigate a revolution there."

"Bloody hell," Michael and Ryan muttered in unison.

Alexandra just stared at William. "We have to warn Wellington," she told them in a clear voice of determination. "Do you know where Bonaparte intends to strike?"

William's eyes met hers and exhaustion suddenly seemed to swamp him. This whole business had taxed his energy more than he'd realized. They couldn't stop now though. Alexandra was right. They had to warn the duke. "I can't be certain," he said with an almost defeated shake of his head. "But if I were to venture a guess, then I'd imagine he'll attack at Mons. This will cut off all access to the ports Wellington relies upon for supplies."

"Sounds like a logical strategy," Ryan said, offering William his support. "When do you propose we leave?"

"Well, we have two options. We can leave now and ride ahead of the army, or we can leave in a couple of days and trail behind." William looked at each of their faces, waiting to hear their suggestions.

"I think we ought to trail behind," Michael said. "We're less likely to be tracked by scouts that way, and we'll have a better chance of keeping an eye on any possible changes in Bonaparte's plan that may occur along the way."

William nodded. "My thought exactly."

"I think it's an excellent plan, Will," Alexandra told her brother, jumping to her feet and sweeping him into a hug. He wasn't sure what startled him more—the hug or the endearment that she hadn't used since they were children. As odd as it felt, it also felt good in a way, in spite of the fact that he couldn't help thinking that the alcohol must have muddled her brain.

"Then it's settled," Ryan said, nodding toward the quickly diminishing bottle of whiskey. "Another one before bed?"

And so it went until there wasn't a single drop left.

CHAPTER NINETEEN

Alexandra still felt a slight tingle from the whiskey, though she'd stopped drinking long before her brothers. They were already fast asleep, and she was back in her designated room, alone and unable to sleep. With a sigh of exasperation, she got out of bed and put on an oversized shirt that practically hung all the way to her knees. She wanted company, she decided brazenly—even if she had to wake someone up in order to get it.

No more than a minute later, she was standing outside Michael's bedroom door reevaluating her decision. What was she thinking? She was about to sneak into Michael's room and . . . what exactly? He was probably asleep already and wouldn't take kindly to being woken up by a drunken woman. It was probably best if she left well enough alone and went back to bed. But no sooner had she turned away, than she heard the door open.

"Alexandra?" Michael's voice was barely a whisper—as if he couldn't quite believe that she was standing there. And why would he, when she could scarcely believe it herself. "What are you doing here?"

"Er—" She turned around to face him. She needed an excuse. "Sleepwalking?"

He stared back at her, looking anything but impressed with her answer. "Sleepwalking?" he repeated. "You don't honestly think I'm going to believe that do you?"

She had to admit that it didn't sound nearly as plausible as it had done inside her head. "Very well then. I was bored."

Michael's eyes narrowed. "And?"

"And what?"

He rolled his eyes. "Alex," he said, following her name with a heavy sigh of exasperation. "You've been standing outside my door for the past five minutes. I assumed you might knock at some point, but that clearly wasn't going to happen, so I decided to come out here myself and see what on earth you might be up to this time."

She stared back at him blankly.

"On your last midnight walk, you cut your feet, if you'll recall. I thought it prudent to rescue you from harming yourself further."

She considered that for a moment, and then remembered what he'd said a short while earlier. Her eyes narrowed. "How do you know how long I've been standing here?" It hadn't felt like five minutes, but perhaps she was wrong about that.

"I could see your feet beneath the door, Alex."

Oh.

He watched her for a moment, and she couldn't help but wonder if he was deliberately trying to make her feel as uncomfortable as she now did. "You're not very sharp when you've been drinking, are you?" He then said crossing his arms and leaning against the doorframe in a manner that made Alexandra's stomach tie itself into a giant knot. He really was entirely too handsome for words.

"Forget I came," she said, her mind already on her immediate escape back to her own bedroom.

He smiled at her then, as if he were the keeper of a very juicy piece of gossip. "You know I can't do that," he murmured.

Alexandra stiffened. "You can't?" She wasn't even sure if she'd said anything, her senses were so numb to anything else but his presence—which suddenly seemed to be much too close for comfort if the effect he was having on her was any indication. Her mouth had gone dry, her skin tingled in the most unexpected places and a slow heat had begun creeping over her.

He shook his head slowly. "Come," he said, taking her hand and pulling her toward him. "There's really little sense in standing around out here."

She read his intent in his eyes, and her breath caught. This wasn't why she'd come. Or was it? She no longer knew, but whatever the reason, she was powerless to turn away, so instead, she did as he suggested, sweeping past him on her bare feet until she stood in the small room that was his. When she turned around, she couldn't help but gasp, for he was looking back at her, his eyes blazing with intensity, and then he shut the door.

Michael was beginning to find it very difficult to keep his composure. And who could blame him? After all, Alexandra was sitting before him in his bedroom (on his bed of all places), dressed in nothing but a white shirt that was putting an alarmingly large amount of her legs on display. He felt his blood stir as it coursed through his veins. His stomach tightened while flames flew down his back, gripping his chest and settling within him a smoldering mass of desire. He could not move. Hell, he could barely breathe. Conflicting thoughts assaulted his mind. He wanted to grab her, toss her back against the bed and bring to life all the fantasies he'd been having for the past couple of weeks. But what would she think of him? He'd meant to send her back to her room, to tell her to get some rest, and instead he'd done the complete opposite, and with her brothers sleeping a very short distance away no less. He had to be mad. Besides, he'd promised her a proper wedding night, and instead he was letting his carnal instincts overrule his common sense. She wouldn't possibly be able to respect him for such a lack of discipline—she who thrived on that very thing.

Discipline.

He looked at her, sitting there with her ankles crossed as her legs swung back and forth. He understood that she must be nervous. He also understood that she couldn't possibly know the effect her movements were having on him. *Lord, give me strength.*

Crossing the room, he sank to his knees before her, taking her feet in his hands to still them. He gazed up at her, knowing all too well that his need for her must be blatantly clear in his eyes. And as he held her gaze, he watched in amazement as she began to transform. Her lips parted ever so slightly, her eyelids grew heavy, and when he ran the pad of his thumb along her instep, she sighed with pleasure. He could see the desire as it grew in strength behind her eyes. It almost seemed to leap across the space between them and sink beneath his skin, igniting embers of desire so searing that they seemed to brand his very soul. The heat coiled and swelled within him until he felt himself consumed. "Alex." Her name was but a breath upon his lips. "I've tried to restrain myself," he muttered, feeling the softness of her skin beneath the palm of his hand. "God help me, I've tried. But, Alex, this need I have for you . . . it's like a beast, raging to be set free. I don't know how much longer I can hold it back."

"Then stop trying and set it loose," she said, her voice was no more than a murmur.

His heart thumped erratically in his chest. "But your wedding night?"

"If you recall, I wanted to give myself to you before there was any talk of marriage. I think that saving my virtue for my wedding night was always more important to you than it ever was to me. Perhaps if I were to marry someone else, I might be able to see the reasoning behind it." Her eyes met his in a dead on stare. "Who knows how this mission of ours will turn out? One thing I'm certain of, however, is this—I don't want to die a virgin."

Michael grinned, allowing for some of the tension to ease. "You're not going to die a virgin, Alex. Hell, if I know you, you'll live to be a hundred."

The edges of Alexandra's lips curled upward into a playful smile. Her voice was hushed when she spoke again. "It's the excuse you're looking for, Michael. Don't put too much thought into it or it won't work."

As if Michael's arousal hadn't been hard enough to begin with, it was now as firm as steel. All thoughts of waiting as much as a second longer flew out the proverbial window the moment Alexandra had said her piece.

Firm hands slid along the length of her thighs, rumpling her shirt as they went. Alexandra sucked in a breath when they roamed over her belly, sending darts of fire straight to the very tips of her tightening nipples. But he didn't touch her there. His hands were everywhere except where she wanted them most. Instead, they moved steadily upward, to her shoulders.

He leaned toward her, his lips brushing gently against her neck. "Come." His voice was a soft whisper against her ear as he took her hand in his and helped her to her feet. She couldn't for the life of her imagine his intent, but he'd surprised her before, and so she couldn't help but thrill at the anticipation of what was to come.

They didn't move, but just stood there for the longest time, watching each other somewhat hesitantly. And then his arms were suddenly about her, pulling her against him as he finally kissed her.

It was a kiss to rival all kisses—a kiss so full of passion and desperate desire that it may as well have been their last. Heat wrapped itself around them as they delved deep within each other's mouths, their lips bruising while their tongues tangled in the confines of the moist heat.

They both gasped for air when Michael pulled away, but his lips were upon her again in an instant, placing blistering sparks of pleasure along the rise of her breasts. She raked her fingers through his hair and pressed herself against him. His hands gripped at the fabric of her shirt, gathering it, pulling it upward. She lifted her arms and the garment was gone.

Cool air encased her.

"Let me see you," he said, his voice raspy with want. She stepped away from him, her blonde curls cascading over her shoulders.

"Venus," he murmured, his face filled with awe.

Never in her life had Alexandra thought herself more beautiful, more feminine, or more desired. It intoxicated her senses in a way that nothing else ever would.

He reached out his hand toward her and she went to him—their embrace less fervent this time. Instead, it was more controlled and measured as he hugged her against him, his erection pushing itself against her belly—a constant reminder of what he was after. It surprised her how pleased she was to discover how powerful her effect on him was, and it occurred to her that she ought perhaps be frightened by it. But she wasn't. This was Michael, and something about the way he touched her told her that he would treat her with care.

His hand fell to her hip, tickling her lightly in a downward motion. He took hold of her thigh and raised her leg until her knee rested against his waist. Alexandra gasped in response to the swarms of tingling delight that hummed along her nervous system. "Oh God," was all she could manage to say when his right hand clasped her bottom and forced her against him "Please." Her voice was breathless. "Please touch me. I need you to touch me." She couldn't believe what she was saying, but neither did she care. It was just too much.

"God, Alex . . . you've no idea . . . no idea at all how I've dreamed of this moment." He gave her earlobe a tender nibble as he reached down and ran his fingers along the crevice between her buttocks . . . down, down, down . . . to the soft, wet folds of her womanhood. His fingers paused. "Say it again."

It was the sweetest moment of torture imaginable. "Please," she begged as her hips rose against his hand, silently imploring him to continue. And he did. With a moan and a shudder that seemed to drive him equally wild with desire, Alexandra arched against him, offering up her breasts as well.

"Do you like this?" He circled one pert nipple with the tip of his tongue. A faint *yes* was all the encouragement he needed.

"Then how about this?" With gentle ease, he drove two of his fingers inside her.

She almost buckled, clinging to him for dear life, a loud groan of pleasure escaping her lips. "Don't stop," she begged, pressing herself against the thrust of his fingers, her muscles clenching as she sought for release. And yet, he did—to her utter disgruntlement.

"Lay on the bed." It was more of a command than anything else, though the words were spoken tenderly. "I want to taste you."

"You *what?*"

Alexandra's eyes flew open so wide that she felt they might pop right out of her head. "You . . . you can't be serious." There was a distinct stammer to her voice. "I mean . . . *really?*"

"Trust me, Alex. This will be a treat—one you will thank me for later."

"But I . . ." She suddenly felt horribly shy at the thought of this handsome man's face being in such close proximity to a part of her that even she had never seen up close.

He must have sensed her distress, for he pulled her close and kissed her forehead. "Go ahead," he urged her. "Make yourself comfortable against those pillows over there, and I'll get undressed as well."

As self-conscious as she was, she straightened her back, lifted her chin, and climbed onto the bed. Once settled, she turned her full attention on Michael, her breath catching at the sight of his naked torso. Muscles rippled and flexed with every move he made. She'd known he was solidly built, but by God, this defied all of her wildest dreams and expectations. When he pulled down his breeches and her eyes swept over his sinewy calves, along his lean looking thighs and across his fully engorged manhood, her eyes widened, and she drew in a shaky breath.

Her gaze shifted uncertainly to his face when he drew near. There was a wolfish grin upon his lips.

As if another force controlled her eyes, she helplessly returned them to his fully aroused flesh, marveling at how splendid he looked. A slow and gradual ache settled in her loins, stirring to life a wantonness she'd never known she possessed. Insecurity abandoned her, and she eagerly spread her legs, opening herself wide to his perusing stare.

She couldn't begin to imagine what he might be thinking, but if the thrill of excitement in his eyes was any indication, then his thoughts as he crawled onto the bed, his eyes riveted upon the ultimate prize, must have been very wicked indeed. It sent a small shudder down her spine as heat poured through her. "So beautiful." His voice was but a low murmur as he lowered his head and stroked his tongue against her.

A million sensations buzzed like tiny sparks of electrically charged energy, assaulting her all at once. She clutched his shoulders with all her might as he licked her, afraid she might die if she let go. "Oh, Michael . . ." She dug her nails against him. "I feel . . . oh God I . . ."

"Soon," he promised as he broke from her grip and climbed on top of her. "Very, very soon."

She knew what would come . . . partly at least—she felt terribly close already. But this time would be different. This time it wouldn't be just about her, but about them, together, and it was suddenly terribly important to her that he should find fulfillment too . . . not that she knew exactly how she might facilitate that, or if it was even possible for them to share in the experience simultaneously, but she would definitely try her damnedest to please him. Accepting his mouth in a hungry kiss, she felt his weight as he lowered himself between her legs and entered her welcoming warmth. On a sigh of pleasure, she felt herself expand around him as he eased his way forward.

He paused, as he took a deep breath, then lowered his head and began placing small, searing kisses upon her cheek. His fingers stroked the softness of her breasts as she moved her body restlessly beneath him. Why was he torturing her like this? If she could only . . . she tried moving her hips toward him, but he remained quite still, his whole body frozen in place.

"Please, Michael," she whispered as her hands splayed

across his back. "You mustn't stop now. Please . . . not now. Take me Michael, for the love of God, just—"

"This might hurt a little." He warned her. "But the pain will be brief. I promise."

"I don't care." Her voice was as desperate as the need she felt roaring through her veins. If he didn't claim her soon . . . Her train of thought faded as he covered her mouth with his own, thrusting his tongue inside her, just as he plunged forward, burying himself to the hilt. Whatever cries she might have made were never heard—not that it hadn't hurt like blazes, but the pain she'd felt was quickly forgotten by the sense of fulfillment that followed.

"God, you feel so good," Michael muttered against her parted lips. "How are you, Alex? Are you all right?"

"Yes, yes, I'm fine." Her voice was close to a gasp. "I feel . . . full . . . complete . . . and about a thousand other things that I can't possibly begin to describe."

"How about now?" he asked, pulling back a little, then plunged back inside again.

Her legs wrapped themselves around him in a silent response while a soft moan of pleasure escaped her lips. This was what it meant to be alive.

With slowly increasing speed, Michael drove in and out of her, his steady beat, lifting her upward and coiling around her until he drove her over the edge, and she fell, spiraling downward in a dazzling burst of light.

Hot ecstasy poured through her, gripping every particle of her body as she shuddered beneath him. She cried out his name and felt him tighten, a wave crashing over him as he groaned between clenched teeth before finally collapsing on top of her in a heap of heavenly bliss.

It took a while before either one of them made an effort to speak. "Do you know, I believe you've turned me into a very naughty woman indeed." Her voice had a mischievous edge to it.

Michael grinned openly and pressed a kiss against her cheek. "Oh, Alex, I think you were always naughty. You just needed the right man to help you express it."

"Well, I do feel as if I could get quite used to expressing it." She giggled while she hugged him against her, her lips meeting his in a tender kiss.

Rolling them over until she was on top of him, he gazed up at her face, and she looked back, seeing there, the same stirring of passion that she suddenly felt swamping her once again. "I thought you might like a different perspective," he said, waggling his eyebrows in a most teasing fashion.

"Why, Lord Trenton," her voice was thick with her newly awakened hunger. "I do believe you're a very wicked man."

"Perhaps . . . with the right woman."

Alexandra lay awake later that night, still unable to sleep. All she could think about was Michael and their wondrous experience in his bedroom a short while earlier. She didn't want to think about him right now, but she couldn't help herself. He'd awakened something in her—a longing of some sort. She'd already acknowledged to herself that she cared about him, but since their coupling, she was no longer sure that her feelings for him weren't developing into something more—something much more powerful.

Once again she felt that familiar fear tugging at her soul as her mind's eye focused on the dreaded abyss. They were all moving toward it, some faster than others. But no matter how much she wished it, she could not stop them from falling into it. Sooner or later the people she loved would die and her heart would break. Wasn't it better then, not to love at all and to save herself from misery? It was a question that she was too afraid to answer.

She woke the following morning to a loud knocking at her door. "Time to rise, sleepy head!" It was Ryan's voice, shouting so loud he was likely to raise the dead. Alexandra groaned. She was confident she hadn't slept more than a couple of hours—three at most. Throwing back the covers, she sat up and stretched.

Five minutes later, she entered Ryan's and Michael's room, her disgruntled mood only marginally better. Feeling like she'd just been whacked over the head with a sledgehammer was doing very little to supply her with a cheerful disposition.

"You certainly look affright," Ryan remarked as he sipped what Alexandra could only presume to be tea. This was confirmed a second later when William offered her a cup of her own. "Didn't sleep much?"

A quick retort sprang to her lips, but she forced it back and drank her tea instead. No sense in rising to his bait this time. Besides, all she had to do was cast one look at Michael who was seated in the opposite corner of the room, and all that had transpired between them in the early hours of the morning, came flooding back to her. She looked away, hoping that her tired expression would deter her brothers from jumping to conclusions.

"I certainly enjoyed a good night's rest," William said with an annoyingly pleased smile. "Not much space, but perfectly comfortable all the same. Wouldn't you agree, Ryan?"

"I would indeed," Ryan said. "Though I did find myself awoken at one point during the night—it was almost as if somebody was screaming, or shouting . . . I'm not quite sure which."

Alexandra's cup clattered noisily against her saucer as her eyes flew to Michael's. He was watching her with the most appalling look of amusement on his face as if he was truly enjoying her show of anxiety. "Re— really?" she asked, clamping her mouth shut at the sound of her broken voice.

"What sort of a scream?" Michael asked, a look of mischief bobbing about his eyes as a crooked smile slid its way across his face.

"A stray cat, no doubt." Alexandra's voice was clipped, her jaw clenched as she glared across the room at Michael, silently willing him to put a stop to the topic immediately.

"No . . ." Ryan grinned suddenly while a steady blush of crimson rose to his cheeks. "This was not the sort of sound one might expect from a feline. In fact, I imagine it must have been one of our neighbors having a rather good time, if you know what I—" He blinked and turned to Alexandra, her mouth hanging open as she gaped at her brother in disbelief.

"Forgive me, Alex," Ryan said. "That was thoughtless

of me. I have the tendency to forget that you are a lady. We ought not discuss this sort of thing when you are present."

He doesn't know.

She'd never felt more relieved in her life. "That's quite all right, Ryan," she muttered, with a hint of embarrassment as she dropped onto a chair. "But perhaps we ought to talk about something else instead."

"I didn't hear a thing," William ventured.

"I doubt you would have woken if the roof had fallen on your head," Ryan said. "I dare say I've never known anyone to sleep so soundly."

"Yes . . . well," Alexandra interjected. She was quite determined to steer the conversation on a smoother course. "Shall we discuss our plans instead? We'll need horses and provisions."

They spent the next hour trying to determine how they might best go about thwarting Napoleon. Given their experience, William and Michael did the most talking while Alexandra and Ryan patiently listened, only occasionally adding their opinions. Through it all, however, Alexandra remained painfully aware of Michael. His whole countenance and bearing were different somehow—he seemed . . . content. And each time his eyes met hers, there was a knowing look behind them that made her heart flutter.

That evening, as she was combing out her hair in front of the mirror in her room, she saw her door open. Michael stepped inside, closing the door silently behind him. She watched as he walked toward her, a steady warmth rising within her with every step he took.

"I'm sorry, I didn't knock," he said as he came to stand

behind her, his eyes locking onto hers in the mirror as he placed his hands upon her shoulders. A soft wave of heat rippled through her at his touch. How was she ever going to be able to walk away from him?

"What are you thinking?" He brushed away her hair with his fingers and proceeded to press soft kisses against the side of her neck. His hands left her shoulders in search of her breasts.

"Nothing." Her voice was breathy in response to his caress, her skin already tingling while her stomach flipped in anticipation. She couldn't say no to him. Not tonight when she so desperately wanted to feel his touch. She would allow herself this final luxury, because tomorrow, she would start rebuilding the wall around her heart.

Chapter Twenty

Bertrand paced about his study with wild agitation. Damn Sandrine Laurant—if that was even her real name, which he by now very much doubted that it was. She and her cohorts had made a complete fool out of him. How could he have been so stupid? He'd had his suspicions, yet she'd still managed to help his prisoner escape, right under his very nose. If word got out about his inexcusable lapse in judgment, he'd be the laughingstock of Paris, if not all of France. Fortunately, he'd managed to shoot the man, though it might have served him better if he'd have lived so he could at least have questioned him. What a dratted nuisance.

And the doctor!

He'd been given direct access to the Imperial Majesty himself. It was outrageous! To think of what he might have heard—every aspect of the Emperor's plan of attack in Brussels might reach the Coalition armies at any moment. He glanced across at Pierre Dupont. The lieutenant sat perched on the edge of his seat—ready to jump to attention the minute he was given the order to do so. He looked about as nervous as a young lad waiting to have his bottom smacked. Served him right. If it weren't for him, Bertrand wouldn't be in this mess.

"Explain yourself." The command was barked, Bertrand's face was red with anger as he turned on Pierre who was looking more and more ashamed and embarrassed by the second, his eyes flickering hopelessly toward the door. "How can it be, that one of my finest soldiers allows for something like this to happen? Do you have any idea of the ramifications? I gave you a simple order to keep an eye on one prisoner, and instead I find you locked up in a cell wearing nothing but your underthings. It's disgraceful!"

"I was attacked, my lord," Pierre stammered.

"You were attacked?"

Pierre shifted uncomfortably in his seat.

"Speak!" Bertrand yelled, becoming increasingly enraged from just looking at his lieutenant. "How did this happen?"

"There was a woman . . . she looked distressed . . . hurt. One minute she was running toward me and the next . . . I suspect she must have been aided by one of her friends, but it's difficult for me to say, my lord."

"And why is that?"

"Well, because I was unconscious at the time, my lord," Pierre told him regrettably.

"Unconscious?" Bertrand stared at his lieutenant with complete and utter dismay. "*Unconscious?* How the bloody hell did you manage to render yourself unconscious?"

"Oh no, my lord, you misunderstand," Pierre quickly added.

"Oh?" Bertrand pinned the man with a stare. "Then by all means, please enlighten me."

Pierre took a deep breath, somewhat shakily. "As I was saying earlier, I was attacked. The woman practically lured me toward her with her deceiving ways—as I said, she looked injured. I thought it prudent to try and help her, and before I knew it . . ." He gave a helpless shrug.

"No no no . . ." Bertrand raised his hand to silence him. "Please, for the love of God and all that is holy, do not tell me that you—one of my finest lieutenants—was bested by no more than a mere slip of a woman." He turned to glare at Pierre, hoping that he might deny it, but he could not. Indeed it did seem as if Sandrine Laurant, or whoever she was, had not only deceived this man, but that she or one of her companions had also knocked him out cold before humiliating and disgracing him in the worst possible way by stripping him of all his clothes. This did not reflect well on him. Indeed, it was an outrage that Bertrand could not allow to go unpunished.

"She must have been a very skilled actress to pull it off," he muttered as he sank down into his armchair.

"She was quite believable," Pierre remarked.

"I should certainly hope so—for your sake. As it is I've a good mind to have you stripped of your duties for the foreseeable future. Perhaps, it will do you good to scrub a few floors as a reminder of your irresponsible actions."

Pierre paled, but said nothing, apparently, reluctant to anger his commander any further.

Bertrand groaned. The woman was most likely English

if her primary objective had indeed been to find the spy and aid him in his escape. But the fact that she'd escaped together with the doctor was unnerving to say the least. He'd ridden all the way to the bloody Bois de Boulogne before he'd realized that the carriage he'd been pursuing had long since been abandoned. It was deplorable.

Bertrand raked his fingers through his hair and considered the matter once more. They were up to something, and he could only hazard a guess as to what that something might be. She had to be found immediately and stopped before she could do more irreparable damage.

"You may leave," Bertrand told Pierre with a wave of his hand.

Visible signs of relief flooded the man's face as he scrambled to his feet, only too eager to escape any further punishment that he might receive.

"Oh, and Lieutenant Dupont?" Pierre froze—his hand already on the door handle. "Have Colonel Martinet sent for, will you? I wish to have a friendly word with him."

Affirming the orders he'd just been given with a curt nod, Pierre departed from the room.

Bertrand reached for his carafe and poured himself a glass of red wine, then leaned back in his chair to await the colonel. He had made his decision, and could not help but feel as though a great weight had been lifted from his shoulders—in spite of whatever reservations he might have. The fact of the matter was that Sandrine Laurant would soon be dead and would trouble him no more. He couldn't help but smile.

CHAPTER TWENTY-ONE

Over the course of the next three days, it became increasingly clear to Michael that Alexandra was trying to avoid him. She was always in her brothers' company, and he couldn't help but wonder if this was a tactical maneuver on her part, with the primary goal of keeping him at bay. If so, it worked.

The rest of the time she would always succeed in slipping away before he managed to approach her, spending an annoying amount of time alone in her room in whichever inn they happened to be staying at.

Michael, was beginning to grow increasingly desperate at the sudden change in their relationship and eventually felt completely out of sorts. Though he had a faint inkling of what lay behind Alexandra's sudden retreat, he wasn't ready to accept it. He needed to talk to her, but it was impossible for him to have a moment alone with her. He knew that she probably planned it that way—that she was intentionally avoiding him (though it was a painful admission to make), but he wouldn't continue to let her do it—not indefinitely. He'd long since admitted to himself that he loved her more than he'd ever hoped to love anyone and once they reached England he *would* marry her.

The thought filled him with nervous trepidation.

They'd become friends in Paris and grown close, especially during the week when she hadn't been able to leave her bed because of her own carelessness. He smiled at the memory of it. They'd talked for hours on end during those days and he'd shared thoughts with her that he'd never shared with anyone else before. He knew that she was an honorable woman and that she wouldn't run from her responsibilities, but he was beginning to ask himself if he would make her face them even if it wasn't in her heart to do so.

On the fourth day, he finally managed to catch her alone. She must have let her guard down because he found her completely by herself, taking a walk in the garden behind the inn they'd arrived at just half an hour earlier. "Do you mind if I join you?" he asked.

He heard her catch her breath as if to protest, but she finally shook her head.

They walked for a while without either of them saying a word. "I miss you, Alex," he then confessed as they passed under a large oak.

"I'm sorry, Michael, but I can't allow anything to distract me from our goal, and neither should you."

"Why are you doing this?" It hurt that she wasn't being honest with him.

"I already told you, I—"

He held up a hand to stop her, his face suddenly set in

stone and his mouth drawn tight in a grim line. "I know. I heard you. I just thought I'd give you a chance to tell me the truth, Alex." He paused for a moment as he searched her face, looking for some small sign that she cared—some trace of the affection she'd so readily shown for him in Paris. There was a glimmer, but it came and went so fast that he wasn't sure if he'd imagined it or not. "Take your time. I'll be here whenever you're ready to talk."

He turned to leave, but she stopped him. "I'm honor bound to marry you, Michael, but I thought I'd ask you all the same."

"Ask me what?" A cold sliver ran down his spine. He suddenly knew what was coming, but he didn't want to hear it and he certainly had no desire to face it.

"Will you insist I marry you, even if I don't want to?" There was pain in her eyes now and it told of an inner turmoil so arduous that Michael's heart wept for her.

"No," he said simply. It was an honest answer, but the look of relief that flooded her every feature at the sound of that one word was like a punch to his stomach. With nothing more left to be said, he turned around and walked away, his heart struggling against the pain.

He wasn't giving up though—far from it. He was just as stubborn as she was by nature, if not more so. He'd already decided that she was the woman he wanted by his side for the rest of his life and nothing was going to change that. She'd just made it more difficult for him to accomplish it, but hey, he'd always loved a good challenge.

It was too bad that all his efforts had been for nothing. He'd been so certain of himself, so confident. He grinned as he recognized in himself her greatest fault—cockiness. Well, perhaps it wasn't entirely for nothing. He'd laid the groundwork, now he just had to set about tearing down that damn wall she was so adamant about building around her heart. But more than that, he had to make her face the way she truly felt about him. He knew she cared for him and that she desired him . . . now, if only he could make her love him.

He needed help, he realized, and he knew just who to ask. Well, there really wasn't anyone else, but as it happened they were perfectly suited for the job. "Ryan, William." Both men looked up at him as he came toward them. They were sitting on the terrace, each with his own glass of beer. "I'd like to speak with you for a minute."

William eyed him momentarily before a grin spread its way across his face. "Is this about our idiot sister?"

"Oh, this is going to be fun," Ryan chimed in as he pulled a chair out for Michael to sit on.

"She's not an idiot," Michael admonished half-heartedly while he took the proffered chair and sat down.

"Yes, she is," William insisted. "She's lying to herself and if we can all see it as clear as day, then why the hell is she unable to?"

"Do you know why she's acting this way?" Michael asked, ignoring William's question. He placed his elbows on the table and rested his chin against his folded hands. "At one point when we talked, I got the distinct feeling she's terrified of something—something relating to your mother's death."

William looked suddenly wary. "Look, it's just a theory, that's all."

"Please tell me," Michael said. "I need all the help I can get."

"Has she bolted?" William asked. When Michael nodded, he let out a long sigh. "How did she do it?"

"She just asked if I'd force her to marry me. I wouldn't have it in me to do that to her, in spite of the duel. I couldn't lie about it, so I imagine the wedding's off."

William seemed to consider this turn of events for a moment. "Let her go," he finally suggested. "Give her the freedom she wants and keep your distance. Refrain from talking to her if at all possible. Give her the illusion that you've completely retreated, and then wait for the right moment to strike."

"She might think that he's lost all interest if he does that," Ryan said.

"Yes, but showing interest will be worse. I think Alexandra's terrified of falling in love. She recognized the possibility for it with you, Michael, so she cut all emotional ties to you before it was too late. I'm not sure why she's so afraid exactly, though I do believe it's related to Mama's death, just as you have suggested." William leaned forward in his chair, his arms folded before him on the table. "You have to understand—things have been very difficult on the home front since she passed, especially for Alex, I would imagine. Papa was a wreck for a long time after, and while Ryan and I were able to escape back to school, Alex remained behind with a father who barely had enough energy to get himself out of bed in the mornings. As unfortunate as it is, she was neglected at a time when she should have been introduced to society."

"He should have made more of an effort," Michael said, suddenly quite angry at how Bryce had ignored his daughter.

"He sees that now," William said, with a sad look in his eyes. "And he blames himself for it every day. At least he's making a real effort to make it up to her though."

"And he's doing this by allowing her to go on this mission?" Michael sounded appalled.

"You know her character," Ryan put in. "Papa wouldn't have stood a chance of putting her into a ball gown, much less of actually dragging her to a ball. Instead he focused on mending their relationship. When this situation arose, he probably saw an opportunity to indulge a longtime dream of hers."

"By sending her into harm's way?" Michael's voice was dubious to say the least.

"She's the best, and our father recognizes that," Ryan paused for a moment. "He's a good man, Michael, but even good men make mistakes."

"Ryan and I are on your side," William said. "We'll do what we can to help, but it will have to wait until we return to England. Let her realize how much she already cares for you. I can't promise anything, but knowing our sister and how willful she can be, I believe it's your best shot. Until then, just keep out of her way. She needs space."

With that in mind, Michael refrained from seeking Alexandra's company. He agreed with her brothers' reasoning, so he did his best to set his mind to the task at hand. He'd just never considered how impossibly difficult such a feat would be.

When they reached Thuin on the fifteenth of June, right on the heels of Bonaparte and his army, they were forced to acknowledge that the French general's plans weren't at all what they'd thought them to be. Instead of heading toward Mons, he was now gunning for Charleroi.

"What do you suppose Bonaparte's up to?" Alexandra asked while her mare tossed her head in an eager show of impatience. They'd found a grove of elm trees upon a hillock from which they had a clear view of the French as they busily went about setting up camp.

"It looks as though he might be aiming for a more centralized position between the two opposing armies," William muttered, before adding hastily, "There's no time to lose. We have to inform Wellington right away. If he expects an attack to come from Mons, just as we did, then his troops will be gathered in completely the wrong place."

Fully aware of the already darkening sky, they turned their horses about, hoping to make it to Brussels by nightfall. They didn't get far, however, before the sound of approaching hooves was upon them. Someone had seen them and the alarm had been sounded. There were now five French soldiers barreling after them at top speed, dirt churning beneath their horses' hooves.

Their intent was unmistakable.

"Yah!" Alexandra cried, spurring her mare into a faster gallop. She sensed another horse coming up beside her and knew without looking that it was Michael. But where were Ryan and William? With a quick glance over her shoulder, she spotted them. Their horses had been slower to start and the French were rapidly closing in on them. Rather than flee, they were now pulling on their reins and turning their mounts around, drawing their swords and preparing to do battle.

"They need our help," Michael called, clearly as aware of the brothers' precarious situation as Alexandra was. He pulled roughly on his own reins with the apparent intention of turning back so he could assist them. "Ride on, Alex."

And what? Ride to safety while you three get yourselves killed? Not bloody likely.

Burying her heels in her horse's sides, she pulled on the reins with all her might until she felt the mare skid to a halt. Turning about, her heart began a frantic gallop at the sight that greeted her. Horses and men seemed to thrash about, swords flashing, slicing the air before clanging together as metal touched metal.

"I thought I told you to ride on," Michael yelled in annoyance when Alexandra joined in.

They'd been three against five only a moment earlier, but her arrival had evened the score. "You can't seriously have thought I might listen to such a ridiculous command." She dove forward, slashing at the Frenchman in front of her. A wide gash appeared in the sleeve of his jacket.

"Our primary objective is to reach the duke," William called out as he parried a blow from his opponent. "All will be lost if we get ourselves killed."

"What do you suggest we do?" Ryan asked. He was fighting two men at once and was rapidly beginning to tire.

"Group together on Michael's side—when I give the command, we'll have to make a run for it," William replied.

It was a dangerous plan indeed, for the French were quick

to react. If they happened to grow suspicious, they'd kill them all with ease before they managed to get away safely. Alexandra maneuvered her way over to Michael, her sword still engaged with the same Frenchman, though he'd now lost a few brass buttons on his jacket as well.

And then William gave his command. Alexandra didn't hesitate one second. Spurring her horse onward, she flew forward. A second later, she sensed another rider at her side. It was Michael. But then a shot sounded, and then another. Realization dawned. Her brothers didn't stand a chance. They were too far behind and were losing ground fast. She had to help them. "Take the lead," she yelled at Michael. "My horse will follow."

As soon as he was in front of her, Alexandra slowed her horse to a steadier pace. Then, with practiced ease, she wound the reins around her hand to tighten the grip and hold the mare steady. Grabbing onto the front of the saddle, she swung herself around, her knees braced hard against her horse's flanks for support. She could see the look of horror on her brother's faces as they saw what she was up to, but she ignored them. This was a matter of life and death—common sense didn't factor in.

Drawing her pistol, she took steady aim and fired, her shot felling a soldier who'd closed in on Ryan. But it was a single shot pistol and she would have to reload. Not only did that take time but it was also a difficult task to accomplish while riding backward.

She had an idea.

"Hand me your pistols," she shouted across at her brothers as they came up beside her.

"What the hell are you thinking, Alex?" William yelled, though he wasted no time on doing what she asked.

There was no time left to talk. The French were upon them and they were mad as hell now that one of their own had been hit. Two were getting ready to fire, so Alex aimed, and took her best shots, felling both of them. Two remained.

Unwilling to risk her life to reload, Alexandra judged the distance between herself and the oncoming soldiers. She might just be able to do it if she dared. No time to think.

Swinging back around, she ground her heels against her horse's sides and hauled with all her might on the reins, bringing her about to face their attackers head on. At little more than a moment's notice, Alexandra reached for her sword and dagger, holding one in each hand and thrusting them out at the oncoming men as momentum carried them forward. She saw the fear in their eyes the second before her blades touched them. They knew what came next and then it happened—blood splattered across her as each man was sliced open, their screams of despair dying in a horrific gurgle of bubbling liquid. Alexandra closed her eyes and dropped her weapons—she could not bear to have a reminder of such an awful moment, but at least it was over. Ryan and William were safe.

Michael had pulled his horse to a stop when he'd heard the air splitting screams. He could only pray that it didn't belong to someone he knew. There was a bend in the road behind him, so he couldn't see—he could only hear. Horses were coming toward him and again he prayed. If those were the French approaching, then everything he loved and cared about in this world would be lost. He had no power to move as he sat there upon his horse, his eyes fixed on the bend while he held his breath.

"Did you see her?" Ryan yelled, rounding the corner with William close behind him.

Michael shook his head, his throat tightening.

Where is Alex?

He couldn't seem to get the question out. All he could do was sit there and stare as Ryan and William slowed their horses, bringing them to a walk.

"She was magnificent," Ryan said, his voice filled with excitement as he related Alexandra's unbelievable feat to Michael.

"She *what?*" Michael shouted, suddenly finding his voice. "She could have been killed. Speaking of which . . . Where the hell is she?"

No sooner had he asked the question, than he spotted her coming toward them at an almost sedated gait. Her shoulders were slumped and her head hung forward, lolling to the beat of her mare's walk. A whoosh of air escaped Michael's lungs as he let out a deep sigh of relief. But as Alexandra came closer, his stomach clenched itself into a knot and his heart ached at the sight of her pain. Gone was the strong and fearless hoyden he knew. Before him sat a trembling woman, her face wracked with anguish as tears poured freely down her cheeks.

"Thank you," William whispered as he reached out to grab her horse's reins. "Had it not been for you . . . thank you."

All Alexandra could do was nod. She was too overcome by the enormity of her own actions to be able to speak. She'd taken life without a second thought—just like that, as if it had meant nothing. Yet somewhere, each of those men had a set of parents, a wife, perhaps even children, all of whom loved them and worried for them. And in the blink of an eye, she'd altered the lives of all those people—people who were just now going about everyday things without a care in the world, until news of their son's, husband's, or father's death would finally reach them. Then they would know grief, and the knowledge of having delivered such pain to the doorsteps of people she did not even know, was more than Alexandra could bear.

She felt an arm close about her waist and before she knew what was happening, she was being hauled onto another horse. Looking up, she saw Michael. The closeness of him, and the tenderness that shone in his eyes was enough to make her cry all the more. He hugged her against him, apparently not caring about her disheveled state or the blood staining her shirt. "You had no choice," he whispered in her ear. "They would have killed your brothers. You did what you had to do, and you did it brilliantly."

His words of praise brought on yet another wave of shaky tears, but in her heart, Alexandra knew that he was right.

Easing his horse into a slow trot, Michael started forward just as a loud crack split the air. Alexandra jerked against Michael's chest when a second shot followed to the sound of whinnying horses. The frightened animals skittered about while their riders pulled frantically on the reins to steady them.

"What happened?" Alexandra yelled, looking about for the source of the sound.

"It seems one of Bonaparte's men survived, Alex. Somehow he managed to stagger after us. He fired a shot, but it must have missed," William told her as he looked toward the soldier who was now sprawled out upon the ground with his pistol still in his hand. "Ryan and I are both unharmed. How about you?"

"I'm fine," she replied. "I—"

"Hold still!" Ryan yelled, turning his mount about and hurrying to her side. He reached Alexandra's, side just in time to stop Michael from falling from the saddle.

"What the—" Alexandra gasped with horror when she turned to see Michael's face, completely ashen, staring back at her.

"I'll be fine," he muttered, bracing himself against Ryan for support. "It's merely a flesh wound, I'm sure."

"You'll be riding with me, Ashford," William told him sternly. "Alex can ride with Ryan."

"I said I'll be fine. It barely even hurts. I'm sure it's just a graze."

"You were hit?" Alexandra's voice came in a small whisper of disbelief.

"No need to trouble yourself about it, my dear. All things considered, there's really . . . no reason for you to concern yourself about me now, just because I happen to be slightly injured." He shot her a cheeky smile before turning his attention to William. "Come along then and give me a hand. I'm not sure if I can dismount gracefully without your assistance."

Alexandra was simply stunned. She couldn't quite believe

that even though he'd just been struck by a bullet, Michael put her in her place. She felt as if she'd just been smacked.

As he slid from the horse with William's and Ryan's help, Alexandra finally caught sight of the blood. It was pooling beneath his shirt at the very top edge of his shoulder. Perhaps the bullet had just grazed him like he'd said. Still, there did seem to be an awful lot of blood. "Shouldn't we tend to him before we do anything else?" she asked. She had no experience with this sort of thing. All she knew was that it looked really bad.

"Not on my life," Michael growled. He hoisted himself up onto William's horse a little awkwardly, wincing, no doubt in response to the pain. "We're not risking the chance of failure because of this. Not after everything we've all been through, and not with all the people who depend on us to succeed. Pull yourself together, woman, it's not as bad as it looks."

Alexandra blinked. Was she just imagining it or did Michael seem brusquer with her than usual? Very well then, she thought as she grabbed hold of Ryan's waist and felt the horse move beneath her. If Michael Ashford wished to bleed to death, then why the hell would she care? It wasn't as if she loved him or anything. Besides, if he wanted to be in pain, then that was his prerogative. Still, she couldn't help herself from thinking him a complete ass for being so damn stubborn.

It was almost eleven by the time they entered Brussels. Only a few people were about at that hour, all of them local citizens who were unable to help in locating Wellington's whereabouts. They rode from street to street, hoping for some sign of where he might be staying, but soon discovered the enormity of such a task. Michael was looking visibly worse, though he did his best not to show it, but they all knew better and Alexandra didn't miss the look of concern on William's face.

At eleven forty-five, they came across three young men, all dressed in military uniforms and heading back to their quarters for the night. They were finally able to point them in the right direction, no more than a few streets away. By the time they arrived at Wellington's headquarters, it was midnight, though candles still flickered from within.

William banged loudly on the door, and they were soon admitted by a young man whom they guessed to be the duke's valet. Once inside, they wasted no time in stating their purpose and were quickly brought before the very man they'd been seeking.

"Your Grace." William's greeting echoed through the room as he bowed before the Duke. Righting himself, he gestured toward his companions. "May I present Lady Alexandra Summersby, Mr. Ryan Summersby, and Lord Trenton?"

All three made a courteous bow, including Alexandra who found it odd to courtesy without a dress. She cast a nervous glance in Michael's direction and was relieved to see him standing straight and surprisingly upright.

Wellington nodded politely at each of them, but he did not smile. "I understand you've brought some news for me." He eyed Alexandra who knew she was looking more and more like something that had just been dragged behind a cart.

"Yes, Your Grace," William said. "If you'll forgive our appearances—we decided time was of the essence."

"Quite right." Wellington squinted as he took in Michael's bloodied shirt. "Will Lord Trenton be requiring medical assistance?"

William turned a questioning gaze on Michael.

"It's very kind of you to offer, Your Grace," Michael replied. "But I think we would all prefer to be on our way as soon as William here has said his peace. I thank you though."

Without further ado, William conveyed what they knew as quickly and concisely as he was able to. Wellington stared at him for a silent moment afterward, before turning on his heel and marching across to a large oak table to look at a map. He murmured a few words to another military man dressed in equally prominent attire, pointed to a couple of places on the map and then looked across at them once more and frowned. "I wasn't sure I ought to believe it until now," he admitted. "But you have just confirmed how wrong I've been."

Alexandra's mouth fell open in shock at the duke's show of self-deprecation. She'd heard rumors about him of course, but she'd never suspected he'd so openly admit to a tactical blunder. She had no clue as to what that blunder might be of course, but she felt that she was about to find out.

"Earlier today, I issued orders for my troops to gather at Nivelle in order to head off any attack coming from Mons," Wellington said.

"But that will . . ." the words were out before Alexandra could stop them. She clamped her mouth shut and shifted uneasily as Wellington's gaze met hers. An uncomfortable silence followed.

"Yes," Wellington agreed with quiet firmness. "That will open the road between here and Charleroi, just as Bonaparte undoubtedly planned it." He let out an agitated sigh before turning toward his companion. The other man was surprisingly unmoved by the sudden turn of events, his face set in a mask of sternness. "General, have a dispatch sent this instant to Nivelle." Wellington told him. "I want the troops moved to Quatre Bras without further delay."

"Yes, Your Grace." The general bowed, turned sharply on his heels and departed with swift steps that rang through the air.

"Thank you," Wellington told them. "I suspect you plan to return to England now."

"You're quite right," William replied. "I think we're all a bit eager to get home."

"Well then, I wish you a safe journey. Will you please give my best to Sir Percy? It seems I would have been quite lost without his assistance. He has the best men . . . and women"—he added as his eyes moved to Alexandra—"working for him. You may tell him from me that you four might just have saved the day. We'll see tomorrow, and the day after that, but I want you to know how grateful I am for your efforts."

"That's very kind of you, Your Grace," William said.

"Now, if you will excuse me, it does appear as if there's a battle to be won."

"Good luck," the four of them told him in unison before bowing and making their exit. Wellington merely inclined his head in response before returning his full attention to the map that lay stretched out before him.

CHAPTER TWENTY-TWO

It was difficult for Alexandra to believe that all their efforts—the lies they'd lived for the past four weeks and all the risks they'd taken—had culminated with no more than a ten-minute audience with the Duke of Wellington. It not only baffled her but it also left her with a deflated feeling of disappointment. Somehow she'd expected more. She wasn't sure what exactly—just that it was very surreal to now be riding toward England without any purpose.

They rode until they reached Gent, hoping to put some distance between themselves and any eventual battle that might take place in the morning. By the time they'd found some lodgings and been assigned to their rooms, they were all bone tired. It was after two, and they'd been on the road since early morning. Still, Michael's injury needed tending to, and Alexandra was beginning to lose her patience. She quickly called for some hot water, some towels, and a pitcher of wine.

"My lord," she told Michael firmly while she pointed to a chair.

He sat down with a loud groan that clearly indicated

his resignation—he didn't look as if he was the slightest bit pleased about the way in which he was being treated. Alexandra really didn't care. She was going to tend to his wound whether he liked it or not.

"Good," she said once he'd taken his seat. "Now take off your shirt."

Judging from their pinched expressions, William and Ryan were doing their best to hide the ridiculous grins that played upon their faces, albeit with a tremendous amount of difficulty. Removing themselves to the other end of the room, they must have decided that it was best to stay out of their sister's way, for which she was thankful. She certainly wasn't in the mood to be trifled with right now.

With a glowering look of displeasure, Michael followed her orders, revealing a wide gash upon his shoulder. Closing her eyes, Alexandra took a deep breath before letting out a sigh of relief. It was only a graze, just as he'd said it was. The bullet had merely clipped him. Still, it had to be cleaned and the sooner she did that, the sooner they could all be off to bed.

Wetting a fresh linen towel, Alexandra dabbed at the blood, gently wiping it away as she cleaned it to the best of her abilities. When she was done, she asked that William and Ryan come and inspect her work. They both gave their approval before nodding in the direction of the pitcher. The worst was yet to come. Discarding the blood stained towel, Alexandra picked a clean one and poured a generous measure of wine over it. Without wasting time to think of how much it was sure to hurt, she pressed it against Michael's wound. He barely even flinched.

"I apologize," she said. "But I have to do this."

"I'm not so sure about that," he grinned. "I imagine this might be your pay back for when I tended to your feet in Paris."

She hesitated for a moment, her hand resting upon his shoulder. This was the closest she'd been to him since departing the city. Her fingers trembled as the heat from his body flowed through them. The effect that he had on her had not lessened. If anything, it had risen to a new level of maddening frustration. How she longed to wrap her arms about his chest and hug him against her. But fear persisted, bellowing for her to beware.

"Just grit your teeth," she heard herself say in a distant voice as she let her hand fall away from him. "It will be over before you know it."

Once the wound was firmly bound and Alexandra was confident that it would remain so while Michael slept, they thanked the sleepy innkeeper and began to make their way upstairs. Alexandra was certain that she would sleep until ten, unless someone happened to wake her—she was so exhausted.

On the landing, Michael caught her arm, stopping her gently in her tracks. "A word if I may?" They quietly waited as both of her brothers said their good nights, each of them departing to their respective rooms.

"What is it, Michael?" she asked warily.

He saw the glimmer of hope that shone in her eyes, but there was still that trace of dread that lined them. He knew what he had to do, but it wasn't going to be easy. However, if they were to stand a chance of happiness together, then she was not only going to have to face her greatest fear yet, but she was going to have to overcome it. For that to happen, he would have to back away, give her space and allow her the chance to fight her demons alone.

"Thank you for everything you did for me this evening, Alex. I just wanted to tell you I'm so very, very proud of you. You're the strongest woman I know, and I've no doubt you can do anything you set your mind to. I know we've had our differences, but you have made me see that you truly are a remarkable woman. You're one of a kind, and I . . . well, I want you to know I hold you in the highest regard." He hoped that she would consider the meaning behind his words in the weeks to come as memories of the last few weeks filled her mind. Then hopefully, in time, she would come back to him.

Caught between two needs, that of pulling her into his arms and kissing her with all the longing that he felt and that of letting her go, Michael reluctantly released his hold on her arm. "Good night," he whispered as he leaned toward her and placed a tender kiss upon her forehead.

She looked as if she might say something, but Michael didn't wait to hear it. Instead, he hurried to his room, closing the door firmly behind him before he lost his resolve.

Alexandra stood for a long moment afterward, staring at the solid oak door through which Michael had so quickly vanished. She wanted so desperately to go to him, but what was the use? She would only be prolonging the inevitable. She could not allow herself to love him and because of that, she would not marry him, so then really . . . what was the point? It would be better this way. Eventually, he would forget about her, move on, and find someone else.

Alexandra forced away the unwelcome wave of emotions that shook her at the thought of Michael in someone else's arms. But then, they'd known each other for only four weeks, the man would hardly be in love with her. And even if he were, she was determined to push him away.

Eager for the escape sleep offered, she snuck inside her room to undress before climbing into bed.

A couple of larks perched on a tree branch just outside Alexandra's window woke her with their twittering just after ten on the following morning. Stretching her arms out behind her head, she considered calling for a bath. She'd been too tired the previous evening and too unwilling to set the whole inn on its end at such a late hour that she'd gone to bed filthy. But now it was a new, bright, beautiful day. Her mission was over, and it was time to get cleaned up.

Moving to the bell pull, she rang for a maid. A slip of a girl appeared at her door five minutes later. Alexandra made her request and within twenty minutes a tub filled with steaming hot water was brought into her room.

With a sigh of contentment, Alexandra eased herself into the water, reveling in its warmth. She found the soap and eagerly covered herself in a thick lather, washing away any remnants of blood and dirt that might still be upon her. That done, she washed her hair, dunking her whole head underwater until she resurfaced with a splash of delight.

When she went downstairs for breakfast fifteen minutes

later, she felt like a new woman. She wore a clean white shirt, a pair of light grey breeches, and her newly polished boots— her damp hair held loosely together at the nape of her neck with a red velvet ribbon.

Stepping outside onto a small sunny terrace, Alexandra noticed her brothers sitting at a round, iron wrought table. Ryan spotted her immediately and waved for her to come over and join them. "Tea or coffee?" he asked as she took a seat.

"Coffee," she replied, just as a maid brought her a plate. Taking a roll of bread from the bread basket, she allowed Ryan to fill her cup.

"I'll let you add the milk and sugar yourself, shall I?"

"Yes, thank you, Ryan."

He leaned back in his chair to look at her. "You're looking a whole lot better today than you were last night. Don't you agree, William?"

"Hm?" William brought his attention away from the newspaper he was reading, waving away a boisterous fly as he did so. "Yes, absolutely."

"Well, so do you," Alexandra grinned as she spread a thick layer of jam across her bread. She licked her fingers as she glanced about. "Any sign of Michael yet?"

She'd aimed for a casual tone, but her brothers apparently knew her well enough to realize that there was nothing casual about it. They glanced at each other for a brief moment before Ryan excused himself and headed back inside. William folded his paper and turned a steady gaze toward his sister. "Ashford left early this morning," he told her simply.

Alexandra froze in mid bite and stared across the table at

her brother. She didn't care; she reminded herself. This was after all what she'd wanted—to push him as far away from her as possible.

Then why did it feel as if her world was suddenly crumbling all around her? "I see" was all she could manage to say, even though she didn't really see at all. It hurt that he'd gone without saying good-bye, and there was something else—a sudden feeling of emptiness that she'd never known before. She felt hollow.

"It's probably for the best, you know," William told her. "You clearly don't care enough for him or you wouldn't have broken off the engagement. What reason would he possibly have to stay?" The words sounded harsh, and Alexandra couldn't help but serve him a disgruntled frown in return. She knew that he thought she was being an obstinate little twit, and he probably reckoned she'd do well with some blunt truths.

"I don't know. I just thought—"

"What did you think, Alex? That you could string him along indefinitely to pamper your own ego? Surely you hold him in higher regard than that."

"Of course, I do, William. You know that I . . ."

William raised an expectant eyebrow and watched while she struggled with her own emotions. She wanted to tell him how she felt, but how could she when she barely knew it herself?

"Never mind . . . it's nothing," she finally said, cringing at her cowardice.

"Good." William's voice was suddenly clipped with annoyance. "Then by all means let us be off. We can't sit about here all day eating pastries, no matter how tempting it may be."

"Yes, of course," Alexandra agreed, finishing the last of her coffee and rising to her feet. There was a sudden smile on her face as she pushed in her chair and walked around the table to William's side. "Papa will be terribly pleased to see us."

"Indeed, he will, Alex," he replied, throwing his arm over her shoulder and steering her toward the doorway. "Indeed, he will."

Caught up in her own thoughts, Alexandra was too distracted to notice the woman who was just then stepping out onto the terrace. A second later, she turned right into her, almost knocking her off her feet.

"Pardon!" Alexandra exclaimed, startled by the woman's sudden appearance and quite embarrassed at not having noticed her soon enough to avoid running into her.

"Please, forgive my sister," William said kindly, offering the woman his arm to steady her. "Her head is somewhere in the clouds today."

Alexandra mumbled a few words of denial before pasting a bright smile on her face and turning her attention toward the helpless victim of her clumsiness. She appeared to be no more than eighteen years of age, shorter in height than Alexandra, but with a slim figure and ample bosom that any number of women might envy. Her hair was dark brown and straight in appearance, tied back into a taught knot at the nape of her neck. Her face was not exactly beautiful, but could certainly pass as pretty. Looking her up and down, Alexandra had to conclude that her greatest flaw had to be her taste in clothes. Her garments were simply drab and did very little to flatter her figure, but then, who was she to judge? After all, she was standing there in men's clothing while the woman before her was at least wearing a dress.

"It's quite all right," the woman replied, stretching her neck to get a better view of the terrace. "I was just looking for my papa. Have you perhaps seen an older gentleman with graying hair and a big, bushy moustache?"

"Afraid not," Alexandra said.

"Perhaps, he went for a walk in the gardens?" William suggested.

"Yes, I believe I'll take a look. Papa does enjoy the flowers." Thanking them for their advice, the woman hurried off toward the other side of the building.

"That was odd," William muttered a moment later after they'd gone inside.

"What?"

"That woman you just ran into . . . there was something odd about her."

"What do you mean?"

"I can't put my finger on it just now, but I'm sure it will come to me."

"Very well then," Alexandra said. "Let me just pack the last of my things so we can be off."

They continued on toward Dunkerque, with another overnight stay at Lichtervelde, enjoying the lack of haste. "Isn't it beautiful?" Alexandra asked as they stopped in Veurne to marvel at the neo-gothic architecture surrounding the town square.

"Hm . . . I believe extraordinary might be a more apt description of it," Ryan said as he stared up at the splendid display of color in the stained glass windows of the church.

"I need a beer," William muttered from behind them.

Alexandra couldn't help but sigh in response. "You don't have a cultural bone in your body, do you, William?"

"Of course I do," he grinned. "It's just limited to alcohol and food."

"And women," Ryan chuckled.

Alexandra rolled her eyes. "Don't you think it's impressive?" she asked as she pointed out all the lacework adorning each façade.

"I suppose so," William admitted. "But to just stand about gawking at it for hours on end seems a trifle pointless."

"Honestly, Alex," Ryan cut in. "I don't know why you bother. He simply doesn't get it."

"I certainly do," William said. "I would just appreciate it more if I were having a cold drink at the same time."

"Come along then," Alexandra grinned, pulling William along with her by his arm. "There's a brewery just over there where we can get some refreshments while enjoying our surroundings."

"Now you're talking!" Hurrying ahead of them, he quickly secured a table with a bench on either side. A waiter appeared a moment later and William placed an order on all of their behalves.

"Ah . . . that's more like it," William exclaimed five minutes later as he set his beer mug on the table and wiped the foam from his mouth

"I couldn't agree more," Ryan admitted.

"It certainly does hit the spot," Alexandra agreed. She studied her brothers for a moment. "Tell me Ryan, what do you want to do with your life?"

The question clearly surprised him for it had come from out of nowhere. "What do you mean?"

"Well, you're just about the smartest person I know. In fact you're better read than William and I put together. I thought you might want to—"

Ryan chuckled. "Just because I've read close to every book in creation, doesn't make me smarter than either one of you."

"Perhaps not, but I still think you're too hard on yourself at times," Alexandra told him. "Back in Paris for instance, *you* saw to it that Michael and I did our duty. *You* encouraged him to challenge me, knowing it was very likely the only thing I was going to learn anything from. I learned a valuable lesson because of you, Ryan. I learned just how dangerous a game it was I was playing. Now that I'm free again, I'll keep that lesson in mind."

"But do you really want to be free again?" Ryan asked cautiously. The painful reminder of what she'd given up on rose to the surface. She pushed it back, forcing a smile for Ryan's and William's benefit alone.

"What a silly question," she whispered. "Of course I do."

Setting her mug on the table with a hard clunk, she got up and walked away in search of her horse.

"You must admit, she has a point," William said as he handed some money over to the waiter and got to his feet.

"Have you considered going back to Oxford and actually getting a degree?"

Ryan winced. He'd been studying all his life it seemed, but he just wasn't capable of sticking to one area of expertise long enough to become certified. "Of course, I've considered it. After all, I'm not the eldest and will have to make my own way somehow." There was no resentment or bitterness in his voice. "Still, I'd like to pick something that will make me happy. I suppose that's why I've drifted so much. I wanted to try it all to make sure I made the right decision. After all, it would be a permanent one."

William considered that for a moment and couldn't help but agree. "It's rather like choosing a bride I suppose."

Ryan grinned. "Trust you to make such an analogy." They continued after Alexandra to where they'd left their horses.

"I've finally got it!" William suddenly exclaimed.

"What are you on about?" Ryan stopped in his tracks to look at his brother.

"That woman Alex and I ran into at the inn in Lichtervelde . . ."

"What woman?"

"Oh, Alexandra almost knocked a woman to the ground because she was so distracted by her thoughts of Ashford."

"The point is that something about this woman struck me as odd, and I've just now figured out what it was." William felt as excited as a child on Christmas morning. "She had a surgeon's badge pinned to her arm."

"A female surgeon? But that's impossible, William. Surely you must be mistaken."

William shook his head with amusement. "I assure you I

am not. And she was young too. I had her pegged as no more than eighteen at the time, but given her profession, I suspect I'll have to add a couple of years."

"Good heavens," Ryan said. "Imagine that . . . I must say that's quite remarkable. She was Belgian I take it?"

"I've no idea. We spoke French, but that's hardly an indication."

"Well, they certainly do seem to be more liberal over here on the continent. A female surgeon or doctor or whatever it is she claims to be would never fly back home in England."

"You're certainly right about that," William agreed.

"Still," Ryan continued. "One cannot help but admire her courage. Do you suppose she'll be attending to the wounded?"

"The wounded? You mean Wellington's and Bonaparte's troops? I hadn't considered it. Who knows what her destination might be? She was looking about for her father when Alex ran into her."

"Ah. Well, let's hope the man will keep a watchful eye on his daughter then. Lord knows the world has fostered enough willful chits."

William caught a glimpse of Alexandra brushing down her horse's flanks. "Amen to that," he muttered.

They reached home five days after leaving Brussels.

"Look!" William pointed ahead of them, his voice ringing with excitement. "It's Papa!"

Alexandra spotted him instantly, his back turned toward them in the gig he was driving as he headed toward the manor. He couldn't have heard them yet, she realized—not with that much distance between them and the sounds that his own horses were surely making. Kicking her heels against her horse's sides, she quickened the pace, hoping to catch up. "Papa!" he continued on his way, so she tried again. "Papa!"

This time, her father must have heard her. He pulled on the reins and then turned in his seat, shading his eyes with his hand as he looked back in her direction. Alexandra waved with great enthusiasm, her heart leaping with joy at his happy expression. A moment later, she pulled up beside him, leaped from her horse, and dashed right into his open arms.

"Alex." Bryce sighed, gripping her in a firm embrace. He released her to welcome his boys. "I see you have brought William home with you."

Alexandra barely caught the hint of tears in her father's eyes.

How difficult this must have been for him.

"And Alex appears to be in one piece," Bryce added as he turned to Ryan, patting him fiercely on the back. "I knew I could count on you to keep an eye on her."

"I did my best," Ryan replied. Alexandra couldn't help but note the look of apprehension in his eyes though. Well, at least he was being somewhat honest, for which she was thankful.

"And Trenton? I trust he's no longer chasing after William?"

"Indeed, he's not," Ryan said, "I think you'll be happy to find that everything has been resolved and that Michael has returned to London to give his report to Sir Percy."

"Excellent! Then let's return to the house shall we? I want to hear all about your adventure. Who will ride with me?"

"I will, Papa," Alexandra said, tossing her horse's reins to William and jumping up into the gig.

"What do you suppose Papa will say when he discovers you didn't keep such a good eye on Alex after all?" William asked Ryan as they watched the gig roll away. They'd both had enough of riding and chose to walk the remainder of the distance instead.

"Perish the thought," Ryan muttered in response. "He'll probably have my head. However, I don't intend to play the coward. Besides, Papa needs to know what's going on. Without his help, our plan has no chance of succeeding."

CHAPTER TWENTY-THREE

During the course of the next couple of weeks, Alexandra began to feel as though she were under assault.

On one occasion, she came downstairs to find the parlor filled with several bouquets of bright yellow tulips. A smile came to her lips as she asked her brothers who had sent them. "Oh, nobody," they replied. "We merely thought the room needed a touch of color, so we asked Mrs. Barnes (the housekeeper) to buy whatever struck her fancy."

"I see," Alexandra replied with a sullen look upon her face before departing the room.

A few days later when she went in search of William, she found her older brother in his room, busying himself with a painting. "Is that a new acquisition?" she asked while she watched him tear away the brown paper in which it had been wrapped.

He looked up at her as she leaned against the open doorway, and threw her an impish smile. "Yes. It's from Paris. I found it in a small out of the way place and simply fell in love with it. It was much too big and awkward for me to bring along, so I asked the shop owner to have it shipped."

Alexandra regarded her brother for a moment as she mulled that over. "That was very kind of him. He could just as easily have taken your money and kept the painting."

"Hm . . . I suppose he could have, but then again I did say it was for a friend and that I'd be back if he didn't receive it."

Alexandra smirked. "Yes, of course you did."

"So? What do you think? Isn't it the most beautiful piece you've ever seen?"

But it wasn't the obvious display of artistic talent that had Alexandra catching her breath and feeling rather faint—it was the subject matter. Before her, on a canvas of medium size, was painted the very same scene that she'd beheld as she'd gazed out over Paris from the top of Montmartre. Michael had taken her there and in doing so, he'd given her a memory that she'd treasure for the rest of her life. Now, an actual, true-to-life depiction of that very moment would hang upon William's bedroom wall. It was simply too much to bear. "It's very moving," she told her brother, dabbing at her eyes.

"You're welcome to come and look at it whenever you please, if you truly like it as much as you seem to do."

"Thank you, William. I just might take you up on that."

Fearing she might soon be reduced to a puddle of tears, she quickly left with a desperate need to go for a ride. Was she imagining it or did little reminders of Michael appear to be popping up in whichever direction she turned? It was quite alarming to say the least.

The next week during afternoon tea, Ryan appeared to be

aimlessly flipping through a book when he suddenly stopped. "Oh look," he said. "I haven't read this one in ages."

"Which one?" Bryce asked as he sipped his tea. "Mind telling us what the devil you're on about now?"

"Oh, not much, just a poem I'd completely forgotten about—*My thoughts by night are often filled with visions false as fair, for in the past alone I build my castles in the air. I dwell not now on what may be night shadows o'er the scene, but still my fancy wanders free through that which might have been.*"

"Hm, not bad," William remarked. "Who's it by?"

"Thomas L. Peacock," Alexandra said without a moment's hesitation.

"Oh, I take it you're familiar with it?" Bryce asked with some degree of curiosity. "I didn't think you enjoyed poetry unless it happened to be by Burns."

"That is true," Alexandra agreed a bit more cautiously. "However, this particular one happens to be one of Ashford's favorites. He was kind enough to share it with me."

"Indeed," Bryce muttered as he took another sip of his tea.

Things continued in much the same vein for almost three weeks until Bryce finally walked into his study one day to find Alexandra sitting in a chair, more teary-eyed than he'd ever seen her before.

With one look at his daughter, he stepped slowly inside and closed the door behind him. "Is there something that you would like to talk about?" he eventually asked after a moment's silence.

Alexandra nodded between sniffles as she drew a shaky

breath. She began rummaging around after something that Bryce could only presume to be her handkerchief, but was apparently unable to find it. He offered her his instead, and she accepted it, then quickly dabbed at her eyes.

Feeling like a fish out of water and with little idea of how to handle his weeping daughter, Bryce seated himself with a comfortable distance between them. "Now then," he told her softly. "What seems to be troubling you?"

"Oh, Papa . . ." Alexandra sobbed. "I can't think of what to do. I believe I may have made the most terrible mistake and as hard as I've tried, I just cannot seem to escape it. I'm forever reminded and . . . and . . . oh God, Papa, I'm so scared and . . ." she choked on another onset of tears.

Bryce studied his daughter carefully. Despite knowing all that had happened in France, he still needed to determine the cause of her fear. "Perhaps, if you were to start at the very beginning, Alex." His words were gentle and kind. "Tell me what's causing you such distress."

"I . . . er . . . while we were away in Paris, Lord Trenton and I spent a great deal of time together, in each other's company and . . . Well, I couldn't stand him to begin with. He seemed so arrogant and judgmental. He was not at all happy about bringing me along—at least not to begin with. Of course, it didn't much help that Ryan and I deceived him. He didn't at all care to discover he'd brought a woman along."

Bryce chuckled as he reached for a cigar and cut the cap before lighting it. "Yes, I can only imagine how displeased he must have been."

"You have no idea, Papa. He was furious about it and I was so angry with him too. He kept patronizing me and treating me like a spoiled child who insisted on having her way, but somewhere along the way I managed to get to know him and . . . well . . . I'm not sure how to put this but I—"

"You developed a *tendre* for him?" Bryce concluded, letting out a puff of smoke.

Alexandra raised her eyes to meet her father's for the first time and quietly nodded as she twisted the handkerchief between her fingers.

"And you're upset because he doesn't share your feelings?"

She shook her head as she lowered her gaze once more. "No . . . well, I don't believe he does share my feelings, but that's not the issue. I know he likes me . . . he offered to marry me though the circumstances surrounding his proposal were a bit out of the ordinary."

Bryce did his best to hide a grin. He knew all about the duel of course and had long since come to terms with it—so much so that he was able to see a bit of humor in it all. He also knew that Alexandra was completely wrong about Michael's feelings toward her, but this was something that she would have to discover for herself. And she would, with a little helpful prodding from her family.

"Then why not marry him, Alex? If you like him and he likes you, enough to offer for you at any rate . . . why not take the leap?"

This was it. The moment of truth. Bryce gripped the armrest and braced himself for his daughter's reply.

"I'm scared," she whispered.

No explanation followed—just those two simple words. Now what was he to make of that? After several minutes he felt compelled to say something. Ryan had told him he suspected she'd lost her innocence already but . . . maybe she hadn't? Bryce nervously cleared his throat. "Alex, I know there's much your mother would have discussed with you if she were still with us. After all, marriage can be very daunting for a young lady. I imagine . . . the thought of a wife's duties may be quite frightening. But I assure you my dear that it can be quite . . . um . . . enjoyable . . . especially when the two parties are attracted to each other and—"

"No, Papa . . ." Alexandra cut him off with a shake of her head. "Michael and I have already . . ." Her hand flew to her mouth, but not quick enough for her to shove the words back in. She stared aghast at him, presumably worried that her life was about to come to an early end.

Bryce cleared his throat as he shifted uncomfortably in his chair. "I . . . er . . . I see," he mumbled.

"I wish your aunt were here," he heard himself say before continuing in a firmer tone. "Look, Alex. You and I aren't the sort to beat about the bush. I realize our conversation has touched upon a rather sensitive topic, though I assure you it's far more embarrassing for me than it is for you. So I'm just going to ask you point blank. Was your encounter with Lord Trenton . . . disturbing?"

Alexandra gaped at her father as if he'd just turned blue. Words eluded her. Was she really discussing something as taboo as sex with her very own papa?

"No! No, not at all," she stammered, hardly believing that such an odd conversation was actually taking place. She wondered how long it might take for her cheeks to burst into flames.

"Good." He paused for a moment to take another puff of his cigar. "Then what the bloody hell is the matter?"

"I love him, Papa. I love him so terribly much that my heart literally aches. I can't stand it. And I've tried so hard . . . so damn hard not to love him, but I just can't seem to stop myself and . . . oh God, Papa . . . what good will it do? In the end, it will only cause more pain and suffering, and I don't want that." A chocked sob escaped her while Bryce watched her in what could only be construed as stunned silence. "For the last nine years, I've sworn never to marry. I don't want more love in my life. As it is, I can't stand watching everyone I care about as they move steadily toward death—and I can't save any of you, I just can't. It doesn't matter what I do. One day, I'll eventually have to bury another loved one. I think about it every single day, living the moment in my mind and feeling the pain that's yet to come. It torments me, Papa, and to add one more worry like that . . . to wonder every time I watch Michael ride off, if that will be the very last moment I see him . . . it's just too difficult a burden to bear."

Alexandra shook her head, her self-control completely abandoned as tears streamed down her face. "I know I'm not making much sense . . . I'm sorry, but it's the best I can do to describe what I'm going through."

"Actually, Alex, you've made quite a bit of sense, though, perhaps in a rather muddled sort of way."

Alexandra gave a miserable laugh.

"Your mama died nine years ago, Alex."

Alexandra bit on her lip, then wiped away the tears with the back of her hand. "I was there, you know . . . when it happened."

Bryce regarded her for a long silent moment, a tortured look creeping into his eyes, and then he said, "What are you talking about?" His voice was unusually quiet—as if he dreaded what she might now tell him.

Alexandra let out a deep, quivering sigh as she allowed her mind to travel back all those years to her mother's bedroom. "I'd picked some flowers for her in the afternoon—violets. She loved violets." She smiled at the recollection—happy to have brought her mother some measure of happiness in her final moments.

"I sat with her for about an hour, telling her all my secrets, afraid I suppose that another opportunity might not arise. She was weak, but not too weak to tell me she was ready to go." Alexandra paused for a minute to steady herself against the fresh tears that stung behind her eyes. "She said she'd accomplished everything she'd ever dreamed of—that she'd found true love with you and left behind a legacy in us.

"When she grew tired and went to sleep, I stayed, holding her hand as if by doing so I might keep her from slipping away. At some point I must have dozed off, for when I awoke, all the candles in the room had burned out, save one . . . the one you held.

"I've no idea when you arrived at her bedside, but your candle gave off such a faint glow that I remained shrouded in darkness. When I heard you baring your soul to her and whispering prayers of forgiveness . . . I had no wish to intrude. So I sat there, still holding her hand as her life slowly ebbed away. But the sorrow I felt at her passing was quickly outshone by your heart wrenching display of grief."

Alexandra sat in silence, doing her best to gather her emotions under some form of control. She could hear her voice quiver and quake as she spoke, and she knew that once she allowed the grief to grip her, she'd lose her ability to speak. Trying to avoid her own feelings surrounding the subject, and aiming for a detailed account of the facts alone, she took a deep breath to calm herself.

"You're a military man, Papa. You've led countless numbers of troops into battle without a moment's hesitation and without ever considering your own safety. You're strong and fearless—nothing can harm you. But when I saw you so easily defeated . . . so easily crippled by something as intangible as love . . . I didn't really give it much thought. I just knew that love, the sort that binds your soul to another . . . I knew it wasn't for me, and from that moment on, I would do everything in my power to always avoid it."

"Oh, Alex." Bryce's voice was filled with a mixture of pain and compassion. "I had no idea. And you were so young. I can't begin to imagine the sort of impression such a moment must have made on you."

Snuffing the last of his cigar in a nearby ashtray, Bryce got up and walked across to his daughter. He sat down next to her and pulled her into his arms, giving her all the paternal comfort that she needed. When the tears had passed and she drew away with a trembling sigh, he reached out and took her hands in his. "You mustn't turn your back on love, Alex. Life is meaningless without it."

"But the way you suffered . . . not just then but for years afterward. I could see it in your face, the way you pulled away from us, feel it in your demeanor . . . I still can. How can you ask me to embrace something that has caused you so much grief?"

"Because, it's also been the source of great joy for me. And though the grief was intense, the joy always lingered. You have to understand, where there is love, true and unblemished love, the sort most people only ever get to dream about, grief is the price you have to pay. But speaking as one who's been fortunate enough to know that kind of love, I can promise you it's been worth it all. Never in a million years would I trade the pain for all the happiness your mother brought me." He squeezed Alexandra's hands—his eyes were glistening and his voice had begun to wobble . "And I count my blessings every day that I've known what it feels like to be held in her arms, to walk hand in hand and steal a kiss from her below a willow tree. Yes, your heart will be on constant alert, just waiting for disaster to strike, but such is love, Alex. The best you can do is bury your fears and focus on all the good it will bring you. Because I promise you, if you don't follow your heart, you'll wake up one day, knowing you squandered the most precious gift life has to offer you, feeling nothing but emptiness inside and with a mind filled only with regret. This should be your greatest fear, Alex. Not love."

Alex sat, stunned and shaken. She'd been so busy focusing on all the pain and heartache that came from love that she'd completely missed the point. Worse than that, she'd spent the last nine years running from the only thing that really mattered and straight toward that which promised true anguish—the knowledge that she'd deliberately spurned a chance for true happiness.

"I need him, Papa," she suddenly whispered as she gazed up at her father. She felt suddenly struck by an overwhelming sense of wonder, as if she couldn't quite believe what she was saying. It soon fled as worry took over. "What if he doesn't feel the same? What if I'll always love him and he'll never love me? Oh God, Papa . . . what if he won't have me anymore? I've been so stupid, so selfish . . . I've made such a mess of it all. He'll never forgive me. How can he? I've treated him terribly and now . . ."

Bryce held up his hand to quiet his rambling daughter. He looked serious, though, she couldn't help but notice the beginnings of a smile. She could hardly imagine what a mess she must seem in his eyes as she aimed for what she hoped to be a less besotted expression. The tears were gone, that was true, but she still wasn't her old self. No, she was acting like a nervous lovesick girl mooning over her own prince charming—probably with big red hearts glowing in her eyes.

"Pull yourself together, woman," her father told her firmly. "Now that you've got your head back on straight, I'm quite confident everything will work itself out."

"Really?" she asked with genuine concern as she bit down on her lip. "I'm just so . . . I've never felt like this before . . . this need to chase after him as fast as I can while I shout my love for all the world to hear."

Bryce grinned. "Steady on, Alex, or you'll scare him off. Now I know how you feel, because I felt the very same thing after meeting your mother."

"Really?"

"Oh yes. Well, it would hardly be love if you *didn't* feel that way, but you see . . . it's never good to just charge ahead. Take your time and make a statement that won't leave him wondering about what's in your heart. Now, I do believe an opportunity has presented itself."

"An opportunity for what?"

"For you to make your statement."

Alexandra's jaw dropped. Was her father seriously forging a plan for her to win Michael's heart? "What are you up to?" she asked cautiously.

"Nothing. But I did receive this invitation earlier today from the Duke and Duchess of Willowbrook. They've invited us to attend a ball they're hosting a week from today. It promises to be the highlight of the season if I am not mistaken."

"I'm sure it will be," Alexandra replied with a rather bland expression. "But I don't see why their ball should be of any interest to me. You know how much I despise dressing up in frilly dresses and such."

"It should interest you, my dear," Bryce said with an almost victorious smirk on his lips. "Because the Duke and Duchess of Willowbrook, are none other than your beloved Michael's parents."

"Bloody hell!" Alexandra exclaimed as she plopped back in her seat to digest this new piece of information.

"Yes, well . . . I do hope you'll watch your language when you venture out into public."

"Hm? Oh . . . yes, of course, Papa . . . sorry." Michael Ashford was the son of a duke. Why the devil hadn't she heard about this before? Or maybe she had and she just hadn't given it much thought. She wasn't sure. In any case, her father was right in strategizing. Michael was probably the most sought after bachelor on the marriage mart. Young women would be swooning at his feet, and if he thought his relationship with her was over, then . . .

Oh hell!

There was nothing for it. She would have to dive into the

middle of the London season and stake her claim before it was too late. "I'm going to London tonight," she announced as she sprang out of her chair. "I need to pay Aunt V a visit."

"Calling in the cavalry are we? Well, I'm sure she'll be delighted to see you, especially once you tell her you're finally giving her a shot at making a presentable lady out of you."

Placing her hands on her hips, Alexandra gave her father her most convincing *do not mess with me* stance. "I *am* a presentable lady. I just need a bit of guidance that's all."

Sticking out her tongue in a way she hadn't done since she was five, Alexandra sauntered from the room. A second later she popped her head back in. "Thank you for listening, Papa, and for all the advice." She then served him her brightest smile before closing the door behind her.

Things were finally beginning to look up.

Lady Alexandra Lindhurst. And it...

CHAPTER TWENTY-FOUR

Virginia Camden, the Viscountess of Lindhurst, was just finishing dinner with her husband, Henry, when a rather bewildered butler entered the dining room. "My lady ... ah ... er ... well ..."

"Whatever is the matter, Pierson?" Virginia asked as she set her crystal glass back down upon the table after taking a very tiny sip. She never overindulged in anything.

"I'm terribly sorry, my lady, but you appear to have a visitor."

"A visitor?" Lord Lindhurst asked in obvious disbelief and not without a great deal of annoyance. "Whoever would call upon us at such a late hour? Is there an emergency of some sort?"

"I don't believe so, my lord. The lady . . ." Pierson looked as if he might turn purple from his effort to complete his sentence—he certainly appeared rather distressed. He took a deep breath, apparently finding it quite a challenge not to let his otherwise perfectly collected facade slide. "She says she's a relative and that she wishes to see you, my lady, on a matter of some importance."

"Good heavens." Virginia quickly dabbed at her mouth with her napkin as she rose from the table. "I'd best see what all of this is about."

As she came closer to the butler, he leaned toward her and subtly whispered, "She's wearing breeches, my lady."

Virginia stopped in her tracks. She had only one female relation who was daring enough to show up on her doorstep dressed like a man and that relation had run off the last time she'd been there. "Alexandra," she muttered, hurrying past a visibly shaken Pierson in order to greet her niece.

"Well, this is an unexpected surprise," Virginia exclaimed as her eyes settled on Alexandra's slim figure. She turned back to frown at Pierson. "You didn't even offer to take her cloak?"

"No, my lady. I didn't expect her to stay for long," he said as he sent a disapproving glance in Alexandra's direction.

"Pierson, this is my brother's daughter, Lady Alexandra. You will treat her with respect, or I shall have to ask you to personally polish every piece of glass in this house, including the windows. Do I make myself quite clear?"

Looking as if he'd just swallowed something very unpleasant, Pierson inclined his head toward Alexandra. "Please accept my sincerest apologies, Lady Alexandra. I had no idea that . . . ahem . . . may I take your cloak?"

With a crooked smile, Alexandra obliged, unclasping the heavy folds of fabric from around her neck and draping them across Pierson's outstretched arm. "Thank you, Pierson," she told him with a ring of amusement to her voice.

"Please have some tea brought to the parlor," Virginia told

him. Then, after a moment's hesitation and giving Alexandra a quick once over she added, "And some sandwiches. I'm sure her ladyship must be quite famished."

"Yes, my lady."

As Pierson strode off with a stiff gait that belied his befuddlement, Alexandra turned toward her aunt. "Aunt V, I must apologize for disturbing you at such a late hour, but I simply couldn't wait until morning."

"Oh? And why is that my dear? Come, let us go to the parlor and you can tell me all about it." Taking Alexandra by the arm, Virginia guided her toward a room that had been tastefully decorated in shades of muted greens and creams.

Alexandra spent the next half hour detailing to her aunt the particulars surrounding her relationship with Michael. "So you see, Aunt V," she finally concluded. "I'm in desperate need of your help."

Virginia responded with a small chuckle that eventually morphed into a warm smile. "You did the right thing in coming here, my dear. I'll be absolutely delighted to help you as long as you promise to follow through this time. I won't have you running off again, is that understood?"

"Perfectly," Alexandra laughed. "As long as you promise to do your very best to help me choose a gown that will make his lordship's eyes pop."

"Oh," Virginia winked. "By the time we are through, it will do much more than that, I can assure you."

"Aunt V!" Alexandra exclaimed, feigning surprise at her aunt's insinuation.

"Hush, dearie, and come sit next to me." Virginia patted a

spot beside her on the loveseat as she pulled a towering pile of fashion plates into her lap.

Alexandra scrutinized the pile as if it were a ten-foot high wall that she was suddenly expected to scale. "Perhaps, we ought to get some rest. It's late and there'll be plenty of time for this tomorrow."

"Rest?" Virginia's voice shrilled. "My dear girl, there's no time for rest. Why there's only a week until the ball. We have much too much ground to cover before then if you're to have the desired effect. No. One cannot face a battle lying down. Your dear papa will attest to that." She patted the space on the loveseat again. "Now come along."

Alexandra drew a heavy sigh and armored herself with all of the patience that she possessed as she took her seat beside her aunt.

Two hours later, they'd finally made their decision. "We shall visit the *modiste* in the morning to pick out fabrics and discuss the final cut," Virginia said, as she carefully sorted the illustrations into a series of neat piles, tying each together with a blue satin ribbon. Looking up, she eyed Alexandra carefully for a moment. "Are those the only clothes you brought?"

"No, I did bring one dress, though it may need some pressing after being rolled up in my saddlebag for the last few hours."

"Never mind." Virginia sounded much relieved. "One of the maids will see to that in the morning. I'm just glad I won't have to endure walking down Bond Street with you dressed like *that*."

Alexandra didn't take the least bit of offense to her aunt's comment. The woman was clearly uncomfortable by Alexandra's unconventional selection of clothes and as comfortable as those clothes might be, she had to recognize that they weren't for everyone. Her aunt was also a true lady in every sense of the word. She never wore as much as a single strand of hair out of place. Though she might not be above alluding to certain things that ladies weren't supposed to even think about, as she'd clearly demonstrated earlier that evening, she certainly wasn't about to invite unnecessary gossip of any kind.

The following day turned out to be more grueling and exhausting than anything else Alexandra had ever experienced before in her life. By the time they returned to Virginia's house in the late afternoon, she was positively sure that she'd require assistance in climbing the front steps. Her aunt on the other hand practically skipped up the steps like a bright young school girl, all the while chattering about all the things they'd accomplished thus far and everything else that still needed attending to. Alexandra groaned, grabbed hold of the banister and hauled herself upward by sheer determination before staggering inside the house. There she managed a meager three steps before collapsing onto a small bench that stood in the hallway.

"Whatever is the matter?" Virginia asked as if they'd merely taken a turn about the garden rather than cover every inch of Mayfair on foot.

"I'm positively exhausted and my feet are killing me," Alexandra gasped as she stared back at her aunt, half expecting the woman to do a pirouette or burst into song. She seemed to have more energy than a puppy.

"Not used to women's shoes I suspect." Virginia nodded as if she was fully aware of the difference between the comfort of men's boots and the painful contraptions that were presently blistering Alexandra's feet. "Not to worry, I'll ring for some tea and ask Pierson to bring up a footbath for you."

Fifteen minutes later, Alexandra found herself planted in a very comfortable chair, sipping tea and eating biscuits while her feet soaked in the heavenly warmth of lavender scented water.

"There's a letter here that appears to be from your father," Virginia announced as she leafed through a pile of correspondences that Pierson had brought her. "He says he's taken up residence in town and that he wishes to know if he ought to be expecting you."

Alexandra kept silent. She knew that her aunt would continue on with her own ideas on the topic at any moment and decided to wait before offering an opinion on the matter.

"I think you're better off here for the time being," Virginia said, folding back the letter. "That is of course if you would like to stay. I merely wish to let you know that you're more than welcome, and with everything still left to be done, it would be so much easier than traipsing back and forth between here and Grosvenor Square every day."

"It's just around the corner," Alexandra pointed out with a hint of a smile.

"Yes, I suppose it is, but—"

"Aunt V, I'd be happy to stay if Uncle Henry doesn't mind."

"Uncle Henry?" Virginia brushed the name aside as if she hadn't the faintest idea who that name belonged to. A bright smile shone upon her face. "What on earth does he have to say about the matter? You are my niece, and I have just invited you."

From that moment on, every waking hour of Alexandra's days turned into a frantic frenzy—a race against time, so to speak. People hurried in and out of the house—seamstresses, dance instructors, cobblers, maids, and milliners, all united in the common goal of turning a duckling into a swan.

Two days before the ball, Alexandra's gown arrived for the final fitting. It was made from the finest white Indian muslin, beautifully embroidered with little white flowers that flowed in a wide panel from the bustline to the hem. The fashionably low neckline was underlined by a wide satin ribbon that tied at the back in a voluminous bow and the sleeves puffed airily just below the shoulders. Over this, Alexandra intended to wear a robe of cream Egyptian silk that, since it did not close and was held together only with a ribbon, was designed to reveal the gown beneath. "Well?" Alexandra asked her aunt as she turned back and forth before the full length mirror. "What do you think?"

Virginia studied her niece for a few moments while Alexandra did her best to keep her enthusiasm under some measure of control. She knew that this was the sort of gown to draw attention and she wasn't too modest to recognize that she filled it out very nicely. "I think it suits you remarkably well," Virginia said. "But I also think we ought to lower the neckline."

"But it's already rather low . . ."

"Yes, but if you have the courage for it, I'd recommend removing another . . . shall we say quarter of an inch?"

"But my breasts will be practically spilling over the edge of it if we do that. I won't even dare breathe!"

"My dear," Virginia said quite seriously. "You're about to make your debut. You're no young miss anymore, so you'll want to make a dramatic statement. There's no harm in turning a few heads."

"Papa will most likely be horrified and my brothers . . ." Alexandra suddenly grinned. "When we were in Paris, we attended a ball at the Tuileries Palace. Ryan intended to keep me covered up all night and that dress was far less risqué than what you're proposing here."

"Take my advice, Alexandra. The man you desire will be there on Saturday. Let's get his heart pumping a little shall we?"

"Very well," Alexandra agreed with an impish smile.

"Wonderful!" Virginia clapped her hands together with glee. "And as for jewelry . . . I have just the thing." Crossing to a nearby table she picked up a velvet box and snapped open the lid. "These were your grandmothers. I think they'll add the perfect finishing touch."

"Oh, Aunt V!" Alexandra stared down at the pearl necklace and matching pearl drop earrings. "Thank you. Thank you so much. Yes, I think they'll be absolutely perfect."

"Good. Now let's get you out of this dress so the seamstresses can get back to work on it, and then we'll have some lunch while we talk about your hair. I have quite a few ideas on how we might best tame those curls without removing from the natural beauty they offer."

Alexandra grinned as she shook her head in surrender. "Of course, you do, Aunt V, I wouldn't have dared think otherwise."

CHAPTER TWENTY-FIVE

Flickering torches lined the steps of Willowbrook house as Lady Lindhurst's carriage drew up and the steps were set down. A handsomely dressed footman helped the ladies alight, bowing to Lord Lindhurst as he too emerged from the carriage. They were deliberately late of course. Virginia had strategically planned to be the last guests to arrive so that everyone might be present as her niece made her entrance.

Alexandra knew that there was no doubt in her aunt's mind that she would render even the most talkative ladies of the *ton* speechless this evening, and her unwavering support added to her confidence as she now stepped forward. She felt utterly divine in her gown and robe, which her aunt had remarked, brought out a pink hue to her creamy white skin. They'd solved the problem of her rioting curls with a couple of tortoise shell hair clips that seemed to work wonders for Alexandra's overall appearance.

"Go ahead, my dear," Virginia urged Alexandra. "We'll be right behind you."

Taking a deep breath as she glanced toward the stairs, Alexandra lifted the hem of her gown and began her ascent. When she reached the top, a footman asked for her name before leading her through to a grand staircase that descended into the ballroom. "Lady Alexandra Summersby," he announced in a voice that rose above the music and the murmur of the crowd.

Holding her head up high, Alexandra ignored the butterflies that had just been unleashed in her stomach. She moved forward instead.

A hush spread like wildfire through the masses as every single head without question turned toward her. Only the occasional whisper could be heard. She might as well have been standing there stark naked, she realized, because it was highly unlikely that she would ever feel more uncomfortable than she did at that very moment under the scrutiny of the *ton*. In truth, she wanted to turn and run, but instead, she straightened her back, slapped a smile on her face, placed her hand upon the banister and started down the stairs.

She hadn't gone down more than a couple of steps however, before she found herself surrounded. It seemed that every eligible bachelor in London and beyond was ready to assist in any number of ways imaginable. They all wanted to dance with her and each was equipped with more questions than the last so that Alexandra eventually gave up answering them altogether. It was quite dizzying really when in reality all she wanted to do was find Michael. "Perhaps a glass of lemonade," she finally suggested to no one in particular. And just like that, they were off to do her bidding. No doubt twenty glasses would turn up, but by then Alexandra hoped to have vanished into the crowd.

"Alex," a familiar voice sounded from just behind her right

shoulder. She turned her head to find William and Ryan both staring at her with roguish grins upon their faces. "For someone who hates the spotlight, you certainly have a way of making yourself noticed. You look stunning."

"Thank you, William." Alex paused, not wanting to appear too eager, but unable to help herself. "Have you seen Michael?"

"Yes, we spoke to him about half an hour ago. He introduced us to his parents and his sisters—all five of them."

"Summersby!" A tall and handsome gentleman strode up to them and placed a companionable hand on William's shoulder. "So good to see you again, old chap."

"Ah, Hamilton. It certainly has been a while."

"Indeed it has," Hamilton agreed as he glanced toward Alexandra. "Might I trouble you for an introduction?"

"Certainly. You remember Ryan of course."

"Of course." Hamilton nodded politely toward Ryan.

"And this is my sister, Lady Alexandra."

"Charmed," Hamilton crooned as he bent toward her in an elegant bow and lifted her gloved hand to meet his lips. "I was hoping to have the next dance if you'd grant me that favor."

Alexandra's lips pursed as if unsure of how to reply. Her eyes flittered past him to half a dozen gentlemen, all eagerly moving toward them as they did their best not to spill the lemonade they each carried—her lemonade. "I would be delighted," she heard herself say and was swiftly marched off in the direction of the dance floor.

"It's the waltz," Hamilton noted. "I take it you have permission to dance it?"

"Yes, of course." Aunt V had seen to it that every minor detail had been taken care of during the past week. It hadn't hurt that she was close friends with all of Almack's patronesses.

Placing her hand in Hamilton's as he placed his other hand against her waist, she couldn't help but think how odd it was that she'd never danced with Michael. He was the only man that she had any interest in dancing with and yet she always seemed to be dancing with complete strangers.

"You look ravishing this evening," Hamilton told her with a faint smile as he led her about the floor. He was a graceful dancer and seemed polite enough to allow Alexandra to relax a little.

"Thank you, sir. I did my best."

"Might I ask for *whom* you did your best?"

Looking up, she found herself staring into coal black eyes that held an almost frightening intensity. "I beg your pardon, but that's hardly your concern."

"Quite right," he told her after a moment's pause. "My apologies. It's just that when a woman of your beauty dresses so . . ." He leaned in close to her ear. "Provocatively . . . one has to wonder if she's looking for a bit of fun."

That did it. The man clearly hadn't a clue as to whom he was dealing with. Releasing her hold on her dance partner, Alexandra pulled back, placed both hands against Hamilton's chest and gave him the hardest shove she could manage. It caught him completely off guard and happened so swiftly that nobody else had a chance to see what actually happened. The effect however, was that Hamilton was instantly removed from Alexandra's immediate line of sight as he fell backward, arms flailing before landing with a thump at her feet. She stood over him for a moment afterward as she regarded the man who was now sitting on his bottom in the middle of the dance floor with a stunned expression upon his face. "I believe he must have slipped and lost his balance," she remarked to nobody in particular as she turned and walked away. "It seems the floor is quite wet."

Now where the blazes was Michael? She still hadn't caught the slightest glimpse of him. Surely, he must have seen her arrive. Perhaps he was avoiding her? The thought sent an immediate chill down her back. Considering how badly she'd treated him, he had every right.

"Alexandra!" She looked up to find Sir Percy beaming down at her. "What a lovely surprise. I'm so pleased to see you here. Might I add that you really do clean up rather well, my dear."

Alexandra grinned. "You don't look so bad yourself, you know."

"Still trying to charm me I take it?"

"You know I always am."

He laughed merrily at that before turning a bit more serious. "On a different note, I wanted to commend you for your fine work in Paris. Ashford told me everything in his report, and I must say I was quite impressed. You certainly lived up to my every expectation. In truth, I couldn't be more proud."

"That means a great deal to me. Thank you," she told him sincerely as she picked a glass of champagne from a tray that was just then passing by.

"And because of how well you did, I thought I'd take it upon myself to offer you a more permanent job within the agency. What do you say?"

"That's very generous of you, Sir Percy, but I'm not sure I can give you an answer just yet. I have a few loose ends to tie up first."

"Hm . . . I don't suppose any of those loose ends would have anything to do with Lord Trenton?" he asked with a wry smile.

"How did you—"

"Well, you tend to blush and get this distracted look upon your face whenever his name is mentioned. As for him . . . I do believe that during the two hours in which he and I spoke, only half an hour was spent discussing his assignment. The rest of it was used in singing your praises."

"Truly?"

"You have my word," he told her with a wink.

"Then if you'll please excuse me, I think I'd better go and see if I can find him."

Leaving Sir Percy behind, Alexandra headed back into the crowd. She hadn't made it far before she heard her name called once again and turned to look in the direction from which it had come. She saw her father, handsomely dressed in black evening attire and waving for her to join him. "May I present your hosts, the Duke and Duchess of Willowbrook?" he asked as she sidled up next to him.

"Your Graces," Alexandra replied in greeting as she presented the lord and lady before her with a graceful curtsey. "It is indeed a pleasure. Thank you so much for inviting us."

"Thomas," Bryce said, addressing the duke in the informal

manner that spoke of many years of friendship. "This is my daughter, Alexandra."

"Well then," Thomas exclaimed as he studied Alexandra with much interest. "The pleasure is entirely ours. We've heard a great deal about how you aided our son in his very important assignment. Indeed, Wellington himself has told me he'd undoubtedly have lost the battle if it hadn't been for all of you."

Alexandra cringed inwardly. Just how much did they know exactly? Well, she supposed that if they were aware of just how cruelly she'd treated their son's heart, she very likely wouldn't be standing there before them right now. "I did what I could to be of assistance. It was no more than anyone else might have done."

"Oh, come now, my dear, you mustn't be so modest," the duchess chided her. "Michael has done nothing but recommend you for your excellent swordsmanship."

"Perhaps you ought to give my daughters some lessons," the duke added. I've always considered it useful for a woman to be able to defend herself. London's hardly getting any safer. I should find it quite reassuring if they could at least fire a pistol with some degree of accuracy."

Alexandra's eyes lit up instantly with the prospect of imparting her skills on others. "I should be delighted to teach them," she said.

"Thomas, I never knew you were quite so liberal in your thinking," Bryce told his friend with an honest smile.

"No? I would have to be to marry a woman like Isabella." He cast an adoring look at his duchess. "She was quite the willful little devil in her youth. I've seen her fight a bull, you know—not the sort of thing we like to discuss in polite conversation, but you are certainly the sort of friends who might appreciate such a tale."

"Thomas, really . . ." Isabella admonished.

"Now who's being modest? You should have seen her—dark hair streaming out behind her as she faced the beast without a single sign of fear upon her face. She was beautiful, strong, and undefeatable. I do believe I lost my heart to her that very moment."

It was Isabella's turn to blush.

"That's quite remarkable, Your Grace," Alexandra said with much admiration. "Ashford never mentioned it."

"Oh, I don't believe he even knows about it—he's not the sort of man who'd approve of his mother having done such things."

Alexandra grinned. "I believe you're right about that. Well, your secret's safe with me."

Isabella offered Alexandra her arm. "Would you be kind enough to walk with me?" she asked. "You don't mind, do you gentlemen?"

"Not at all, my dear," Thomas replied as he leaned closer to Bryce and whispered something incoherent in his ear. They both chuckled as the women walked away.

"What Thomas doesn't seem to realize," Isabella remarked when they were safely out of earshot. "Is that bullfighting's quite a commonplace thing where I come from. It's true that women don't usually participate in the sport, but I insisted on being taught, and my papa eventually indulged me."

"I must say that you and I appear to have quite a lot in common, Your Grace," Alexandra ventured.

"Please, my dear, you must call me Isabella."

Alexandra nodded in response to that and they walked on for a while in silence, regarding all the guests and admiring the various gowns.

"My son's a great admirer of yours, you know," Isabella suddenly said. "To the point where one cannot help but wonder if there are other feelings at play."

Alexandra felt slightly uncomfortable at that statement. She liked the duchess a great deal and wished to be friends with her—she did not want to lie to her. "I'm afraid I may have wounded him deeply."

"Ah, so I'm correct then. Do you mind if I speak plainly?"

"Indeed, I would encourage you to do so."

"Well then, it's my impression that you're just the sort of woman who would make an excellent wife for Michael. I wish for you to know that you have my blessing and my support, should the two of you decide to marry."

"And you know this from speaking to me for a mere five minutes?" Alexandra asked with a significant amount of shock.

"Of course, I know a great deal of you from Michael, but yes, I know my son and what his needs might be in a life companion. You fit the type so extraordinarily well."

"Really?"

"Really. Listen to me. Michael needs someone with whom to spar, so to speak. He needs a wife who'll not only speak her mind but also who'll be brutally honest with him. He needs not only a challenge but an intelligent and adventurous woman or he'll tire of the marriage in no time. Now, if you've wounded him as deeply as you say, then your reason for coming here this evening and having to face him can only mean you're ready for the chase."

"You are correct." Alexandra admitted. "I've come because I've realized how wrong I was to run from him. I love him more than I would ever have imagined loving anyone."

"Then by all means," Isabella told her gently and with a warm smile. "Don't let me keep you at my side. You must go and find his lordship immediately so that all may be resolved."

Taking her leave of the duchess, Alexandra began winding her way through the crowd in search of Michael. Without any luck, she eventually decided to get a breath of fresh air before diving back in. Four sets of French doors stood open, and the cool breeze beckoned for her to abandon the heated ballroom.

She'd taken no more than a couple of steps before she saw him standing before her. He was just as handsome as she remembered him, if not more so, but then her eyes registered someone else—a beautiful dark haired woman whom he held firmly in his embrace. "You know, I love you right?" the woman said, just as Michael replied, "I love you too."

Alexandra's world came to a screeching halt. Her mouth fell open in order to scream or shout or say something . . . but no words would come. And her feet remained frozen to the ground. She wanted to run as fast as her feet would carry her, but she could not move. This had to be her worst nightmare come to life—worse even than Ryan catching her with her hand in the proverbial cookie jar.

Michael had seen Alexandra arrive about an hour earlier, but had chosen to stay back for a number of reasons. For the past week, he'd been hoping she'd take the bait and come to him. After all, she'd never attended a seasonal ball before, so what reason would she possibly have for attending this one that happened to be hosted by his parents, unless it was to see him? She knew he would be there, and she had come. Nothing made him happier, and nothing filled him with more hope than when she'd finally made her entrance. Of course, he'd been a nervous wreck by then, because of how late she'd been, but when he finally saw her . . . oh how he longed to wrap her in his arms, to whisper words of endearment in her ear and to kiss those kissable lips.

But then he'd seen the eager men rushing to her side, and he'd restrained himself. Alexandra had never had any gentlemen callers or admirers before, she'd never been appreciated by men for her beauty . . . surely it wouldn't hurt to allow her to bask in all the attention a little. And if she did choose to push them all aside in favor of him then . . . well . . . it could only mean that she really loved him, couldn't it?

So he'd found himself a glass of champagne and ventured out onto the terrace only to find his sister, Cassandra, crying quietly to herself in a corner. "Cass?" he'd asked as he'd carefully approached her. "Whatever is the matter?"

"Oh, Michael, it's no use. I don't believe I'll ever marry. You'll see. I shall wind up an old spinster—the kind aunt who likes to read or embroider and always takes her naps at ten."

He offered her his handkerchief and put his arm around

her shoulders for comfort. "Surely it won't come to that, Cass."

That had apparently been the key to opening the flood gates. Between sobs his sister had told him how she'd fallen hopelessly in love with Lord Barton and how sure she'd been that he would one day return her affection. She delivered a long list of examples to this effect until she eventually hit upon the very heart of the matter. It seemed that Lord Barton had just proposed to Lady Jayne Greaves. Well, if this wasn't a pickle, then Michael wasn't sure what was.

Pulling his sister into his arms, he did the only thing he thought might help. He offered comfort.

"Oh, Michael," she told him after all the tears had dried away. "You truly are the best brother in the whole wide world. You know I love you right?"

"I love you too," he'd said.

And that was when he'd spotted Alexandra.

If looks could kill, then Michael was just about to be obliterated. Alexandra was practically foaming at the mouth, eyes blazing with an overwhelming amount of fury.

He quickly distanced himself from his sister and took a tentative step toward Alexandra. "It's not what you think, Alex," he said as he held up his hands as if hoping to somehow placate her.

"Oh, is this her, Michael?" Cassandra's voice rang out in the night and Michael instantly winced. Of all the times to ask the most damning of questions.

"Ah," Alexandra sneered as she cast a vehement look in Cassandra's direction. "So you've been discussing me. How very cozy."

"Alex, I'd like to present my—"

"Stop Michael," she snapped. "Please stop." The last word came out shakily, and Michael saw that she was trembling. She was clearly close to hysterics.

"Damn," she cried. "Now look what you've done. You and your . . . your little Cyprian."

"Good heavens," Cassandra exclaimed. "She certainly has quite a mouth on her."

"Shut up before I challenge you," Alexandra screeched.

"Challenge me?" Cassandra's eyes opened wide. "To a duel? Dear me, she can't be serious, Michael."

"Alex, that's enough," Michael all but shouted. "You're jumping to conclusions and making a fool out of yourself in the process."

"Really?" Alex's voice was filled with sarcasm as she raised a mocking eyebrow. "So this woman is not your lover?"

"Good God no," Michael exclaimed in a horrified tone of voice. He cleared his throat before turning and gesturing for Cassandra to come forward. "This, Alex, is Cassandra my sister."

Alexandra paled. Her eyes seemed to flicker back and forth between the two siblings, as if she was trying to compare them. Michael knew they looked similar, and as he watched Alexandra's eyes widen, he realized that she finally saw it too. With a mortified groan, she buried her face in her hands and muttered a muted "I'm so sorry." She remained thus, apparently not daring to look at either one of them.

"Cass, would you please give us a minute?" Michael implored.

Giving her brother a reassuring smile, Cassandra hurried

back inside. Michael moved closer to Alexandra. "Look at me," he said as he reached for her hands and removed them from her face. He nudged her head upward with his fingers until she was looking him straight in the eye. That old familiar sense of desire, that only she was capable of evoking, stirred to life in his belly. She looked dazzling even now, with her eyes all puffy from crying and her lips quivering with remorse. "Come. Let's take a walk in the garden. I think it's time that you and I talked."

Chapter Twenty-Six

As if in a daze, Alexandra nodded, linked her arm with Michael's and allowed him to guide her away from the terrace and toward the darkness. "Won't this be frowned upon?" she asked as the music faded behind them. "Our being alone like this . . . unchaperoned . . . in the dark?"

"If someone sees us, then yes, it will." He tightened his grip on her. "But you've never been one to pay much heed to what other people might consider inappropriate have you?"

"No," she agreed. "I haven't. But I wouldn't want my aunt or my father to be affected by any sort of scandal I might cause."

"Alex, I'm quite confident that by the time we return to the ballroom, any chance of a possible scandal occurring as a result of our being alone together, will be made null by what we're about to discuss." He sensed her hesitation and paused for a moment before pushing for what he wanted to hear. When she gave a slight nod, he continued. "Now then, would you please tell me why you, who never attend any balls whatsoever, have decided to come this evening?"

The darkness was almost complete as they continued to walk to the sound of gravel crunching beneath their feet. The air was pleasantly warm and filled with the sweet scent of honeysuckle. From somewhere nearby, Michael could hear a few lonesome frogs croaking while a group of cicadas were happily strumming a tune.

"Well," she said, averting her gaze as if to admire something or other that they happened to be passing, though, he couldn't imagine what that something might be—it was too dark to see anything. "Your parents invited us and as it happens, my papa and yours are quite good friends."

"That doesn't really answer my question though, does it?" he teased. "You see, I have it on good authority that you're not interested in marriage, but then . . . based on that daring gown of yours, I can't help but wonder if there might not be a gentleman whose interest you're vying for? Or perhaps, I am mistaken, and you seek to take a lover?"

She didn't answer, but he could practically see the steam coming out of her ears, no matter how dark it was. He held back a chuckle and wondered how long it would take for her to tell him why she'd really come.

"No," he continued in a lighthearted manner. "You don't strike me as the sort of lady who would entertain a lover."

"Really? Because that's exactly the sort of woman Lord Hamilton took me to be."

"And I suppose he was sufficiently punished for his inaccuracy?"

"He took a spill upon the dance floor."

"Did he indeed?" Michael grinned. "I'm sorry I wasn't there to see it. He's not usually the sort of man who takes to offending young ladies. I'm surprised he made the attempt with you."

"Well, I can only hope it will be his last attempt. He did appear to be a touch humiliated when I left him there."

"Hm . . . So if you didn't come in search of a potential lover, then I'm left with only one assumption. I do believe you must be in love. Am I correct?"

He felt her stiffen beside him just as a small gasp escaped her lips. Ah yes, he'd finally struck a chord. "Is it possible? Are you in love, Lady Alexandra?"

"I . . . I . . ." Alexandra stammered, trying desperately to free her arm. So she could run back to the safety of the ballroom perhaps? Michael held her firmly in place.

"Would it help if the gentleman you're in love with were to confess that he's undeniably and madly in love with you too?"

"I . . . maybe," she finally managed to say. He couldn't be. Could he?

Before there was time for any further consideration, Michael's lips came crashing down on hers, the warm heat of him wrapping itself around her. Her lips parted of their own accord and the moist warmth of his tongue, as it filled her, sent her heart racing in seconds. "I love you, Alex," he murmured against her neck as he trailed scorching kisses over her. "I love you with a desperation I can't quite begin to fathom, and I assure you I'll never stop doing so."

Clinging to him, her nails dug roughly against his back as he nibbled lightly on her earlobe. How could she ever have thought to deny herself this? "Michael," she murmured while a tingling heat flowed down her spine. "I want you . . . I need you . . . I . . ." She needed to say what was in her heart. As much as it frightened her, she owed it to him to be honest. "I love you, Michael. I love you so terribly much."

A small murmur of pleasure erupted in the back of his throat at the sound of those words. "I love you too," he whispered against her ear. She pulled him closer, reveling in the knowledge that he felt as strongly for her as she did for him. Her heart swelled with instant happiness until she thought it might burst with joy.

Taking her hand, Michael pulled her along with him, stepping between rows of bushes until they reached a large oak tree. He leaned her carefully against the trunk of the tree, his hands placed on either side of her as he bent his head toward her.

Her breath was ragged with passion as she waited expectantly for him to make his move.

"Say it again," he told her as he ran a finger along the edge of her neckline and felt her flutter.

"I love you," she whispered.

"And?" He dipped his finger between her breasts. She drew a tight breath. He wasn't going to make this easy for her she realized, but she could hardly fault him for that. After all, she was the one who'd backed out of their proposal, not him.

"I know I've treated you unfairly, Michael, but I was so scared . . . I still am, but perhaps . . . I was hoping you might help me overcome it. Please, Michael, I need you more than I've ever needed anything or anyone else before in my life, and as terrified as that makes me, I can't turn my back on it. I want you by my side for the rest of my life, Michael.

"Will you marry me? Please?" She could feel her heart hammering against her chest as they stood there, but all she could do was wait.

"Why, Lady Alexandra," he placed a kiss against her cheek. "I thought you'd never ask."

"Is that a yes?" she asked with a note of desperation in her voice.

"Indeed, it is," he replied as he lowered his lips to kiss the swell of her breasts. She responded with a soft sigh as she arched against him, encouraging him to take more. The movement forced her breasts to rise, producing a hard outline of her perky nipples as they pressed against her gown. His desire for her was evident in every part of his being—his eyes, his touch . . . his arousal, which seemed to be growing increasingly hard with need.

Pushing her neckline down, he bent his head to her nipples. Nothing in the world could have stopped the gasp that escaped her lips at the feel of his tongue teasing its way around each bud, or his teeth tugging them gently a moment later. She moaned her response.

Desperate hands pulled and tugged until her skirts were up around her waist and the front of his breeches had come undone, freeing the whole length of him. He ground himself against her, and she reveled in the erotic feel. "More," she whispered.

Responding to her wishes, he stroked a finger between her thighs. Heaven help her—she might just burst into flames. "You're so very, very"—he dipped a finger inside her, and she almost buckled—"wet, Alex."

"For you, Michael," she breathed. "Only for you."

Without another moment's pause, he removed his finger and pushed himself inside her, gripping her buttocks and thrusting against her as if his life depended on it. There was nothing gentle about their coupling this time—they both had too much built up passion for the patience and restraint that such a mating would require.

Instead, they felt the wave of pleasure crash over them with a mightier force than ever before. For moments on end, they soared together among the stars, completely sated and joined, in the sparkling sensations their love had wrought.

They stood for a long moment afterward, just wrapped in a tight embrace, enjoying the closeness. "I'd better help you adjust your gown," Michael grinned after a while as he eased himself away from her.

"Do you think I might be pregnant yet?" Alexandra suddenly asked as she pushed her breasts back inside her dress and tugged her bodice back in place.

"I suppose you might be," he answered hesitantly. "Would that worry you?"

"No, not at all. I long to have your children. I was merely wondering what a child of ours might look like, that's all."

"I suppose that he, or she, shall be very handsome indeed."

She smiled at that. "That will be very true as long as the boys take after their father and the girls after their mother."

"If the girls take after their mother," Michael mused. "Then I fear the lads of tomorrow will have their work cut out for them."

"And is that such a bad thing?" Alexandra asked as she smoothed away the wrinkles in her skirts.

"Not at all, my dear," he said, kissing the top of her head. "They'll soon discover that it's well worth it."

They looked at each other for a long moment, both incredulous that it was possible to feel as much happiness as they suddenly felt just then. It was overwhelming. "Shall we go back to the house and announce our engagement?" he asked as he took her hand in his and placed an endearing kiss upon her knuckles. "Or would you rather keep it as our own little secret for the present?"

"I'm not much prone to the idea of torturing people, you know," Alexandra told him seriously. "And I do believe your mother and my father might soon expire from the anticipation of it all."

"Then we ought not keep them in suspense," Michael remarked. He offered her his arm. "Shall we?"

"Indeed we shall," she replied.

They were just climbing the steps to the terrace when they heard a couple of familiar voices talking to each other. It was Ryan and William who were practically hanging over the railing to get a better look at Alexandra and Michael as they made their approach. "Good heavens, where have you two been off to?" Ryan asked.

"You'd better not let Papa catch you looking like that, Alex," William laughed. "Do you know you have leaves sticking out of your hair? And your gown . . . well, all I can say is that you two had better be getting married since you've clearly been up to no good. Oh look, here comes Papa right now."

Alexandra froze as she stepped onto the terrace. Not only was her father making his approach but he was also bringing the Duke and Duchess of Willowbrook as well as Aunt V and Uncle Henry along with him. She grasped hold of Michael's arm as if he was a lifeboat about to rescue her from drowning. "Do I really look as bad as William says I do?" she asked Michael quietly.

"Not at all," he said, plucking a bit of grass from her dress. God only knew how that had gotten there.

"Ah, my dear, there you are," Bryce remarked as he walked up to her, his brow furrowing disapprovingly as he took in her overall appearance. "I dare not even begin to guess why you suddenly look so . . . tousled." His gaze went to Michael. "I hope this isn't your doing, Ashford."

"If I were you, Papa, I would certainly hope it *is* his doing," Ryan said. "For if it's not, I'm quite confident you'd like that even less."

"When the devil did you become so mouthy, Ryan?" Bryce growled while Virginia appeared to try desperately and quite unsuccessfully to hide a smile. Alexandra hoped she'd just tripped on the stairs, hit her head and was presently having what could only be considered a nightmare—from which she would soon awaken to find herself still engaged to Michael, but without the judgmental stares of her entire family hanging over her.

"Well? What have you to say for yourself, Alex? Really, you've gone too far this time. Every single person of the slightest importance is here tonight and yet you insist on causing a stir, not only with what you're wearing, but—"

"Sir—"

Michael started to say.

"And I'm sure it was a shock for you when Alexandra said no to your proposal, though I have since learned of her reasons for doing so. But really, to . . . to run off between the bushes when someone might happen upon you at any given moment . . . scandal would be too mild a word to describe such a catastrophe and—"

"I'm sorry, but I really must interrupt," Michael quickly cut in. "I don't intend to be rude, Lord Moorland, but before you go any further, I was hoping you might all be able to congratulate us. We're finally engaged and wish to be married as soon as it can be arranged."

A deafening silence followed.

"Well why the devil didn't you say so sooner?" Bryce suddenly exclaimed.

"I don't believe he was able to get a single word in edgewise, Papa," Alexandra muttered.

"Oh come here, sweetheart," Bryce said as he stepped toward his daughter with open arms, his eyes misting over with tears. He hugged her tightly against him. "I wish you a lifetime of happiness together, Alex. I know you've made the right choice for yourself, and I truly couldn't be happier for you."

"Thank you, Papa," Alexandra sniffed as she wiped at her own eyes.

"Take good care of her, Michael," Bryce added as he shook Michael's hand. "We'll be keeping an eye on you."

Michael grinned. "I have no doubt that you will, my lord."

A string of good wishes followed from the duke and duchess, Alexandra's aunt and uncle, and finally from Ryan and William. When they eventually decided to go back inside after making Alexandra a bit more presentable, Michael put his arm about her, holding her close. "Now, we just have to find my sisters," he grinned as his hand slipped down to grip her hand.

"All five of them I suppose?"

"Yes, my dear, you'd better arm yourself with patience because I do fear we'll be here all night."

"Michael?" Isabella suddenly asked, holding him and Alex back for a moment.

"You said you wish to marry quickly . . . is there . . . ?" her meaning was unmistakable of course, and Alexandra felt herself blush for the hundredth time that evening.

"We don't know, Mama, but we thought it best to play it safe," he replied.

"Yes . . . I see your point," she murmured though she did not sound the least bit surprised. "Well then, we'd best get started right away."

With a helpless look of desperation at Michael, Alexandra found herself hauled away by his mother to discuss the very last thing she wished to talk about at that very moment—her wedding dress, the cake, the invitations, the guest list, and just about a thousand other things that seemed to play a vital role in a society wedding. Alexandra could do nothing but take it in stride. She would gladly sit through endless days of fashion plates and fittings if she could only marry the one man who had managed to capture her heart.

Epilogue

Whickham Hall
October 10, 1825

Alexandra waited anxiously for Michael to return from London. He should have been back three days ago, but there was still no sign of him. Logical reasoning told her that any number of things might have happened to delay his return, yet she could not stop herself from fretting over his safety.

He had gone to see Sir Percy with the sole purpose of discussing his retirement from The Foreign Office. Since their marriage ten years ago, he had engaged in no less than fifteen assignments. Most of those had consisted of nothing more than delivering important messages to foreign dignitaries abroad, but they had still kept him away from home too long for comfort.

Alexandra had been unable to accompany him on a single one of these trips, no matter how much they had both wished it. Eight months after their wedding, she had given birth to their firstborn child—a boy whom they had christened Richard. Three more children had followed after him—a daughter named Claire and then two more boys named Andrew and Henry. Needless to say, Alexandra had enough on her plate to keep her busy with four children vying for her attention.

She loved it though—the joyous sound of their voices ringing throughout the house as they played hide and seek or chased each other around the long dining room table. She understood now what her mother had meant when she'd told her that she'd accomplished everything that she'd ever desired in life. She also knew how empty and meaningless her life would have been without her husband and her children about her, and she was glad that her father had made her see reason.

Still, she could not help but worry as she walked over to the lead paned windows and looked out over the fields once more. Why wasn't he back yet?

Perhaps, I ought to go and check up on my students.

It would at least serve to distract her from the long list of tragic incidents that might have befallen her husband and that was presently being compiled at the back of her mind, entirely against her own will. Throwing a heavy woolen shawl over her shoulders, she headed out of the library, just as the front door crashed open with a thunderous bang.

"Where's my little hoyden?" A loud voice bellowed.

Alexandra squealed with delight as her heart leaped into her mouth, her stomach fluttering with nervous energy as she raced down the corridor and straight into Michael's open arms. "You scoundrel!" she chided, punching a fist against his chest as she looked up at him with a smile that still told of her troubled state of mind. "What on earth took you so long? I thought something terrible might have happened to you. After all, you only went to London—there's hardly any reason for you to be late, or at the very least not to send a letter to inform me you'd be arriving later than expected."

"I know, my dear," he agreed, lowering his head to kiss her forehead. He drew her against him in an attempt to soothe her, and there was an intimacy about the moment—about knowing that he understood her well enough to realize that she must have driven herself half mad with worry. "I'm so sorry. I was called upon to perform one last task—a matter of some delicacy which required my complete discretion. I remained at Carlton House until the issue was resolved."

"Would you perhaps be able to tell me why?"

"I'm sworn to secrecy, my dear, but I can tell you a young lady of questionable birth and desperate circumstances was involved. I tell you this not only because you are my wife, and I know I can trust you implicitly, but also because you have that look in your eyes that tells me I'm in a great deal of trouble. Do you think you might forgive me?"

"I do believe I might. If you kiss me." Alexandra grinned as she looked up into those wonderfully dark eyes of his.

"My dear woman, nothing in the world would give me more pleasure." Their lips touched and that old familiar heat filled them both as they reveled in each other's closeness. It was a tender kiss that spoke of all the years in which they'd loved each other and of all the years that they still hoped to share, wrapped in each other's arms. When they finally pulled apart, the strength of their emotion was deeply etched in their eyes.

"Come," Alexandra told him as she took his hand in hers. "I was just about to visit with my students when you arrived. Now that you're here, I thought you might like to join me. They've made a lot of progress during your absence."

Michael grinned. "Yes, I can imagine they would have under your tutelage."

Stepping out into the courtyard, they both watched as teams of young girls sparred with one another, some more proficient with their swords than others. Alexandra noted that Michael's gaze went quickly to his daughter, Claire. His face brightened with a crooked smile. "Oh Alex," he muttered as he put his arm around her shoulders and pulled her against him. "There's so much of you in her. It's absolutely remarkable to watch."

Alexandra followed his line of vision until her gaze settled upon her daughter. "Yes, she's only eight and yet it seems like this is precisely what she was born to do."

"Well, of course it is. She's your daughter. What did you expect? That she'd be a bluestocking?"

Alexandra couldn't help but laugh. "I suppose not," she admitted. "I'm so proud of her you know, though she'll undoubtedly give some unfortunate man a run for his money."

"Ah, you are mistaken, my dear. He'll be the most fortunate of men, he who manages to win her heart. I only hope she'll manage to find a man as handsome and charming as I am. We're quite rare you know."

"Yes, I know," Alexandra replied, unable to help a smile.

"But hopefully, she won't have to join The Foreign Office in order to meet him."

"Oh? Would you be against that by any chance?"

"Well, of course, I would!" Alexandra exclaimed. "It's much too dangerous."

Michael laughed as he draped his arm about her shoulders. "Then I predict we must prepare for open war within these very walls. I tell you, Alex, she won't allow you to have your way forever. Mark my words."

"We'll just have to see about that," Alexandra smirked as she leaned her head against his shoulder.

They stood quietly for a while in a comfortable silence as they turned their attention to Richard who had happily joined in the lesson, even though his partner did happen to be a young girl of nine years of age. Andrew and Henry were still too young to attend, though Andrew eagerly chased his nurse around the nursery with a wooden sword that his father had once made for him.

"Are you happy?" Michael suddenly asked.

"Absolutely."

"So you're glad you gave up spinsterhood in favor of all this?"

Alexandra chuckled. "I wouldn't have it any other way, my lord."

"Then you admit that I was right and you were wrong?"

Alexandra raised a haughty eyebrow. "Are you trying to goad me into a duel?"

"Never," Michael gasped with exaggerated horror.

"Well, I fear you've managed to do so all the same. And

before you get any ideas into that arrogant head of yours, it's for *you* I fear, not I."

"That goes without saying," he quipped.

Holding out his arm for her, he gave her that dazzling smile of his—the very one that always made her heart quicken and her knees weaken. "Shall we show them how it's done?"

"We certainly shall, my lord. We certainly shall."

Acknowledgments

A special thank you to my good friends Monika, Vicky, Laura, and Ida who patiently critiqued my first draft—your advice and insight have been invaluable.

Like last time, my editor Esi excelled—this novel wouldn't be what it is today without her help.

And to all of my lovely readers out there—thank you!

Loved LADY ALEXANDRA'S
EXCELLENT ADVENTURE?
Here's an exclusive peek
at the next book in the Summersby series,
available Fall 2012.

Then keep reading
for an excerpt from Sophie Barnes's
amazing first novel,
**HOW MISS RUTHERFORD
GOT HER GROOVE BACK.**

An Excerpt from

THE NEXT SUMMERSBY TALE

CHAPTER ONE

London 1816

Mary stared in disbelief at the thin little man who sat across from her at the heavy mahogany desk. His hair had receded well beyond his ears and his face was pinched. His eyes, lacking any definition due to his pale eyelashes, were set on either side of a nose that would have been perfect, had it not been for a slight bump upon the bridge.

Mary watched quietly as he adjusted his spectacles for the hundredth time. She then posed the only reasonable question that she could think to ask. "Are you quite certain that an error of monumental proportions has not been made, Mr. Browne?"

In response to her question, Mr. Browne nodded so profusely that Mary couldn't help but envision his head suddenly popping off his neck and bouncing across the Persian carpet that lay stretched out upon the floor. She stifled a smirk to the best of her abilities, but feared that her eyes betrayed her. In any event, Mr. Browne did not look pleased.

"Quite certain, your ladyship. Indeed, your father was very adamant about his wishes, and as you can see for yourself," he added, handing her the final amendment to John Croyden's will. "He made certain that there would be no doubt about his intentions. Indeed, it's really quite plain to see."

"So it is," Mary muttered, still unsure of how to respond to the enormity of what her father's lawyer had just told her. She leafed through the crisp white pages of her father's last wishes, before pausing at the one that bewildered her the most. There, right before her very eyes, was a petition, made by her father and signed by none other than The Prince Regent himself. Her gloved fingers traced the outline of the royal insignia as she read the request—that John Croyden's daughter Mary be made his sole heir and a peeress in her own right, inheriting all of her father's worldly goods, including his title.

His title?

Half an hour ago, Mary hadn't even known that he had one. She'd grown up in a modest house in Holborn, which had also served as her father's medical practice until she was old enough to accompany him on his never-ending travels; his constant companion in his thirst for knowledge. Still, they'd kept that two-story house with its much too low ceilings and worm-eaten beams, returning to it whenever they happened to be passing through. It was home to her somehow, and yet, here she was now, sitting in a lawyer's office, smack in the middle of Mayfair. A part of her wanted to jump up and down with delight, while another, much stronger part, wanted to scream at her father for lying to her all of these years. She let out a deep sigh of frustration before biting down on her lower lip. "You mentioned my father's title," she said, rustling the pages of the will as she leafed through them. "But, I don't see it mentioned anywhere, other than in the petition. Which title did he hold, if you don't mind my asking?"

Mr. Browne looked momentarily startled. "Why, he was a marquess, my lady—of Steepleton, to be precise."

Mary gave Mr. Browne a blank stare. "And that would make me what exactly?"

A couple of creases appeared on Mr. Browne's forehead from out of nowhere. Clearly he wasn't accustomed to explaining the ranks of nobility to the daughters of his clients. He adjusted his spectacles once more. "It makes you a marchioness, my lady—not quite as prestigious a title as that of duchess perhaps, but more esteemed than that of countess, to be sure."

"I see," Mary said, though it was quite obvious she didn't see at all. She'd never had the slightest interest in the nobility, least of all in understanding what titles outranked others.

Mr. Browne coughed slightly into his fist as if he hoped to somehow fill the silence that followed. "Shall we discuss the financial aspects of the will?" he eventually asked as he leaned forward to rest his folded arms upon the desk.

Mary's head snapped to attention at that question. "What financial aspects? My father was a man who made an honest living as a physician and later on as a surgeon. He had a respectable income, but he was by no means wealthy. Even so, he did his best to set aside whatever he could for me, and I have legal rights to those funds. If you're about to suggest otherwise, then I promise you I will contest it in a court of law. Other than that, I don't quite see what—"

"No, it is becoming increasingly clear to me that you obviously do not," Mr. Browne blurted out.

Mary's eyes widened with astonishment. She was momentarily taken aback by his remark, but quickly recovered, noting that he too seemed rather shocked. She said nothing however, but merely watched as he leaned back in his chair and drew a deep breath.

"Lady Steepleton, I am not suggesting that you must forfeit any of the money that your father left you." He spoke in a measured tone that told of more patience than he truly possessed. "I'm merely trying to inform you, that your inheritance is substantially larger than you believe it to be."

"How much larger?" Mary asked with a great deal of caution as she shifted uneasily in her seat. Her face was plain beneath her auburn colored hair, which was pulled back into a tight knot—a style she'd stubbornly adopted for the past ten years. Her chestnut colored eyes seemed unusually large for a woman of her size. Not that she was particularly small, but she would quite easily be considered petite. Thankfully, she'd been blessed with a flawless nose, though her lips were much too full for her own liking. However, she wasn't unpleasant to look at by any means, although her drab mourning clothes didn't exactly bring out the best in her.

Twisting the coarse graphite colored cotton of her dress between her fingers, she waited solemnly for Mr. Browne to continue.

"Lady Steepleton, your late father has left you with a sum of no less than fifty thousand pounds," Mr. Browne announced, in a manner that might suggest that he himself was somehow personally responsible for her dramatic increase in wealth. "He has also left you with a very comfortable house on Brook Street, not to mention Steepleton House in Northamptonshire, which I gather is a very large estate indeed. Suffice it to say, you are now a very affluent woman, Lady Steepleton."

Mary simply gaped at the man as if he'd sprouted a second head, a pair of horns, or perhaps even both. Her mouth had fallen open at the mention of the fifty thousand pounds, but by the time Mr. Browne was finished, her eyes seemed quite compelled to leap out of their sockets at any given moment. "You must be joking," she stammered, for want of anything better to say.

"I assure you that I am *not*," Mr. Browne told her in a tone that conveyed just how offended he was by her suggestion that he might actually consider joking about such a thing. "I take this matter quite seriously, and as you can see for yourself, it is really quite plain—"

"To see," Mary finished with a lengthy sigh as she stared down at the last page in the stack of papers Mr. Browne had given her. Sure enough, there was the indisputable bank statement valuing her father's assets at just over fifty thousand pounds, including a brief mention of his properties. At the very bottom of the page, was a quickly scrawled note, identifying the members of staff whom were currently employed at the two locations.

Mary shook her head in quiet bewilderment. "Could I perhaps trouble you for a glass of water?" she asked as she sank back against her chair, her mind buzzing with an endless amount of questions that would in all likelihood never be answered. "Or better yet—make that a brandy."

At that exact same moment, a landau rolled past Mr. Browne's office, swaying gently from side to side before taking a sharp turn onto Duke Street. It continued on to Grosvenor Square where it slowed to a steadier pace before finally coming to a complete halt outside a white brick town house that was separated from the pavement by a black wrought iron fence. The coachman stepped down from his seat, hurrying around to the side to open the carriage door and set down the steps with speedy efficiency. A moment later, Ryan Summersby appeared, his dark blonde hair brightening as the sun cast its rays upon his head. His eyes were as blue as a tropical lagoon; pools sparkling with the promise of boyish mischief. His nose was well defined, set above a pair of lips that edged slightly upward at one corner to form the beginnings of a crooked smile. The jawline was chiseled, the cheekbones solid, and if one were to take a moment to tear one's eyes away from the beauty of his face, one might be struck breathless by the width of his shoulders. Indeed, Ryan Summersby had an exquisitely masculine body, yet he alighted with remarkable grace and ease for a man of his height. After all, he did measure an astonishing six feet and five inches.

"Welcome home, my lord," Hutchins remarked as he reached for Ryan's bags. The aging butler, who'd been with the Summersby's since Ryan's older brother William had been born, still maintained a youthful spring to his step.

"Thank you. It's good to be back," Ryan said as he started up the front steps of his father's London home. "Has Papa arrived yet?"

"No, not yet, but he should be here no later than tomorrow evening. He's just tying up a few loose ends back at Moorland—the usual business when he's planning on remaining in town for an extended amount of time," Hutchins replied. "And your brother will most likely be unable to join you before next week at the earliest. He was recently called away on an urgent assignment which I believe has taken him to Scotland. But there's a guest waiting for you in the drawing room. I won't say who, as I've no desire to spoil the surprise, though I'll wager you won't be too disappointed."

Ryan eyed the butler with a large degree of suspicion as he peeled off his calf-skin gloves and handed them to him together with his hat. "What are you up to, old chap?"

"Oh, nothing but the usual," Hutchins told him, his face completely lacking any kind of emotion. Still, there was a twinkle in his wise old eyes. "Just keeping you on your toes, my lord."

"Then by all means, carry on," Ryan told him cheerfully as he headed for the drawing room door.

It took him only a second to spot the man who was standing by one of the tall bay windows, looking out onto the street as he waited patiently for Ryan to arrive. He was almost as tall as Ryan, though his frame was frailer. His hair, which had turned gray in the space of one week roughly six years earlier, had surprisingly enough retained its thickness. Turning his head away from the window at the sound of the door opening, a pair of light brown eyes came into view, creasing slightly at the corners as they locked onto Ryan.

"Sir Percy!" Ryan exclaimed, unable to hide his enthusiasm as he crossed the floor and reached out to shake the older gentleman's hand. "It's so good to see you again. By Jove it's been far too long."

"Almost a full year," Percy agreed, allowing his mouth to widen into a broad smile. "You look well though. Indeed it does appear as if Oxford agrees with you."

"In some aspects it certainly does," Ryan agreed with a lopsided smirk.

"And would that be the social aspects by any chance?"

"You know me too well," Ryan sighed as he made his way across the room to the side table. "Can I perhaps offer you a glass of Claret?"

"Certainly. But only if you'll join me."

Ryan curled his fingers around the cool neck of a crystal carafe. "I do believe a drink might serve me well after suffering through all those bumps in the road for hours on end."

"Whatever excuse works for you," Percy quipped. "As far as I'm concerned, it's essential to my good health. In fact, I'm quite convinced it's what keeps me from knocking at death's door."

"I'll be sure to keep that in mind," Ryan said with a smile as he handed Percy his glass. He studied the man who'd always been like an uncle to him. Percy was one of his father's oldest and closest friends and if that wasn't enough, he was also the permanent secretary for The Foreign Office. It was unlikely that, with Ryan's father out of town, he would pay a visit for no other reason than to be sociable. Something was afoot—Ryan was certain of it.

"As glad as I am to see you again, Percy, I have the distinct feeling that you're not here to inquire about my health," Ryan said as he gestured toward one of two green silk clad armchairs. "Please have a seat and tell me why you're really here."

Percy took a brief sip of his brandy. "Nothing gets by you, does it Ryan?"

"Not very often," Ryan remarked. "But then again, I have you to thank for that. You've taught me well."

Percy paused for a moment while the hint of a smile played upon his lips. He gave Ryan a short nod. "Very well then," he said as he sat down in the proffered chair and placed his glass on the small round sidetable next to him. "I admit that I have an ulterior motive for coming here today."

"Well, I am all ears," Ryan told him with genuine interest as he sat down in the other chair and turned an expectant gaze on Percy.

"A number of years ago," Percy began. "I made a promise to an old friend of mine, that if anything were to happen to him, I'd keep a watchful eye on his daughter. Apparently, this friend of mine was under the impression that his daughter would be in some sort of terrible danger if anything were to happen to him." A pensive look came over Percy's face. He paused, narrowing his eyes on Ryan. "As it happens, he passed away almost a year ago from a gunshot wound he sustained at Waterloo. From what I understand, he was hit by a stray bullet while attending to a wounded soldier—dratted business really. He was a good man and an excellent surgeon— the best I've ever seen—such an unfortunate and unnecessary loss.

"The funny thing is, in spite of my inquiries, there hasn't been the slightest trace of his daughter since then. I sent word out to a couple of agents who were already stationed in Belgium at the time, but they were unable to find her. It almost seemed as though she'd evaporated into thin air—until yesterday that is, when she finally resurfaced right here in London after a two year absence." Percy paused for emphasis as his eyes met Ryan's. "I was hoping I might be able to convince you to assist in this matter."

"You do realize I no longer work for The Foreign Office, right?"

"First of all, if this were an official matter, it wouldn't be handled by The Foreign Office. The Home Office would take care of it. And second of all, this is a private matter regarding a promise I'm honor bound to keep. I'd like to keep it off the books as much as possible."

"You're leaving me with very little choice here, Percy," Ryan argued. "I was hoping to sow some oats this summer, perhaps even attend a few mandatory balls if I have to. What you're suggesting hardly sounds like any fun at all."

"Stop your bellyaching, Ryan, and man up," Percy told him fiercely. "I'll wager you've sown a whole granary full of oats by now—enough at any rate for you to wait a while before jumping into bed with the next actress who comes along. Damn it, boy, I'm asking you for a personal favor here."

"Very well then," Ryan said, still lacking any sign of enthusiasm for this unexpected venture. "What's the chit's name? And more important, who is she?"

Percy took another sip of his claret. A slow smile began to spread its way across his face. There was an impish gleam to his eyes as he turned his gaze on Ryan. "I'd be careful about calling her a chit if I were you," he said. "After all, being The

Marchioness of Steepleton, she *is* a couple of steps above you on the social ladder. And to answer your question, her name is Mary Croyden."

Ryan stared at Percy with the very unpleasant feeling that he'd just been had. He should have known that Percy would keep an ace like this up his sleeve until he'd already agreed to help. If there was one thing Percy loved, it was the element of surprise. But Ryan was not about to be played the fool, especially when he very much doubted that The Marchioness of Steepleton was even a real title. "How on earth is that even possible?" he asked dubiously.

"Do I really have to explain it to you, Ryan? I would have thought that your father might have seen to the matter by now."

Ryan groaned. "You know perfectly well what I mean, Percy. I've never heard of a Marquess of Steepleton and now there's suddenly a Marchioness? Forgive me if I'm reluctant to believe such a thing, but it hardly makes much sense."

"Hm . . . I suppose you're right. You see, here's the thing of it—the title went into obscurity for a number of years through lack of usage. For whatever reason he might have had, Mary's father was bent on making his own way in life, as far away from the social constraints of the upper classes as humanly possible. All the same, he did manage to ensure that his daughter would one day inherit the title from him.

"The point is, if he believed her to be in danger—for whatever reasons he might have had, then she's more likely to be so now that she's returned to London and claimed her inheritance. The sudden appearance of a marchioness is going to make the headline in every gossip column this country has to offer. If someone's out to get her, they'll be crawling out of the woodwork before you know it, mark my word."

Ryan nodded thoughtfully. Perhaps this wouldn't be so boring after all, he mused. As it were, he rather liked the image he envisioned of himself dodging bullets as he saved the marchioness from imminent danger. There might even be a swordfight or two, perhaps a race across the countryside at breakneck speed while a group of ruffians chased after them, and . . . he suddenly blinked when he heard Percy's voice practically yelling at him.

"Ryan? Are you even listening to what I'm saying?"

"Hm? Oh, I was just wondering how I might best handle the matter."

"Yes, I'm sure you were," Percy told him with a frown. "You need not worry yourself about that however. I will ensure that Lady Steepleton receives an invitation to the first ball of the season, which happens to be this Saturday evening at Richmond House by the way. As charming as you are, I'm confident you'll have no trouble at all in befriending her."

"And once I find her—may I tell her why I suddenly have such a keen interest in her?"

"Ryan, you and I both know that women hate the feeling of being watched, even if it is for their own good. If she so much as suspects that your interest in her lies only in protecting her from supposed harm, she'll most likely make it her mission in life to avoid you for the remainder of her days."

"I see your point," Ryan muttered as he mulled that over.

"You're a handsome lad, Ryan. Surely it won't be impossible for you to convince her that you are genuinely interested."

"But I'm not." Ryan said with a frown. "Am I to understand that you wish for me to give this woman a false impression of my true intentions?"

"It is for her own good, you know," Percy remarked.

"Look, you know how much I despise dishonesty, Percy, and to take advantage of any woman's desire to form an attachment just feels wrong."

"Well, I hate to break it to you, Ryan, but spying is a pretty dishonest business."

"Must you always mock me?" The frustration in Ryan's voice was practically scratching at the walls. "Fine—if it will keep her alive, then I'll agree to do whatever it takes— though, I'm by no means pleased about it; I'll have you know."

"I am so happy to hear it," Percy remarked rather dryly as he drained his glass of its last few drops before jumping to his feet. He looked eager to be gone, no doubt before Ryan changed his mind. "I'll see to it you get an invitation to Richmond House as well then shall I?"

"That would certainly be an excellent idea," Ryan replied, his words dripping with sarcasm as he walked his father's friend to the door.

"Listen," Percy said, turning back around on the threshold and placing a solid hand on Ryan's shoulder. "I know this isn't exactly the sort of thing you want to get tangled up in right now, so I appreciate your help."

Ryan nodded. "It's my pleasure."

"Oh, I hardly think so," Percy chuckled, turning about and starting down the steps that led toward the pavement. "But thank you for saying so."

Ryan remained in the doorway a moment longer until

Percy had hailed himself a hackney and climbed in. Well, perhaps he ought to ask Hutchins to press one of his black tailcoats then. After all, he now had a marchioness to impress.

An Excerpt from
HOW MISS RUTHERFORD
GOT HER GROOVE BACK

CHAPTER ONE

E$mily clutched her canvas and easel tightly under her right arm as she quickened her step, her box of paints held firmly in her left hand. She realized she must look terribly awkward as she struggled along, trying desperately not to drop anything.

As the rustic little cottage with its climbing roses spread across its façade came into view, Emily hurried ahead. She was eager to return home for there was much to be done today. She and her sisters had been formally invited to attend the yearly ball at Coldwell Manor. It had of course been Adrian's doing, for nobody would have thought to invite them otherwise.

The invitation had arrived a little over a week ago, and the three sisters had talked of nothing else since. It was the only invitation that they had received in the last year, as it had been the only one they'd received the year before that, and the year before that. And since it was only once a year that they were invited out, it had become the occasion they looked forward to with unparalleled eagerness and anticipation.

Bursting through the front door of the cottage, Emily immediately set down her cumbersome load on the floor to rest against the wall. She untied the green ribbon of her bonnet and removed it, running her fingers lightly through her hair.

She was all jitters, she knew—something that would suit a young girl but hardly a fully-grown woman. So she took a moment to calm herself and smooth over her dress before quietly opening the door to the parlor.

Claire and Beatrice were both seated within, animatedly conversing with a guest that Emily recognized immediately. "Kate!" she exclaimed, forgetting herself and her composure as she rushed forward, her arms spread wide. "How good of you to have come! I've missed you terribly, and not a day has gone by where I haven't wondered about you. How long has it been?"

"Far too long, I suppose," Kate replied. She was a stunningly beautiful woman with a tall, shapely figure and light blonde hair. Her eyes were the clearest blue, her lips full and rosy. She and Emily had spent much of their childhood together in one another's company, though they'd seen less of each other in recent years now that Kate's family had moved to Stonebrook, the estate that her father had inherited from his brother.

At present, Kate had just returned from her annual two-week visit to her aunt and uncle. As they happened to live in London, Kate thoroughly enjoyed her visits.

"Tell me about your stay, Kate," Emily said, as she took the last remaining seat. "It must have been thoroughly splendid. Was it?"

Kate gave a slight nod followed by a broad smile. "It was indeed. I was just telling Claire and Beatrice that Aunt Harriet and Uncle Geoffrey took me to the theatre a number of times. We saw Tchaikovsky's *Sleeping Beauty* on one occasion and very much enjoyed *Romeo and Juliet* on another. And the parties! Oh Emily, you would have loved it . . . all the lovely dresses, the music, and the dancing."

Claire and Beatrice both raised an eyebrow. "The dancing?" Beatrice asked. "Did you happen to meet any young gentlemen who sparked your interest?"

It was no secret that the main reason Kate's parents encouraged her to visit London was in order for her aunt and uncle to introduce her to the *ton*. Her parents hoped that she would find herself a suitable husband there. She was, after all, approaching her twenty-fourth year. Still, she had returned from her visit earlier than intended, in order to attend the Carroway ball that evening.

Kate giggled shyly as a bright pink hue flooded her face. "I must admit that there was one particular gentleman who . . ."

A squeal of delight filled the air, cutting her off, and before Kate knew what was happening, Emily had sprung out of her chair and was throwing her arms about her in a tight embrace. "That's wonderful news! You must tell us everything at once! Who is he? Are you engaged?"

"As a matter of fact, we have formed an attachment." Kate peeled herself away from Emily, her cheeks even redder than before from all the attention. "However, I did intend for this to be a quick visit. After all, there are a lot of things that need my attention before the ball this evening. I understand from your sisters that you shall all be attending?"

Emily's face brightened at the mere mention of that evening's event and found it impossible to hide a brilliant smile. "Oh, absolutely," she said. "We wouldn't miss it for the world."

"Then I shall tell you everything later," Kate said, looking at each of them with a secretive smile. "Now, I really must be off." She rose to her feet and reached for her bonnet.

"Well, it was lovely to see you again," Emily told her. "I

shall look forward to seeing you this evening and finding out more about this elusive gentleman whom you plan to marry."

"As shall I," Kate told her with a small smile as she gave Emily a quick hug.

Emily and her sisters stood in the doorway and watched her walk away. She turned once to wave to them, still tying the ribbon of her bonnet below her chin.

"Her parents must be relieved," Beatrice remarked as they went back inside. "Considering her looks and the fact that her mother is the Duke of Bedford's sister, I'm surprised it took her this long to form an attachment."

"She's a romantic," Emily said. "She believes in true love and a happily ever after just as much as I do. Finding that can take time."

"At least you don't have to worry about that, dear sister," Claire said with a teasing smile.

Now it was Emily's turn to blush. Her sisters were both aware of her undying love for Adrian. She had in truth pined away endless hours, daydreaming of what her future would be like if she were married to him.

"When do you suppose that he will offer for you?" Claire now asked. "From what you have told us, it seems that the two of you have some sort of understanding?"

"Yes, we do," Emily said with a thoughtful smile. "I do not know if he is *in* love with me, as I am with him, but I do not doubt that he loves me in some way or he would not have suggested that we should one day marry."

"I've told you too many times to count, surely he must be *in* love with you if he suggested as much," Beatrice told her. "How could he not be?"

Emily regarded her sister for a brief moment. The concern was clear in her eyes. She was clearly worried that Emily would end up unhappy in her marriage if Adrian didn't love her wholeheartedly.

"Oh, Bea," Emily said, wishing she could wash away her sister's fears. "You do so worry about us, don't you?"

"It is my job to worry about you, and I do believe that it has kept you safe from harm thus far."

"Well, Adrian would never hurt me. He has been my truest friend for as long as I can remember. I do not mind if he is not *in* love with me. I should find myself fortunate indeed if I became his wife, and I should be thoroughly happy. Aside from the fact that I can think of no other man that I would rather spend my life with, do you not see what my marrying him would mean for us?"

"Of course we do," Claire told her. "We just don't want you to give up on finding true happiness on our account. Emily, you must not agree to marry him just because it will reinstate us to our rightful positions."

Emily gave an exasperated sigh. She knew how much her sisters loved her, but they were taking this too far. "Do you not see?" she asked them. "Marrying Adrian would be a dream come true for me—it would be *true* happiness. I love him with all my heart and I know that he loves me."

"Then by all means, let us hope that he will soon honor your agreement and offer for you," Claire told her.

"Yes, let's," Beatrice agreed with a warm smile. "Who knows? Perhaps you and Kate will both be married before the year is out."

ABOUT THE AUTHOR

Born in Denmark, SOPHIE BARNES has spent her youth traveling with her parents to wonderful places all around the world. She's lived in five different countries, on three different continents, and speaks Danish, English, French, Spanish, and Romanian. She has studied design in Paris and New York and has a bachelor's degree from Parson's School of Design, but most impressive of all, she's been married to the same man three times, in three different countries, and in three different dresses.

While living in Africa, Sophie turned to her lifelong passion: writing. When she's not busy dreaming up her next romance novel, she enjoys spending time with her family, swimming, cooking, gardening, watching romantic comedies, and, of course, reading. She lives on the East Coast.

Visit Sophie Barnes's website at www.sophiebarnes.com. You can also find her on Facebook and follow her on Twitter at @BarnesSophie.